TALES OF BIGFOOT

EDITED BY
ANTHONY GIANGREGORIO

OTHER LIVING DEAD PRESS BOOKS

THE TURNING: A STORY OF THE LIVING DEAD * MEN OF PERDITION
THE DEAD OF SPACE BOOK 1 AND 2 * THE BABYLONIAN CURSE
PLAYING GOD: A ZOMBIE NOVEL * THE JUNKYARD
PLANET OF THE DEAD * THE HAUNTED THEATRE
ZOMBIES IN OUR HOMETOWN * NOVELLAS OF THE DEAD
NIGHT OF THE WOLF: A WEREWOLF ANTHOLOGY
JUST BEFORE NIGHT: A ZOMBIE ANTHOLOGY
THE BOOK OF HORROR* KNIGHT SYNDROME
THE WAR AGAINST THEM: A ZOMBIE NOVEL
CHILDREN OF THE VOID * DARK DREAMS
BLOOD RAGE & DEAD RAGE (BOOK 1& 2 OF THE RAGE VIRUS SERIES)
DEAD MOURNING: A ZOMBIE HORROR STORY
BOOK OF THE DEAD: A ZOMBIE ANTHOLOGY VOLUME 1-6
LOVE IS DEAD: A ZOMBIE ANTHOLOGY
ETERNAL NIGHT: A VAMPIRE ANTHOLOGY
END OF DAYS: AN APOCALYPTIC ANTHOLOGY VOLUME 1-5
DEAD HOUSE * CLAN OF THE BIGFOOT
THE ZOMBIE IN THE BASEMENT (FOR ALL AGES)
THE LAZARUS CULTURE: A ZOMBIE NOVEL
DEAD WORLDS: UNDEAD STORIES VOLUMES 1-7
FAMILY OF THE DEAD, REVOLUTION OF THE DEAD
KINGDOM OF THE DEAD * DEAD HISTORY
THE MONSTER UNDER THE BED * DEAD THINGS
DEAD TALES: SHORT STORIES TO DIE FOR
ROAD KILL: A ZOMBIE TALE * DEADFREEZE * DEADFALL
SOUL EATER * THE DARK * RISE OF THE DEAD
DEAD END: A ZOMBIE NOVEL * VISIONS OF THE DEAD
THE CHRONICLES OF JACK PRIMUS
INSIDE THE PERIMETER: SCAVENGERS OF THE DEAD
BOOK OF CANNIBALS VOLUME 2 * CHRISTMAS IS DEAD…AGAIN
EMAILS OF THE DEAD * CHILDREN OF THE DEAD
ETERNAL AFTERMATH: A ZOMBIE NOVEL * THE END: A ZOMBIE NOVEL

THE DEADWATER SERIES

DEADWATER * DEADWATER: Expanded Edition
DEADRAIN * DEADCITY * DEADWAVE * DEAD HARVEST
DEAD UNION * DEAD VALLEY * DEAD TOWN * DEAD GRAVE
DEAD SALVATION * DEAD ARMY (Deadwater series book 10)

TALES OF BIGFOOT

Table of Contents

BIGFOOT'S FOOT

ALAN SPENCER

Today's speech would be what insiders of the paranormal trade would jokingly call a Probing Convention. The speech was to be given by Caleb Anthony, the award winning writer for the tabloid magazine The Weekly Spectacle. He traveled the states searching for stories similar to The House That Dripped Blood, Bat Boy Seen Shopping at the Mall of America, or his latest article, Talking Dogs Takes Vow of Silence. He'd been writing fake journalism for six years, and he was asked by the group T.A.P.A. (Those Against Probing Americans) to give a speech on the prevalence of alien probing in America. It would turn out he wouldn't just be late to the convention room at the Million Dollar Hotel in Las Vegas, he'd fail to give the speech altogether.

He arrived at the hotel's parking garage in good time. He'd just traveled from a town twenty miles south of Las Vegas where he met Martha Dilday, the owner of the talking basset hound who'd taken the vow of silence, when he was called up by his boss to give the speech to T.A.P.A. He'd be paid five hundred dollars for less than an hour of his time; also included was lodging at the fine hotel and one hundred dollars to gamble on the gaming floor. He was eager to check into his room and go over the bullets of his probing speech when a man who was parked about ten cars down from his called out to him frantically:

"You see it come your way? It was huge, man. *Huge*. And it stinks!"

The man was dressed for a fishing trip in a tan vest and undershirt that had a picture of a carp on a hook. The caption across his beer belly read: **HOOK 'EM AND COOK 'EM: FISH FEST 1998**. He was in his late sixties with a white balding nest of wiry hair. His ashen face was curled up as if he'd not only smelled excrement but had witnessed the culprit eliminate in his presence.

When Caleb didn't reply, the man amped up his distress. "It tore up my Winnebago. Wanna see? You gotta see the damage. The thing that did it is in the building right now. I don't know what the hell it is, but I know it's covered in lots of hair. It's like a bear, but it has an orangutan's face. Look at my camper if you don't believe me. I swear I'm not crazy. What I saw is real."

He was grabbed by the arm and dragged to the alleged vehicle. The man was correct. The back part of the Winnebago was peeled back like a tin of sardines. Punched and peeled through, it seemed. Glass and aluminum remains were mixed with tufts of cotton and springs from either a fold-out bed or a couch from inside.

"Did this just happen?" Caleb asked. "Did you actually see the perpetrator walk into the building?"

"The damn thing took the emergency stairs." The man pointed at the damaged vehicle again and blathered, "I-I didn't know it was in my car. I mean, it stank inside like someone wiped their ass with a tortilla in there. And my Pepperidge Farm Milano cookies are missing, but I thought it was my mother-in-law; she lives next door and eats all my stuff, so I didn't think anything of it. I drove from Forest Hills in Wyoming, and the car reeked, end of story. The second I park here, something makes a grumble and yawns like it just woke up from a deep sleep, and here's my ride smashed to hell!"

"Did you call security?"

"They're on their way."

Caleb heard the elevator ding, and when it opened, a group of suited security guards with their walkies held high approached the scene. He eyed the emergency stairwell and ran to it before anyone could stop him.

He had to get a picture of this thing—whatever it was!

Caleb dug out his digital camera, ready to take a picture of anything that didn't look like a happy set of tourists or a high-rolling gambler. If he was being honest, he'd forgotten about the T.A.P.A. speech once he saw the damage done to the Winnebago. Something powerful was in the building, and no one was safe. It was his duty—and his chance to get paid for a good shot of something scary—to keep everyone protected.

Beyond the thing taking the stairs, he didn't have any real leads to its location except the smell. It reeked of excrement; it was a mix of horse, cow, and dog feces. He immediately noted the dark, fudge-colored footprints. The footprints were at least a twenty in shoe size. There was a large foot pad then five distinct pads for toes, along with marks as if left by jagged nails or talons. The last time he'd seen a foot resembling this was on one of those 'Bigfoot is Real' shows from a print taken out of a concrete mold.

This had to be a hoax, though he couldn't explain why someone would throw down poop on the stairs. *I guess publicity stunts for a Vegas casino have no moral boundaries*, he decided. *I have to find this thing, and fast.*

He tracked the prints, and he was already winded after two flights of searching. Too much traveling on the road, eating fast foot and hotel quality meals, and not enough time on the treadmill, were catching up to him. He stopped at another pile of feces; it was shaped like a cow patty, but the thing had stepped in it. There was a medley of ingredients in the mess. The skull of a fish. Strands of hay. A fox tail. Then he paused on the bag of Pepperidge Farm Milan cookies that had seen better days before sent through a digestive system.

This wasn't a casino hoax.

This was a real creature, and it was free and roaming the building. If it could smash through a Winnebago like that, what could it do to a person if provoked? There were lots of drunks and excited people inside the hotel right now, and if they saw a giant hairy beast, they wouldn't react in a calm fashion.

He increased his step, the prints carrying for half a flight. He heard a wide array of screams from a large group of people, and he burst through the nearest door in search of the source. He rushed down a burgundy carpeted hall and darted into a conference room with a boxing ring erected in the middle of it. About two hundred people filled the room.

He read the banner hanging at each of the walls: **AMATEUR SLUG FEST SEMI-FINALS.**

The crowd was chattering in dismay. Horrified faces exchanged words of concern. Caleb ran straight up to the ring, seeing the chairs that had been busted up and one side of the ring had the poop prints that could only belong to the monster. One of the boxers wearing red silk boxers was clutching his face. His nose was oozing blood out of both nostrils and both his eyes were purple slits.

Caleb urged aside the boxer's coach and demanded, "Who punched you?"

"Everyone saw it." The coach, what could have been the same coach from the movie *Rocky*, said. "One big motherfucker, too. Had humps on his back to make a camel blush. The beast pummeled his way into the ring, and he nearly took Carlos Mendez's head off with his left hook."

The coach pointed at the other fighter who was being carted off on a stretcher with a neck brace.

"My boy threw a few jabs at the thing, but it didn't do shit. Then the thing pounds his face into his nose and down he goes. When the crowd screamed, it bolted out the door."

Caleb was already following the lead. Rushing through the crowd, he threw open the doors, and raced down a new set of hallways where the poop prints were fading fast. They lasted long enough for him to know the thing had entered the gaming area.

The place was in chaos. Gamers ran to every exit, colliding into each other in a mob frenzy. Security was bumbling about, trying to secure the perimeter.

Meanwhile, the buzz of machines continued at ear-blasting levels. The soundtrack of fun clashed against the increasing sense of personal danger. A roulette wheel had been uprooted from the table and hurled across the room like a bowling ball. It had also shattered an ice sculpture of Wayne Newton standing erect in the middle of the room; the singer had been performing on stage in the The Lion's Den auditorium before the commotion began.

Slot machines had been punched and tipped to their sides, bleeding out coins. Some players fought over the spilt profits, while others decided to cut their losses and beat their feet the hell out of there.

By the time he gave the room a good once-over, hardly a soul was in the area. Security kept darting about the place, shouting codes, warnings and questions into their walkies. He stopped to help up an older woman who'd been knocked off her walker. She was frightened and couldn't move. He supported her until she was back on her walker.

She kept saying on her way out of the exit, "It's the Sasquatch. I've seen it before in Kansas. It was rooting through my garden, and it stepped on my begonias." She was out of sorts, and he noticed she'd taken a blow to the side of the head; she must've hit it against the wall when she fell, he believed. He tried to consol her when a security guard, an ex-linebacker who was even more frightened than the woman, helped escort her safely through the nearest exit.

The security guard delivered commands at him, but Caleb continued to scout the gaming room for the beast. "Hey—you need to leave the premises! It's not safe here. Please come with me, sir—sir—*SIR!*"

If it's really Bigfoot, this picture will be worth thousands of dollars. If I make this shot I can quit writing bullshit articles and take on real journalism. Diane Sawyer and Tom Brokaw will take me under their wing. I'll finally be taken seriously.

The clatter of pots and pans rattled against the floor from across the room, and he knew the beast had taken a side trip into the kitchen area. Caleb dashed through the double doors and caught two cooks splayed out on the floor, both clutching their bellies as if they'd been punched. Another cook, a younger woman with the reddest hair he'd ever seen in his life, was holding up a frying pan and was about to bludgeon anyone who got too close to her. She wanted to say something to him, but her lips were frozen in shock.

"Are you okay?"

She said nothing. That's when he noticed the urine at her feet; she'd wet herself in fear. He decided to leave her alone and checked on the other two cooks on the floor. They groaned and complained, but they seemed okay. One said, "I've never been socked in the gut so hard. Did you see what hit us? Whatever it was, it was fucking *ugly*!"

Caleb raised his voice to the woman. "Call security to help your friends."

She didn't come out of it, so he dinged the bell at the short order window. "I said call for help, *now!*"

That got her awake, and she did as she was told.

One of the cooks gave him a skeptical stare. "And who do you think you are?"

It slipped out of him as force of habit. "Caleb Anthony, Weekly Spectacle Digest. I'm a paranormal expert."

The cook uttered a bunch of other things, one of which being, "A damn ghost didn't punch me in the guts," but Caleb ignored him as he followed the path of culinary destruction. There were the shells of boiled lobsters on the floor, partially devoured t-bone and rib eye steaks scattered around his feet, plus six different Italian dishes, the messes splattered everywhere. Six different cakes had been defiled; a large hand had swiped down the middle of them. It was a hit and run cake sampling. He moved deeper into the kitchen to the very back where the dish machine churned out steam. The machine was unmanned, but there it was standing over a trashcan and picking and eating through various leftovers from hundreds of plates.

Bigfoot.

Its hair was bristle thick and blonder than he would have imagined, though the hair was matted and stained from foraging and surviving in wooded areas. Its eyes were barely visible, covered in hair, but he caught sight of those black beady eyes honing in on him. Its hands were disproportionate to its body; large enough to wrap around two heads at once. The stench of excrement was so heavy that his throat wanted to close up. It audibly chomped on food as it breathed out is mouth, taking in a mouthful of spaghetti noodles and a square of lime Jell-o.

It stood up straight, ending its trashcan feast. It eyed the back of the room with disdain, huffing and turning its hands into fists.

Caleb heard the sound of running footsteps from behind him, but he was frozen in place.

"Get out of the way, we're going to shoot it!"

"Get down, you idiot!"

"Move or do something before it gets away!"

Several gunshots popped off despite Caleb failing to yield to their commands. He felt the bullets whiz past him—dangerously close to hitting him. Pings and sparks shot up from the walls from where the anxious shooters missed the creature.

The thing seemed familiar with being shot at, judging by its reaction, Caleb thought. The beast searched the room for a way out, and when it didn't pinpoint an exit, it scanned the walls with its enormous hands and discovered the trash chute opening. Crawling inside, having to bend half of its body to maneuver into the chute, it slid down it without hesitation.

Caleb followed right after it, ignoring the yells of the men behind him.

The chute was a thin metal shaft the size of an air-duct channel, but it was greased with spaghetti sauce and various half-eaten meals. Caleb was slathered in food by the time he landed in the basement wing of the hotel, somehow crashing face-first into a claustrophobic room heaped in garbage. His hands were covered with banana pudding, and he was certain he'd sat on an open-faced hamburger; he had ketchup and pickles stuck on his butt cheeks. He patted the inside of his suit for the tell-tale bulge of his digital camera.

It was still there.

What wasn't there was Bigfoot. It had beaten in a thin metal hatch, and had escaped. He trudged through the sea of stinking food to the other side and managed to escape through the same way. He heard the echo of voices from the kitchen call down after him, but was too engrossed in his pursuit to call anything back. Besides, they'd fired guns in his general direction; he wanted to be as far away from them as possible.

Industrial washing machines cleaned towels and bed sheets in the space he scouted. Mops and cleaning tools lined shelves, but there was no one in the area.

Bigfoot had scared them off.

Instead of feces, there were now barbeque sauce tracks to follow. Down halls with exposed and hissing pipes in the ceiling, he stalked the corridors for the beast. He was gaining on it, he felt, as he heard the grumble of the beast nearby; it was either scared or out-of-breath, or both.

He dodged another heap of feces. They were shaped like charcoal briquettes; he counted easily thirty pieces in the heap.

He thought back to the man he met in the parking lot. The beast had hitched a ride from Wyoming in the back of a Winnebago. How did someone not notice a giant hairy creature sleeping in the back seat?

He wondered what would happen to the creature when it was found. Would it be studied for science? Shaved down? Put on the news? He imagined the relief of those who'd seen Bigfoot over the years finally proven right, and he would be the one to give them that privilege.

A loud crash pulled him from his ruminations; it sounded like a car slamming into a guardrail. He hurried, but then slowed his step when turning onto the edge of a new hallway. He had to stay a calculated distance from the beast to remain safe, but he needed to get his picture, and it had to be in focus.

Diane Sawyer will shake my hand when I break this story. No—she'll give me a hug!

He angled down another hallway, and rushed forward when he discovered a vending machine with its front bashed in. Soda cans were strewn about the floor by the dozens. One of the cans was still rolling; it was orange soda. Eyeing it and the empty hallway, he couldn't help himself to his favorite flavor of carbonated beverage and picked up the can.

By the time he pulled the tab and it went *fzzzzt*, the creature was standing right before him with only an inch of space between them. Its breath was many things: a lake of dead fish, matted shit on damp fur, dead grass, a urine-reek, and as of recently, a Las Vegas hotel trash bin. Caleb was close enough to notice a few of the creature's teeth were chipped and yellow as fool's gold. The tongue was a purple mass in its mouth, the color of a giraffe's, and before he could touch upon any other details, his hand was seized by the wrist.

A gasp escaped him, but he prevented himself from releasing his terror-fueled strength. He could set the beast off, and he didn't want that. The thing could twist off his head at will if it wanted to, he thought.

By the wrist, Bigfoot shoved Caleb's right hand into its mouth.

Oh God, oh God, oh God, oh God, oh God...

All this for a picture of this overgrown ape. I'm covered in food garbage, and I'm about to lose my right hand!

Its mouth was a hot hole, and it sucked once on his entire hand like a pacifier. The beast scrunched its face at the taste of his skin, but it kept sucking as if trying to give him a violent hickie. The next article he'd write would be entitled: ***Bigfoot gives dumbass field reporter a hand hickie!***

At first, the sensation tickled, but now that Bigfoot was sucking harder and harder, as if it wanted to force the blood up through his skin and into its mouth, he began to wince in pain. His bones were beginning to feel the pressure of the pull, the incredible suction.

Please stop, please, please, please stop...

Bigfoot sucks hands right off reporter's arm—all this and more in this month's Weekly Spectacle Digest.

His wrist clicked.

Ahhhhhgaaaaaaaaaaaawd!

The last few sucks nearly dropped him to his knees. He had to think fast, or he'd lose the hand. Lose his life. Lose everything.

All for a goddamn picture!

A smile was in the creature's eyes, beaming with pleasure at his unbearable pain. Was that the face it made when it ransacked campers' food supplies and tents for goodies?

Was Bigfoot a cannibalistic creature?

Reporter's injury proves Bigfoot only likes to eat human hands. The beast is otherwise a peaceful, foraging creature.

Its sharp teeth, jagged as a seasoned wolf's, was biting softly on his flesh. Testing the flesh for breakability, perhaps. Any second it would bite down. Full-clamp, it would break his hand off from his wrist and down the hatch his appendage would go. A froth of creamy spittle surrounded Bigfoot's purple-lipped maw. The floor below them was a wide puddle of goop.

It felt like his bones were being crushed, and Caleb was so overwhelmed he didn't realize he still had the can of orange soda in his other hand. He dropped the can, jerking in a spasm as the pain sent yellow and red stars in his eyes.

The orange soda fizzed between Bigfoot's toes, and the beast gave a *huuuuh?* sound in its throat. Upon spitting his hand out, Caleb dropped to the floor with his wrist bent and dripping in saliva juices.

The beast picked up the can and held it in its large hand as delicate as if the soda was a baby. Turning its head side-to-side, it was captivated. It *sniff-sniff-sniffed* the rim of the can, curious as to its contents.

"Drink it," Caleb grunted in a fit of delirious pain. His wrist was broken, he was certain. "It tastes good, you big ape."

Maybe Bigfoot could understand English, because it tipped the can back into its mouth. It chugged what was left, gulping, masticating, and moaning in pleasure. Its eyes were fixed on nothing after the can was emptied, crushed, and thrown down the hallway. It spaced out. Caleb swore the monster's eyes trembled ever so slightly, buzzing on sugar.

Bigfoot endorses Juicy Orange cola with a big thumb's up. Coming next month from the Weekly Spectacle Digest!

He noticed orange cola fizzing around the hair on its upper lip. Caleb would later tell his co-workers and other believers this was The Bigfoot Mustache. On all fours, he kept his eye on the beast for several seconds when the creature suddenly belched and filled the air with the odor of rotten dead fish offal and Juicy Orange cola.

Before Caleb could react to the bad smell, Bigfoot was trudging towards a nearby exit and making his escape.

No—the picture!

He had to maneuver with his good hand to dig out the digital camera from his suit pocket. Once he had the camera free, he turned it on.

The big ape was almost out the door.

He lifted the camera up, and forgoing shutter speed, clicked four pictures. Getting up and making pursuit, he nearly took a spill on the spread-out cola cans from the broken vending machine.

The exit led to a loading dock. He couldn't find the big creature anywhere. *Did one of his forest friends pick him up in a getaway car?* he wondered. By the time he saw where the beast went, it was too late. The vehicle was well down the street and out of sight. Caleb couldn't identify it, but he caught Bigfoot standing in the back cargo space of a large truck. What turned out to be a Hostess bakery truck.

Caleb's wrist was in fact broken. It was put in a cast, having been treated at the local hospital just an hour ago. Other than having to change his clothes, he was otherwise no worse for the wear. Several policemen questioned him, and he had no choice but to affirm that some man in a gorilla suit was parading around the building causing all kinds of property damage. The officer was accompanied by a mysterious man in a silver suit who wore an FBI badge on his front pocket. This man quickly took over all questioning, the two of them standing in the parking garage alone, where the back of the Winnebago had been peeled off like a tin can. But the vehicle was gone as well as the owner. He faced off with the agent who looked like Clint Eastwood's fat cousin.

"I know who you are, Caleb Anthony. You're in the exposure business, and I'm in the classifying business. I know you believe in monsters and all that bullshit, no matter how ridiculous it is. You've battled against vampires. Bleeding houses. Talking dogs. Babies who can do long division..." His chin puckered like a boiling sunny side-up egg. "...And Bigfoot."

"What of it, Mr...? Uhm, I didn't catch your name."

"Don't worry about my name. Just get out of here and don't write anything about this. You know the drill. This is the umpteenth time this has happened to you, isn't it? You seem to be a magnet that draws in these freaks. Okay, write your fake articles all you want, but when you start telling the truth, I can't allow it. Now get out of here."

After the odd briefing from the agent, he visited the conference room where T.A.P.A.'s meeting was being held. He answered questions and talked to people, but he didn't give his speech. He was worn out, and he kept feeling Bigfoot sucking on his hand, and the sensation was outright creepy.

Before completing his informal Q&A session with T.A.P.A., he was chatting with a farmer from Kansas about crop circles and why aliens went straight for the butt and not the brain. He wasn't sure how to field that question, so he gave the man something else to ponder. The question caused an eerie silence in the room. Somehow, all fifty-eight members had heard his prolific question: "How come there are no women in this room?"

He'd been so busy with Bigfoot and T.A.P.A. that he'd forgotten about the pictures he'd taken with his digital camera. Later, when he was sitting on his hotel bed, his window busy with Vegas night lights, he scrolled through the four photos. He was upset the first three were blurry with motion, and ultimately useless.

Caleb took a deep breath before looking at the last one. A real photo of Bigfoot could get him thousands of dollars...

He scrolled to the last picture, and it was crystal clear.

But there was a problem; a photo of Bigfoot's hairy left foot sticking out of a doorway would get him jack shit.

KEVIN

REBECCA SNOW

"You've ridden the Ferris wheel seven times already, Jill," Megan Turner told her daughter. "It's time to let Uncle Fred and me ride something that we want to ride."

"He's not my uncle," Jill said, her eyes drifting to untied shoelaces as her bottom lip bloomed into a pout.

"Oh, no you don't." Megan propped her hands on her hips and raised an eyebrow at her. "That face won't work this time, young lady."

The little ten-year-old stomped once, blew out a short breath, and crossed her arms over the lime-green turtle dancing on her shirt. Planting her feet in the dirt, she scowled at her mother.

"Fine. You want to act like a two-year-old, then you can't have any cotton candy." Tossing a glance to her date over her shoulder, Megan tapped her foot.

"But you promised." Jill's brown curls swarmed her head as she shook it from side to side. A tear blossomed in the corner of her left eye.

"You're right. I did promise," Megan said, reaching a hand toward her daughter's reluctant form. "Now, come on, Jillibean. Maybe Uncle Fred will win you that stuffed monkey at the ring toss."

"He's not my uncle," Jill said, dragging her sleeve across her face. "And it's not a monkey. It's Bigfoot."

"Whatever." Megan scratched her sweaty neck with her fingernails, the polish chipped. "Can we go now? Uncle Fred's waiting to go on the Tunnel of Love. You can have your own car."

Jill hunched her shoulders and trudged behind her mother, her tiny hand crushed in her mom's perspiring palm. Craning her neck, she swiveled for a last look at the giant rotating wheel. A movement in the bushes caught her eye. As she turned her head, a large man-like creature disappeared into a stand of trees.

"Mom?"

"Yes, dear?" her mother asked, not looking at Jill, her eyes still distracted by her search for the tunnel's sign.

"I think I just saw Bigfoot." She twisted in her mother's grip to peer into the darkness.

"Yes, I know. He's hanging on the wall in the ring toss booth." Megan yanked her daughter's arm. "Now, walk straight. I don't want you to trip me."

"No, Mom, not the stuffed one. This one's real," Jill said. "He went into the woods." She pulled her hand free, rubbing her shoulder.

"That's nice, sweetie. We'll get Uncle Fred to win him for you in a while." She'd found Fred and tapped him on the shoulder. Megan pointed to a line that snaked around several barriers. "There's the Tunnel of Love. The line's pretty long. Are you sure you want to wait?"

Fred's greasy ball cap jerked when he nodded. He'd found the end of the line and faced forward with as much enthusiasm as it took to fill out a form for a new driver's license.

"It wasn't a prize. Bigfoot was real." Jill threw her hands up as high as she could reach. "He was thiiiis big."

Fred whispered into Megan's ear and looped his thumb into a belt loop on her cut-off jean shorts. Jill's mother giggled and covered her mouth with her abused manicure. The line moved and the couple took a step.

"Mooooom!" Jill shrilled. "It was really Bigfoot!"

Fred rolled his eyes and Megan thrust a hand into her purse and pulled out a wad of one dollar bills.

Handing them to the shrieking girl, she said, "Go get yourself some cotton candy, honey. Don't get lost."

Jill shrugged, grabbed the cash, turned, and fled the winding line of couples. Spotting a stand with a peeling picture of the painted pink confection, the little girl skidded to a stop. She pointed to the biggest pink and blue striped bag she could find and placed her money on the counter. Without a word, the teenage boy behind the register rolled her purchase through the window and handed Jill her change.

From the corner of her eye, Jill peered at her mother as she waited in line with Fred. Their fingers interlaced like teenagers in a horror film before the monster showed up to eat them. They whispered and kissed and laughed as Jill turned and walked back to the Ferris wheel. Her eyes scanned the fringes of foliage that lined the carnival's edge. A rabbit darted under a bush. Fireflies flashed their neon green lights. A branch snapped.

She inched closer to the shadows and opened the hulking bag of spun sugar. Pulling out a pink, fluffy hunk, she waved it at the spot where she thought she'd seen the furry man.

"Mr. Bigfoot?" she whispered. "Are you there?"

Squinting past the dark branches, she tossed a bit of candy into the bush. The wind caught it and whisked it into a high bough.

"Shoot," Jill said, pouting.

She reached into the bag and grabbed another handful. When she looked back to where the cotton candy had lodged in the tree, the splash of pink had disappeared. Searching the ground, she found no trace of the pastel floss mingling with the dark green moss.

She heard a grunt and caught a whiff of wet dog mixed with the scent of the cotton candy-filled plastic bag. The first thing she saw when she peeked up from the ground was an enormous pair of hair-covered feet. The toes wiggled in the soft soil. Lifting her head, her eyes followed the line of furry legs to a fuzzy chest, then to an outstretched shaggy arm. A large, hairless palm opened like a flower to reveal the missing confection. Jill blinked and stared up into a tilted, unkempt face. The creature's bushy eyebrows crunched as if concerned.

"Bigfoot?" Jill gasped.

His head swiveled to tilt in the opposite direction, and he pressed his palm toward the little girl.

"I brought that for you," she said. "To eat."

Demonstrating the intended action with the piece of candy in her hand, she placed the pink wisp in her mouth and let it dissolve on her tongue.

"Mmm." She rubbed her stomach and smiled, then arched her eyebrows and watched the large creature lift his hand to his face. His nostrils flared as he sniffed her offering. Sticking out his tongue, he licked the sweet substance. His face flinched at the taste of the sugar. After a moment, his eyes met Jill's. The corners of his open mouth turned up into the semblance of a grin. He licked his sticky hand until the small gob of candy was dissolved, then produced a guttural moan and rubbed his belly, imitating Jill's gesture.

"Do you want some more?" she asked, holding out a bigger chunk of spun candy.

The beast's eyes flicked from the cloud of sugar to Jill's eyes and back again. Inching forward, he snatched the puff from her hand and stepped back. The treat disappeared into the creature's toothy maw. When his hands were empty, his gaze returned to Jill. Flecks of blue clung to the hair on his chin and cheeks. Jill giggled. His beady eyes disappeared in a wide, smiling grunt.

"I'm Jill," she said after retying the plastic bag. "Jill," she repeated, patting her chest with her fingers before pointing to the Bigfoot. "Who are you?"

At first, the shaggy monster seemed confused as the little girl patted her chest and repeated the same noise. Then, he patted his own chest and snorted a sort of growling burp.

Jill smiled. "Well, I don't think I know how to say that." She tapped her pinched lips and searched the starry sky. "I know," she said with a snap of her fingers. "I'll call you Kevin."

Reaching up, she grasped one of Kevin's fingers and pulled.

"C'mon," she said. "Let's ride the Ferris wheel."

Kevin stood as if rooted as the girl strained against him. She released his hand and watched his arm drop. She pointed to the blinking lights that spun above them.

"Don't you want to go up there?"

The child looked at the monster and back at the lights twice before Kevin took a step back into the forest. With sticky fingers, she fumbled with the knot she'd tied in the plastic bag. Thrusting her hand into the multi-colored cloud of candy, she ripped off a chunk and shook it in front of her new friend.

His eyes widened and sparkled in the glowing lights of a nearby popcorn stand. Kevin took a step toward her. Jill retreated, baiting the Bigfoot with the promise of sugar. He followed the girl and her candy, baby step by baby step, until they had reached the edge of the midway. The Ferris wheel loomed above them when Jill relinquished the bribe.

After more sugar tendrils wove themselves into Kevin's facial hair and the rest of the sample was gone, the creature's muscles tensed. Jill had both arms wrapped around one of his gigantic hands and began to pull him toward the short line that waited to board the swinging carriages.

Kevin gawked as the last trio of teenagers laughed after the bar was lowered and the cart pulled away from the ground. Jill released her grip just long enough to rip two tickets from a small stack in her pocket and hand them to the man at the gate.

The tiny pieces of paper fluttered to the dirt as Jill dragged Kevin past the attendant. The man stared slack-jawed and rubbed his eyes, the tickets on the ground all but forgotten. Shaking his head, he turned back to the line, telling himself what he'd seen couldn't be true.

"I'll give you some more cotton candy when we get settled," Jill said, still tugging on Kevin's hair-covered arm.

A shrieking rider on the wheel above them startled the wary Bigfoot. Kevin's frantic flailing threatened to send Jill tumbling to the ground, but she held on with every ounce of childhood tenacity that she possessed.

Having looped the tied end of her cotton candy bag around her wrist, she managed to hold on to it as well.

With one foot resting on the rocking platform, Jill bobbled and began to lose her balance. Kevin caught her as she fell and placed her onto the hard, fiberglass bench. Before he could back off the teetering bucket, she pulled him down beside her, procured another piece of candy, and held it in front of her. The attendant locked the metal bar in place as he tried not to look too closely at Kevin, and the wheel began to move.

Jill heard the metal sides squeal under Kevin's grip. Placing a hand on his trembling arm, she petted his shaggy hair as if he were the runt of the litter.

"Shhh. It's okay," she told the frightened beast. "You can't fall out." Pressing a bit of pink fluff to his mouth, she added, "Just sit back and enjoy the ride."

Kevin's lips quivered as he opened them just enough to accept the sticky treat. Jill poked it in and patted the side of his face. As the rest of the riders boarded and the carriage climbed higher, the boiling terror drained from the Bigfoot's eyes. His fingers still curled around the twisted metal frame, but he began to scan the festive scene below them. Jill pointed to the winding line leading into the Tunnel of Love.

"That's where my mom and Fred are," she said with a scowl darkening her face. "I'll bet they don't even know I haven't come back."

Sticking out her tongue, she blew a raspberry at where she thought her mother was. Kevin blubbered an imitated attempt beside her. She chuckled as the Ferris wheel picked up speed, while beside her, the seated creature slumped down onto the bench as the fair flew past them, the wind in their ears.

"Fred's a moron. I don't know why my mom likes him." Jill handed the huddled monster another ball of light pink puff. "He eats all my cereal and doesn't leave enough juice in the bottle to fill a glass." Lowering her voice into a hissing whisper, she added, "And he drinks from the milk carton. Straight out of it." She shook her head. "I don't want his cooties."

Kevin stared at her as he crimped the metal bar in front of him and shook his head in reply. His wild hair spun in a whirlwind around them and tangled in the chunk of cotton candy Jill was stuffing into her mouth. Realizing aromatic Bigfoot hair was mixed with the sweetness she tasted, she spit and wiped at her tongue with the back of her hand. Her nose crinkled in disgust at the foul flavor. Refusing to release the crumpling bar, Kevin just blew his hair from his face in a mimicking gesture.

"She left my dad last year, but I don't know why. I don't know where he is, but I want him to come back." She looked at the tiny crowds of people gathered below them. "He could be somewhere down there for all I know."

The wheel began to slow, and Kevin's hold on what was left of their cart loosened. Jill slithered out from underneath the bent metal safety bar before the attendant reached them. She beckoned to Kevin with a wave of her arm, and he sprung from the destroyed seat and vaulted over the barrier. As the two skirted the carnival, Jill spurted gleeful giggles. Kevin let out a few gurgling snorts as he loped along beside her. When they stopped, the girl dropped the bag and doubled over to catch her breath.

The creature retrieved the knotted plastic and tore a hole in the side. Pressing his face into the opening, he devoured the pink and blue clouds. When Kevin lifted his head, his face resembled an Impressionist painting of wildflowers. Jill howled with laughter. Dabbing her thumb in her mouth as she'd seen her mother do many times, she began to rub the monster's dirty face.

"Hold still," Jill said as Kevin dodged her poking fingertip.

Running her fingers through his matted hair, she picked out most of the pink and blue strands.

"Okay, that'll have to do." She wiped her hands on her shorts. "Ready to have some more fun?"

Kevin licked the remaining sugar from his fingers as he trod along behind the skipping girl. Heads turned toward the pair as they wound their way through the thickening crowd. A group of teenage girls pointed and whispered as they passed the furry beast. A toddler screamed and thrust his face into his father's thigh. The two revelers remained oblivious to the chaos they'd created. Most who passed them barely gave them a glance, assuming the Bigfoot was a man in a costume, paid to run around the carnival scaring people.

When they reached the funhouse, Jill produced two more tickets and pulled the Bigfoot into the spiraling tunnel. Kevin ducked and growled as the floor toppled him sideways. Trying to take another step, he fell to his knees and rolled, while Jill stood outside the spinning cylinder.

"C'mon," she said. "You can do it."

Kevin crawled over the edge of the rotating tube and flopped onto the floor beside her. Heaving a sigh, he rose. Jill led him into a room filled with swinging sand bags. She bobbed and wove her way around the obstacles. Kevin followed, pummeling the bags with his fists. Sand seeped onto the floor as they passed into the Plexiglas maze.

As Jill darted through the narrow openings, the creature squeezed himself into tighter and tighter spaces. Trying to reverse, Kevin warped three walls and hopped over the rest as he exited the maze ahead of her.

Then he found himself in a pitch-black room. Black light flashed, illuminating geometric shapes painted on the walls. The strobe went dark, leaving the room unlit and the Bigfoot's eyes trying to adjust. The monster bellowed and thrashed, terrified.

"Kevin, calm down," Jill said. "Just keep walking."

She pushed his furry rump until he began to move. The black light flared and Kevin screeched. Barreling into the nearest barrier, he fell. The room went dark. Patting the floor, Jill felt her way around his hairy form.

"Crawl this way," she said, yanking him by the scruff of his neck.

When they reached the hall of mirrors, she collapsed into her squashed reflection. The person looking back was a foot tall and looked to be three feet wide. Kevin stood in front of another Bigfoot that was twice as tall as he was but much thinner. Pressing a finger at the other creature, the reflection pointed a slender digit back at him. When Kevin roared a warning, the taller creature screamed a threat. Kevin scurried through the next door without a second glance.

The crash and tinkling of broken glass made Jill dart through the hall behind him. Several mannequin arms littered the floor along with torn clothes and shards of what looked to have been a glass vampire head. The coffin in the corner was on its side, the mechanics of the jumping demon torn to pieces.

"Uh-oh," Jill said.

Kevin had disappeared.

Jill hurried through the last few rooms, looking under anything that could harbor a terrified Bigfoot, but Kevin was gone. When she found herself standing outside the swinging exit door, she spun in a quick circle, surveying the immediate area.

A man darted around the side of the funhouse and shouted, "What was that racket!"

Jill shrugged and pointed back into the modified trailer, then trotted away in the opposite direction, all the while searching for her friend.

A furry foot peeked from under a funnel cake cart as Jill rounded the food stand and waited at the window.

"Can I help you?" a tattooed woman asked.

"I'd like two funnel cakes and a hot dog."

Jill peeked beside the booth to make sure Kevin was still there. He tucked his toes farther into the cart's shadow.

"Do you want berries or sugar?" the woman asked.

"Berries on one, sugar on the other," Jill said, kicking a rock from under her shoe. After taking the last of Jill's money, the woman passed the food over the counter and pointed to the side of the Formica edge.

"Fixin's for the dog are on the corner." The woman pulled a dirty rag from an apron pocket and began to wipe the surface in front of her.

"Thank you." Jill nodded and dragged her food across the food-stained surface to the condiments. When she was done and picked up the hot dog, it was a pound heavier, piled high with relish, onions, and everything else that had been available. She balanced the paper plates as she waddled around the side of the stand. Dropping to her knees, she tapped Kevin on the sole of his foot. It curled out of sight.

"Kevin," she whispered. "I'm sorry you got scared."

The creature didn't respond.

"I brought you some food."

She tore a piece of mustard loaded bread and held it under the food cart. After a moment, she felt hot breath on her fingertips. Then the food was nibbled from her hand. Kevin's furry face emerged and he stared at the piled plate.

"Okay. You can have the rest."

She slid the plate toward him. Kevin crawled from beneath the stand and squatted in the dirt as he gulped the foot long in two quick bites. He grunted and pointed a ketchup-soaked finger at the funnel cake Jill was nibbling.

"Don't worry. I got you one, too."

She pushed the paper plate through the dust. A strawberry toppled off and rolled through the dirt. Kevin lunged at it and popped it into his mouth.

"Kevin," Jill said. "That was gross. You don't know what was on the ground."

The beast didn't care. His funnel cake and half of hers was gone by the time she looked back at her own powdered sugar-covered plate. The monster looked at her, opened his mouth, and produced a rancid belch.

"Gross," she shrieked. "No more. All gone." Checking her pockets, she added, "And I'm out of money."

"Jill," a familiar voice called as Megan searched for her.

The little girl shot to her feet. "Oh-no. I've got to go." She reached out, grabbed Kevin's grimy hand, and shook it.

"It was very nice meeting you, Kevin. Maybe I'll see you again."

Jill grabbed the beast under his arms and shoved him to his feet. Kevin's eyebrows creased as she pointed back to the woods.

"Time for you to go home now," she said.

"Jill, where are you?" her mother called.

Kevin shook his shaggy head and grabbed Jill's hand.

"I'm sorry, Kevin but my mom wouldn't understand. She won't even let me have a dog." She pointed to the dark, shadowed edge of the carnival. "You've got to go."

Kevin turned and took a few steps. Looking back at Jill, he raised his eyebrows. She waved to him. The monster veered away and loped into the brush.

"There you are," Megan said. "We've been looking for you everywhere."

"I've been waiting for you," Jill said sweetly. Her eyes darted across to the shadowy trees.

"Look what Uncle Fred won for you," her mother said.

Fred trudged toward the little girl and dropped a large stuffed animal into her arms.

"The giant monkey," Megan said.

"Thank you," Jill said as she hugged the furry beast to her chest. "But he's not my uncle, and it's a Bigfoot not a monkey. I think I'll call him Kevin."

Megan pushed out a disgusted breath.

"Did you have to name it after your father?"

"Yes," Jill said, looking over her shoulder into the woods. "Yes, I did."

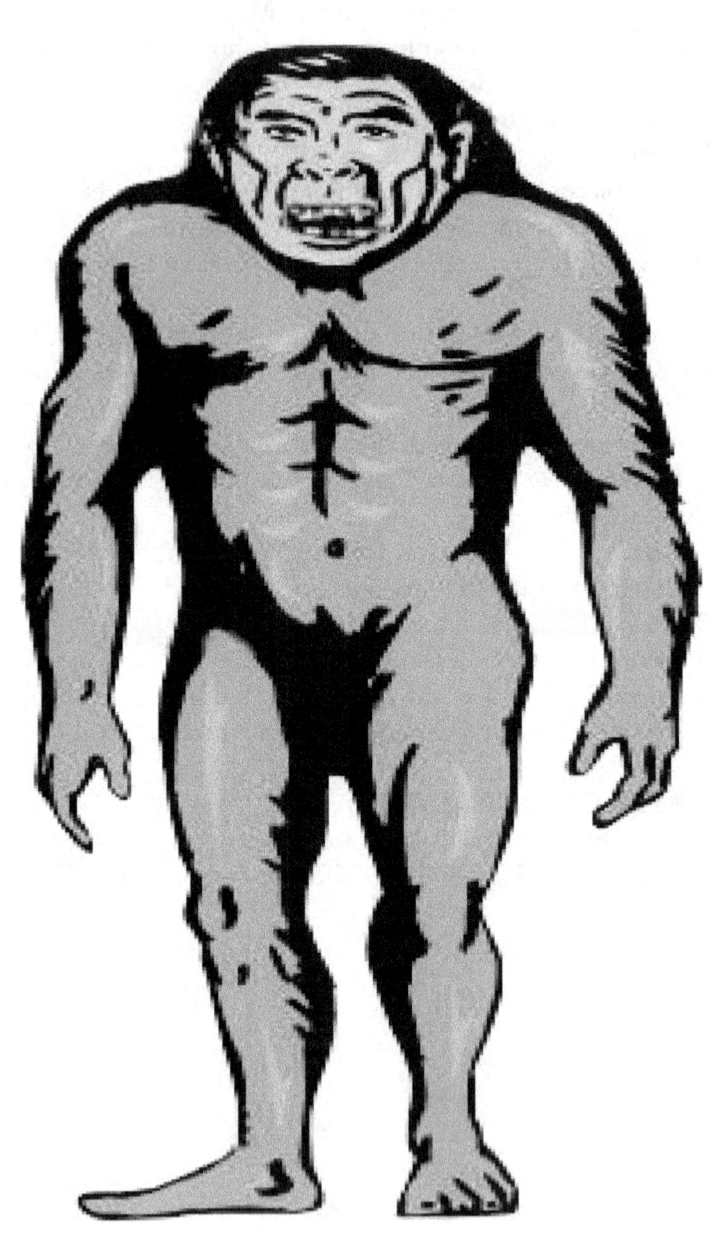

THE STONE GIANT OF
SHELVING ROCK

ADAM P. LEWIS

Looking down from the cliff edge at the river below, Tim made the snap decision to jump. Not knowing if the water below was deep or shallow and bedded with rock, he didn't care. The only thing he cared about was escaping the beast. Just behind him, he could hear the snapping of branches as the beast's heavy footfalls stomped through the brush. He sprang from the rocky ledge and pin dropped into the water below, splashing in, sinking to the bottom.

The section of the river was deep enough to slow and cushion his plunge. His feet planted on the rocky bottom and he sprang up through the water like a rocket. Upon surfacing, he inhaled deeply and kicked his legs, keeping his head above water. Looking up at the cliff, he saw the beast.

It was just as the Iroquois elders from his clan, the Okwáho, described the Ot-ne-yar-heh, 'the stone giant' in their oral story telling. The stone giant stood erect like a man but was hunched over at the mid of its back like a frail woman. Its mane was dark brown, nappy, and thick around its waist, shoulders, back, forearms, and calves. It receded as it spread between body parts. The hairs on its chest, feet and hands were thinner as was the hair growing around its facial features, which gave the beast the impression of an unshaven man. Its face was half-human and half-ape and its skin was black.

Tim measured the stone giant with his eyes and estimated it standing over seven feet tall. The bulk of the stone giant was more impressive than its height. The head appeared to rest on its shoulders, because the neck was hidden under muscle and hair. Its shoulders were broader than two normal sized men standing shoulder to shoulder. Its legs and arms, bulging with dense muscles, twitched under its hide.

The stone giant bellowed, guttural and angry. It hammered its fists into the rocky ledge, breaking and tearing pieces of rock free, to throw them down at Tim. The rocks plunged in, shooting columns of water high into the air. Tim dived underwater to escape the bombardment and let the undertow carry him downstream until he couldn't fight the urge to breathe.

He surfaced for air and looked back at the ledge, now fifty to sixty yards away. The stone giant was gone.

The night before, Tim had been dry, safe and laughing around a campfire with two fellow Okwáho, Carl and Mick. They shared tall tales of their biggest catches which were exaggerated more from the cheap beer they drank than trying to outdo each other's stories.

Tim had bitten off the end of a Churchill cigar, spit it out, leaned into the fire, and puffed. After a few drags to keep the cigar lit, he held it between his teeth and held his hands apart about four feet. "I'm telling you the truth, that son-of-a-bitching catfish had to be this long. The head on that sucker was bigger than my wife's jugs!"

Carl laughed. "Then the fish's body must have been the size of your fist. Your wife's rack underneath her bra is nothing short of powder puffs!"

"You didn't let me finish; bigger than my wife's ass!"

Mick laughed and stood up. "I'm going to take a leak."

"You have our permission!" Carl joked.

"Boy, you sure are full of comedy tonight."

"Do you need one of us to hold it or are you gonna be a big boy and do it all by yourself this time?" Carl joked again.

"Maybe I'll just wiz on you instead of the trees."

Everyone laughed.

Later that night, the men hunkered down in their sleeping bags, talked a bit more about woman, cigars, and fishing before falling asleep. The night was cool, overcast and a slight mist had formed across Shelving Rock which overlooked Lake George.

Startled from what he thought was a cry for help, Carl woke and lifted his head. A hunting guide by trade had given him a keen sense of his surroundings. He could follow a moose for miles just by looking at broken tree branches. Any slight noise would draw his attention, such as now. "Did you guys hear that?"

Mick grumbled incoherently and started snoring. He wasn't much of a woodsman as Carl; he just liked getting away from the reservation and selling duty free cigarettes to non-clansman. Fishing trips were his favorite escape from work and his family. Neither his wife nor kids cared much for fishing and never bothered to ask to tag along. Just the thought of hooking squirming worms made the three most important women in his life gag and shiver.

"I thought I heard something," Tim said. "I think it was an owl or a hawk."

"No, that was no owl," Carl said. "It sounded more like someone calling out for help."

Off in the distance, a bellow echoed from across the lake. "What the hell was that, a coyote?" Tim asked.

Carl shook his head. "No, there aren't any coyotes in this area of the Adirondacks. That was a bear, maybe grizzly, if so it would be a black bear. And from the other sounds, it appears to have attacked something putting up a fight. Those cries sound like a distress call. I can't imagine a grizzly attacking something big enough to cry out like that, though. I've never heard or seen such a thing."

Yawning and laying his head back on the pillow, Tim said, "Well if it's a grizzly, it's eating now, so we won't be attacked."

Carl laid his head down as well. "They'll only attack us if desperate or threatened. They'll run from us before we even see them."

As the sounds faded, the three men returned to sleep.

Before the sun had fully risen, the men were already fishing. Carl and Tim were up to their waists in the water, kept dry by chest-high waders. Mick was about fifty yards offshore in a rowboat just visible through the mist hovering over the water.

"Any luck yet?" Tim called to Mick.

"A few nibbles, no takers though."

"If I didn't know any better, I'd say all the fish grew legs last night and walked ashore," Carl grumbled. "I haven't had a single nibble."

Tim reeled in his line. "Same here. I'm gonna move down the lake a bit. You coming?"

"Nah, I think I'll stay here. Mick is directly in front of me and he's gotten a few hits. The fish may be moving this way."

Tim walked along the shoreline as Mick drifted towards the opposite side of Lake George. Feeling pressure on his bladder, he stood up and relieved himself over the side of the boat. Then he felt the urge to take a dump. He rowed ashore, pulled the boat onto land, and walked twenty feet into the woods.

Once there, he dropped his pants as well as the refuse of last night's dinner onto the ground. After he finished, he swore in annoyance; back across the lake was the toilet paper. Still squatting, he searched in the brush for leaves large enough to wipe, when he suddenly jumped up in fear.

Like a scared rabbit running out from under a bush, he fled the woods with his pants only halfway pulled up to his waist. Before he even had his pants up, he was a good fifteen feet from shore, rowing the boat as if he was competing in an Ivy League boat race.

By then the mist had lifted just enough for Carl to see everything that was happening across the lake. Not knowing what exactly was going on with his friend, he laughed.

"Son of a…" Mick repeated, as he rowed full steam across the lake. He was fifty feet from shore when Carl realized something was wrong. The look on Mick's face was one of terror. Tears streamed down Mick's chalky face, his knuckles turning white from tightly gripping the oars that shook within his trembling hands.

"What happened to you?" Carl asked.

Mick stood and pulled his pants up, jumped out of the boat, and yanked it ashore. Ignoring his friend, he ran to the campsite and started packing his camping and fishing gear. By this time, Tim had seen what was going on and ran back from where he'd set up his new fishing spot.

"What's wrong with him?" Tim asked, pointing his fishing rod at Mick.

"Don't know. The only thing he keeps saying is we have to get the hell out of here, right now."

Tim grabbed Mick by the arm and spun him around.

"Let me go, before I end up like that guy across the lake!" Mick yelled.

"What guy across the lake? What're you talking about?"

Carl grabbed Mick's arms. "What did you see across the lake?"

Mick ripped his arm free and continued to pack his gear in a hurry, as if he were saving precious items from a house fire. "Across the lake, there's a man, or what I think is a man. His body's ripped up, head bashed, guts all over the place with claw marks. He's all chewed up…hell…just don't stand there and stare at me, we've got to get out of here!"

Trying to grasp what their friend was saying, Carl and Tim looked at each other thinking Mick had turned crazy on them overnight. "I think he saw a dead deer or something like that," Tim said.

"I know a deer when I see one and that mess across the lake wasn't a deer. It was human."

Carl looked back across the lake. "The only way to find out is to row across and take a look."

"I'm not going back there. If you two want to die like that guy then go 'head, but I'm stayin' on this side of the lake," Mick said, pointing down at the ground, adamant he was staying put.

"If what you saw was a human, then we've got to find out for sure," Carl said.

"He's right, Mick," Tim added. "We just can't let a dead body rot out here in the woods. We have to at least find it and get help, or bring the body back with us."

Mick froze and looked at his friends. "Something over there ripped that guy apart and it could still be out there waiting to get us next."

"Then that something could've swam or walked around the lake and gotten us by now. Or maybe it's waiting in the woods behind us and waiting for the right moment," Carl said.

"Knock it off. You're gonna freak him out even worse," Tim said, nudging Carl in the back. But Carl continued, knowing that if he frightened Mick just enough, then he'd join them instead of staying alone at camp.

"So you stay if you want to and fight off the animal that got the guy across the lake," Carl said.

Tim knew that moment Carl was using reverse psychology on Mick. "Come on, Tim, help me get the boat in the water," Carl said.

The two men pushed the boat into the water and started to row across the lake. Within five feet of leaving shore, Mick darted from the camp, high stepped through the water, and jumped into the boat.

On the way across, Mick mumbled to himself. Only a few words could be comprehended: *doomed, all going to die, end up mutilated, damn.* The jokester around the fire last night, Carl, cracked a few jokes as he rowed but soon shut up, knowing there was no way he could lighten the mood.

When the boat reached the far shore, Carl and Tim got out and pulled the boat onto land. Mick was shaking in fear so much that ripples from under the boat scattered on the water's surface.

"Where'd you say the body was?" Tim asked.

Mick raised a shaky hand and pointed to the right of where he'd stopped off to crap.

"Are you going to sit in that boat or are you gonna help us find it?" Carl asked.

Mick nodded his head. "Yup, I'm stayin' right here."

Carl and Tim approached the treeline and a smell resembling puke and crap filled the air. At first, they thought that's exactly what Mick had done there a short time ago—puked and crapped. Hopefully they both agreed that was what he mistook for a body. Even though they knew Mick wasn't stupid enough to confuse a body with his excrement.

Searching the area, they couldn't find any sign of a body, not even a trace of blood. Fifteen minutes went by and all they found was where Mick had dropped his pants and his excrement.

Carl did find a few broken twigs and patted-down moss, suggesting something big did in fact make its way through the area. The ground was covered with too much brush to determine what animal species had left the impressions.

"What do you think?" Tim asked.

"I don't think he saw anything, maybe a light trick of some sort. It was foggy this morning," Carl reasoned.

The two men reemerged from the woods, grabbed the end of the boat, pushed it into the water, and climbed in.

"Did you see it?" Mick asked.

"We didn't find anything except where you crapped," Tim said.

"And by the smell of it," Carl added, "it looks like you crapped out a dead body. So that must be what you saw."

Tim laughed as Mick barked in anger, "Shut up, I know what I saw and it didn't come out of me!"

"We saw that there wasn't any toilet paper around, so you didn't wipe," Carl joked. "How 'bout you save your dirty underwear and we take it to the police and use it as a sketch so they know what they'll be looking for after you file a report!"

"Screw you both," Mick snapped and crossed his arms.

The remaining boat ride across the lake was more teasing at the expense of Mick. Instead of defending himself, he sat motionless and stewed. Whatever he saw was real to him and he wouldn't be confused with anything but a gutted body.

By the time they arrived back ashore at camp, Mick was no longer giving his friends the cold shoulder. Instead, he was scolding them like a father on how teasing could hurt a person's feelings.

During the lecture, all three pulled the boat from the water and carried it back to camp. Within fifteen feet from camp, they dropped the boat to the ground and quickly sprinted to the campsite. Their eyes darted back and forth like surprised children scanning presents on Christmas morning at what they found.

The camp had been ravaged. Everything they owned was in ruins. Sleeping bags were torn to shreds, tents shredded, the cooler crushed in on itself, and even their carbon fiber fishing poles were snapped into a dozen pieces.

"What in the name? Why would someone do this?" Tim asked aloud. "Damn kids!" he yelled in anger, kicking at pieces of a fishing pole. "I bet it was those teenagers we passed about half a mile down the lake when we drove up here the other night. They didn't look of age to be drinking. I bet they got drunk and trashed the place while looking for beer."

"If it was those teenagers, then they would've stolen the beer rather than crush the cans without opening and drinking them first," Tim said, holding up a crushed can.

Mick picked up a pair of his torn-apart pants that were still somewhat wearable. Rather than stand around in soiled pants, he changed into the ripped pair.

"Kids my ass, I bet it was that thing that killed that guy!" Mick said.

Carl ignored Mick and searched the area for supplies that weren't destroyed. He bent down and looked at the tracks covering the campsite, his tracker intuition taking over. The tracks were humanlike, but two times wider and nearly twice as long as a human footprint.

Tracing the outline of the footprints with his fingers, he found a hair within one impression and picked it up. His eyes squinted as he studied the hair and rolled it between his fingers. The hair was short, thick, coarse and ended in a dull point. He sniffed it. It smelled of dead skunk.

Mick picked up a cooler; each side was cracked open like a walnut and caved in as if a sledgehammer had been taken to it. "There were human footprints next to this cooler," he said, holding it up. "So maybe it was those teenagers."

"These tracks are human, the shape anyway. But…" Carl paused.

"But what?" Mick yelled, becoming scared once again.

"But," Carl snapped back, "they're twice the size of an adult human. It's almost as if the person or thing that trashed our camp was Bigfoot."

"Stop joking around, Carl, this is no time for comic relief," Tim said.

"It's no joke," Carl replied. "Look at the tracks yourself; the front of the footprints has five large toes and the back an oversized heel. Look at the bump near the middle. That's a midtarsal break. Humans don't leave midtarsal breaks…primates do!"

Tim looked around the ground and saw footprints everywhere. "Maybe we stepped in our own tracks and made them look bigger," he suggested.

"I've tracked animals for too long," Carl said. "I've seen overlapping tracks and these aren't them. They're implanted too deep into the soil to be ours. Only a heavy animal could imprint that deep."

"Perhaps the old stories are true, that there really is a stone giant of the woodlands," Tim whispered under his breath.

Carl searched about for other tracks that could negate his findings while Tim picked up most of the trashed campsite. He didn't pick up the mess in an orderly way. Instead, he took what was left of his sleeping bag and filled it up with pieces of destroyed gear. When the bag got to the point where it almost had to be dragged, he approached his pickup to load it into the back.

"Oh my," Tim mouthed. His face was flash frozen in fear.

Behind him, Carl picked up a handful of dirt that looked as though it was mixed with blood. Carrying it over to get Tim's opinion, his fingers spread apart, releasing the dirt like an hourglass. Like Tim, he froze too.

"Mick, you better get over here!" Carl called out after the shock began to wear off.

Mick approached to see what Carl wanted, but unlike his friends, he began shaking in fear

Sprawled out on the truck's hood was the body Mick saw when he was across the lake. The body looked as though a grizzly bear had performed an autopsy. A deep claw wound had ripped the chest open down to the pelvis. All the organs inside showed signs that they were either chewed or eaten away. What was left of the ribcage had claw and teeth marks dug deep into the bone. The throat had teeth punctures on each side where the animal had crushed the man's windpipe, suffocating him to death. The man's arms and legs had smaller chew marks where much smaller animals, possibly skunk or opossum, had fed on the carcass after it had served as a meal to its killer. The top of the skull was cracked open and hung off the side of the pickup's hood. Gravity worked on the skull's contents, forcing a mushy pile of brains to slide out and plop onto the ground.

"Believe me now?" Mick gasped.

"Shut up, Mick," Tim snapped. "You're not helping the situation."

"I'll never doubt you again, Mick. I swear to it," Carl said, walking around the pickup and examining the body. "Whatever did this was no grizzly."

"You think so?" Mick asked sarcastically. "No grizzly carries a dead body around a lake and places it on top of a truck."

"I think we're dealing with a Bigfoot here," Carl said in a shaky voice. He'd never bought into the elders stories of the stone giants until now.

"That's what we heard last night from across the lake; the screams and howls. That wasn't an animal fight, it was this poor bastard being attacked by Bigfoot," Tim said.

"If it's smart enough to do this, then it knows we're here. For all we know it could've been watching us all night long," Carl said.

"Whoa, wait a minute," Mick broke in, raising his voice in anger. "You two knew that this thing could've been out there watching us, waiting to attack us? And all you did was continue ignoring that fact, then put on waders and started fishing in the morning."

Carl raised his voice in reply. "We didn't know what was out there, Mick! It sounded just like a grizzly and that's all I figured it to be!"

"A grizzly that carries a dead body around a big lake within thirty minutes, drops it on Tim's truck, trashes our camp, and runs back into the woods to let us know it's watching us?" Mick yelled. "You're nuts! Whatever beast did this was a Bigfoot, Sasquatch, stone giant or whatever the hell you want to call it! It's obvious!" He was becoming annoyed and frustrated with his friends.

"Calm down and stop yelling!" Tim snapped. "If there is a Bigfoot out there, then it's nearby and we don't need to let it know we're here for it to attack us next. We need to gather up what's left of our gear and get the hell out of here in a hurry!"

Wanting to get out of the woods sooner, Mick grabbed the corpse by the arm and pulled it off the pickup's hood. The body slid down the bloody hood to the ground with the ease of a hockey puck gliding over ice. Not wanting to be the next victim, he jumped into the driver's seat and turned over the engine. "Get in or I'll leave you both behind!"

Tim reached into the cab and turned the ignition off. "Get out and help us load the truck or you'll be walking back home through these woods."

"Bigfoot is out there, stalking us, and you want to pack up our gear…are you two crazy?"

Angrily, Carl pulled Mick from the truck.

"We don't know what's out there, but just in case it isn't anything but a prank we aren't leaving our stuff behind," Carl said.

"Pranks don't involve mutilated bodies!" Mick yelled.

"Damn you, Mick, no one knows what the hell's happening here, just help us get the truck loaded. Stalling is going to get us all killed," Carl said, while dragging Mick by the arm to the camp. "Now help us load the damn truck!"

It took ten minutes, but the men got the pickup loaded and started driving away from the camp. Tim drove slowly over the bumpy and potholed dirt road.

"At this rate," Mick sneered, "it could take about an hour or more to get out of the woods to the main road."

"No worries," Tim reassured him, "we'll make time once we hit the main roads. We'll leave Shelving Rock behind us soon enough."

During the ride, Mick rocked back and forth in the backseat of the double wide pickup, muttering obscenities. Carl shook his head at how annoying Mick had become. Both Carl and Tim knew Mick was somewhat paranoid but not to this extent.

"Whoa, whoa, whoa… stop!" Carl yelled.

Tim slammed on the brakes and skidded to a stop. "What—what's the matter?"

"Back up about ten feet."

Tim shifted into reverse.

"It's that campsite those teens set up, all their gear looks trashed, too."

Carl got out of the pickup and walked over to the camp, followed closely by Tim. Too scared to join them, Mick stayed in the cab, still rocking back and forth with his eyes closed.

Looking over the camp, they found more Bigfoot tracks. There were no signs that the teenagers were killed or harmed in any manner. Both cars they'd drove up the mountain in were gone. Deep tire skid marks were found, suggesting the teens had left in a hurry. Carl and Tim returned to the pickup and continued the drive back down the dirt road.

"Well?" Mick asked.

"Looks like they left in a hurry. There's no sign of foul play so hopefully they're safe."

Keeping a sharp lookout into the woods on both sides of the pickup, each of the men scanned for Bigfoot. They prayed they wouldn't see the beast charging from behind a tree before they reached the main road.

If Bigfoot attacked, the slow moving vehicle would be a sitting duck.

Almost forty minutes passed until Tim reached the main road. He accelerated, pushing the engine to its limit, which nearly blew a head gasket as the RPMs were pushed into the red. Burning engine oil could be smelled and on every turn the tires squealed like hungry pigs.

"Slow down some, Tim, you're gonna roll over and kill us all. I'd rather take my chances with that Bigfoot than your driving right about now!" Carl said as he held tight to the dashboard.

"If that's the case I can pull over and let you out!" Tim shouted, his hands gripping the steering wheel tightly.

"Don't stop, just open the door and jump out!" Mick yelled. "I don't want Tim stopping for anything."

Tim sped around another turn and slammed on the brakes, sending the vehicle fishtailing thirty feet until it came to a stop. "Hey, I was just joking!" Carl yelled.

Tim responded by pointing a shaky finger out the windshield. There, standing down the road before them, was the stone giant, Bigfoot.

It stood hunched over, arms spread out from the sides of its body like a wrestler waiting for his opponent to lunge forward. Then, without warning, it lowered its head and darted towards the pickup.

Tim yanked on the stick shift, putting the vehicle into reverse and flooring the gas pedal, driving backwards up the mountain road.

Carl and Mick yelled in fright, ordering Tim to do what he was already doing…drive.

Gaining ground was Bigfoot; every stride drew the stone giant inches closer until it was only twenty yards away. Tim slammed on the brakes, stopping the pickup in a spray of dust. The sudden stop caused Bigfoot to stop and crouch close to the ground. It was ready to pounce.

Slamming his foot on the gas and shifting into 'drive,' the pickup surged forward towards Bigfoot. Carl and Mick yelled for Tim to turn around but instead, Tim continued to drive straight at the monster. The beast didn't flinch as the pickup sped toward it. Closer and closer the truck came upon Bigfoot, and seconds before the moment of impact, the creature jumped forward at the pickup and landed on the roof.

Swerving across the road, Tim tried to fling the beast off the roof but failed. For a brief moment, Tim lost control, nearly driving off the edge of the road and into the trees.

When the pickup was under control again, he slammed on the brakes, screeching to a halt. All three men stared out the windshield, hoping to see Bigfoot falling off the roof, rolling down the road and away from them, but all they saw was an empty road.

"I must've shook that thing loose back up the road a ways," Tim said between heavy breaths.

Mick turned and looked up the road. "Unless it went off into the woods, I don't see it anywhere. Let's not find out where..."

A loud crumpling sound rang through the inside of the pickup as the beast ripped open the roof. A flash of brown blurred into and out of the cab. The creature grabbed Mick's throat with its large hands and yanked him out. Fierce and hungry bellows drowned out Mick's choking as his lungs filled with blood.

Frightened, Tim ran from the pickup and into the woods. Carl was left alone. He hopped into the driver's seat and sped away.

The beast crouched down and held tightly to the roof while ripping Mick's esophagus from his throat with its mouth. With its fingernails, it tore through Mick's clothes, gripping the flesh and swinging him over the vehicle.

Mick's body slammed through the windshield, causing Carl to veer off the road and slam into a tree. Before the pickup collided with the tree, the beast leaped off it and landed on its feet, then began to walk towards the vehicle. The last thing Carl saw as he opened his eyes for the last time was the creature's hands wrapped around his temples as it squeezed, crushing his skull.

Running faster than he ever had in his life, Tim dashed through the woods, hoping the beast wasn't trailing behind. After about fifteen minutes, he stopped and leaned against a tree. He looked back and could no longer see the road, or the beast. As his breathing slowed to normal, he thought whether Carl had escaped or not, and how stupid it was for Tim to flee into the woods.

Cursing himself for not staying behind and helping, Tim punched a tree and nearly broke his hand. Then he thought that maybe fleeing was for the best. If he could hike through the trails of Shelving Rock safely, he could get help. Even though his legs felt like wet spaghetti noodles, he continued running.

More than an hour went by of him running as fast as he could and Tim was now dragging his feet, figuring he had a safe and untraceable distance between himself and the creature.

Thoughts of that very beast were few and far between as the feeling of thirst, hunger, and exhaustion took its toll.

Instead of wanting to get out of the woods for help, he hoped he would stumble upon other campers, a creek, or a cabin to replenish his body and be safe from the creature.

However, the only thing he came across were trees and small animals that startled him every time they ran when he got too close to them. Soon he realized his wandering around for a stream, campers and shelter was leading him in circles.

Three times in the past hour he had came across the same large, broken rock with a tree growing from within a crack. Tim was lost and the sun was setting, nightfall soon upon him. He sat down on the rock with the tree to rest.

His breathing slowed and his legs felt better, though they were sore from so much running. This rest was exactly what he needed to clear his mind. Now he was able to ignore his need for water and food, and he shifted his attention back to escaping the beast and making it to safety.

He stood up, and after making it through a bout of dizziness from standing too fast, he figured out which way was north and began moving off in that direction.

Daylight succumbed to darkness and Tim was a good mile from where he'd rested. Instead of running full speed, he jogged to conserve energy. He would need it if the creature found him or if he stumbled upon *it*.

In his left peripheral vision, he thought he saw movement in the woods. At first, he thought they were tricks of light and shadow, but tricks of light don't make guttural moans, break tree limbs, and crush dead leaves on the forest floor. The shape of the figure, bulky, tall and hairy was all too familiar. Bigfoot had found him.

The beast was shadowing Tim's movements, waiting for the right moment to strike. Tim picked up his pace, hoping he could somehow elude his hunter in the darkness. In spite of this, he knew it was his scent that led Bigfoot to him.

He'd watched *The Legend of Boggy Creek* many times, and he knew the creature had a bloodhound sense of smell. There was no room for escape unless he could shield or hide his scent. Every step he took as he ran made him perspire. His sweat was like a pheromone and the beast, being closely related to humans, reacted to it. Tim's only option was to find a water source and travel within it.

Thinking like his tracker friend Carl, Tim figured out Bigfoot's hunting habits. It only pounced when threatened, an unwelcomed person or animal entered its territory, or if its prey sensed its presence. Avoiding all contact and urge to look over his shoulder to see how close the beast was to him, he continued moving through the forest and soon heard what he was looking for.

Just through a clearing in the forest, he saw the moonlight dancing off the breaking of water upon rocks. He found the water source he'd been searching for in order to take a chance at escape.

Sprinting, he took off through the forest. The sudden burst through the woods alarmed the stone giant and it began running after him, breaking branches and uprooting ground growth with every step. Branches cut Tim's face, arms, and legs, leaving a fresh blood scent behind for the creature to follow.

Trailing close by, the creature was only a few body lengths behind when Tim came to a small rocky incline. Like a crawling baby, he clawed his way up the rocky slope on his knees and hands. Suddenly, he was stopped dead in his tracks by Bigfoot. The stone giant dug its fingernails into Tim's shoe and pulled him down the slope. Kicking his feet at the beast's grip, Tim tried freeing himself. By doing so, he slowed the creature down, giving himself enough time to slip out of his shoe and kick the monster in the face, causing it to lose its balance and roll down the rocky incline. Tim got to his feet and ran the rest of the way up the slope. When he reached the top, he ran from under the brush and screeched to a halt. He found himself at the edge of the cliff overlooking the river below.

Tim contemplated jumping into the water. Behind him, Bigfoot charged up the slope, screaming in anger. The rock cracked and split open as the creature dug its fingernails and toenails into the slope. Upon reaching the top, it sniffed the air for Tim's scent. Once the scent was found, the beast looked in the direction it came and saw Tim stepping back away from the ledge. It dashed forward, unleashing hairsplitting growls that echoed throughout Shelving Rock. Salivating at the thought of sinking its teeth into fresh prey, Bigfoot could taste Tim's scent lingering in the air. Tree branches broke off as Bigfoot pushed through the brush, and just as it leapt out onto the ledge, Tim jumped. Bigfoot stopped at the ledge and sniffed the air for Tim's scent but all it could smell was the forest. It turned and began searching once more.

Tim dived underwater to escape the bombardment and let the undertow carry him downstream until he couldn't fight the urge to breathe. He surfaced for air and looked back at the ledge, now fifty to sixty yards away. The stone giant was gone.

He floated downstream, where the width of the water narrowed and the depth lowered to ankle height, causing him to continue through the water on foot. Turning a bend in the stream, he noticed straight ahead moonlight gleaming off a cabin window. Heading towards the cabin, he heard Bigfoot bellowing in the distance. With each scream, the beast drew closer.

When he was standing before the cabin, he screamed out, calling for help, but received no answer. After pounding on the front door, he again received no reply. Circling around the exterior, he looked in the windows. The cabin was empty, except for wooden furniture, a gun rack above the fireplace, and an unlit oil lamp on the mantel.

He kicked in the front door and began reinforcing the cabin. He placed the heavy oak-framed bed in front of the door and the wooden dressers and a table in front of the windows. The only way in and out was the fireplace, which he lit ablaze to keep Bigfoot from climbing down, though due to the beast's size it was highly unlikely. After he barricaded the cabin, Tim took down the shotgun from the gun rack and loaded it with slug shells. The shotgun was his only plan of defense if Bigfoot got inside or if he had to make a dash from the cabin.

It wasn't long after Tim fortified the cabin, that he heard Bigfoot's footfalls pounding the ground around the cabin. Seconds later, he heard scraping sounds as the creature dragged its sharp nails on the cabin's long exterior, sizing up the dwelling.

The beast let out snorts of anger as it pounded its fists on the framework. The log frame was hard, thick, and would take hours to hammer through. Every slight noise Bigfoot made on the outside, Tim pointed the shotgun in that direction. Then he heard loud poundings on the roof as the creature stomped about, trying to smash through.

Tim pointed the shotgun at the roof and pulled the trigger, firing slug after slug. Each shot caused the beast to jump back at every exit point exploding through the roof. One lucky shot grazed its hide, knocking the creature off its feet where it tumbled to the ground.

It grew quiet. Tim listened carefully, trying to pinpoint Bigfoot's whereabouts but all he heard was a ringing in his ears from the loud gunfire. He lowered the shotgun and crept towards one of the windows to see if the fall had killed the creature. He pushed the dresser away a few inches and looked out, seeing nothing.

A loud and startling crash came from the front door, causing Tim to jump. Without hesitation, he swung around and pointed the shotgun at the front door. The beast was slamming its body against the door, forcing its way inside.

With every slam into the door, the heavy bed skipped an inch across the floor. When enough space between the door and the frame was created, the hairy beast pushed its clawed hand inside, trying to grab onto the bed and push it away. Tim's hands shook as he pointed the shotgun at the creature and squeezed the trigger.

The slug tore through the door. Wood shrapnel exploded off it, scattering about the room. Outside the cabin, Bigfoot let out a loud, distressed howl. The slug had entered its left shoulder. The impact knocked it onto its back where it lay in pain.

Blood poured from the wound. Its left shoulder blade had shattered when the slug exited, rendering the arm useless. Rising to its feet, the wounded beast swayed back and forth, pacing the cabin perimeter, still looking for a way in.

Inside the cabin, Tim broke open the oil lamp. He ripped curtains from the windows, tearing them into strips. With oil from the lamp, he soaked each strip. Next, he poured a portion of the oil around the cabin and dowsed the floor in a circular pattern, then backed into a corner. From this corner, he had a view of every possible angle if the creature tried to enter through a window or if it managed to once again push open the door.

Or if he had to, Tim would light the oil-soaked floor to slow the beast down so he could fire off more slugs.

With shotgun in hand, he was ready for the inevitable showdown. There was no escaping the Stone Giant of Shelving Rock and he knew what he had to do next, wait for it to enter and kill it.

Silence surrounded the cabin as the creature walked around, pacing back and forth. The only way in was through the windows. Thick walls and only one good arm to climb on top of the roof prevented Bigfoot from an easy attack. It would have to jump through a window or doorway with enough force to topple over the dresser or table propped up as a barricade. It backed up and began running.

Startled, Tim jumped to his feet as window glass shattered, followed by the loud bang of the dresser falling to the floor. Tim aimed the shotgun at the window. His finger twitched on the trigger nervously and fired off a round that blew through the cabin wall under the window.

Not knowing if he'd hit Bigfoot or not, he pumped the action, loaded more rounds into the chamber, and aimed at the window. Bigfoot didn't rise into view and all was quiet.

The weight of the shotgun tired his arms. He lowered it and quickly brought the barrel up when a second window shattered. Bigfoot had broken through the window, knocking over the barricade. The creature grabbed onto the window frame and tore it loose, creating a large enough hole to crawl through.

Muzzle flashes from the shotgun lit up the cabin like flickering lightning. Unfazed by the slugs that found their mark, the beast kept inching forward.

Panic set in as Tim tried to reload, his hands shaking in fear and causing him to drop the shells.

Growling, Bigfoot staggered like a drunkard while reaching out with its hands. Tim pulled matches from his pocket—which had been found next to the oil lamp—and struck one on the side of the box, and dropped it to the floor.

A quiet popping whoosh was followed by a wall of flames. Bigfoot jerked back, covering its face as the sudden brightness blinded its eyes. The beast shook off the surprise and inched forward. With every bit of remaining energy, it leapt through the flames, tackling Tim to the floor.

Pushing his hands up on the beast's jaw, Tim used all of what was left of his strength as well and rolled over, pushing the creature back into the flames. Normally this would have been impossible, as the beast was much bigger than Tim, but the creature was weak from all the gunshots and so Tim was a close match in strength.

The creature screamed as fire licked at its back, the odor of singed fur filling the cabin. It released Tim and rolled across the floor in pain as its flesh burned.

Unable to smother its flaming body, the beast rose up, staggering about the cabin. Melted flesh dripped like candle wax, spreading the fire throughout the cabin. Embers of hair floated in the air, sticking to the ceiling, causing sporadic fires to burn through to the dry roof. The cabin became engulfed in fire, a wall of flames blocking every exit.

Catching sight of Tim through the raging flames, Bigfoot lumbered forward. Tim wrapped the oil soaked strips around the shotgun barrel and held them over the flames, igniting them. Waving the burning rags between himself and the creature, he kept the monster at bay. Soon however, the rags had burned away and Bigfoot again found the strength to attack.

The beast tackled Tim to the floor and its melting flesh sizzled through Tim's clothes, setting him ablaze as well. Unable to extinguish his burning clothes as he fought for his life, he felt his skin begin to blister. He yelled out in intense anguish but was soon silenced as Bigfoot clasped its jaws around his windpipe and bit down.

Weakened from the violent fire, the roof collapsed. Blazing ceiling beams and shingles fell, crushing to death what little life Bigfoot retained.

When the cabin was consumed, the fire then spread across the mountainside, burning everything trapped within its blazing path. Days went by as the fire burned uncontrollably. Fire departments, volunteers, and the National Guard fought the blaze. Members of each perished trying to control what was now classified as a wild fire.

Nearly two weeks went by until the fire was finally under control in part to the efforts of man and a rainstorm that swept across the area.

Fire investigators and cleanup crews worked the area, finding no signs of the cabin or Tim. Only small fragments of the Bigfoot's skeleton were found.

Not wanting to upset Tim's family, investigators passed those remaining bones off as being Tim's only remains.

The fire itself was contributed to an accident that occurred miles away. Two badly burnt bodies were found inside a pickup truck. The vehicle in question was registered to Tim.

BIGFOOTED

PATRICK MACADOO

The dry snap of a twig outside his tent jolted Darrin awake. With a raspy hitch, he broke off inhaling and listened hard. Shadows shifted across the walls of the blue tent, humanoid shapes materializing and disintegrating in the pre-dawn murk. He reached for his rifle; it should have been beside his sleeping pad, where he placed it last night. The breeze rippled the unzipped tent-flap.

He knew he'd zipped the flap shut before bedding down.

He swallowed and forced himself to take a slow breath through his nostrils, as he continued to grope for his rifle. It could be one of the others, he thought. But they never got up before sunrise. He was always the first one up. It could be an animal wandering through their camp. Where was his gun?

He could picture Scott slipping into his tent while he was dead asleep, some noise in the night scaring the careless jerk into snagging the rifle, and Scott too frightened and too drunk to remember to zip the flap back up.

A furtive *scritch* sounded outside the front of the tent. It could've been the flap bustling in the breeze. It could have been a bear easing onto the dirt, preparing for a blitz-style attack. The sudden acceleration of his heartbeat, the throbbing in his ears, deafened him, and prevented further scrutiny. He inhaled again, hoping to catch the musk of a harmless forest creature.

A shaggy, snarling face thrust through the tent flap. Darrin screamed and scrambled backwards. He propelled himself upwards, his back crashing into the rear wall of the tent, his feet tangling in his bedding. The entire tent came down around him, aluminum rods clattering, the animal roaring. The bedding was wrapped around his ankles. The nylon tenting tangled around his torso and hooded his head, for a moment becoming constricting, making him helpless and blind. Then he tore free, stumbling for balance, the lumpy, hard-packed dirt bludgeoning his sock-covered feet, the low-hanging, pliant branches whipping his face and outstretched palms.

As he crashed through the trees, he heard an eruption of laughter behind him. Donna called out his name. He stopped. Blood boiled into his cheeks so fast that it made him dizzy.

The urge to keep going, to leave them to find their own way out of the wilderness, roiled inside him. He shuddered. They called for him to come back, that it was just a joke. He hung his head, took a deep breath, and manufactured a smile. He turned around. Scott was wearing a Chewbacca mask. Donna wore an old Mariners cap with her long black ponytail flowing out the back.

Cruel mockery only made her dusky features more beautiful. Darrin swallowed the bitter lump in his throat and trudged back to the campsite.

Donna glimpsed a flash of neon-orange safety vest among the deep green leafage way up the trail. Darrin had been ranging further and further ahead all day long. Most of the time out of eyesight, sometimes out of earshot. She berated herself, for the umpteenth time, for going along with Scott's prank. At the time she'd convinced herself that the joke would lighten the mood, which seemed to grow heavier with each passing mile. Now she accepted the fact that she'd simply been thrilled to conspire with him.

She ducked a caterpillar hanging from a gossamer thread. She knew she'd avoided the creepy-crawler, but couldn't help running a hand over the brim of her hat just to be sure. They freaked her out, hanging from a strand usually about head-high, usually in the middle of the trail.

Neither of the men could give her a satisfactory explanation for this phenomenon, but Darrin claimed it sometimes happened after an unseasonable chill. Scott just shrugged. In a nutshell, that was the sum of the last couple of days, camping with these two so-called 'best friends,' Darrin full of esoteric information and dead serious about doing things the right way, and Scott so laid back that sometimes he went hours without speaking, and often lagging far behind, which she was now certain, was so that he could take furtive hits off his flask.

She glanced behind her and saw Scott lagging once more. She'd broached the subject of Scott's drinking, but Darrin had snorted and said, "That's Scott for ya," while walking away, showing nothing like the concern a best friend should. They claimed to have never missed the Hunt for Harry, the annual half-assed dragnet to capture Bigfoot, since before high school. Usually it was just the two of them, camping for five days, searching their allotted zone, and likewise about two dozen other teams, searching for any sign of Bigfoot, every spring. It sounded like a good time when Darrin had invited her.

She squinted but couldn't see Darrin ahead. She looked back and Scott was out of sight. She slowed down. A gnat buzzed her ear. She swatted the pest away and tugged her cap lower, grimacing. The damn bugs forced her to swaddle herself head to toe, in order to prevent infestation. The long pants, cuffs tucked into her boots, and the long sleeves overheated her. By their first break, sweat slimed her entire body. Worse, she'd only packed one stick of deodorant, which gave off a flowery scent that attracted swarms of biting insects, so she had to go *au naturel.*

She checked ahead and behind. The men were still out of sight. She raised her right arm and took a quick sniff. Her armpit was damp, but so far, no odor escaped the double layer of t-shirt and rugged flannel. She'd taken pains to rinse the stink out of the pits of both shirts the night before. This excursion was nothing like she'd pictured it, imagining the three of them sitting around the campfire, laughing, gossiping about the office, and most of all, the chance to show Scott how cool she was, and as things progressed, perhaps the two of them would end up sharing a tent.

Donna lifted her cap and wiped sweat from her brow. Now that the sun was up, the temperature had soared. It was too cold at night, and too hot in the day. She grimaced again. She knew she was bitching to herself about the heat to avoid facing the truth. She knew Darrin had the hots for her. She'd hoped that out here, without the distractions and decorum of the office, he would figure out that she had the hots for Scott. Maybe it was her fault that they weren't all buddy-buddy, with Darrin pressing far ahead and Scott dallying far behind, leaving her stuck in the silent and resentment-filled middle.

Donna pulled her cap down tight and reminded herself that she came out here for a reason. She stopped, crouched, and pretended to examine a delicate purple blossom. When she heard footsteps, she looked up and hoped for a smile.

He was so beautiful when he smiled, but Scott's angular face, made rugged by his blonde stubble, was blank. He looked down at her, and his eyes, usually a warm blue and playful, were bloodshot and watery. In a flat tone he said, "You know he likes you."

Scott ignored Donna's wince at his statement and kept walking. He didn't want to hurt her, but damn it, he wasn't the one who'd invited her. He swatted a branch away from his face and stomped onward, sensing her trailing behind him. Damn Darrin. The conniving prick had set it up this way, set it up so that it was Sherri all over again, so that it was their senior year all over again.

Their friendship had barely survived. One drunken night, Sherri was all over him, and it was morning before he knew it, his best friend's ex snoring next to him.

The only difference this time, besides their age and supposed maturity, and the fact that Darrin had never dated Donna, was that Darrin was orchestrating the betrayal, dangling this bubble-butted, dusky horndog in front of him, so that the prick wouldn't feel bad about stealing his rightful promotion.

Rage sizzled up within, making his head rush. He closed his eyes and a sneer stretched across his lips. His prank last night had scared Darrin shitless. He should screw Donna, who was begging for it anyway, and do it loud enough so that Darrin could hear her moans from his own tent. It would serve the bastard right.

Scott exhaled a shivering breath. He opened his eyes, and took another shaky step. He had to stop drinking so much. He knew he was a mean drunk. The crap about the promotion, the truth was, Darrin deserved it, the truth was, Darrin was smarter than him.

Always was, always would be. Scott reminded himself how much Darrin had helped him, studying together as far back as freshman year in high school and right on through college. And still, after all these years, Darrin's office door was always open if Scott had a question or needed some advice.

Scott picked up his pace. He wasn't going to do a damned thing with Donna. He ground his teeth, thinking how stupid it had been to make Darrin look like a fool in front of her last night.

He had to stop drinking so much. The booze always made him into an asshole. He promised himself he'd find a way to make it up to Darrin. Maybe he could find a way to hook him up with Donna.

Darrin yelled from up ahead.

Scott hadn't heard such an electrified tone out of him since they were boys. Scott ran, his pack jouncing on his back. He blasted through a shady, narrow section of trail and into a sunny clearing.

Darrin was aiming his rifle, his erratic shaking causing the barrel to blur, at a monster. Scott gaped, blinking in shock.

Darrin was babbling something.

Scott shifted his eyes up and down, searching for the zipper, the Velcro, any sign that the giant of a man was wearing a Bigfoot costume. His eyes kept coming back to the wiry gray hairs speckling the creature's lush brown fur. Who would think to fake that?

D arrin stared at the furry creature, which returned the stare.

After the initial fright of seeing the creature for the first time, Darrin quickly found out the beast meant him no harm, or at least wasn't going to attack him.

The beast was basically docile, though still a wild card and one they were wary of.

The sun was about to drop behind the mountain. The shadows were thicker, longer, cooler, darker. They had maybe half an hour of daylight left. All they had to do was head east. But somehow, they kept going around in circles. His eyes flickered away from Bigfoot, and he watched Donna swat another mosquito away from her face, before cursing and shooting him an evil glare, like the bugs were his fault, too.

"We'll go a little farther, then camp for the night, start out fresh in the morning," Darrin said.

"Just make sure we go in a straight line," Scott said. He waved a hand towards Bigfoot. "Seems to understand English, doesn't he?"

Darrin nodded. Bigfoot did seem to understand their commands. Walked when they said so, stopped when they said so, but there was no way they could dare to tie him up, or even to veer within arm's reach.

Bigfoot was huge, at least eight feet tall, four hundred pounds or so, Darrin judged, factoring in his massive chest and thighs, although it was difficult to tell under all the gray-tinged brown fur. For Bigfoot, tearing a person's head off would be no more difficult than popping a dandelion bloom off its stalk. They would have to take turns guarding him all night long.

Scott sidled over to Darrin. They stared at Bigfoot, who stood motionless, his humongous head bowed, as if he could no longer bear its weight.

"We should kill it," Scott whispered out of the corner of his mouth.

Darrin nearly screamed when Donna whispered the same suggestion in his other ear. He hadn't heard her creep up on him. He swallowed the lump in his throat. So it was true. All day he'd watched them, oh, they thought they were slick, but he saw them. They were colluding, conspiring.

"You can tell it wants to murder us all," Scott said.

Darrin tensed. He hated when Scott called Bigfoot 'it.' Bigfoot was a he. One glance at its crotch verified gender. "We're not gonna kill him," Darrin said. "He's not gonna hurt us." He sensed them stepping back and exchanging a knowing look behind his back. So that was their scheme. "We'll take precautions, we won't be stupid, but we're not gonna kill him."

Why couldn't they see the truth? Bigfoot had more or less surrendered to them. He was tired of hiding, tired of the whackjobs constantly scouring the woods for any trace of him. He was ready to give up, and it was their good fortune that he gave himself up to them. Darrin saw now that he couldn't trust them. They'd probably already had a plan to shoot Bigfoot in the night and claim that he tried something, maybe claim self-defense. His furrowed brow was starting to ache, when the answer popped into his head. "There's no way we could carry his corpse anyway."

Scott chopped a branch out of his way. The day's sweat had cooled into a salty crust that crackled over his entire body. It was getting too dark to hike. Darrin should've called a halt for the night at the last decent campsite, but he insisted they push on, and now they were marching into the darkness in the company of a monster. It was damned stupid. Also, he hated leading the way. He couldn't take a drink with them watching his every move. He was getting a headache, and all he needed was a shot or two, and the pain would go away.

But he could feel them watching. Darrin didn't care, but he saw the way Donna was looking at him, with a mix of pity and scorn, as if she were his mother. He knew she saw him as a project, a fixer-upper.

But Bigfoot's constant stare was worse. Those inky, alien eyes, all pupils. Scott could feel them boring into the back of his head. He could feel the creature's murderous intent. The first chance it got, it would go on a rampage. He knew it.

Scott glanced back and met its homicidal gaze. It might have Darrin fooled, but he knew better. He…

His right foot plunged downward into an animal den, then slammed to a stop. He stumbled forward, trying to take his weight off his right leg but he reacted too late. He could feel the tiny snap within his ankle. He cried out and fell to his knees, then rolled over onto his back and clutched his damaged ankle. He looked up through slitted eyelids and saw the malice shine in Bigfoot's black eyes.

Donna knelt beside him and began asking half-formed questions. When she took a breath, he hissed, "It made me do it."

From the other side of Bigfoot, Darrin called out, "Can you walk?"

Donna helped Scott up and he tried the injured ankle. When he put weight on it, he howled. He shook his head, the fresh sweat flying from his forehead.

"We'll have to stop here for the night," Darrin said, the annoyance in his voice rankling Scott.

D onna blinked then she snorted in a harsh breath. She couldn't believe that she'd almost fallen asleep while staring into its bottomless eyes, which glistened darkly in the moonlight. She could only imagine what Darrin would say if he found out, after the sexist pig argued against her taking a watch while the others slept.

She hefted the rifle from her lap and stood up. She paced, trying to get her blood going, trying to wake up. She glanced at Bigfoot. The beast didn't move a muscle, but just sat there, its legs crossed, a stinking, hairy mound in front of the dead campfire. It stared at her.

She tore her eyes away and looked at the two tents. She couldn't help feeling that she was on some twisted game show.

"Behind tent number one, the man of your dreams, children, contentment, and growing old together in perfect happiness. Behind tent number two…the booby prize," she muttered softly.

Her eyes narrowed. All their friends knew how Darrin, the sneaky little bastard, had gone behind Scott's back to get the promotion. Except Scott. He was too good to believe the worst of his 'best' friend, who would keep on stabbing him in the back on his way up the ladder. That was why Scott drank. His best friend was two-faced, and deep down, Scott knew it, but he would drink himself to death before he'd accuse Darrin of a double-cross.

She looked down at the rifle in her arms. A woman good enough for Scott would sacrifice herself for him. She gnawed on her lower lip. There was no need for her to go to jail. Accidents happened all the time in the woods. People shot each other, shot themselves, all the time and by accident. A careless handoff, her finger still on the trigger, Darrin gut-shot, and they would make a heroic but ultimately failed effort to get back in time to save him.

She set her jaw as Darrin stirred in his tent. This was her best chance. She trembled. She hated the way he leered at her with his beady little eyes.

She raised the rifle to her shoulder. She hated the way he made the flimsiest of excuses to linger in her office, wasting her time, seemingly unaware of the uncomfortable silences that put all the pressure on her to think of something to say. He would be out of the way. Scott had made it pretty clear that he was staying away because his best friend had the hots for her.

She curled her index finger around the cold metal of the trigger. Scott would sense the truth. He was a lot smarter than people thought. He would hate her, wouldn't he? Maybe. Maybe not. Maybe he'd be relieved. Probably deep down he'd be grateful. If she played it right, Darrin's death would bring them closer together, and he would get to know her, see her inner beauty and fall in love with her. Not like all the others.

She flinched. All the others. When they'd gotten to know her, they couldn't get away fast enough. What if Scott saw the same inner ugliness that the others did, that hideous thing that allowed her to contemplate murdering a man in cold blood?

She swung the gun down from her shoulder and pointed it at the dirt, her shoulders slumping. When Darrin emerged from his tent, she thrust the gun into his hands without meeting his eyes, ignoring his questions while crawling into her tent.

Darrin stared at Bigfoot, who stared right back at him with his lively black eyes. The creature's intelligence was obvious to Darrin. So was his massive depression. Darrin guessed that was the factor tamping down his excitement, the profound loneliness of Bigfoot.

He could relate.

Sure, he worked too much, but everyone did these days. Everyone else, however, seemed to also fit in some kind of social life. He used to have an illusion of a social life, back when he and Scott hung out more often, but as things got more serious at work, they'd spent less time together, to where this trip was the first time they'd seen each other outside of the office in weeks, maybe months. It was hard to remember, exactly, with all the days blurring together like they did.

Bigfoot's massive chest rose and fell, the hiss of escaping air stupendously long. Darrin had to fight to keep from mimicking his captive's sigh. Yeah, he knew how Bigfoot felt. Over the last few months, he'd realized that if it wasn't for Scott, he would have never had anything like a social life. He'd always drifted in Scott's wake. Going all the way back to high school, the cool kids invited Scott to their keggers, and Darrin just tagged along. If he was being totally honest with himself, he could recall instances of arrival, the way they glared at him, the uninvited guest.

After a while, though, the party-givers understood that to invite Scott meant that Darrin would be there too, hovering around the edges. Then in college, the whole rigmarole had to be re-established, and once again when they landed jobs at the same company. As long as he kept to the background, most of the cool people tolerated him. It seemed a necessary evil if they wanted to bask in Scott's radiance.

But his parasitic relationship to Scott had tapered off after they fell into direct competition with one another. His life had become a gray wheel of work and nights home alone, vegetating in front of the TV, meaning to read, but always too tired to get a book going. He went to bed earlier, slept more, but he only felt more tired.

Bigfoot tilted his mammoth head to one side, without breaking eye contact. "Oh yeah, I know what's going to happen," Darrin muttered. Fame and fortune. Yeah, right. He knew how it worked. *They* would be a sensation. Interviews on the morning talk shows. Selling their stories to the highest bidders. Maybe even book deals. And once again, he'd be the tagalong. Once again, his best friend would coast on his hard work. The cameras would love Scott and Donna. They'd be the ones that Dave, and Jay, and Conan would want to talk to, and as they reaped the rewards, he'd be relegated to the background, a sidekick at best.

They'd spend weeks together on the press junket. It would be Sherri all over again. They'd fall in love, get married, have children, and live happily ever after. He would make some money, sure, but not enough to quit his job, not like them. The gray of his life would spread and deepen.

Bigfoot appeared to nod. Darrin laid the rifle across his lap and rubbed his stubbly face with both hands. There was an elegant solution. He knew the woods. He could stay out here, disappear, live with Bigfoot, cure each other's loneliness. He'd often daydreamed about it. Screw the rat race. Live off the land. He'd have to force Donna to go along, at first, until she acclimated, until she went all Stockholm syndrome. Then they'd live like hippies, raising their children as Mother Nature intended. It was either that, or give her up to Scott.

People vanished all the time out here. Amateurs made mistakes. They'd search for a while, but he figured it wouldn't take much to bury a body so that they'd never find it. Bigfoot had to know good places to hide, since he'd evaded capture for so long. It could work. It really could. He could almost see his children, healthy and happy, dancing around their cave, listening as he told stories around the campfire, stories including his adventures with Uncle Bigfoot.

He snorted and looked away from Bigfoot. He squeezed the rifle's stock. None of his problems were Scott's fault. He looked back at the silent creature and understood that all he had to do was drag Donna by the hair into the woods and Bigfoot would take care of the rest.

He stared long into those unfathomable eyes. Bigfoot would make it quick and as painless as possible. He was no sadist. All he needed was the go ahead. Just a nod, and seconds later, it would be done. Scott would pay for his crimes.

He closed his eyes as he thought of the past.

The stench of unwashed gym-clothes and cheap disinfectant in the boys' locker room, Scott laughing with the jocks, who ignored Darrin's brand-new blue tracksuit while making fun of his ratty old sneakers. A pick-up game at Yocum's Field, Darrin's cousin Bo, starting varsity quarterback, lofting another tight spiral to Scott, who was double covered, while Darrin stood wide open on the goal line. In front of the reception desk, Scott and three of Darrin's clients, flushed and back-slapping, bursting into the lobby, fresh from a liquid lunch, yet another informal meeting from which Scott excluded Darrin. Then back at college in their cramped apartment, three hotties drinking around a flimsy card-table, giggling at one of Scott's asinine jokes, their delight in his wisecracks tinkling and true, as was Donna's, as was Sherri's, like when she and Darrin were heading out the door and Scott squeezed in a one-liner, and she *laughed*, and kept bringing Scott up on their dates, her eyes shining every time.

But still, he hadn't seen it coming, that sunny Sunday brunch when she told him she loved his best friend, when tearfully, she fled their table and he sat there stunned, until he was able to gather enough of his wits to stagger to the nearest bar.

The same dive where weeks later, while he was in the middle of picking another fight with a pack of muscle-bound frat-boys, who would've beaten him within an inch of his life, Scott showed up and stared the frat-boys down.

He'd taken a swing at Scott, clipped his chin, and Scott had stood there and endured it, like he'd endured weeks of the cold shoulder interrupted only by slurred insults.

Scott had a billion chances to turn his back on Darrin once and for all. Instead, he made sure that Darrin got back to their apartment, unbeaten, undefiled…safe.

The metallic *ratch* of a zipper unzipping snapped Darrin out of his fugue. He didn't remember sitting down on a log. His eyes darted toward Bigfoot, who stared back at him.

Scott emerged from his tent and limped toward him. Darrin ran his tongue around the inside of his mouth to work up some moisture.

"How's your ankle?" he asked.

"It's better," Scott said, lying. "Get some sleep."

Darrin handed him the rifle and with a grunt stood up from the log. Scott watched his friend stoop down and enter his tent, like he was bearing the weight of the world on his back. Scott sat down on the log and looked at Bigfoot. He was amazed that he wasn't more amazed to be staring into the creature's bottomless black eyes.

Darrin should have been the most excited of all, fulfilling perhaps their wildest childhood dream. Instead, hunched and sluggish, he moved like he did back in college during those dark days after Sherri had ripped his heart out.

Scott blinked at Bigfoot's oil-spill gaze, then looked down at his bad ankle. He wasn't going to make it back easily; not without help. But they couldn't carry him and guard Bigfoot at the same time.

In the morning he'd admit that he couldn't travel, that they'd have to send back help. He scoffed at Darrin's no-cell-phone rule; it was really biting them in the ass this time.

"Darrin's rules," he murmured. He supposed he'd better get used to Darrin making the rules. Wouldn't be long before Darrin was his boss. Just the other day he and Darrin and a couple of bigwigs were laughing and joking in a conference room, and then the laughter died down into an uncomfortable silence, which stretched until he realized that they were waiting for him to vacate the room so they could get down to serious matters with Darrin.

Scott knew what they called him behind his back. Pretty Boy. Mascot. Airhead. His career had stalled mid-ladder. He could no longer disguise his lack of brainpower with charm and good looks. It was like back in school, when Darrin got A's and B's, and he got B's and C's, but because they hung out together, everyone thought he was smart, too. Everyone except the professors.

But the company bosses knew the truth, as did a few of their colleagues, and pretty soon, they'd all know that he'd been riding Darrin's coat tail all along.

And Darrin just *loved* it, *reveled* in it. Back in college, Darrin had kept the secret, but when they'd studied together, the bastard talked to him like he was an idiot! Scott could imagine the day in the distant future when Darrin, biding his time, waiting for Scott's looks to fade, maybe for a paunch to develop, waiting until it was too late for him to do anything else, would summon him into his corner office, a mask of sympathy barely disguising his glee, telling him that they had to let him go, that it was nothing *personal.*

Darrin deserved much more than that morning's prank. Scott glanced at Donna's tent. He knew he would meet no resistance if he wanted to go to her. He knew that he could make it so Darrin heard her ecstatic moans. Maybe the bastard would come running.

He squeezed the rifle tightly. He'd blow Darrin's brains out.

The pain in his ankle flared up and he realized that he'd gone rigid all over, that he was gnashing his teeth. He turned his head and saw the moonlight glimmer across Bigfoot's greasy-black eyes.

"Damn," he whispered and swung the rifle around.

Donna refused to roll onto her back. She wasn't going to change position again, no matter how uncomfortable her bedding was. She felt hot, sweaty and stinky. No wonder Scott wasn't interested. She was gross.

The gunshot jarred her alert. She jumped from her bedding and rushed out of the tent. Darrin was standing by a log, looking at the ground. She saw the soles of a pair of hiking boots propped up on the log. She knew Scott's boots. She sobbed, knowing what she would see, but she had to look, so she staggered over and dropped to her knees beside Scott, who was splayed out, his face a mess of blood and exposed bone.

With shimmering eyes she looked up at Darrin, who wouldn't meet her gaze. She looked back at the sticky red wreck that used to be beautiful Scott. She wanted to cradle the shreds of his face, but she couldn't bring herself to touch the gore. It was all ruined. She would never find true love, never have a family, never be happy.

She had to look away. She locked eyes with Bigfoot. The creature sat motionless on the ground. Her tears rolled down her cheeks. Darrin had done this. She *knew* it. His glassy, half-lidded gaze flashed through her mind, the way he'd looked all pervy when she'd caught him staring at her ass. He had to murder Scott so he could rape her to his heart's content, then he would murder her, too, out here in the middle of the woods where the bodies would never be found.

She looked down at Scott's waist. Her fingers found the clasp to the sheath on his belt. She unsnapped it, then eased out his big hunting knife. She wrapped her fingers around the hilt. The knife fit good in her hand.

She glanced upward. Darrin was staring at Bigfoot, pointing the rifle at the creature. Now was her chance.

Standing up, she lunged for him.

Darrin gazed down at Donna's twitching body. From the neck up, she was a bloody pulp, same as Scott. Grey and red spattered chunks of skull dappled the grass beside her head. He wasn't sure how many times he'd stood over her and shot her in the face. His eyes stopped on the un-bloodied knife, its hilt in her open right palm. His stomach throbbed where she'd tried to stab him. He was lucky and there was no wound, the tip of the knife had hit his belt and the leather was too thick to penetrate.

He dropped the rifle, turning away from the slaughter. He took stiff-legged steps, awkward footfalls planted too hard onto the grass. Each step brought a greater degree of coordination, and soon, he was running over the grass, crashing through high weeds and low-hanging branches.

Ignoring the lashes to his face, he took one whippet across his left eye and his vision blurred, but he didn't slow.

He burst into a clearing, the numb blankness in his mind turning a viscous red. He saw green-jacketed Forest Rangers finding the bodies. Two plus two equals a double murder followed by a suicide. He saw his coworkers sipping coffee in the break room, whispering about how they saw it coming, about how Darrin was obsessed with Donna, but she loved Scott, and that something bad was bound to happen with the three of them alone in the woods.

He saw his enemies, stretching in a line devolving from professional rivals all the way back to boyhood bullies, telling anyone who'd listen that they always knew there was something off about him, that he was a sociopath, a psychopath. He saw opportunists, blow dried and slathered with orange makeup, hawking their books on talk shows. He saw tabloid reporters harassing his ashamed parents to death.

Then he saw puffy white clouds mottling the blue morning sky and jagged rocks in the ravine below as he fell off the edge of the cliff, thanks to him not watching where he was going.

He twisted off his back foot, jumping straight up and spinning in midair, and he lunged for the grassy ledge. He slammed down hard on the edge and it knocked the wind out of him. He felt crumbles of dirt trickle down his dangling body as he dug his fingers into the soft earth and jerked himself forward. Hauling his belly up on solid ground, he took a rattling breath, knowing he could pull himself to safety.

A shadow fell over him. Darrin looked up into Bigfoot's glistening black eyes, as if the beast was communicating with him. The creature had allowed himself to be captured. Images flashed through Darrin's mind, and the reasons why Bigfoot hated humans, gushed one after another, a movie playing out in his head.

A scene reoccurred, a half-sized Sasquatch, a toddler in a cage made of uneven wooden bars, gap-toothed, urine-stinking trappers wearing half-cured beaver skins taunting the miserable child, jabbing it with sharpened stakes, before their stunted brains turned to darker sports. Puppy mills, dead fish floating in bright orange runoff, exploding derricks, bear traps, smoldering campfires sparking blazing acres of old-growth forests…and so much more.

The current of images shifted and Darrin gasped. He scrunched his eyes shut, but he couldn't block out the flickering collage of snuff-film climaxes dominating his mind. Cruelty, greed, cravings for the forbidden, feverish urges slicing through the thin plastic masks of virtue.

Bigfoot wallowed in turning such truths back on their possessors, the beast relished witnessing the destroyers destroying themselves, mothers and daughters and sisters 'seducing' sons and fathers and brothers, the men raping their children, grudges erupting into murders, and regrets fueling suicides.

Darrin saw it all in one big information dump.

"What are you?" he whispered.

Then his mind went blank and he licked his lips in anticipation. His interior field of vision quivered. Now he would know the full truth. Bigfoot would reveal himself.

Warm pressure enveloped Darrin's right index finger. He opened his eyes to see Bigfoot crouched by his hands as he held onto the edge for his life. The beast began snapping the fingers backwards. Darrin screeched, the pain shooting up his arm. The creature seized his right middle finger and tore it free from the earth. Darrin screamed again and grabbed Bigfoot's shaggy arm with his left hand.

The beast surged upward and Darrin clung to Bigfoot's arm as the sudden recoil yanked him away from the cliff's edge. Bigfoot leaned forward and shook Darrin over the drop. Darrin thrust his right hand into the thick, wiry fur covering the beast's arm, and he gritted his teeth against the pain while twining his fingers into the thick pelt. The creature clouted Darrin on the side of the head.

The blow dazed him and he knew he couldn't withstand another. He swung his feet onto the soft ledge and yanked backwards, feeling Bigfoot's immense mass give an inch.

He roared the primal joy of prey chancing upon a predator's vulnerability. His blind flurry of backward jerks drew Bigfoot closer to the edge. He coiled, tightening his grip, and with a violent lunge, threw himself over the edge.

He felt Bigfoot teeter.

Harsh laughter raked his raw throat. Darrin knew he was going to die, but he would take the bastard with him. Bigfoot pin-wheeled his free arm for balance. Under the monster's feet, a grassy clod broke free and tumbled into the chasm.

Darrin kicked at the crumbling ledge as the beast emitted a distorted growl, then straightened and grabbed both of Darrin's wrists in his gargantuan free hand.

The creature clenched his hand, crushing Darrin's wrists together, then the beast ripped Darrin loose, separating them.

Almost as if it was a casual gesture, Bigfoot flicked Darrin into the chasm. As he fell, Darrin stopped screaming and watched Bigfoot grow smaller. As he stared into those depthless black eyes, he made a silent plea to Bigfoot to show him the truth.

The creature stepped back from the ledge and out of sight before Darrin smashed into the rocks.

THE HOLLOW

DUSTIN READE

The part of town where the loggers came to spend their money on women and alcohol was known as the *skid row*. It was an ugly, boisterous part of town. The streets were sawdust over mud, and a few boards had been laid over it all to create sidewalks. The houses and saloons were all built on pilings, the storefronts pushing up against the sawdust with their back ends hanging out over the river.

Many of the local businesses had trapdoors built into the back rooms, so anyone who couldn't handle his booze could be dumped into the river for a sobering swim. The place crawled with pimps, muggers, murderers, and thieves. They skittered between the buildings like rats.

The rest of the town was small, inoffensive. It was mostly old homesteads, built back when the town was new, and before the logging industry had taken over, there had been a small Methodist church. There was a General Store, where the locals bought their sundries and the loggers fresh off the train purchased prophylactics.

Skid row was separated from the rest of the town by a thick patch of wilderness known as Black Ape Hollow. Heavy trees loomed over both sections of town, creating a threatening umbrella under the perpetual gray sky. A small path cut through the woods to connect the two parts of town, though few people dared to use it. For the most part, the two sections kept their distance from one another, separated by the forbidding Hollow.

Michael Winslow had been on the row for three years, longer than almost all the other loggers in town. Most came and went when the summer ended. Few chose to stay on during the winter months, and even fewer chose to call the area home. Mike stayed on because he liked the rain and seclusion the area allowed. If a man wanted to, he could completely disappear into the woods.

Stepping out onto the rain-soaked sidewalk one morning, he scanned the treeline for signs of deer. His supplies were running low, and he would have to make a trip into the Hollow soon if he wanted to stay in meat much longer. He couldn't afford to buy his food from the General Store, and anyway the owner, Mr. Jimson, had told him he would shoot him where he stood if he ever set foot in the store again.

There were no deer grazing that he could see. He would have to go hunting.

"Well shit," he said, rolling a cigarette. Just as he lit it, the clouds opened up and released a wall of rain. The streets bubbled, puddles forming almost instantly. Several sidewalk planks came loose and floated down the middle of the road.

He cursed the weather for the thousandth time as he plodded through the mud to gather his hunting gear from the shed. There was no point in putting off the trip any longer. Along with the rifle, he packed a canteen, extra ammunition, some ancient bear jerky, his pocket knife, and a sleep roll. He didn't figure on staying out all night, but in this area one never knew what might happen.

He walked into the Hollow. After a few minutes, the rain stopped and the sun came out. The air grew hot and moist, weighing down on his wet clothes and adding about ten pounds to his pack. Wet leaves slid under his feet and he had to tread carefully or risk taking a fall. He stopped to eat some jerky near a clump of boulders overlooking the town.

He was on his third piece when he heard something moving behind him.

Carefully, he picked up his rifle and brought it to his chest. With one hand, he slowly, slowly pulled back the bolt and loaded a round into the chamber. He still wasn't sure what it was behind him, but he knew it hadn't been a bird. The noise was too loud. Birds skittered through branches, disturbing leaves only rarely, and rabbits rarely made any sort of noise at all. Whatever it was, it was big enough to make a significant sound, and it didn't seem to be aware of his presence, as it continued rustling about in the bushes.

Mike slowly turned around to get a look at the thing. He hoped it was a deer and not a bear, as his single shot was no match for game that big. He raised the rifle as he turned, prepping for the shot.

It wasn't a deer.

It wasn't a bear.

It wasn't a fox, or a bobcat.

It was a monster.

Mike froze. The thing was easily nine feet tall. It was bulky and stocky, with a barreled torso so enormous he might have mistaken it for a tree had it not been moving around so much. It was covered from head to toe in shaggy hair, matted in places with feces and mud. Two small, dark eyes peered out from beneath a heavy brow ridge. The head was small and pointed, with no discernible neck or forehead.

Mike watched as the beast stooped and plucked berries from a nearby bush. He'd never been so scared in all his life. The beast stank. It gave off a rancid odor somewhere between a wet dog and a rotting corpse. The smell reminded him of cemeteries, of death.

Not knowing what else to do, Mike continued to raise his rifle. It was as if his body was on autopilot, still unconvinced that the creature was real, that he was really seeing a deer, no matter how many times his brain screamed he wasn't. Before he knew what was happening, he fired. The shot echoed off into the surrounding trees, scaring numerous birds from their nests, and snapping him out of his daze.

The beast reeled back as the bullet tore through its muscular shoulder. It spun in a half circle, screaming, bellowing out an inhuman howl that shook the very rocks Mike was on. The beast searched about for the cause of its pain, scanning the treetops briefly before lowering its gaze on Mike. It bared its long, razor-sharp teeth and screamed again.

It charged.

Mike forced himself down into a crack between the rocks. Stumbling and grabbing for his supplies, and trying in vain to load another round into the rifle. His fingers shook.

In no time the beast was upon him, scratching and clawing at the rocks surrounding his body, the blood from its wound running down the rock sides and dripping onto his face and neck. All the while the beast roared, filling the space between the rocks with its rotten breath, the red of its eyes shining like two exploding suns.

Mike screamed. The rifle slipped from his hands and clattered beneath him. With his body twisted as it was, he couldn't reach it, and with every swipe, the beast's claws came closer to his face, the nails scraping long, jagged lines into the soil beneath his feet. Mike screamed again, and attempted to curl into a ball, trying to force himself farther into the cold, wet earth. Tears streamed down his face.

He got to his knees, jumped to his feet, and ran, the beast following. There was a large grouping of boulders to his right and he made for them. Upon reaching them, he dived into a small crevasse.

The beast continued its attack for over an hour, scratching and clawing at the rocks, hoping to get at the human that had hurt it so much, wanting to tear the human into pieces in its large hands, pulverizing the prey against the very stones it now hid between, so frustratingly close but still just out of reach.

It began to rain again. The water poured into the space between the rocks, soaking Mike to the bone and mercifully washing the hot, stinking Sasquatch blood from his face.

Finally, the beast backed away from the rocks. Mike listened as its heavy footfalls receded into the distance. He waited until the rain stopped, lying there between the boulders, half-drowned, half-insane from fear, willing his legs to move, but they didn't respond. He was paralyzed.

The sun went down over the distant mountains and the moon cast a cold blue light across the land. Mike climbed slowly, cautiously, from the rocks and scanned the trees for any sign of the creature. He was hungry, tired, and beaten. His clothes clung to his wiry frame, completely soaked with rainwater.

There was no sign of the creature, so he climbed down from the rocks. His sleeping bag and hunting gear were scattered all over the wilderness floor. He decided to leave it. He tore off down the trail, heading for town. All the way back, he imagined an army of the beasts chasing after him, nipping at his heels, frothing at the mouth as they swiped at his head, hoping to sever it from his neck and release a fountain of blood into the chilly night air.

The town was quiet. The recent rain had created a boot-sucking stew of the muddy street. A few lamp posts, housing candles, flickered and wafted, casting eerie shadows over the wooden front of saloons and cat houses. Except for in the tavern, few lights were visible in the windows. With so many of the lumbermen gone, the whores and pimps had been reduced to hawking their good times to the locals on the other side of the hollow. They had left the day before, leaving skid row all but deserted.

Mike stumbled onto the street, still frantic and terrified. He raced for the one business he knew would be open—the tavern. All the way there he looked over his shoulder, checking for signs of being followed, sure the imagined army of creatures was right behind him.

They weren't.

He threw open the swinging doors and raced inside the tavern. Big Ed Matheson was fishing from the open trapdoor near the piano, and Bill Wilson, the owner, was polishing a glass behind the bar. He looked up when Mike ran in.

"Jee-zuss, Mike!" Bill said, setting the glass down and placing his meaty palms down on the bar. "You look like you've just been through hell and back! What happened?"

"Do you have any weapons in here?" Mike asked frantically. He raced over to the bar and grabbed Bill by the collar. "There's things in the woods!"

Bill Wilson fought to separate Mike from his collar. He'd seen a lot of drunkards babble on about this and that, but he'd never seen anyone look as scared out of their minds as Mike Winslow looked right now. It scared him.

He helped Mike over to a table and poured him a shot of whisky. Once Mike had calmed down enough, he said, "All right, Mike, now, why don't you tell me what happened."

Mike told him everything. He told him about going hunting that afternoon, and about the noise behind him. He told him about shooting the creature, and how he'd hidden in the rocks until nightfall. When he was finished, Bill walked over to the bar and poured them each a shot. He'd heard tales of the 'Ape Men' that lived up in the Hollow, some of the stories went all the way back to the Indians, but he'd never believed in them much. Hell, he'd lived on the row nearly forty years now, and he'd never seen anything more wild or frightening in those woods than a mountain lion. But still, looking at the expression on Mike's face made it hard to doubt his sincerity. Whatever he'd seen up there, it'd rattled him.

Bill waved his hand around in a complicated gesture. "It was probably just some kind of bear or something," he said.

Mike shook his head.

"That was no goddamned bear, Bill! I've seen bears before, and whatever this thing was, it wasn't a bear." He walked over to the bar and helped himself to another drink. "I tell you," he said, "when I shot that thing it got mighty upset. It looked like it would've liked to kill me, and it had all the parts necessary to do it, too! If there's more of those things out there, we're all in big trouble!"

Bill was just about to say, "I'm sure there aren't any more of them," when the trapdoor in the back room slammed shut. The two men looked over.

"Where'd Big Ed run off to?" Bill asked.

Mike shook his head. "I didn't see him leave, did you?"

"No, but then again I was so wrapped up in your story I don't think I would've noticed if he had."

Slowly, the two men walked over to investigate. The first thing they noticed was Big Ed's cigar still smoldering in the ashtray. A full beer sat on the table, barely touched. The fishing pole was lying on the floor by the trapdoor, the line snapped and frayed.

Bill held up the line. "Looks like he caught something big!" he said.

The trapdoor flew open suddenly and something small, red, and round flew through the air. A terrible stink filled the room. When the smell hit his nostrils, Mike Winslow pissed his pants in terror. He knew that smell; he'd smelled it all day. In fact, he doubted if he'd ever stop smelling it, burned as it was into his brain.

The red thing came to rest at Bill's feet. It looked like a peeled watermelon with two melted marshmallows stuck into it. Bill spun around and vomited after looking at it.

It was Big Ed's head; a frayed bit of spinal cord jutted from the bloody neck stump. The tongue dangled obscenely from the lipless mouth, and the entire head looked like it had been skinned.

The trapdoor slammed shut. From outside there came a horrible screech, followed by the sound of dozens of heavy footprints.

"What's that?" Mike asked, afraid he already knew the answer.

"Maybe it's the pimps?" Bill offered, totally aware of how stupid it sounded.

Screams filled the air as the few residents in the town were dragged from their homes and slaughtered in the streets. The two men crept to the swinging doors and peered outside.

The Ape Men were everywhere. There were dozens of them. They raced in and out of homes, shattering windows, bellowing heinously as they slaughtered the townsfolk. One of them exited a home, dragging a pretty blonde woman by the hair. Mike and Bill watched as the beast stepped on her stomach. The woman's stomach ballooned under the weight of the beast as her entrails were forced into a tight ball, before erupting from a wide split in her side. The exploded entrails coiled around the Bigfoot's ankles as it continued to jump up and down on her limp corpse, splattering the mud with gore.

This scene was being repeated endlessly up and down the row. Blood mingled with the mud as yet another torrent of rain was released from the heavy clouds overhead. Three of the beasts sat in the middle of the road, peeling the flesh from a dead child's back in long, sinewy strips.

Bill gasped, "My God," while choking and backing away from the door and searching frantically about the tavern for some sort of weapon. "It's like hell out there!"

Mike raced over to Bill and the two men clutched each other, huddled against the counter of the bar in fear. Secretly, they were both ashamed of themselves. They were supposed to be tough, rugged men—loggers. Tough as the very wilderness they chopped down. Yet, here they were, in the middle of a slaughterhouse ruled by monstrous, ape-like creatures, and what were they doing? Fighting back? No. They were huddled together in fear like children.

The building rocked violently as some of the beasts began battering the walls with their beefy fists. The walls leaned in, slanting the room at an odd angle.

Bill leapt to his feet. "What's that?" he screamed, tears streaming down his unshaven face. "What's happening now?"

Several beer mugs slid from off the counter and crashed at their feet. Paintings fell loose from their nails and clattered to the floor. The ceiling bent and bowed in the middle as the entire structure was forced back on its pilings. Mud seeped up through the slats in the floor.

"They're trying to push the building into the water!" Mike yelled.

"No!" Bill shouted. "No, they can't do that! Not my bar!"

He reached behind the counter and pulled out a dusty, worn shotgun. Without thinking, he loaded it, clicked the barrel into place, and charged out the door. Mike remained huddled against the counter, the urine in his pants stinging and burning his thighs. He listened as Bill fired into the burly animals. He heard their cries of rage and pain. It didn't sound like any of the beasts were harmed. There was a brief scuffling, followed by another shotgun blast, this time much closer.

The swinging doors opened and Bill stumbled into the tavern. His shirt was ripped, and Mike clearly saw the gaping wound in his abdomen, spilling blood and bits of intestines onto the rickety wood floor.

Bill ran behind the counter and tore his shirt off.

"Hand me that bottle of whisky," Bill said.

Mike handed him the bottle and watched as Bill emptied the contents onto the gaping wound in his stomach. Bill clenched his teeth, fighting back a scream. His eyes welled up with tears and the wound bubbled and oozed for several seconds before returning to a calm, liquid state.

Mike helped him tie his shirt around his stomach. The war against the building had intensified, and it looked to Mike as though the tavern would soon fold in on itself completely. He looked to Bill again, hoping he'd done more damage with the shotgun than it had sounded like. If so, maybe they could make a run for it.

"How many of them are out there?" he asked.

Bill shook his head. "Dozens. Hundreds…hell, I don't know."

"How many did you kill?"

"None."

"None?"

"Nope," Bill replied, moving around the counter and crossing the room. He opened a closet-sized door beside the one to the bathroom. "Not a one."

He disappeared into the room and emerged a few moments later carrying a small wood box. He was smiling. The blood on his face and torso made the grin seem frightening, as though his mind had snapped and he thought he was at a party, rather than a massacre.

"What's in the box?" Mike asked as Bill put the box down on the bar. The top came off it and Bill removed a long, red stick with a fuse at one end. He held it up for Mike to see.

"It's dynamite," Bill said happily. "I forgot I had it. It's been in the closet for months. One of the logging outfits left it at the train depot."

The ceiling beams began to snap and dust and dirt drifted to the floor. Outside, the creatures redoubled their efforts, pushing against the walls of the tavern in an attempt to flush out the people within. Mike wondered why they didn't just come through the door or windows. Maybe they didn't know about doors or were too big to fit through the windows? Another beam snapped and the entire building groaned as it slid back several feet closer to the water.

Mike grabbed a stick of dynamite. "Do you think it's still good?"

Bill shrugged. "I hope so."

Another beam snapped. The rain had stopped.

With a final roar, the last beam cracked in two and the tavern went sliding down the hill into the river. Mike grabbed onto the wooden counter as the building crashed into the water, spilling glass and boards down onto the two men. The dynamite slid down the bar as the water worked its way icily into the tilted room.

A table came loose and pinned Bill against the back wall. Water poured in through the trapdoor, windows and cracks in the walls and rushed up to the man's neck in seconds.

"Save the dynamite!" Bill screamed. "Don't let it get wet!"

The water rushed in over Bill's head. It filled up his lungs. His heartbeat raced as he struggled against the weight of the table; he was drowning in the freezing water. His vision faded and he knew no more.

Mike dove into the frigid water. The box of dynamite slid to the end of the bar and nearly toppled over the edge. He reached out a soaking wet hand and caught it before it could hit the water. Fighting against the swirling current, he climbed up the bar and leaped to the door, managing to jump out before the entire tavern slid into the water. He could hear the continuous screams of the townsfolk as he clambered up the shoreline.

In the darkness of the trees, he made his way into the forest. No birds called out. No animals skittered through the treetops. The only sound was that of the chaos taking place on skid row. There were human screams mixed with animal bellows, all full of inhuman pain and rage.

He could see the clump of boulders up ahead, the same ones where he'd been attacked. Still clutching the dynamite to his chest, he muscled his way over rocks and fallen trees. He could hear something charging up behind him, following his trail.

Quickly, he removed a handful of the dynamite sticks from the box and clambered down in the space between the boulders, exactly where he'd hidden before. He positioned the sticks around the bottom of the rocks, and climbed out again. He repeated the process several times, until the crack in the boulder was literally stuffed full with explosives.

The creature following him was getting closer.

Mike searched his pockets for matches, praying he would find them and they would not be too wet to use. He found none.

He was just about to give up when he remembered his hunting pack. It was still nearby, hopefully where he'd left it. Running to his gear, he saw that the beast had scattered his belongings but it all seemed to be there. He always kept a pack of matches rolled up in his bed roll.

Climbing down from the rocks, he began searching desperately amongst his scattered hunting gear. He found the bed roll near the base of a tree. Unrolling it quickly, he prayed the matches would be there. They were.

He hurried back up onto the rocks. The footsteps were thunderous now, so close he could smell the heavy stench of matted fur and spilt blood. Frantically, he struck the first match. It went out. The footsteps came closer. He could hear the creature's breath escape its mouth in deep grunts. The second match flared up and sputtered out. The smell of sulfur filled his nostrils. The beast let out a tremendous roar. It was close.

One match left. It lit. Slowly, carefully, he lowered the flame down to the coiled fuses. It flickered. The fuses caught the flame. They flickered.

He leapt from the rocks and tore off down the trail as fast as his legs would allow. He didn't care if he ran into the monsters; he only knew he needed to get as far away from the coming explosion as possible.

When he confronted the beast in the middle of the path, it grabbed him by the arms and raised him over its head. Its beady, black eyes bore into his face, searing his pupils with primitive hatred. The monster opened its mouth, exposing several rows of serrated, rotten teeth. Bits of human flesh could be seen between the fangs.

Mike noticed the gaping wound in the beast's shoulder. This was the same one he'd shot earlier that afternoon. The blood had matted around the wound, forming a pulsing, infected scab.

With one final scream, the beast dug its teeth into Mike's shoulder. He screamed. The pain was intense. White spots exploded behind his eyes as the monster tore the flesh away from his bones and chewed it greedily, smacking its lips with delight.

The dynamite blew just as the beast went for its second bite. The force of the explosion flung both hunter and prey through the woods. The boulders rocks came loose and began rolling down the hill toward the town. Mike slammed into a tree and lost consciousness.

The boulders lumbered through the town, knocking down the rickety dwellings and crushing beast and human alike. Blood gushed from the flattened bodies.

Mike dreamed he was floating down the river, surrounded on all sides by otters, their bellies rumbling hungrily.

When he awoke, the creature was standing a few feet away. It had lost an arm in the blast, and most of its hairy body was badly burned. Drool fell from its thick, monkey-like lips. Blisters swelled and popped, oozing thick, yellow pus down over its blackened flesh.

Mike knew it was over. There was no use running any longer. He had a large, bloody gash in his side, and he could see a few loops of dark intestines poking through. But at least he felt no pain.

He raised his hands to the beast.

"Come on, big fella," he said. "Come and get it."

The creature took a few awkward steps forward. Mike could tell it was dying, too. It had lost a lot of blood, but with its final breath it wanted to devour him, to rip him apart with its teeth. He couldn't see the harm in giving it what it wanted.

Then, something hot and heavy landed beside him in the mud. He looked over at it.

It was his rifle.

Somehow, the explosion had thrown it from the boulders, where it then landed in the tree branches above him, where fate had brought it back to him now. The barrel was buried in the mud, but it looked undamaged. With a groan, he plucked it from the ground.

Using a finger, he cleared the barrel of dirt, pulled a bullet from his shirt pocket, and loaded it into the chamber. The bolt locked with a satisfying click.

As the beast lowered down over him, Mike lifted the barrel and placed it directly under its chin. The creature froze. For an instant, their eyes met.

"You can't eat me. I'm a man!" Mike yelled and pulled the trigger.

Brains erupted from the back of the large, bushy cranium. The beast collapsed on top of him, vomiting gallons of blood and drool from its gaping mouth.

He listened as the gunshot echoed off the distant rocks and mountains. Soon, the sound faded. Dawn was breaking. The scattered chirps of birdsong could be heard in lieu of screams and bellows. A light rain began to fall as calm washed over Black Ape Hollow.

Mike listened to the birds until he could hear them no more.

GRAMPA'S STASH

J. D. STANTON

"Put another log on the fire, please, Bill?" Rosie rasped before she leaned back in her lop-sided rocker, lit a Marlboro, and sucked on it hard. Bill lumbered over to the potbellied stove, methodically inserted a neat wooden column into the faltering embers, then fished out his Barlow and sawed a wedge off a bald Michelin tire propped up against a bookshelf crammed with knick-knacks.

Bill tossed the wedge into the stove, closed his eyes and blew on the embers till the fire jumped to life. He stood back and watched the flames dance for a moment. There was a distance in his eyes, and a slight twinkle that flashed and then faded before he dared to remember.

Bill closed the door to the stove, then made the arthritic trek to the chair that had long since molded to his form. He had barely faded into the upholstery before five-year-old Chucky ran past him screaming, tripped over the cat, and fell headlong into the coffee table. The boy had time only to gulp enough air for a good scream before Tara landed on his back and knocked the wind right back out again.

"Tara-Ann! Tara-Ann!" Cassie whined as she peeled her eight-year-old daughter off the back of her frantic son. Cassie puffed as she raised her own bulk with her daughter's. She was only twenty-four, but she could have passed for twice her age.

They would stay the night again as it was too late to venture outside. Cassie and the kids would sleep in her old bedroom, and hubby Sy Adams would begrudgingly take the couch. Only the foolish or the brave would even think of walking farther than the outhouse after the darkness had descended.

A lone streetlight shone over the house at night; from the road, the Stahl house appeared to be centered in the base of a cone of dull, dusty light. Country music seeped from the cracks and crevices, to echo from the hills and return as an eerie, warped harmony. Kerosene had given way to electricity, but little else had changed here in the past fifty years. For generations, few had ventured past that cone after dusk, and the stories of those who did were still told in the hollow, late at night, usually to naughty children and the newly in-lawed.

The screen door swung open, squeaked and slammed shut. Twelve-year-old Norman, Rosie's baby, was home from school. Norman tossed his books on the couch, scooped up Chucky, and two Twinkies from the coffee table.

"What's for supper, Ma? I'm starved!" Chucky giggled gleefully as Norman teased him with a Twinkie.

"You put that back, Norman," Cassie groused. "You're gonna spoil his dinner and rot all his new teeth out."

"Aw, dry up, sis," Norman said as he handed Chucky to Bill. "It's okay if you spoil him rotten."

"So, how was school today?" Sy asked with a wink.

"Same as ever," Norman replied reluctantly. "How's work?"

"You better watch yourself there, boy," Sy grumbled. "I could tell a few stories on you."

Rosie placed a worn marker in her novel, put it back in her purse, took out a huge ring full of keys, and jingled them. All heads turned. "Norman, set the table."

Norman flashed an evil look at Sy, then slowly made his way to the kitchen. "Yes'm," he replied solemnly.

Rosie followed Norman into the kitchen, unlocked the freezer chest, removed two huge brown paper packages, and locked it back.

"When you gonna stop this foolishness, and quit locking up all the food around here, Rosie?" Sy asked from her shoulder. He tugged at the keys while Rosie tucked the frozen packages under one arm.

"When you get a job, and quit eatin' us out of house and home," she grumbled, forcing herself to look away from Sy's infectious grin.

"Ol' Stinkpot's on the prowl again," Norman drawled lazily. "Killed thirteen chickens out at Angie's last night. He'll eat anythin' that's too dumb to run from him—you better watch out, Sy!" he said as he strained with a stack of chattering china.

"No such thing..." Rosie muttered to herself as she touched the gold filigree cross on her necklace.

Soon, the kitchen was warm and steamy. Pots full of greens, corn and potatoes bubbled on the stove, and Rosie hummed to herself merrily as pork chops sizzled in an old iron skillet. Beads of moisture broke like sweat on the October window. The aroma of cornbread rose from the oven and she sniffed the kitchen scents. When the kitchen smelled just so, dinner would be ready. Peach cobbler would bake during dinner.

"You remember Ray, don'tcha, Sy?" Bill and Sy were already seated at the dining room table.

"That old drunk?" Cassie said as she hauled Chucky from her chair and plopped him on her hip. "Ain't nobody believes what that old fool has to say."

"Never forget the time old Ray's hair turned white," Bill continued, unfazed. "He was huntin' rabbit with his best dogs, Hank and King. Damn dogs cornered somethin' at the edge of the hollow. The dogs went plum crazy, and Ray thought he'd cornered Peter Rabbit himself before he cut loose with that .410." Bill poured himself and Sy another glass of home brew while he paused for dramatic effect. "Just then, he heard this God-awful growl, and old Stinkpot himself came stomping out of the briars, ripping branches this way and that. Hank ran smack into an oak tree and killed himself dead on the spot. Then King turned tail and ran straight up a hill—that was the last Ray ever saw of him. If you go out back and listen at the right time…" Bill leaned over toward Tara and lowered his voice. "You can still hear old King a-howling at the full moon."

Tara stared at Bill through wide eyes. She scooted closer to his chair, her eyes darting to the windows, searching for a hairy face and dripping fangs.

"Wolves," Rosie grumbled from the kitchen. *Ain't no such thing as 'Stinkpot,' Bigfoot or whatever they want to call it,* she thought while absently stroking her cross again.

"Ray don't quite know how he got home," Bill continued. "But when he got there, his hair had turned ghost white, and he never did go back and look for his shotgun."

"Old fool probably got drunk and shot both his dogs thinkin' they was rabbits," Cassie announced with a huff. She took a plate piled high with pork chops from Rosie and placed it in the center of the table.

Chucky giggled and scrambled into his chair. "Eat!" he ordered gleefully.

"My old man thinks Stinkpot's just a crazy man who let his hair grow," Sy announced authoritatively. "Told me a plane crashed near Potter's Hill—said everyone on the plane was killed, but they never found the pilot. The old man thinks he got knocked in the head and went crazy. Bet he lives in one of those caves 'round there. Probably went wild, just like an animal."

"Could be," Bill added thoughtfully. "Pets and farm animals go wild when they get lost in the hills. Guess people could, too."

"Like Blackie?" Norman asked.

"Yeah," Bill replied. "Blackie was the sorriest excuse for a cat I ever did see, till he wandered off one day. We all thought somebody ran over him,"

Bill remembered, "I saw Blackie, oh, about six months later, while I was hunting squirrel. Thought he was a panther at first. Damn thing snarled at me from a tree and I tried to shoot him."

"Not *Blackie!*" Tara started to cry.

"No, sweetie, I didn't shoot Blackie. He got clean away before I could even draw down on him," Bill reassured his granddaughter. "He's still out there, living the life he was meant to, I suppose."

By now, all the food was on the table. Cassie tucked a napkin under Chucky's chin and Bill muttered a short prayer. Several arms drew back quickly as Rosie added a few lines to the prayer, then everyone feasted on the country fixings.

Halfway through dinner, Cassie excused herself to use the bathroom. "Better take a flashlight," Norman suggested ominously. "You wouldn't want Old Stinkpot sneakin' up on you while you're takin' a dump!"

"Norman!" Rosie boomed. "You watch your mouth at the dinner table."

"Can't," Norman replied, then stuffed his mouth full of potatoes.

"Great eats, Ma," Sy said as he reached for seconds.

"Why, thank you, Sy. I'm glad somebody appreciates all my hard work," she responded with genuine gratitude. "That reminds me, Sy. There's no more rabbit in the freezer. Do you suppose you could round up some more soon?"

"That all depends." Sy stretched and yawned. "Need a box of shells."

"Bill's got plenty of shells, don't you, Bill?" Rosie asked. Bill shrugged and sawed his pork chop. "You can have a box of .410s, Sy," she said with a frustrated sigh. "I can't seem to get him to do any hunting here lately, anyway."

"I've been fishin', woman," Bill boomed abruptly. "I know where the bass are bitin'. You wait and see—I'll bring a mess of 'em home this weekend."

"That's what you always say," she muttered beneath her breath.

"Damn it, I'm getting' too old to chase rabbits up and down these hills, Rosie," Bill huffed.

Tara eyed Bill suspiciously. "I'm not hungry anymore," she announced and left the table.

"You finish every bite, or you don't get no cobbler," Cassie called after her daughter in vain.

"Maybe her tummy's still botherin' her," Rosie suggested. "Might have to keep her home from school again tomorrow."

"Just wait till she comes back whining for desert," Sy laughed, smacking his hands together. Rosie glowered over her glasses at him. He looked down sheepishly, and went back to swabbing his plate with cornbread. He washed down the cornbread with a long gulp of water, then changed the subject. "Gonna have to borrow that dog of yours, son," he said to Norman. "Need to flush out some bunnies for your ma."

"Why don't you just use your own ugly face—then you wouldn't have to shoot them!" Norman retaliated.

"You ought to let that mutt earn his keep," Bill said. "Besides, it'd be good for him to get his lazy rear out from under the porch."

"Not while Stinkpot's about!" Norman stated emphatically.

"You can just forget that nonsense," Rosie ordered. "How many times do I have to tell you, there aren't any hairy monsters in the Bible, or in the Hollow. You two have scared this boy silly." She looked accusingly at Bill and Sy. "It's your own fault for tellin' stories." She swatted Sy on the shoulder, then helped Cassie clear the table.

The sound of nails being pulled from wood was followed by a clatter and the shatter of ceramic. Tara whimpered from the next room, knowing she was going to be in trouble.

"What the hell!" Bill jumped from his chair and ran to his bedroom.

Sy sauntered across the dining room, placed his arm around Norman's shoulders, and whispered to him, "You cut school again today, didn't you, boy."

Norman could feel his ears flush, turning red.

"You're crazy," Norman managed to say. "You're just tryin' to get me in trouble again."

"Don't lie to me, boy. I saw you and Angie out behind the barn this mornin'."

"So, who died and made you a truant officer? You got no business followin' me," Norman said, replacing fear with anger.

"Now, I wasn't exactly followin' you. I got better things to do than spy on a little twerp like you. I was tryin' to follow your old man to his fishin' hole, when what do I see, but Norman and Angie, playin' doctor."

"Thought you promised Cassie you'd give up drinkin' the hard stuff," Norman said sarcastically.

"You just shut up that kind of talk, boy. I was just tryin' to find your old man to tell him somethin'." Sy was aggravated now. "Tell you what—you let me borrow that good-for-nothin' hound of yours, and I'll just forget I saw you at all this mornin'. Deal, kid?"

"I *saw* those chickens. They was torn up all to pieces..."

"Forget the damn chickens, son. Maybe I just better tell your ma." Sy turned toward the kitchen.

"Well, okay," Norman said reluctantly. "But you take good care of Fred, or I'll tell sis you're huntin' the old man's stash of booze."

"Now, did I say anythin' at all about booze? You heard your ma ask me to hunt some rabbit for her—and that's what I'm gonna to do."

"Yeah, sure. Jack Rabbit Daniels, I bet," Norman mumbled.

A wail followed by short bursts of hysterical sobs came from Bill's room. Tara emerged, rubbing her rear with both hands, sniffing and choking back tears.

"What the hell did you do this time?" Cassie towered over her daughter, fists on her hips, tapping her right toe. Her own mother had struck that very pose over her countless times when Cassie was a child, and now it came as automatically to her as a Southern accent.

"I... I was lookin' at Grampa's things again," Tara sniffed.

"She climbed up on my shelves and tore them all to hell. Busted my old shaving mug, and the cuckoo clock I brought back from Germany," Bill grumbled from the bedroom doorway.

"Bill, that old clock ain't worked for twenty years," Rosie said from the dining room.

"Damn it, that was the only thing I brought back from the war, 'cept for my rifle and a bum leg." Bill's face was flush. He steadied himself against a chair.

"If you hadn't been drinkin', you wouldn't give a damn about that stupid old clock," Rosie huffed.

"Don't you git on me about my brew, old woman."

"Hope you get the shits, you old fart," Rosie muttered just low enough that Bill couldn't make out what she'd said. "Come on into the kitchen and help your grandma dry the dishes, sweetie," she said and took Tara by the hand.

"I'm gonna put Chucky down for the night." Cassie hoisted her boy. "Give your Grampa a kiss."

"Yeah," Bill said as he lowered himself into his chair. "Tear the hell out of my stuff and I can't complain in my own home," he grumbled.

Can't get nothin' out of the old man when he's pissed off like this, Sy thought. He sat at the dining room table and stared off into space for a moment. He fished deep into his pocket for his Barlow and Arkansas whetstone, then reached for a can of 3-Way oil from a shelf behind him. He carefully oiled the stone, opened the knife, and drew the blade slowly across the stone in a steady rhythm.

"I don't think Grampa likes me," Sy overheard his daughter say to Rosie in the kitchen.

"Oh, he just gets that way sometimes, sweetie, You know your Grampa really loves you."

"No, he *don't*," Tara stated emphatically. "He wouldn't even take me fishin' with him today."

Rosie raised her eyebrows. "Did Grampa say he was goin' fishin' today?"

"Sure did," Tara replied. "Soon as you all were gone, Grampa got his fishin' pole and tack—tackier box, and, and, and then he told me it was high time that I learned to take care of Chucky all by myself."

"Oh, he *did*, did he. What did he tell you then, honey?"

Sy quietly picked up his chair and moved it near the door to the kitchen. Tara lowered her voice. "Well, Chucky was takin' his nap, so I followed Grampa to his fishin' hole."

"You went all the way to the creek after him?" Rosie asked.

"Nope," Tara answered with finality.

"Well, where did you go then, honey?"

"I followed Grampa all the way to the backwater over by Potter's Hill."

"Oh, *really*..."

Tara's voice was almost a whisper now, and Sy leaned to his left to hear better.

"And, you know what, Grandma? Grampa *didn't do no fishin' at all!*"

Sy spied Cassie's shadow precede her into the dining room. He straightened up and went back to sharpening his blade.

"He was *drinkin'*, Grandma."

"What's that I hear?" Cassie stomped past Sy into the kitchen.

"Did your Grampa take a bottle with him?" Rosie urged Tara to continue.

"Nope," Tara shook her head slowly.

"Was the bottle hid there?" Cassie asked.

"Grampa found it in the river."

"Oh, come on, Tara," Cassie said. "He must have had it hid somewhere; you just don't find booze floatin' lazy like down the river."

"It's *true*," Tara insisted. "Grampa found a rope tied to a big old oak tree. He pulled on the rope, and up come these baskets. There were three baskets." Tara glanced into the dining room, just in case Bill was there listening, then turned back and whispered, "They were full of bottles and cans, every one!"

"Oh, really!" Rosie exclaimed.

"And where was your brother all this time, young lady?" Cassie inquired.

"He was takin' his nap, Ma. Soon as I saw Grampa with them bottles, I ran home to watch Chucky. Honest, Ma!"

"Damned old fool!" Cassie was tapping her foot nervously. "Don't he know kids need watchin'?"

"He don't know nothin' when he's got a bottle hid somewheres," Rosie said angrily.

I lost him behind Keller's, Sy thought. *No wonder I couldn't find him at the creek. I got carried away watching Norman and Angie playing doctor.*

"I'm gonna tell him what for, goin' boozin' while he's supposed to be watchin' the kids," Cassie said ominously. "Suzie Farnsworth's baby choked to death on a bottle cap last month, and she only left him alone long enough to go to the toilet!"

"Now, just calm yourself down, Cassie. Your babies are fine. What we're gonna do is teach that old buzzard a lesson he won't soon forget," Rosie said with a gleam in her eye. Cassie grinned, pulled up a chair, and mother and daughter began plotting revenge.

"Let's see, now. We'll tell your Pa you gotta be to work early tomorrow. We'll leave a couple hours early, and park over by Crabtree's house..."

"Yeah, then we'll go smash every bottle," Cassie chimed in.

"No, I've done that a hundred times, hon. Now, this is what we're gonna do...first, we get Sandy to watch the house and get the kids as soon as he leaves."

"Yeah, maybe she could knock things around a bit, make it look like they've been kidnapped!" Cassie added enthusiastically. Rosie grinned, but shook her head.

"Could, I suppose. When he gets to the backwater, he's gonna find that the rope cut loose on a rock, and two of them baskets just sunk to the bottom..."

"There's *three* of 'em, Grandma!" Tara interjected.

"I know, honey," Rosie continued. "Seems like the cove got a little choppy last night, 'cause all but one of them bottles in the first bucket broke..."

"And..." Cassie said in anticipation.

"And that last bottle of Jack tastes like somebody poured a whole bottle of Tabasco sauce in it!" The three generations of women broke out laughing.

"And when he gets back, seems like the kids done wandered off into the Hollow!" Cassie added.

"You got it!" Rosie said. "He's gonna be frantic by the time we get home."

"Yeah, and we happen to have found the kids just wanderin' on the road to town!"

Sy was hatching a plot of his own as the women folk savored their scheme. *Only one thing to do*, he thought as he folded his Barlow. *Gotta go rabbit huntin' tonight.* He licked his lips as he thought about the old man's stash. *'Sides, I'll be doing him a favor...it's a shame to let all that good liquor go to waste. Maybe he'll learn to share next time, if I save him some. I'll have to think on that one.*

Sy stretched lazily, then tip-toed into the living room. Bill was asleep in his chair, snoring softly. Sy stoked the potbellied stove, and rattled the rusty handle a few extra times until Bill stretched and opened his eyes.

"Huh...?" Bill said sleepily.

"Boy, were you sawing a log there!" Sy said. "I just ain't tired enough to sleep tonight. How about some of them .410 shells?"

"Huh? That fox back again?" Bill wasn't quite awake yet.

"Hell, no. I'm huntin' rabbit tonight."

"Oh, yeah, sure." Bill stood and stretched again. He dragged his fingers through his thinning gray hair. "You want a whole box?"

"May as well," Sy said as he lifted the .410 from the wall rack. He drew his finger slowly over the length of the barrel, then sniffed. Gun oil. "You sure take good care of your guns. This old cannon could have rusted away years ago."

"Army..." Bill said, then trailed off as he rustled through a drawer in the bedroom dresser.

"Got a box of .410s here, never been opened." He placed the box on the coffee table and eased himself slowly, luxuriously, into his faithful chair. By now, Sy was flipping through the coats in a small closet hidden from view by the potbellied stove. Bill's worn red hunting jacket and Elmer Fudd cap had worked their way back to the far right of the closet; no one had been cold-weather hunting since last winter. He pulled on the heavy hunting jacket and patted the half-dozen or so odd pockets. He removed two .12 gauge shotgun shells and a jack knife from a lower right pocket.

"Bet you wondered where this was," Sy waved the knife at Bill as he rounded the stove. "I'll have to clean it up and sharpen it for you."

"Found that old thing in the Hollow. No tellin' how old it is."

Sy pocketed the knife and reached beneath the coffee table, retrieving a waterproof lantern flashlight. He clicked it on and off to test the beam. Satisfied, he put it on the table. He methodically rolled the cuffs on his jeans, then distributed the .410 shotgun shells throughout the numerous pockets in the hefty jacket. He then glanced at his watch, shook his wrist a couple of times, and checked it again.

"Guess I better get goin'," Sy said, doffing the hat at him. Bill nodded. Sy checked the shotgun one more time—still unloaded.

"Lots of rabbits out by Potter's this year," Bill said.

"Yeah, I think I'll head out in that direction." He strolled past Bill to the dining room, then he paused for a moment and turned back to face Bill. "If I was you, I don't think I'd go fishin' tomorrow mornin'. Carrie's on the warpath again."

Bill opened his mouth to speak, but Sy was at the kitchen door before any words formed. "Damn it," he finally managed. Bill scooted down into his chair, closed his eyes and moments later stepped from the fog into a London pub, circa 1943.

Dinner dishes done and put away, Cassie was sweeping the kitchen floor and Rosie was humming 'Rockytop' softly, when Sy entered the room. Tara was sitting at a card table covered with a red and white-checkered tablecloth. Her head was propped up with both hands; her eyes were fluttering, and she was nearly asleep. Sy reached down and messed her hair. "Better get to bed, young lady, before you fall outta that chair." Tara gave her father a sleepy kiss, hugged her mother and grandmother, and headed off to bed.

Sy pecked Cassie on the cheek. "Bring us back some rabbit," Rosie smiled.

"How 'bout anythin' foolish enough to move!" Sy boasted.

"Just you be careful," Cassie said with a pause. "There's a bad moon tonight." She shuddered at her words, realizing she'd voiced a nagging feeling she hadn't allowed herself to acknowledge. "You won't catch me out of this house tonight."

She threw her arms around Sy, and hugged him tightly. The barrel of the shotgun clattered against the card table as he took a step back to catch his balance.

"Gracious!" Rosie exclaimed.

"You'd think I was goin' off to war!" Sy grinned at Cassie. He looked deeply into her eyes for a long moment. He sensed that the embrace conveyed something closer to fear than passion. "Don't scare yourself, woman. I'm just goin' huntin', like I have a thousand times." He said it with some finality in his voice, then stepped out into the cold night air. He stood on the back porch, the dry wooden clack as the screen door closed behind him giving him an unexpected start.

Damn woman gave me the creeps. He rolled his shoulders back and fingered the trigger guard of the shotgun. As his eyes began to adjust to the darkness, he saw a familiar shape come into focus. Norman was leaning over a porch rail, dangling his feet off, sulking. Sy drew in a deep breath. It was a brisk October night, perfect for hunting—the kind of night that he normally liked—but the air seemed colder than it really was. It smelled like a bitter morning in January.

"I heard you getting' ready," Norman said slowly, still staring out into the darkness.

"Where's Fred?" Sy asked. "We gonna have some fun tonight."

"Under the porch... but you ain't gonna get him out. No way."

"Come on now, boy. Fred and me's old friends. You know how he loves to chase those rabbits. Here, Fred!" He whistled for the dog as he strolled down the steps. He heard a whimper and shined his flashlight under the porch. Fred was on his haunches and scooted backwards when Sy reached for his collar.

"Acts like somebody done whipped him," Norman said dully from the porch.

"Come on now, Fred, we gonna chase the bunnies!" The light from the lantern stabbed through a shredded spider web. Fred scooted further back into the darkness. "Come on, Fred... here, boy!" Sy whistled again. Another whimper. "Fred, get your lazy ass out here on the double!" The dog's whimper changed into a low growl. "Screw you, too, dog!" he yelled and stood up. He looked at Norman. "I don't need your damned chicken dog," he grumbled hoarsely. "Just thought the exercise would do him good."

"The dog *knows,*" Norman said ominously.

Sy shrugged, and turned away from the house. "Don't need no damn dog anyway," Sy chuckled to himself as he walked into the night.

"The dog *knows*," he heard Norman say again. Sy could feel the boy's stare on his back, eyes unblinking.

Thought it might look a little more convincing, though... Sy's thoughts trailed off as the hill took a steep downward turn. As he rounded the pile where Bill and Rosie had dumped their trash for the past twenty-three years, he saw something move next to a scraggly blueberry bush.

He quickly raised the gun, then lowered it. He reached down into one of the jacket pockets, fished out a couple of shells, and deftly slid one into the slot underneath the barrel of his borrowed Mossberg.

Guess I ought to pop a couple of 'em while I'm at it, he mused. As his thumb shoved the second cartridge in, a cottontail bounded through the flashlight beam and made it to the briars to Sy's left. "Wouldn't you just *know* it!"

He turned and looked back at the Stahl house. Smoke curled up from the chimney in a lazy spiral. *The old man's gonna let the fire go out... house'll be half-frozen by the time I get back,* he thought. He watched the light from Cassie's bedroom go out, and felt a chill as the darkness surrounded him. Above, a pale, yellow light filtered through heavy clouds, the moon mostly hidden. A dark blotch scooted quickly through the hazy frame of his vision. *If I didn't know better, I'd think it was gonna snow.*

He raised the red fur collar to his throat and slowly turned back to the path that led downward into the Hollow. *Can't stand still for too long,* he thought as he felt a sudden breeze drag icy fingernails down his back. He clicked his flashlight once again, and his gray eyes soon adjusted to the milky illumination.

He tucked the butt of Bill's shotgun under his right armpit and rested his hand on the barrel. This way, he could quickly raise and fire the weapon, his hand sliding to the trigger guard. He stepped stiffly as the path he followed took a steep incline, bent to the left, and vanished into the woods.

Shouldn't take more than half an hour. He fixed his thoughts on his destination, the cove on the cliff-side of Potter's Hill. Damp leaves mashed and rustled, sticking to his boots as he stepped into the woods. He stood still for a moment and listened to the night. Cool, dark and silent, a light breeze drifted over from the hill and dropped downward; to his left, a row of blue spruce swayed gently at the top. Sy continued his mission. He passed the remains of an ancient white oak. The stump had been a marker to him since his childhood.

From here on in, things get strange, he thought to himself as he remembered his superstition. Everything south of the stump was familiar. Normal woods, normal sounds and shapes. Everything north of the marker was forbidden, strange and ominous. He was at the border once more. An owl screamed hideously nearby. He looked up, and saw the wall of fog ahead for the first time. He hesitated for a long moment, then stepped into the swirling mist.

Well, nobody's gonna follow me tonight, that's for sure. He maneuvered the path as it curved and twisted. It had started as a brown clay groove, but now the path was a sidewalk of trampled straw grass and weeds, narrowing as he stalked deeper into the Hollow. Hills rose up and passed by, dark giants outlined by the dull, cold moonlight. Twice, something had scurried across his path, and twice he leveled the shotgun too late to fire. He used his flashlight sparingly, just in case there were any game wardens in the area. Not likely, though; the rangers didn't make it out this far much. It had been at least five years since his pal Ray was arrested for hunting deer.

Sy heard a branch crack to his right, spun and sidestepped into a spiderweb. The web was every bit of six feet high, and at least eight feet wide, suspended between a cedar and a tall beech. He pawed his face—he had somehow wound himself in the web.

"Damn!" he yelled, and "Damn!" echoed back mockingly a moment later. He clawed the webbing from his face, feeling the thick, sticky strands break like carpet thread. The silken trap glistened with dew, and as he pivoted again, he saw the web's master—a nasty arachnid with a weird double hump, perhaps three inches across, scrambling down a cord that was still wound around his throat. He swung the shotgun up, and a thin red flame scorched the webbing as he blasted the spider into the treetops.

"Damn thing, come at me like that." He stomped down the path, flailing at the webbing on his clothing. He ripped a thick strand of it from the barrel of the shotgun. His heart was still thumping, and he choked on something thick that didn't want to be swallowed.

"*Hate* those damn things!" He grinned as he replayed the shot in his mind. *Women are scared of spiders, men just hate them.*

He stopped at the edge of a creek bed. Inch-high water slid across shelves of shale that jutted out from the water, forming hundreds of tiny waterfalls. He unloaded the shotgun, then stepped carefully through the stream, slipping several times, but not falling on the slimy wet rock.

A hundred yards or so north of the creek bed, he came upon a tiny cabin, weathered and worn with age. He sat on the front step to catch his breath. He wondered if anyone back home had heard his shot.

At least they'd think I was doin' my job! he mused. Sy turned and shined his light into the rectangular hole where a door had once been. He scanned piles of trash and bottles in the front room of the little cabin. As he had when he first discovered it when he was twelve, Sy again wondered what kind of person had built this home, and what had happened to the people who once lived here. He'd envisioned a tall, muscular mountain man, and a ruggedly beautiful, raven-haired woman living in the cabin.

The summer after he'd turned twelve, Sy and his older brother Cravens spent a night in the cabin. They went through every inch of the abandoned home. In the kitchen, someone had once papered the cabin shelves with newspaper. He and his brother had removed the shelves, and read the crumbling funny pages. Sy remembered the date he saw in the corner: 'August 25, 1923.'

The boys decided that no one had lived in the cabin since. They had walked through the small cemetery atop the hill behind the house, wondering if these were the people who had lived there. He remembered there were five graves in a row, each with a small wooden marker that was too worn, warped or rotten to read. Above each grave was a flat piece of shale covered with moss. The brothers turned one of them over—it bore only the inscription: **MacDonald**.

Sy roused himself from his memories. To his delight, he realized that his throat was dry. *Damn, I forgot my canteen. Now I'm gonna have to go down to the cove and find myself somethin' to drink!* He was quite satisfied with his justification. He stretched and yawned, then looked for the path that left the MacDonald clearing and headed toward Potter's Hill. Down, around, left and then right, the path slithered on. Soon, the fog was dense, damp and cold. He knew he must be getting close to the river. Still thirsty, he had by now completely forgotten about hunting rabbits.

Abruptly, he stepped out of the woods and into a clearing. Ahead was the cove. His ears popped, and he could hear the rushing 'shush' of the river in the distance, and the gurgling laps of water in the cove.

Looks like a fine place for a thirsty man to rest his bones. He looked down, found a likely-looking forked tree branch, then strolled up to the edge of the water. He shoved the stick into the soft earth, then propped up the shotgun barrel as he would have a fishing pole. He then fingered the button on his lantern, and a bright white beam leapt out into the fog. He slowly traced the shoreline with the beam, past weeds and chunks of driftwood, looking for a taut nylon cord. Across the shimmering black water loomed Potter's Hill. Jutting out from the base of the hill, just above water level, was a humongous oak, its massive roots reaching down into the cove.

Sy hoisted his shotgun and followed the shore to a footpath at the base of Potter's Hill. The footpath twisted along the edge of the craggy hill. Past the oak, the path curved upwards sharply, ending on a bluff that jutted out like a jaw line above the massive tree. He parked his shotgun by the American baobab and scooted out on one fat root-tentacle. He scanned the roots with his lantern beam. Sure enough, tied around the next root to his left was the dingy nylon cord he'd been anticipating since he'd eavesdropped on his daughter.

He held the lantern between his thighs, balanced himself with his left hand, then stretched over and snagged the cord. He leaned back against the tree and slowly reeled in the cable, pausing occasionally to scrape moss off the line and fling it into the murky lagoon.

Too feeble to hunt rabbits, huh! He grimaced as he strained to haul in the first basket. Bottles clanked noisily against each other as gray water whooshed out of the basket. He dragged the dripping basket onto his lap and leaned back against the tree, laughing out loud.

He fumbled nervously at the latch, grabbed the flashlight, and peered inside at his treasure. Inside were four hefty bottles—the screw caps on each had been replaced by long corks, each strong enough to keep the water out, but not long enough that a corkscrew was needed.

The old fox thought of everything, Sy mused. He held up each bottle in turn for inspection. Though the labels had soaked off, he identified each bottle by its shape. "Jack...Beam...Old Crow...Grandad...my, what a nice mess of fish!"

Sy leaned back and carefully placed each bottle securely on the ground. He pondered for a long moment, then picked up the bottle of Jack Daniels.

Guess I better make sure these ain't gone bad.

He wiped his fingers on his faded jeans and tugged on the cork. The cork came out with a resounding pop. He put the bottle to his lips.

Damn cold, he thought as he swallowed. Nope, no river water in this. He replaced the cork. *Gonna have to study on this.* He pondered which bottle to sample next. When he leaned over to replace the bottle on shore, the basket slid from his lap and plunged into the lagoon.

"What the hell..." Curiosity got the better of him, and quickly he hoisted up the empty basket and placed it by his side. He then hauled up the second container, a heavy collapsible wire basket. Sy immediately recognized it as the potato basket Cassie had given Rosie last Christmas. "Can't find it nowhere, hon," he remembered Rosie saying to Cassie some months before. He'd wondered how she could manage to lose such a big thing as this.

Sy's respect for the old man continued to grow. Once again, he inspected his catch with the red lantern.

"Damn!" he exclaimed out loud. Inside, he counted fifteen cans of beer: Bud, PBR, a few yellow, generic cans that simply said 'BEER,' a dark German brew with a name he couldn't pronounce, and a lone bottle of 'Little Kings.'

"Hot damn!" he hooted again. He hadn't really allowed himself to hope for such a bountiful find. He leaned back and reached deep into his pocket for his Barlow. Just as his fingers touched the knife, he felt his rear slide off the slippery-wet oak root. His head snapped back.

"Shit!" His legs caught the root, and his body sprung like a hanged man out of rope. He still had the basket clutched in his left hand, but the right hand was trapped in his pocket.

"Jesus H. Christ Almighty!" he bellowed as he caught his breath.

Then he began to laugh. He hung there for a moment, laughing, swaying in the breeze, feeling the blood rushing to his brain. He rolled his head up, and his eyes began to focus on a burly arm poised above him. The thick old root turned a right angle, a huge knot forming the elbow. In the crook of the wooden arm, the moon winked at him, then darted behind a black cloud. He let out a long breath.

Sy let go of the knife and slowly withdrew his right hand. His legs, still clamped to the root, were cramping now. His eyes fixed to the crooked arm, he groped for his knee, then the root. He pulled himself upright ever so slowly, his stomach and lumbar muscles screaming from the strain. He scooted up the root, and braced himself securely against the tree trunk.

"It's a damn wonder you ain't drowned yourself out here, old man," he bellowed into the night. "Sure ain't no place for a sorry old geezer with a bad back," he added thoughtfully. He retrieved his pocket knife with great care this time. The gleaming blade sliced through the nylon cord almost without effort, and he congratulated himself on his workmanship. He replaced the knife, wound the cord around his wrist, then placed the basket next to the bottles by the tree.

"One more to go!" He pulled on the rope, and a brown bucket appeared on the water's surface. A moment later, with the bucket on his lap, he squinted at the metal basket that was held inside by two spring-lock snaps.

Can't be much in here, he thought as he sprung the latches and lifted out the inner basket. Water drained out of dozens of small holes, and he waited for the flow to stop before he opened it. He felt something move inside the basket as he popped the lid.

"Well, I'll be... *minnows!*" He poked his finger at the dozens of small silver fish flopping frantically in the basket. Sy closed the basket and fastened it back inside the brown bucket. He tied the cord to a likely-looking root, and lowered the bucket back into the water.

Won't she be surprised! Sy envisioned Rosie opening the bucket, Tabasco in hand, only to find minnows peering back up at her.

He climbed back to the path, feeling a great relief at the firm clay beneath his feet. He rubbed his hands together to warm them.

Jeez, I can't handle all this myself, he thought and struggled with the idea of sharing it with Bill. *Better find a hollow tree, or else I'm gonna have to bury the rest.* He tried to think of hiding places. The MacDonald cabin was definitely out; too many kids and hunters went through that place. He thought of the hollow stump behind the Stahl house. No good. Hornet's nest in there.

While he considered other possibilities, a gust of wind whipped through the cove. Fog swirled in the lantern beam like smoke in the 'He Ain't Been Here' tavern on Saturday night. The chilling gust left the cove with an eerie whistle. Suddenly, he had it, the perfect hiding place.

Sy sat and leaned against the tree once more, shore-side this time. He popped the tab on the can of German beer with the name he couldn't pronounce, drained the can, and tossed it into the water. He reached for another, a generic this time, giggling with satisfaction as he imagined a deep, raspy voice yell, "Blon-die!"

There was Clint Eastwood on the path, legs wide apart, the steely blue stare from beneath his cowboy hat, the barrel of his sawed-off shotgun peeking out from his poncho. *What the hell was that guy's name?* He tried to visualize the wooden grave marker next to *Unknown.* He uncorked another bottle, wet his whistle, then blew the theme to *The Good, the Bad and the Ugly.* Oh, well. The MacDonald slab would do nicely to cover his treasure.

And nobody's gonna believe my little brat anymore! Sy thought of Tara crying to Cassie, "But it was there, Mama, I saw it!"

Cold whiskey burned his throat and warmed his belly.

He was comfortable, and pleased with himself. In the protected pocket of the cove, he could drink and think things out without any interruption, without fear of being caught. He didn't even have to worry about Sheriff Cook stopping him after the tavern closed, smelling liquor on his breath.

He took another sip of Old Grandad, and felt under his cap at the base of his skull. He found the round knot of his pineal gland, and remembered discovering it as he massaged his first hangover.

He could see a golf-ball-sized cancer voraciously gobbling brain cells, and remembered fantasies of surgeons cutting great hunks of tissue from his skull and tossing them on a stainless-steel tray.

Thought I was dead for sure.

He was feeling good, loose and cool. His thoughts drifted from monster movies to bars, drinking buddies, and finally to girls. Then, he felt that something was missing.

He straightened up, steadied himself again against the great old oak, and shifted his focus from memories to the fog bank ahead. The moon had taken refuge behind a cloud; a wave of sadness washed over him, and he found himself alone and cold.

"Only one thing wrong here—there ain't nobody to talk to," he said pitifully. His thoughts turned to Cassie; he remembered her when she hung onto his arm, and every word he said. She was such a sad little thing now, so sad. Scrawny, alone, pregnant with Tara when they'd met.

She looked at me with those fawn eyes, Sy remembered with compassion. *When a deer looks at you with eyes like that, you don't have the heart to shoot it.* The predator was captured by his helpless quarry.

The years unfolded quickly before him, and his fragile love now outweighed him. Her soft, sexy whispers mutated to an unbearable, nagging whine. Sy searched for an analogy for his wife's voice.

I got it. She sounds like the rusty door of my old Ford wagon, creaking and groaning and whining all the time. Her voice, like our marriage, just rusted away from neglect, he thought. He uncorked the bottle of Jack.

He heard a rustling sound from a bush across the lagoon. *Damn rabbits must be following me tonight,* he thought as he felt for the shotgun, *Wouldn't you just know it!* Reaching past the weapon, he fumbled for the flashlight. The dry crack of a dead branch sent a surge of adrenaline into his bloodstream.

"Who's there?" He snapped on the flashlight. The beam plunged uselessly into the fog and vanished. *That weren't no rabbit.*

He raised up slowly beside the oak, leaning into the night and listening intently. For a while, all he heard was the dark water lapping at the roots, then a dull *thrupp!* sounded from across the cove. He panicked for an instant.

Jesus H. Christ, they did follow me!

Images of Rosie and Cassie flooded his mind; hatchets in hand, they would smash his treasure right before his eyes. *Hell, they ain't got guts enough 'tween the two of them to make it to the outhouse after dark,* he reassured himself. He picked up a bottle and toasted Rosie and Cassie in defiance.

"Ya'll be tough as nails, 'long as the sun's shinin'!" Sy staggered back a step. "Wouldn't know nothin' 'bout the night but for bed," he growled out into the darkness.

Sy felt a presence; something was getting closer. He hoped for an instant that the little blond waitress at the 'He Ain't Been Here tavern, the one with the heaving breasts and the roving eyes, had somehow followed him, but he reluctantly dismissed that possibility as absurd. Still...

"Bill?" he called tentatively. Another twig snapped, seemingly in response. "You better help me finish this…" He waved his bottle. "Before Rosie finishes *you*!"

He listened for a long moment—nothing. "You get your sorry ass over here, or else I'm gonna…" A deep, guttural growl rumbled across the water and Sy's words stuck in his throat.

"Oh, *shit*," he finally managed to say. "Wolves," he heard Rosie's voice as he fumbled for the .410. A black, upright shadow flashed from the woods and dived back in. *It's comin' closer!*

He stepped to his left and swung his flashlight down in time to see his foot kick the shotgun's stock. The weapon rolled and clattered as he lunged for it. Flat on his belly now, he pulled up a clump of grass as the shotgun splashed and disappeared; the Jack bottle dived in after it, as if attempting a rescue.

Sy scrambled onto all fours and grabbed the half empty 'Grandad' bottle by the neck. Again he heard the growl. This time it came from the foot of the hill, where the path began. His head was reeling; he felt like he might throw up, and gulped hard.

The growl is too low for a wolf, he assessed. *And there ain't been no bear in these woods for a hundred years.*

Sy inched backwards, then rose slowly behind the oak. A dark form crossed the path ahead of him, too quickly for him to make out the shape. He eyed the path. About three feet wide, it dropped off into the lagoon behind him.

To the right of the path were weeds, a few scrawny beeches, and rock. Almost straight up, nothing but rocks and shale, loose dirt, moss and weeds. He tensed, his eyes following the path as it narrowed and snaked up the hill. He knew where the path ended—atop the bluff, directly overhead.

He heard leaves rustle down the path, and he turned and squinted. He thought of the shotgun at the bottom of the lagoon.

Boy, is the old man gonna be pissed. He would have to give him his father's .10 gauge to appease him. Bill had had his eyes on it since they first went hunting together. *Rabbit shot won't kill no bear, but it might've rattled what's out there enough to let me get by.*

A sickening, fetid stench drifted by his flared nostrils. "You can't be Old Stinkpot," he ordered the shadow. "You're just a fairy tale, somthin' to scare the kids with on Halloween." He envisioned an old man with a long gray beard, wild eyes and tattered clothes; chicken feathers and droplets of blood stuck to his beard. *The crazy man.* Sy took two steps backward. He added up the years mentally.

"Shit, you gotta be at least sixty," he called out at the shadow as it inched closer. "Maybe even seventy. I ain't scared of no geezer, even if you are crazy!" Sy stepped out from the cover of the oak tree and yelled, "Let's get a look at you, old man!"

Two red golf-ball eyes appeared in the shadows ahead. Parallel at first, one rose while the other lowered a bit, studying Sy.

"Follow the bouncing ball," he giggled. "Booga-booga!" he yelled, and then laughed hysterically. "Let's see who scares who!"

Sy raised his bottle over his head. "Yaaaaaaaah!" he yelled, running for the dark shape ahead. "Yaaaaaaaaaaah!"

Above, a heavy cloud rumbled from beneath the moon, and pale light shined on the path, beating Sy to the shadowy figure. Sy stumbled and froze about ten feet in front of his quarry. A miniature avalanche of pebbles, loosened by his feet, tumbled down the bank and plopped into the lagoon. Sy felt the neck of the 'Grandad' bottle slide through his sweaty grip. The bottle exploded on a slab of shale, showering his pant leg with whiskey and shrapnel.

"Jesus God Almighty!"

He stood frozen in catatonic shock, his eyes fixed on glistening saliva dripping down yellow fangs. Next to reach his overloaded senses was a putrid stench, worse than that of a maggoty corpse that Sy and his brother had found deep in the Hollow over twenty years ago. The zombie of that dead mountain man had pursued Sy through a hundred nightmares, but he knew that they were only dreams.

This, however, was all too real.

The creature towered above Sy, over eight feet tall. Coarse black fur, mangy, matted in places with mud, leaves and spider webbing. Beneath the golf-ball eyes was a flat, leathery black snout, the same color as the flesh of the paws. Long claws, so very long...

Every detail of the creature was burned into his memory in the moments he stood face to face with it. A growl, deeper and more ominous than he'd ever heard in all his years hunting in these hills, began in the monster's belly, a distant thunder that rose higher and higher as its chest swelled. The creature swung its arms wide, turned its great head to the sky and released a murderous shriek that split the night.

Sy only realized he was running as he skidded across the shale, groping for something to stop him before the path ended. Fabric and skin tore, stones bruised, but he didn't have the time to indulge the pain, even to assess the damage. Whatever the hell that thing was, it was right behind, and still coming.

Sy scrambled to his feet and rounded the first curve of Potter's Hill. The path narrowed to less than his arm span; now the going was steep and rocky.

The lower path was well-worn and widened by fishermen, but few had followed the trail up Potter's Hill, even in the daylight. Sy's long legs pumped the ground. Behind him, he could feel the steady thump-thump-thump steps of his huge tormentor. After rounding the next curve, he no longer heard the thing. He stopped to catch his breath in the ominous silence.

Mebbe he's tired of chasing me, Sy hoped. A low growl sounded somewhere to his right and he leapt ahead on the path. Behind him he heard crack-crunch-snap. *Guess he don't need no path*, Sy thought as his pursuer tore through the branches behind him, leapt through the air, and landed only yards away with an earth-shaking thump.

Higher and higher Sy ran until the trail became so steep that he had to scramble ahead on all fours. He felt the jagged rocks scrape and gouge his palms and knees. *Forward*, he ordered his body. Only thing to do is to keep moving. The mysterious bluff loomed ahead.

Sy stopped suddenly. The trail had ended and ahead was a sheer facing of solid rock. A smooth groove had been cut into the stone by centuries of rainwater and melting snow streaming from the peak.

He paused, panting heavily. He thought of Fred, spent from chasing rabbits all night. He listened again to the night—the breeze, the hoot of a distant owl—but he dared not to look back; no, he'd find a place to hide on the bluff, and wait till after sunup. *Nobody's ever seen Stinkpot in the daytime*, he reassured himself.

He stood up. His palms and knees were sticky with blood, now drying. He tugged tattered cloth from his knees, wincing with pain. He stepped out on the sheer facing, his back to the cold stone, taking one side-step at a time, very carefully. Five feet, then ten, then twenty.

If he tries to follow me here, he's gonna roll right down the hill! He shortened his steps as the groove narrowed. A small trickle of water soaked through the back of the red hunting jacket, and a glassful spilled over the collar and ran down his back. He slipped on wet moss, and his left foot shot straight out. He clutched a jutting sapling, his head reeling.

A breeze arched effortlessly around the hill, swinging the hunting jacket open. Sy turned and lapped at the little stream of water, his face resting against cold, slippery rock.

The icy stream rinsed salty sweat from his eyes, and sticky blood from one hand and then the other. For a moment, he felt relief, from the pain and the utter impossibility of his situation. He felt astonishingly sober for all he drank and laughed at himself. *Cold showers never done me much good before!*

Sy shook the water from his face and inched on toward the bluff. He stepped gingerly over slick moss and small eddies of water. Thirty feet more and he paused again, at the spot he'd almost fallen years before.

He slid his fingers into a crack that went deep into the hill; as a child he'd peered into the six inch rent in the stone one afternoon, and had seen that it opened into a huge cavern. It would have been a great place to hide when he cut school, or perhaps build a clubhouse, if he could have somehow widened the entrance.

To his left was a small ledge where he'd seen a blue racer sunning itself—that's where he'd slipped, when he tried to shoot the snake.

Guess it just wasn't its time to go. He remembered the snake, lazy and disinterested in him. *Or mine neither, thank God.* He stepped gingerly onto the ledge, just in case one of the snake's descendants was there waiting for him. No growls in the distance, and no branches snapped except for those Sy himself stepped on.

Ahead lay safety—the final ledge jutted out of the ubiquitous mist, and he reached for it. He scrambled up the side of the protruding ledge, kicking wildly for a foothold. He found one, hauled himself up, and somersaulted over, sprawling flat on a thick carpet of grass and leaves.

He lay there laughing out loud. "You can't get me now, you hairy bastard!" He laughed until he could think of nothing else to laugh about. *Boy, am I gonna have a story to tell when I get back home.* He reconstructed his adventure mentally; this time, he'd be the center of attention. He'd tell every detail, except for the booze—he'd save that part for when he was alone with Bill, or at the 'He Ain't Been Here' tavern in Bridgeport.

Maybe, he'd tell his story to the newspapers. In moments, he'd be surrounded with reporters, each poking a camera or a microphone at his face.

He could see himself directing the crew of 'In Search of...' to the best places to hide their cameras, confidentially reassuring Leonard Nimoy, "Oh, he's big and hairy and smelly, but he ain't actually hurt nobody." He saw himself grin and wink at Commander Spock and add ominously, "Yet."

He roused himself from his fantasy and sat up. He squinted at his wristwatch; the crystal had been smashed on the bluff, and it still told the time it had when he'd left the Stahl house.

He wrapped his arms around his legs and placed his chin between sore knees. *Should have asked the old man for his pocket watch, too,* he thought. It was late, but still a long time before sunrise; how long, he couldn't tell.

He began to shiver. In spite of the water and the sweat, he had felt warm while he was moving. Now, he felt as if he might freeze, or at the very least end up with pneumonia.

Bones creaked and strained muscles pleaded for mercy as he forced himself to stand. He jumped up and down, swinging his arms back and forth like a soldier on guard duty at a bleak Arctic outpost. Soon, circulation was restored, and he felt his cheeks flush with warmth. He felt wide awake once more, and somewhat surprised at his alertness.

He surveyed his haven; a thirty-foot-wide plateau just below the very peak of Potter's Hill. He scuffed mud off his shoes and onto the green carpet of grass. "How the hell did you manage to grow so good here, I don't know," he addressed the turf. He strolled over to a huge blueberry bush that grew flush to the rock face of the ridge.

Breakfast! he thought as he remembered a lazy afternoon he'd spent away from school, stretched out here on the ledge, eating blueberries from the very same bush until he'd grown sick of them.

His mouth was watering for blueberries now, but as he rummaged through the branches, he only came up with three shriveled pieces. *Damn varmints,* he thought as he popped the berries into his mouth. Sy spat a piece of stem in the direction of the path; as he swallowed his meager breakfast, his stomach began to churn.

He backed away from the blueberry bush. There was suddenly something ominous about it, though he couldn't quite place what it was. He walked carefully to the far edge of the ledge, all the while listening intently. He turned in a complete circle slowly, scanning each of the three hundred and sixty degrees.

Nothing.

Not a sound, not a suspicious shadow... but still, something was wrong. He felt an uncontrollable shudder as he again faced the blueberry bush.

Ain't nobody gonna believe me, he thought sadly, and he felt fame and fortune slipping away. Now everyone was laughing hysterically as he insisted that he'd told the truth.

He heard a soft rustle behind him. As he turned toward the blueberry bush, a frigid panic electrified every nerve in his body. The bush shuddered in counterpoint as his eyes focused on it.

He remembered the sunny afternoon again; he'd stripped one side of the bush of its fruit, and spied one last, fat juicy berry deep in the branches. He shoved the vines aside and reached for it, but snapped his hand back when he saw a huge spider on the leaf above it.

It was yellow, with black stripes, drooling for the hand that reached for that last berry. Behind the spider was a matted mass of white fibers. A nest full of its offspring, a silken curtain of death shrouding the entrance to... the cavern.

Oh, God, that's why I never went in there. He wasn't afraid of spiders. Only girls and sissies were afraid of spiders. Like most boys, he simply hated them.

The bush shook violently as a mighty hand pulled it up by its roots. Two red orbs glowed from behind the bare branches. The growl again rose from the belly, reached the throat and exploded into a shriek.

Sy took one long step backwards, and plunged into darkness.

* * *

The leaves had turned once more.

Brilliant pastels and earthy, crunchy browns scattered by cool breezes, danced and skittered across the blacktop road, swirling in lazy spirals above the dry creek bed near the Stahl home.

The evenings were chilly again, and the children could smell the holiday season in the air; baking pie dough spiced with cinnamon, and turkey with all the fixings.

A year had passed, and life goes on.

Bill greeted the family at the front door. "Cassie, don't you look fine," he smiled.

She did, too. She'd lost weight quickly after she took a typing job at the sawmill. She sported a new hairstyle and had discarded the dingy fat dresses in favor of skirts and designer jeans, shortly after she first noticed Dan at work.

Gossip informed Cassie that Dan's wife had died of fever three years before and that he hadn't remarried. Besides the new figure and clothes, a smile and a soft voice had helped to capture Dan's attention.

Tara was now a young lady in a crisp pinafore; she primly entered the Stahl home cradling her doll.

Chucky, or Chuck, as he now preferred to be called, wore cowboy boots and his belt bore a huge silver buckle with the sawmill insignia. He took this opportunity to shoot Tara's doll with his plastic M16.

Tara now ignored transgressions she would have slugged him for a few months earlier.

Dan was closing in on forty; quiet, strong and stable. His hair was beginning to thin out on top, and he was a little shorter than Sy, but considerably stronger.

He was kind, a hard worker, owned a pickup truck and a well-kept farmhouse close to town. Dan seemed lonely at first when Cassie took him to meet her parents.

He warmed up quickly, though, and turned out to have a great sense of humor and a fair knack with a banjo. Dan was fun to be with, besides being a good catch.

Cassie and Rosie excused themselves to get dinner started, while Bill and Dan talked about the fishing this fall. Thinking that the women were out of earshot, Bill spiked his orange juice with some white lightning. "Cassie ever tell you what happened to Sy?"

Cassie appeared behind her father. "He got himself drunk on your liquor, staggered off of Potter's Hill, and broke his fool neck, simple as that."

Damn, she's got a lighter step—can't hear her comin' as easily since she lost weight, Bill thought as he palmed his flask and surreptitiously wedged it between the arm and cushion of his recliner. He ignored his daughter's comment.

"Drinkin' brought about his sorry end," Rosie added from the kitchen. Bill glowered at Cassie, and she stalked back into the dining room.

"'Way Cassie tells it, Sy was bound to drink himself to death sooner or later," Dan said.

"Naw, Sy was a good ol' boy. We got along fine most of the time." Bill paused. "Figure I ought to let you in on what really happened, seeing as you're as good as family now."

Norman strolled in from the dining room. "Old Stinkpot killed him— scared him plum to death," he said, before stuffing his face with a hunk of cornbread he'd lifted in the kitchen.

Tara seated herself by Bill; Chuck put down his rifle and climbed onto Dan's lap. Dan could feel how much the children still missed their father, and hugged Chuck. "Come on, Norman, don't take to fooling," Dan said.

"It's *true*, Dan." Bill leaned forward, eyes sparkling as he began to talk. "I seen the footprints by the cove—bigger than any human ever made."

"Oh, really? I thought that was just a fairy tale." Dan looked dubious, but interested.

Bill could see he had himself a captive audience.

As the streetlight ignited the cone of safety around the Stahl house, and the women bustled about putting the finishing touches on a fine country dinner, Bill spun a tale of mountain men and monsters, and Sy Adams became legend to his children.

I THINK WE NEED A BIGGER GUN

SUZANNE ROBB

Ranger Carl Kincaid sat in his office listening to the radio. Static interrupted his easy listening pleasure every few moments, but he didn't mind. He kicked his feet up onto the desk and leaned back in his chair, which moaned on protest.

As he felt himself begin to drift off into nap land, the front door of his Ranger Station flew open, slamming so hard against the wall his sharp shooter trophy fell off the shelf. Carl jerked to full alert, gun drawn and zeroed in on the intruder.

He sighed when he saw Jed Hawkins.

Jed had been hunting in Grim's Woods for close to ten years now, and at the beginning of every season he came rushing in with some sort of emergency. Last year bears dismantled his hunting platform, the year prior ground hogs dug holes to purposely cause him to break his ankle, and so on.

"Jesus, Jed, I almost shot you. What did I tell you about charging in here?" Carl holstered his gun, then walked over to his trophy which now read *harp hooter*.

"I swear I saw it, Carl. Ten feet tall, hair all over, and teeth as long as my arm. I finally found the hunters Holy Grail…Bigfoot!" Jed stared at his friend with a look bordering on psychotic.

"Jed, seriously, just stop before you embarrass yourself anymore. Even the tabloids refuse to take your calls or accept your grainy half-assed photos of this so-called Bigfoot. People have been hunting in Grim's Woods since I can remember, and there's never been a sighting of Bigfoot. You probably just saw a bear."

Jed stepped further into the station, glancing behind his back once before closing the door behind him.

"Carl, I've seen bears before and this wasn't no bear, you gotta believe me."

Jed walked to the front of the desk and leaned his hip on it. He took out his camera and flipped through some of the images.

"Jed, if I believed everything you reported over the years…"

Walking to where Carl was, Jed said, "I can prove it. I have pictures, and I know what direction he went in."

Carl looked at his friend as he stroked his trophy. "Show me the photos." He hoped his voice didn't sound as sarcastic to Jed as it did to his own ears.

Jed put the camera in front of him, and hit the button to scan through the digital images.

Carl watched with a bored expression, then stopped. "You have some great shots of trees, shrubbery, a terrified robin, and a three-legged rabbit. However, I didn't see a single one of Bigfoot."

"Okay, so he's too fast to catch on film, but why do you think the robin is so terrified? Did you notice the gashes on the tree? Where's the rabbit's missing leg?"

"Come on, Jed, I don't have time for a wild goose chase today."

Jed put the camera in his pocket and looked at his friend, "I can see the radio's on the easy listening channel. Nap time huh? Lot's on the schedule today?"

"Hey, I actually work here, you know. If there's an emergency they depend on me."

"Come on, this 'is' an emergency. Just imagine going to the gun club meeting next month and being able to say you bagged Bigfoot."

Carl thought for a moment. It would at least get him out of the station for a bit. And on the off chance his friend was onto something like a bear or what not, it would be cool to brag at the meeting next month. He gathered up his gear and prepared to amuse his friend for the next couple of hours.

"*Ranger Station fifteen, this is Ranger Collins. I need some assistance in sector five as soon as possible.*"

"Sorry, Jed, but duty calls." Carl keyed his radio and answered, "This is Ranger Kincaid out at Station fifteen, on my way to offer assistance, what do you need, Collins?"

Carl waited a few moments for the response. "*Rubber gloves, plastic bags, and you might want to call the State Police.*"

Carl stared down at his radio. "Could you please verify the last transmission, Collins? You want rubber gloves, plastic bags, and the Staties? Has there been a crime?"

Jed stood next to Carl with a grin on his face. "I told you I saw him, and he's a mean looking son of a ..."

"*That's correct, Carl.*"

Carl thought he heard the sound of someone throwing up before the radio clicked off.

"Collins…Harry, listen to me. I need to know what kind of crime to report, the police won't come out for littering, you know."

Carl shook his head and looked at Jed and said, "Harry Collins is a rookie. I hired him three weeks ago and already he thinks he's the long arm of the foliage law."

"Carl, I have no idea what happened. There's lots of blood, some internal organs by the looks of it…but I can't tell if it's human or animal."

Carl was stunned. The last time this happened it turned out to be a cult sacrificing animals.

"All right, just stay there, I'm on my way."

He got the exact location of Collins, then called the police and grabbed the supplies asked for.

"Okay, Jed, you stay out of trouble. I gotta take care of this."

"I'm going with you. I know Bigfoot did this. I can probably catch his trail and hunt him down for you."

"Fine," Carl sighed. "Just don't get in my way."

Before he exited the station, Carl backtracked and grabbed one of the double barrelled shotguns from the weapons cabinet…just in case.

He opened the door and walked over to the Jeep he used while at work, a rugged beat up thing with more rust than metal. He unlocked the door for Jed then started the engine, sector five his destination.

He tried to ignore the excitement on Jed's face.

As Carl pulled into the parking lot for sector five, he began to scan the area for Ranger Collins. He got out of the car and Jed followed behind him. They both began to slowly walk into the wooded area.

When Carl had walked fifty feet into the brush, a smell so rancid hit him that he doubled over. Jed threw up and fell to his knees.

"What in God's name is that smell?" Carl asked, scanning the area for an animal carcass, the only thing capable of putting off an odor like that.

Jed stood up and swayed a bit. "Not sure, but I bet Bigfoot did it."

"Would you stop with this Bigfoot nonsense, really it's just annoying now."

Carl saw the hurt look on Jed's face, but didn't care. He pressed forward when he found a trail of a brownish-red tarry substance he recognized as congealed blood. A hundred feet later he came across a clearing littered with various organs, and other viscera.

Carl took it all in; intestines were strung up on branches thirty feet in the air. A bird of some kind had a severed finger in its mouth, trying to feed its babies in a nest with it. The ground was soggy underneath his feet in certain areas, the smell of blood tangible.

"Ranger Collins, you here? Harry?"

A noise off in the bushes had both Carl and Jed pulling out their guns.

"Over here, Carl."

Looking over to where the voice came from, Carl lowered his weapon. A short chubby man with a rapidly receding hairline came out of the bushes. He was in his thirties, and had a pale complexion.

"Want to tell me what happened here, Harry?"

"Sure." Harry began to walk towards Carl and Jed, getting paler as he said, "I came up here on a routine noise call. I saw them in the parking lot, just a couple arguing like couples do. Then…"

Carl led Harry over to a large rock and helped him to sit down, he seemed as if he was about to fall over.

"Thanks." Harry took a breath and continued. "Then out of nowhere this 'thing' reached out and grabbed them. They were arguing one minute, the next screaming horribly.

"What do you mean a 'thing' reached out and grabbed them?"

Harry looked at Carl with frightened eyes, the terror evident in them. "The thing, a monster, a wild animal of some sort, you have to kill it. It had long arms, covered in hair and razor sharp teeth and claws. The couple were shredded in no time. I can't even find proof these are human remains." Harry fell silent as he stared at the ground.

Carl knew they had gotten everything from him they could. He stood up when he heard a car pull up in the distance.

Must be the Staties, he thought.

Several minutes later, two uniformed State Troopers who looked very worse for wear entered the clearing. They were pale, and when they saw all the gore littering the landscape, they managed to turn paler.

"You the one who called us?"

Carl walked over to the first young trooper, feeling bad for him. He was no more than twenty-three years old, and shaking so bad that the handcuffs on his belt made jangling noises.

"Yeah I am. Seems like we have a wild animal on the loose, probably a rabid bear. It's already killed two people."

Both troopers drew their guns, their eyes darting back and forth. Carl raised an eyebrow as he stared at them. He really didn't understand people; that's why he liked his job, he rarely had to deal with them. Just the occasional lost hiker, or people like Jed who over the years he'd learned to deal with, or at least tolerate.

"The bear's gone now. You guys stay here with Ranger Collins and try to collect as much of the bodies as you can. Here are some bags. My friend and I are gonna see if we can pick up its trail."

Carl dropped the rubber gloves and plastic bags he'd brought next to the troopers. They were scanning the clearing and still hadn't stood up.

"You may want to alert people to be careful in the woods, perhaps ban camping and hiking until we find it." Carl waited for a response. After a full minute and nothing had changed, he joined Jed who was off to the side of the clearing, pointing to a particular spot eagerly.

As he walked over, Carl hoped he was making the right decision. After all, going after a rabid bear wasn't the smartest thing to do, but there were two of them after all. Plus, he had a really big shotgun.

When he reached Jed, he saw what the hunter was so excited about. There were blood drops leading away from the clearing. Carl figured the bear must have carried some body part away with it and left a blood trail.

"Good work, Jed, we'll follow the blood and see how far it takes us."

Jed held his shotgun at the ready and Carl took point, the two beginning their hike into the woods. The blood trail went a good half mile before it stopped at a river. Carl debated crossing to the other side to see if the trail continued or going either up or down river.

"We need to cross the river, he didn't go up or down it," Jed said.

Carl turned his gaze onto Jed. "Oh really, and how do you know that?"

Jed pointed across the river with a raised eyebrow. Carl looked to where his friend indicated and saw a severed human arm. Okay, so the bear had crossed the river, he would have seen the arm eventually. The sun had blinded him to it.

Carl examined the river, wondering how deep it was; he needed to keep his guns dry. "How deep would you say the river is?"

Instead of responding, Jed waded out into the river holding his shotgun above his head. When he was about a third of the way in, the water reached his chest. When he was in the middle, it was up to his chin. His gun was held high, his arms straight up over his head.

Then his head dropped underwater, only the gun not wet.

Carl counted how long his friend stayed underwater—thirty-two seconds. He could do it. Taking a deep breath, he held both his shotgun and his pistol above his head. The water was a hell of a lot colder than he thought it would be.

By the time he reached the other side, it occurred to him that he should have removed his shoes and pants, as well as his coat, and wrapped them around his guns. It might have been the smarter move. He chalked up his lack of foresight to spending too much time with Jed and made a mental note to think clearer in the future.

As he stepped out onto the opposite bank, Jed asked, "Well, what should we do now?" Jed looked like an eager puppy ready to please his master.

"Take a break for now, maybe let our clothes dry a little."

The two men stripped down to their boxers. Carl smiled when he saw the heart-covered ones Jed wore. His were manly and covered with rabbits for hunting. Carl started a small fire to try and speed up the drying process.

A loud growl echoed not too far from them, and they both reached for their shotguns. Carl stood in his rabbit boxers and made his way into the woods, Jed close behind. As they moved forward, the growls got louder, much louder than Carl felt comfortable with.

"Maybe we should turn around. It sounds like it might just be a goat or something,"

Carl suggested as he looked at Jed.

"Don't be chicken, it's Bigfoot and you know it."

Carl shook his head. "I don't know if it's Bigfoot; a bear maybe or just some poor animal stuck in a trap.

As the two men bickered with one another, dressed only in their boxers, a large portion of brush opened up in front of them. In unison, they turned to look at what could only be described as a hairy, sharp toothed, clawed monster.

Carl held his shotgun up with shaky hands and stared into the face of the horrific creature. The teeth dripped pinkish-colored saliva and bits of flesh could be seen caught between its teeth. Carl realized if this was a bear, it had been raised in a tub of toxic waste and bottle fed steroids.

He aimed the shotgun at Bigfoot's head, annoyed Jed had been correct abut everything, and fired. The shot didn't echo as he expected it to. The sound of the blast, and the buckshot, was absorbed fully by the creature's head.

Carl realized he needed a bigger gun, something along the lines of a Howitzer. He had never seen a head so large in his life, it had to be at least two feet in diameter and mostly teeth. He pumped the shotgun to reload it, knowing the effort was pointless, but there was nothing else to try. He watched in horror as the beast leaned forward and swiped at him; he held the weapon up protectively. The claws were so sharp they sliced through the metal of both barrels. They hit the ground with a thunk, the creature's face now inches from Carl's.

Bigfoot let out a growl, sending bits of spittle and rotten flesh into Carl's face. The smell was so rancid Carl tasted bile as he fought not to vomit. With death imminent, Carl's only regret, if they found him, or parts of him, was that he only wore bunny boxers, and it might be interpreted wrong. He didn't want to be remembered as the 'bunny boxer' man.

He closed his eyes and heard the snapping of the jagged sharp teeth in front of him, then a shotgun blast. He opened his eyes and saw Bigfoot looking around in a daze. The right side of its face was bloody and one sharp tooth hung from the side of its mouth.

The monster opened its mouth wide and Carl waited for the growl sound, but heard nothing. Off to his side, Jed moved his lips; no sound came out. Carl could hear ringing thanks to the blast.

"What are you saying? Speak up, Jed."

Jed shook his head and grabbed Carl, pulling him with him. They ran back towards where they had set up the fire to dry their clothes. Carl, still waiting for his hearing to come back, looked at the shotgun Jed held. The damn thing was louder than normal. He suspected Jed was using explosive rounds. At least now he knew where the noise complaints were coming from.

Ready to throw on some clothes, he looked at the fire and saw only a charred pile remained of them, their boots smoking. Carl looked at Jed, who gazed at him and yelled so he could be heard, "I thought putting them closer to the fire would make them dry faster."

"Stop yelling, you moron, Bigfoot could be right behind us." At the thought, Carl turned as if the monster was already there. He saw nothing, so he grabbed his smoking boots and put them on. They were hotter than he realized and he danced around the fire as they cooled down. He looked down and could see his toes through a burnt-out hole on the tops and glared at Jed again. With his bunny boxers, burnt shoes, and a bit of lost pride, he looked towards the area they'd come from.

He felt something on his face and wiped his hand across it. He looked down and saw that his hand was covered with blood-laden saliva, small bits of flesh, and what might have been a popped eyeball. He turned to his right and threw up.

Mustering as much pride as he could, he stood back up. "We can't go back empty handed. This is personal now. I'm taking this Bigfoot character down."

Jed smiled and said, "That's what I like to hear, let's do this."

Carl glared at his friend, but happily realized his hearing had returned somewhat, at least to his right ear.

"You need to give me the shotgun, the ammunition you're using is illegal and you know it."

Jed hung his head and held out the weapon. "Wait, your shotgun shells did nothing but bounce off its head, my rounds actually stunned him, even hurt him a bit. Write me up, but I'm keepin' it."

Annoyed that his friend decided to be smart at this particular moment in time, he let the matter drop and scanned the forest. He knew the creature would be nearby, most likely stalking them. He looked down at their appearance and realized they needed to go commando for this mission to be a success.

"Jed, we need to go to the river and cover ourselves in mud, blend in with the environment. It should also help cover our human smell."

Carl began to march down to the river, confident in his plan; he felt like the lead man in a movie. He knelt down next to the water and began to slather himself in mud. Jed went to his knees next to him and did the same. Moments later, the only thing visible about them were parts of their boxers and the whites of their eyes.

"Come on Jed, time to hunt again."

Bigfoot watched the two men from the woods. One had a loud gun which had hurt his ears and face; he would kill that one first. He wondered why they covered themselves in mud, as it was such a dirty habit. Then again, he found humans utterly disgusting, that's why he planned to exterminate as many as possible.

He knew they planned to follow him, track him, hunt him, but what they didn't know was that 'he' was the ultimate tracker.

Bigfoot would follow the two men for a bit, to learn their habits, until he found the perfect opportunity to kill them.

Jed held onto his shotgun tightly. His friend had been acting erratically, and he didn't know if he could trust Carl's judgement any longer. They were up against Bigfoot, not a rabid bear. Rubbing themselves in mud served no purpose; didn't Carl understand Bigfoot was unlike anything they had ever hunted?

Bigfoot had survived for hundreds of years living by his wits and learning how to hunt with deadly accuracy; an adversary worthy of only the best hunters, and he didn't think Carl was up to the task. Jed knew that if it hadn't been for him, Carl would have been nothing but deli sliced human back there.

Jed watched Carl stand up and scan the area. He shook his head; Bigfoot would be on the hunt for them. He didn't think letting prey get away was something the creature did often.

Jed stood up, grabbed his gun and made sure it had a load in it ready to go. He turned around and walked back to the fire. Jed had left a few things off to the side, out of the prying eyes of his anal-retentive friend. He picked up the plastic bag and pulled out a few sticks of dynamite, two flares, a grenade, and several boxes of ammunition for his shotgun, as well as two handguns, and a book of matches. Checking them over, he smiled when he discovered they were all dry.

"What the hell is that? Do you know how many park laws you're breaking by having those?"

Jed raised his head slowly and looked at his friend, "You saw Bigfoot, right? The big hairy thing that almost ate your face? The thing you thought was a rabid bear?"

Carl nodded. "Yeah, you're right it's Bigfoot, happy?"

"You saw what its claws did to your shotgun, and you really think this is the time to point out rules I might be breaking, even when the items I have are most likely going to save our ass?"

Carl looked chagrined, which wasn't hard considering his appearance. Jed looked away and debated what they should do next. So far letting Carl take charge hadn't led to much action, and Jed wanted action.

"We should go back to where we last saw him and see if we can pick up his trail."

"Okay, you take point," Carl said.

Jed smiled; he could hear the fear in Carl's voice. He knew his friend acted tough, but at heart he wasn't a real hunter. Last year he'd run over a bunny and had felt absolutely terrible for over an hour.

Jed led the way, hating the way the dried mud he was coated with itched. When they had reached the small area again, Jed noticed Carl hanging back. Jed examined the ground, looking for some sort of clue as to where the creature went. He found a broken branch, then another leading away and decided to follow the trail. He led them down a path of destroyed leaves, and very obvious footprints. The two men soon came to a small clearing. Jed looked around and saw the leftovers of an extinguished campfire, some remnants of clothing, and the severed arm which had caught his attention in the first place.

"He tracked us? Christ where is he now? Is he watching us? Give me the gun, Jed."

Carl said and reached for the gun, a pleading look on his face.

Jed shook his head. "Not a chance, but I'll give you a stick of dynamite and some matches."

Carl reached his hand out greedily for the explosives.

Putting the stick of dynamite in the elastic band of his boxers, Carl held tight to the matches. Jed looked around in jerky motions, like he was some sort of mechanical sentinel in need of greasing.

The hairs on the back of Carl's neck rose and he knew Bigfoot had to be near. A snorting noise, and a growl from nearby confirmed his suspicions.

Jed stared at him with wide eyes and raised his shotgun.

Carl didn't know what to do. If he moved, he might run right into Bigfoot, but if he stayed put, the explosive shells Jed was using would tear him to shreds if he was hit.

He felt hot saliva falling on his neck and the decision was made for him. He hit the ground and covered his ears.

The boom echoed this time, and Carl felt warm fluids land on his back. He removed his hands from his ears, thinking Bigfoot would be dead after a direct hit. He stood up to see Jed with a terrified expression on his face.

As Carl looked over his shoulder, he saw Bigfoot standing there, rubbing the front of its chest. Bits of shell casings fell off and a little bit of blood oozed out of the creature's hand.

Carl stepped backwards slowly, then ran when the beast looked up with angry red eyes. "Run!"

The two men took off into the woods, branches slapping them in the face, roots tripping them up, and both narrowly missed a bear trap. When they leaped over it, they found themselves tumbling down a steep hill.

Head over heels, they rolled down the embankment. On one of the turns of his body, Carl caught a glimpse of Bigfoot as he loped down the hill after them.

Seconds later, Carl crashed into a tree, knocking the air out of him as he came to a halt at the bottom. He reached into his boxers and grabbed the dynamite, glad it was still there, though he'd lost the shotgun in the fall.

He stood up on wobbly legs and held the dynamite in front of him to ward off the army of Bigfoots, his vision playing tricks on him.

"Back you beasts, I'll use it I swear."

A shotgun blast let him know Jed had managed to keep hold of his weapon, though he wondered how he could aim after the fall they'd taken. A moment later, he heard his friend screaming in pain.

"Oww, my damn leg!"

Well, that answered that question, Carl thought. His vision cleared just in time for him to see Bigfoot charging him. Acting fast, he lit the dynamite and threw it in front of him. He ducked behind the tree, and when the explosion went off, he heard a howl of pain.

Chancing a look around the tree, he could make out a tall figure in the smoky area. He looked for Jed and saw him lying on the ground about twenty feet from him.

"You okay, Jed?" He waited for a response as the smoke cleared. Bigfoot was clearly visible now, his left arm dangling by a few blood-drenched strands of muscle and sinew. Significant damage had been inflicted on its leg also.

"I think I blew my damn leg off. How do you think I am?"

Carl saw Bigfoot carrying a human leg in its remaining hand. The leg had been severed from the knee down. Bigfoot ran after Carl and raised Jed's leg, ready to use it as a weapon. Carl had no idea what to do: no gun, no more dynamite, all he could do was run.

He circled the tree a few times until the monster stopped. A howl of pain filled the air and Carl knew Bigfoot was at his most dangerous right now, an animal in pain, one that would lash out on instinct. Bigfoot was a beast that had already wanted to kill him, and now it was in great pain as well. He didn't know what it meant, but it couldn't be good for his wellbeing.

Carl ran for Jed, seeing blood squirting liberally out of his friend's leg. He looked around for something to tie it off with but only found a few roots blown loose from the dynamite. Upon closer inspection, he noticed his friend was covered in bits of debris, twigs, and various bits of foliage. He looked down at himself and realized he looked the same, like some sort of forest monster.

"You're gonna be fine, Jed, just hang in there. Where's your shotgun and other explosives?" He was lying of course. Jed was a goner, but it didn't mean Carl had to go down with him.

Jed, delusional from blood loss, handed Carl a rock. "Sorry I didn't make the football team dad." He was delusional.

Carl sighed and looked around. About ten feet away he saw one stick of dynamite, and a few feet away was Jed's shotgun. He lunged for them, knowing time was short. He grabbed the shotgun first and then crawled to reach the dynamite.

When he turned around, he saw Bigfoot approaching him, eyes blazing red. The fear meter lowered a bit because the creature had to hop, and only had one arm. Its face looked scary enough though, and the mere fact the monster still stood was a testament to its will to kill Carl.

Realizing the beast wouldn't stop until Carl was dead, he tossed the stick of dynamite in front of the creature and lifted the shotgun. When the beast was two feet away from the stick, he fired. The resulting shockwave from the explosion echoed for miles, causing a rockslide a quarter mile away, the ground shaking violently. Carl was thrown onto his back after flying threw the air ten feet. He hit a tree and landed hard, his head in a daze.

Smoke hung heavy in the air. Carl coughed for several moments before he got some fresh air into his lungs. Standing up on shaky legs, he had a look around the area.

Bigfoot lay on the ground fifteen feet away. Both its legs were gone and its lower abdomen was exposed. The creature tried to reach out and hit Carl with Jed's leg, still clutched in its hand, but failed.

Carl looked over at Jed. His friend was now dead, a pool of blood surrounding him. Carl watched as the monster took its last breath.

Though death was in the air, he couldn't help but think that he would rock next month's gun club meeting when what happened here had gotten out into the world.

He quickly got to work making a litter, and once done an hour later, he rolled the hairy, bloody carcass onto it. It was heavy but he'd manage to make it to the Ranger Station with frequent rests. He had no choice; he'd need proof after all.

He placed the shotgun on the carcass' chest and began his trek back. He would come back later with help to retrieve Jed's body.

An hour later, as he stopped to rest, he closed his eyes and breathed in, his back muscles aching. When he looked up from closing his eyes, he was shocked to see the angry eyes of a rabid bear standing before him. It was a big one, nearly eight feet tall when standing on its hind legs.

"Of all the dumb luck…" Carl dropped the carcass and stared at the bear; it rose up on its hind legs and growled. Carl stepped away from his trophy carcass. He did make sure to pick up the shotgun, and as he leveled it at the bear, all he got was a dry click for his trouble. The damn thing was out of shells.

"Ah, hey there, listen to me, big fella. You don't want to eat me or my dead buddy here. He's too tough and I'm all stringy, no meat on my bones. But I tell you what you can do. There's a body a half mile back. It's missing a leg, you can't miss it. Go eat that one instead and leave me alone."

The bear simply roared back and dropped down onto all fours. Carl watched it move forward and begin to eat the carcass.

Carl kicked the ground, amazed at his bad luck; to find and take down the kill of a lifetime and to lose it now.

As the bear fed on his trophy, he continued on to the Ranger Station. No one would believe him now, and he had to explain about Jed's corpse in the woods.

As he thought about it some more, he decided to let someone else find Jed's body. After all, people might get the wrong impression about two men running around in the woods in their underwear.

It was hard getting back to the Ranger Station without being spotted. He was surprised to see how many other people were in the woods, especially now that he didn't want to be seen by anyone as he was in his underwear.

Later that day, several calls were made from hikers and campers, all claiming the sighting of a swamp creature in bunny-covered boxers.

Carl chose to let it remain a mystery to the other Rangers, and from then on only wore his manliest boxers when at work.

THE ART OF WAR

DANE T. HATCHELL

Traveling down the river's edge, a creature as old as man himself prowled the boundaries of its territory. It walked upright like a man. Its body was covered in reddish brown hair thicker than that of a grizzly, and towered over nine feet in height.

Its massive feet left deep impressions in the soft earth. Fallen limbs crunched under its five hundred pounds of weight. Folklore gave it the name 'Bigfoot,' but it knew of itself only by what its natural instincts taught. It only thought of itself as *Hunter.*

"Yes, sir, there ain't nothin' better in life than sippin' on a cold beer and catchin' trout while the Arkansas River flows betwixt your legs," Mark said, pulling his beer hugger free from his fishing-vest with the sound of the Velcro anchor ripping away. Taking several gulps, he mashed the hugger back securely in place. "Ah, beer…urp...best drink ever. Ain't that right, Joe?"

"Right, Mark, best drink ever," Joe said. The best way to keep his brother from rambling on while fishing was to answer as quickly as possible. The river was up just over their knees. The cool water helped counter the heat of the noon sun, and sang a serene tune as it rolled across the rocks, heading downstream.

"You think I can get a patent on my invention? The fishing-vest beer holder?"

"I don't know, Mark. All you did was glue a patch of Velcro loops on your hugger and sewed in the hooks on your vest. I don't think you can get a patent on that."

"Well, that ain't right. Maybe I could get some Chinese company to make them for cheap and I could sell them over the internet. You'd buy one of these if you saw how great it worked, wouldn't you?"

"I suppose. Or I guess I'd just do the same thing you did and make one of my own. Unless I needed a new fishing-vest, and the hugger came with it."

Mark whisked his fly back over his shoulder, and then sprang it forward. The bait soared through the air and landed a good distance downriver. He smiled proudly at his cast, and celebrated with another quick sip of beer.

Joe loved getting away from the concrete and steel of civilization and becoming one with nature. Sure, he enjoyed fishing. It brought peace to his troubled soul. Fishing though, wasn't a competition for him as it was for Mark, who was younger by three years, and always felt he had to outdo his older brother.

Joe never gave Mark a reason to feel inferior while they were growing up. In fact, he went out of his way to do just the opposite. Mark took it as a sign of weakness, whenever Joe let him win at things. But Joe didn't have enough of a competitive spirit to care in the long run. An attitude that he carried with him into adulthood. He didn't care about winning or losing, as long as he had a steady paycheck, a place to live, food to eat, and the company of a woman every couple of months.

A horrid smell broke Joe from the spell of the babbling river. "Good grief, Mark, that smells like you ate somethin' dead. Try to fart downwind next time, okay?"

"What? I didn't do nothin'. I don't smell...*whew* what is that? That would gag a maggot." He scanned the river, looking for the floating carcass of a rotting animal.

A trout nibbled on the fly. Mark gave it a little play and waited patiently for it to hit, then pulled back on his rod to set the hook. "Whoo-wee...got me a big'un." He reeled in his prize catch with a grin smeared ear to ear across his face. "Look what I caught! Look what I caught! This one's as big as Jaws!" Mark said and looked back at Joe, who smiled and gave a nod of approval. He reeled his fly back in and trudged through the water over to Mark.

With his prize within reach, Mark lifted the line by the fish's mouth and held it out of the water. "See, it's as big as I thought it was! That there Brown must be twenty inches long!"

For once, Joe thought Mark had a right to brag. "I don't know if it's twenty inches, but it's certainly close to it." He unhooked the fish and held it parallel to the water with both hands for Joe to admire.

"Guess who's coming for dinner? I think it's you, big boy," Mark said.

"I'll go put it in the ice chest. I feel a cramp and I'm gonna find a place to take a dump," Joe said.

"Toss me a beer first, mine's empty." Mark filled his empty can with water so it would be heavy to soar through the air and then tossed onto the riverbank.

Joe's amble out of the water *splooshed* with each step as he headed for land. Once on the bank, he went to the camp area some twenty feet away under the shade of a large willow tree.

The latest addition of their catch brought the number of trout up to nine. They were well over their daily limit. He hoped no one from Wildlife and Fisheries would come snooping by later.

After putting the fish in the cooler, Joe opened the other ice chest and groped through the ice for another beer.

The awful smell again blew his way, and this time the hairs on the back of his neck began to tingle. An ancient instinct triggered by the scent of a wild animal told him to run, but the reasoning of a civilized man forced him to turn and look behind him first.

The mighty behemoth stood motionless beside a water oak, looking like a strange creature from a circus sideshow. At first Joe thought it was a stuffed gorilla put in place by some prankster, maybe looking to scare a couple of fishermen to then upload the event on the internet after filming it.

The creature curled its upper lip, revealing two-inch long canine teeth.

Primal fear trumped rational thought in a heartbeat and Joe turned to run. He made it three steps before the creature overtook him and had him face down in the sand. The breath heaved out of him. He didn't have any air to scream with the weight of the beast's knee pressing down on his back, breaking ribs and crushing his lungs.

The beast reached underneath his face with its clawed hand and pulled Joe's head back until it snapped. Joe's face froze in a death stare, contorted by pain and terror. The creature grabbed his head with both hands and ripped it from his shoulders. It held it by the hair and let it dangle, looking at the head as if it were a mesmerizing jewel; blood drained out of the jagged neck stump to the ground.

"Hey, Joe, what the hell is taking you so long with my beer?" Mark called after making another cast, keeping his eyes downriver.

The beast looked at the fresh meat from his kill, and at the interloper fishing its waters. It chose to wait to fill its belly and ignored Joe's corpse.

"Joe, beer me!" Mark called.

Something wet fell from above and hit him on the cheek, and then something splashed down beside him. He wiped the wet off his cheek with his fingers. It felt warm and thicker than water. He thought a bird had crapped on him. When he looked at his fingers, he saw that it wasn't white like bird crap. It looked like blood. What had landed next to him was Joe's head, the dead eyes locked to infinity as the head bobbed in the river current, floating away from him.

Mark watched in disbelief until the foul stench that plagued him earlier caused him to turn around.

The creature let out a yell that echoed off the surrounding mountains, causing Mark's bowels to quiver. He turned to see the angry beast with its arms spread overhead, standing on the bank. Its mouth was open wide, showing all of its large pointed teeth.

Mark dropped his fishing rod into the river, then crouched in the water until it was up to his nose. In his mind, he thought it might be possible to hide from the ferocious beast, but lost hope of that when it left the bank and waded into the water towards him.

Large rocks on the opposite bank presented an obstacle. He determined that the creature could catch up to him easily if he took that direction. He sprang up and trudged down the middle of the river as fast as he could move his legs through the binding water.

The beast maintained a steady pace and wide stride, gaining on Mark without much effort.

The water grew progressively deeper and the river wider until it was up to Mark's chest. At that point swimming for it became his best option. The current picked up speed the further down river he went. Soon, he found the creature no longer gaining on him.

He chanced a look behind and saw the large beast giving up the chase now that the river was chest high on it, too. Mark stopped swimming, but the current continued to carry him further downstream. "What's the matter you ugly sucker! Can't swim? No wonder you smell so bad."

The creature ignored the taunts and waded out of the water to the bank of the river.

"You go 'head and run! I'm comin' back! I'm comin' back to find you! To hunt you down! I'm gonna have your head hangin' from my wall for what you did to my brother!"

Once on dry land, the beast continued walking downriver at its normal stride, its long arms swaying by its sides in rhythm to its walk.

Mark needed to put more distance between himself and the beast, and pushed himself harder. He had no idea how fast it could travel. He needed to get far enough away that he was out of sight, so that he could double back and make his escape in his pickup truck.

The current carried him even faster. He had to struggle to keep his head above water as the turbulence pushed and pulled at him. Just when he thought he'd regained some control, his head smashed into the side of a boulder hidden just below the surface.

He went under and was so disoriented that he didn't know up from down. His lungs ached for air as he spun around, flailing his arms and trying to regain his bearings. He finally righted himself when his feet came in contact with mud. With no time left to spare, he franticly pushed upward and dogpaddled to the surface as fast as he could.

He broke into the pure air of the river valley as his world began to fade to gray. As he struggled to keep his head above water, the river carried him even faster. Mark found himself bobbing like a cork helplessly caught in the rage of the whitewaters. He needed to get to dry ground or his luck was bound to give out, and he would find himself a victim of another boulder.

The river turned and the roar from the water became even louder. He looked up to a startling horizon. He was heading towards more rocks and what appeared to be the end of the river.

End of the river? he thought. Then realized, *Waterfall!*

He tried with his last remaining strength to swim to the bank, but the whitewaters easily guided him into a huge boulder. It sounded like a raw piece of meat hitting a wall when he hit, the crackle of bones crunching.

Another boulder brought him to a momentary halt. Darkness drifted over his consciousness. His body went limp, no longer resisting the fate the whitewaters of the river had in store for him.

He went over the waterfall, his body becoming mangled and crushed on the rocks below, to then be flung into the air like a ragdoll as the water churned and bubbled.

The Bigfoot watched Mark go over the waterfall from upriver. Satisfied the enemy that invaded its territory would never return, it needed to get back to its kill. Human was by far the sweetest of all flesh the land had to offer. It wouldn't be long before the other predators in the woods would pick up the scent and attempt to challenge it for a piece of fresh meat.

*   *   *

The thin air in the mountains surrounding Arkansas Valley caused Lauren's head to ache. For once, she missed the thick, humid Louisiana air she

111

was accustomed to breathing. She held her hand up to block the sun and was relieved to see Cecil, the climb team leader, hammer in his final anchor into the rough surface of the face of the cliff.

"Okay, guys, I'll be on top soon and anchor in the top-rope. You'll be able to make your ascent quicker. Keep your head in the climb and don't get sloppy," Cecil called down.

Jenny, the second leader below Cecil, took a moment to look down at Abe, Donna, and Lauren below, then gave them a thumbs up gesture. The three responded in kind.

She was angry with herself for letting Cecil talk her into letting him take the lead. She estimated that she could have shaved an hour off the climb. They could already be on top and having a glass of celebratory lemonade-spiked vodka to celebrate.

"Climbing!" Cecil called to Jenny.

"I have you on belay, climb on." Jenny pushed a few feet of rope through the belaying anchor, to give Cecil enough slack to make his climb.

Cecil searched and found a new handhold, and moved another step towards the top.

Lauren regretted taking the fifth position on the rope. Her bladder was full to the point that it felt like a balloon about to burst. "If we don't get to the top soon, I'll wet myself," she said to Donna, who was fourth on the rope.

"Me too. I shouldn't have drunk so much sports drink. I didn't expect this to take us more than a few hours. Next time Cecil is the leader, I'll wear Depends," Donna said.

"Rock!" Cecil yelled from above. A handful of loose dirt and rocks fell harmlessly away from the other climbers.

"Drama queen," Lauren said, intending for only Donna to hear. Abe, who was above Donna and third on the line, snickered at her comment.

"If he doesn't reach the top soon, I'm gonna tell Jenny to cut the rope and find us a quicker way out of here," Abe said.

Lauren looked up again and saw Cecil's feet stick out horizontal from the upper ledge. "Looks like he made it."

"Thank goodness," Donna said, watching the feet disappear.

Once on top, Cecil drove in an anchor, removed the rope from his harness, and tied it securely to the anchor. "Okay, top-rope's in place! You guys can come on up!"

Cecil walked in a circle, stretching his muscles and enjoying the feel of firm ground under his feet. The view was beautiful. Lush and green with tall trees all around, with the Arkansas River winding below as far as the eye could see.

Feeling the call of nature, he walked to the edge and called down, "I'm going to begin looking for a campsite!" Without waiting for a response, he removed his backpack and walked into the woods to find a tree to use a suitable target before searching for a decent campsite.

Coming to the trunk of a tall pine, he unzipped his pants, scrounged around for the head of his manhood, and relieved himself. He let out a sigh as the pent-up pressure slowly melted away. Before he could make the final two shakes before zipping up, the sound of someone approaching broke his solitude.

They sure did make good time, he thought. "I'm over here, guys. Just give me a minute."

A large, thick, padded hand with long sharp nails swooped down from behind and struck him on the back of his head. He fell down, knocked out cold.

Upon finding another trespasser in its domain so soon raised the ire of the hairy creature. Even though its belly was still full with its earlier kill, it saw no need to let this human go to waste.

Meanwhile, Lauren had reached the top and Abe and Donna each grabbed an arm to help her over the edge. She rolled onto her back and took a minute to relax while the two looked down at her. "I never thought we'd make it," she said, then lifted herself up on her elbows and stood up. "I really have got to go *now*."

"Go 'head, we didn't wait for you," Donna said.

Lauren took two steps and stopped. "Hey, where's Cecil and Jenny?"

"Jenny went to look for Cecil. She said he went to look for a campsite," Abe added.

"Cool, I'll want some lemonade soon. I need an attitude adjustment," Lauren said, and headed for the woods.

Cecil awoke hanging upside down looking at the back of a hairy animal. At first he thought it was a bear, but soon let go of that belief when he discovered the creature that carried him was bipedal like man. He glanced down at the thick legs of the beast, and observed the large human-like feet it walked on.

I'm being carried on the back of an actual Bigfoot, he thought. *But that's impossible. There's no such thing!*

The filtered light of the forest soon gave way to cool darkness. He lifted his head to see that he was now entering the mouth of a cave. The creature pulled him off its shoulder and laid him on the uncomfortable rocky ground. He strategized that feigning unconsciousness would buy him some time to formulate a plan, and forced himself to lie still, although a sharp rock he was laying on made it difficult.

I wonder if it thinks I'm dead? He could hear the beast walking away. After a few minutes, he chanced to barely open one eye. The creature was reentering the cave, carrying something in both of its hands. He quickly closed his eye and slowed his breathing as much as possible.

Water splashed in his face and he felt a big toe dig into his side. "Ouch!" *Great, he knows I'm not dead now.*

The creature grabbed a handful of his hair and pulled upward.

Cecil sprang up in compliance until he was on his feet and standing next to the massive creature. "Okay, I'm up. You can let go of my hair now."

It shoved a bowl of water towards him. Cecil took it but hesitated to drink. The water didn't smell right, though he couldn't be sure if it was only the water, as the creature and the cave both reeked with a foul gamey odor.

The creature made an intimidating grunt.

"Okay, don't get mad. I'll drink it." He put the bowl to his lips and took a sip. It tasted fresh, so he drank it all, being thirstier than he realized.

As soon as he finished, the beast handed him another bowl. This bowl was a little larger than the first one. An upper jaw full of teeth was still attached to the skullcap.

I just drank water from part of a human skull. Bigfoot uses human skulls as bowls! He felt his knees go weak. The monster grunted again, obviously growing impatient.

Cecil shook as he brought the skull to his lips and forced himself to swallow the water. He handed the skull back to the creature and prayed that by some miracle someone would show up to save him.

The beast balled up its fist and punched Cecil in the stomach. He'd never been hit that hard in his life. He heaved all the air out of his lungs, and the contents in his stomach erupted out of his mouth and onto the cave floor.

He bent over and spit, moaning like an animal as he tried to catch his breath.

The beast left, and returned with more water.

"Why'd you do that? I drank the water like you wanted."

The creature shoved another skull full of water his way.

"I don't want it. Leave me alone!"

A bone chilling growl and the show of its pointed canines quickly put the situation in perspective. Cecil nervously took the bowl and sipped on it until it was empty. Only to be handed another immediately after.

"We've searched over a hundred yards in every direction. There's no sign of him," Jenny said.

"Where can he be?" Donna's hands rested firmly on her hips.

Abe lifted his cap. "Maybe he heard what Lauren called him and he's making us pay for making fun of him."

"I didn't say 'drama queen' loud enough for him to hear," Lauren said.

Jenny lowered her head. "Well, I heard you. I guess it's possible he heard you, too. He probably picked up vibes from all of us that we were pissed at him for being such a weak leader."

Donna spread her arms. "So what do we do? Look some more or call 9-1-1 for help?"

"He hasn't been missing long enough to call for help. Let's keep looking," Abe suggested.

"Let's set up camp and make a batch of lemonade. Cecil may be pulling a prank on us but the joke's on him. We have his backpack, and his backpack has the one hundred proof bottle of vodka. Maybe if he's out there watching us, he'll come running when he sees that the party is starting without him. Let's go roll out our blankets over there." Abe pointed to a flat area between some trees.

"You guys go ahead. I've got to go to the bathroom again," Lauren said.

Donna laughed. "You mean you have to go the bathroom again, again. I swear girl, your bladder must be the size of a walnut."

Lauren rolled her eyes and shook her head in embarrassment. "I'll be back." She turned and left for some privacy, away from the others. She returned to the camp area after several minutes expecting further berating from her companions, but instead found the backpacks haphazardly strewn about and the blankets trampled upon.

The serenity the beautiful trees and magnificent mountains offered suddenly changed into obstacles, silently standing, hiding her from the whereabouts of her friends. For them to go missing so quickly must have meant that whoever took them must have totally overwhelmed them by sheer force or greater numbers. She couldn't help but feel that they were waiting and watching for her, too, ready to pounce in an unsuspecting moment.

But she was only one woman, standing just a few inches over five feet, though very fit and muscular. What were they waiting for?

She pushed her paranoid thoughts out of her mind and focused on the situation at hand. Her friends were missing. Their backpacks thrown about, indicating signs of a struggle. While searching for clues, she discovered a dark substance on one of the blankets. It was blood, fresh blood. She could only wonder as to which one of her friends it belonged to, and feared for the worst.

Having no faith in her tracking skills, she turned on her cell phone and searched for service, waving the phone over her head. Nothing.

Despite it feeling like a total waste of time, she opened the Friend Locator app on her phone in a chance that the GPS was operational. A map of the area displayed in 2D on the screen, along with both her and Donna's location.

It showed Donna just to the north, and heading away. She could only guess that Jenny and Abe were with her. But what to do now? Her head told her to leave and get help. Her heart said to follow and see if her friends were in immediate need, or at least to pinpoint a location. If her captors discovered Donna's phone and in turn destroyed it, there might be no chance in finding them.

Lauren took a deep breath, a swig from her canteen, and headed north.

The creature made quick time through the dense woods, even though it had a human slung over both its shoulders and one cradled in its arms. Over the years, it had a good amount of contact with the weak creatures. It had learned some of the humans' ways, their nature, and in turn how to use it against them. Now that the beast had expanded its territory, it came into contact with humans more often. Instead of sharing its territory with them, it decided that enough was enough, and that they would pay for trespassing. Plus, it had acquired a taste for the delicate flesh of man.

Upon arriving at the mouth of the cave, the creature laid each body on the ground, side by side, then went inside and moved a man-sized chunk of limestone from a natural nook carved in the cave wall.

Cecil popped his head out as soon as his prison door was moved away. He stepped out of his moist enclosure, scratching his arms and legs, thankful for being released from the claustrophobic conditions. A number of the cave's creepy crawlers had explored various parts of his body during his imprisonment.

Then his situation went from bad to worse. The beast loomed like a giant before him and he wondered if his time to die had come.

The beast reached behind Cecil's shoulder and pushed him towards the mouth of the cave. His heart skipped a beat when he saw three of his friends lying as if they were dead on the ground. Abe looked the worst of all. Blood covered his face from a gash across his forehead. The two girls were free of any obvious external wounds.

Cecil ran to the side of the nearest and fell to his knees. "Jenny, are you okay?"

She stirred when he placed his hand on her cheek.

"Jenny, are you hurt?"

Donna twitched and made a soft moaning sound.

Jenny's eyes fluttered open. "Where am I...Cecil! Where have you been? Why does my head hurt?"

Donna let out a blood-curdling yelp as she returned to consciousness and saw the ominous hairy monster in front of the cave. The creature hissed at her disobedience, showing her its feral teeth as a warning.

"Keep it down. You don't want to get it mad," Cecil whispered.

"What is that thing?" Donna asked.

"As unbelievable as it may sound, that's Bigfoot, or Sasquatch, or whatever people call it," Cecil said.

"Why did it bring us here? What's it going to do?" Jenny said.

"From what I've seen so far, our lives are definitely in question. Our only chance for survival is to keep it happy and hope someone finds us before it gets angry." Cecil dry swallowed. "Or hungry."

The beast picked up a skull full of water and poured it on Abe's face. Abe's hand reached up and rubbed his cheek, smearing the water into the dried blood.

"Abe's alive! I thought for sure he was a goner," Cecil said.

The creature nudged Abe in the side with its thick amber big toenail.

"Can you guys get up? We need to see if we can wake Abe before Bigfoot gets pissed and decides to stomp him into the ground." Cecil took Jenny under the arm and helped pull her to her feet.

Donna stood and brushed the dirt off her and ran her hand behind her head. "Wow, my head hurts."

Cecil spread his hands open by his chest and walked a few steps towards the creature. "We mean you no harm."

The beast turned its head to the side, looking like an inquisitive dog. It pointed to Abe, grunted, and backed away.

"It wants us to get Abe up," Donna said and immediately went to him and grabbed his hand. "Abe, you need to get up. You need to get up now."

Abe stirred and pulled his hand away, then opened his eyes.

"Don't be alarmed. Don't make any sudden moves. You're not going to believe this; just try to stay calm."

Abe blinked, looked around, and sat up quickly. He ran his finger across his forehead, causing the wound to ooze fresh blood. "What happened?"

Cecil stepped forward and pointed. "That big thing over there kidnapped me and decided I needed some company."

Abe jumped when he saw the mighty Bigfoot standing by the cave. "That's not a bear!"

"No, it's not. We might be better off if it was. We've got to figure a way out of this."

"How has it treated you so far?" Jenny asked.

"It gave me a lot of water when I first came to. Funny though, it socked me in the stomach and made me throw up. Then it made me drink tons more water. I've been pissing like a race horse ever since."

"Weird, but that doesn't sound too bad. Maybe it won't hurt us after all."

"Did you see what it poured the water into? It was a human skull."

The other three looked at the bleached white skullcap on the ground.

"Doesn't look good for our team," Abe said.

The beast reached from behind and pulled Cecil away from the others. Both Jenny and Donna rushed to Abe's side. The creature then moved and stood in front of the three.

"What does it want?" Donna asked.

The others remained silent in fear. The beast picked up one foot and put it down, then the other, and grunted.

"Does it want us to walk?" Donna said.

It picked each foot up and down again, while moving its arms. It grunted, nudged Jenny in the shoulder, and moved its feet up and down again.

"I…I think it wants you to dance," Cecil said.

"That's ridiculous," Jenny said, biting on her thumb.

The beast nudged her again, harder this time, and made a grunting noise, sounding impatient. Jenny let go of Abe's arm and slowly began moving her feet to an imaginary beat.

The creature stepped back and nodded its head.

"This is too much," Donna said.

It looked at Donna and Abe, grunted, and pointed its hairy finger at them.

"We'd better do it, too." Abe let go of Donna and started bobbing his head and moving his feet. Donna slowly twisted her hips and moved her arms up and down.

The creature made an expression resembling a smile, then went over and stood by Cecil.

"I actually think it's happy. Who would have thought that Bigfoot liked dancing?" Cecil said. "Don't stop until it wants you to. We need to buy all the time we can."

"I've got an idea." Donna pulled her cell phone from its pouch and selected a song from her stored music.

Deep bass and drums filled the air. The beast opened its mouth in surprise and turned its ear to the music. It slowly began to nod its head to the beat.

"Unreal," Cecil said.

"Hey, you know the old saying, music sooths the savage beast," Donna said, now more animated with her dance steps.

"Maybe we can learn to communicate with it. I bet it's a lot smarter than it looks," Abe mused while doing his stationary two-step.

"Maybe so. We'll all be famous. I bet we'll make a boat full of money." Cecil nodded his head in rhythm, looking over at the creature.

The beast looked pleased and continued jamming to the beat.

"Donna, take a picture of it with your phone," Cecil said, now clapping his hands softly.

"I'll get some video and upload it to the internet as soon as I can. No one is gonna believe this is real." Donna switched to camera mode while the music still played. She zoomed the camera in on the creature and Cecil. *This will give some perspective on how big that thing is,* she thought.

Without warning and lightening fast speed, the beast suddenly snatched Cecil up by his arms and clamped its powerful jaws on the back of his neck. Blood streamed down the man's chest as he hung suspended in the air, held only by the creature's teeth. Then Bigfoot abruptly shook its head back and forth. A sickening snap of Cecil's spine breaking rang above the screams and cries of the terrified humans.

It let Cecil fall to the ground and leaped at them. Abe held the two girls tightly by his side. He closed his eyes and hoped their deaths would be swift.

The beast only hissed and raised its fists. Then, it nudged Jenny again in the arm, bobbing its head up and down once more.

"That bastard wants us to keep dancing," Jenny said.

Tears rolled down Donna's face. "I can't…"

The beast leaned down, narrowing its eyes in anticipation.

"Just do it. Don't think about it, just do it. We've got to keep it distracted until help arrives." Abe gently shoved the girls away from him and started dancing again.

Donna tried to hold back her sobs. She swayed her hips from side to side. Jenny felt her fear giving way to anger. "I want to make this thing famous. Famously dead that is."

Satisfied, the creature returned to its kill. It grabbed Cecil's right arm with one hand and jerked it out of its socket. With the three humans still dancing in front of it, the beast began to shred the meat off the bone with its teeth. It ate with its mouth open, blood dripping from its lips, pieces of meat dangling between its teeth. The human's flesh was plump from hydration, having benefited from all the water it had force-fed him.

Abe threw up. Donna never took her eyes from the ground. If looks could kill, Jenny would have already done the hairy creature in.

Lauren arrived just in time to see the large creature snatch up Cecil and kill him. She hid behind a tree some ten yards away, her mind racing as she attempted to comprehend the situation. Like a lion snapping the neck of a rabbit, a man-ape looking creature had just killed Cecil, while her other three friends danced to music.

Goosebumps rose over her entire body and paralyzing fear traveled up her spine to the back of her head. She couldn't move; she was even to afraid to breathe.

The beast continued pulling parts off Cecil and gnawing the bones clean. At one point, when their dance moved too slow for its liking, the creature threatened her friends with one of Cecil's thigh bones.

The horror that struck Lauren blackened out any rational thought. Her insides quivered and fear gripped her like an iron maiden. The creature continued to eat.

A rattling in the brush behind her broke the paralyzing spell. She spun around and went to her knees to hide from whatever approached.

A bush shook a few feet from her and a tiny pointy face poked its head out from underneath. The armadillo was oblivious to Lauren as it rooted around in the earth with its sharp claws, looking for a tasty grub.

She stood slowly and began to back up. The creature stopped chewing and put its nose to the air, scanning the area in her direction.

As gently as she could, she crouched down and slinked her way through the natural obstacles of the woods, until she was certain she was at a safe distance from being detected. Then she ran as fast as possible back to the campsite.

There was only an hour left before the sun would set and the blackness of the night would make it impossible for Lauren to return down the mountain to find help.

Spreading out the contents of the five backpacks on a blanket, she rummaged through the odds and ends for a possible solution to saving her friends.

She was a double gold medalist, and an electrical and computer engineering major from Louisiana State University. It would only be by her reasoning abilities that she would have any chance against the huge beast that imprisoned her friends.

She pealed open a protein bar and ate it, then put her plan of action into place.

First, she took two safety flares and cut them open with her Swiss Army knife, then emptied the powder into two large plastic cups. Though tempted to tip back the bottle of vodka for a shot of liquid courage, she instead carefully filled each cup.

The inert materials in the flare compound that transformed the explosive mixture into a slow burning torch floated to the top. She used a spork to skim off the plastic polymers and sawdust, leaving only the volatile components in the bottom. Once that was done, she poured the vodka from each cup back into the bottle, then spread out the wet powder on a paper towel to dry.

Abe's flashlight best suited her needs to use as a bomb housing. She removed the batteries and pried the power switch off. Cutting a string off a tampon, she tied one end in a knot, and threaded it from the inside of the battery casing to the outside.

The vodka evaporated quickly off the powder. She shook the powder from the paper towel into the battery casing until it overflowed, then tightened the end cap so hard she thought the skin would peel off her fingers.

With the sunlight quickly fading, she stuffed a backpack with her improvised weapons.

The flashlight was now a bomb, with an explosive force of something close to a quarter stick of dynamite. She'd brought a taser for the climb, a gift from her father in case she came across dangerous wildlife. Lauren preferred carrying her pistol, but other climbers always made a big deal against it whenever they would find out that she was armed.

The makeshift bomb and the taser were her most powerful weapons. Along with them, she included Donna's pepper spray, six of Cecil's condoms, a box of kitchen matches, two eighteen inch ratcheting cargo straps, and the vodka.

She set her watch to wake her in enough time to be at the mouth of the cave before sunup. She needed to have everything in place when she made her move. Surprise would be another element in her favor.

Rolling up a blanket, she made a makeshift pillow for the night, and chuckled to herself. None of her classes in college had prepared her for the situation she now faced. The entire plan of action for the attack came from playing Xbox games and converting a flare into a bomb, she'd learned from a video on the internet.

The next morning, as the sun cast an orange mystical glow over the mountains, Lauren was in position behind a ten foot tall boulder, not twenty feet away from the mouth of the cave.

The beast slept soundly just inside the entrance. She couldn't see beyond its sleeping form into the darkness, but hoped and prayed that her friends were still alive and unharmed.

Raising its arm and scratching its chin, the beast began to stir from its night of rest.

Lauren's heart pounded in her chest and she concentrated on keeping her breathing slow, with long inhales and exhales. Her hands shook so badly she didn't think she was going to be able to go through with it.

As she peered around the boulder, the last thing she ever expected to see deep in the woods of Arkansas wandered in front of the cave's entrance—an ordinary house cat. The large beast stood, stretched, and looked down as the orange tabby walked sideways and started rubbing against its leg. Then it reached down and grabbed the cat by the scruff of the neck. Holding it at eye level, the cat pawed the air and uttered a sweet and innocent *meow*.

The creature wasn't amused in the least. It ended the cat's life by biting off the head, crunching it between its teeth as it chewed. Then the creature curled its upper lip and spat out what was left in its mouth, displeased with the taste.

"You son-of-a-bitch," Lauren hissed softly. *It just killed a harmless cat.*

She was the proud caretaker of three cats, and found that she preferred their company to most people. Finding her resolve, she took one of the condoms she'd filled with vodka and splashed a little on the outside of it. Then she lit a match and set it on fire. She stepped from behind the rock and lobbed the projectile at the beast.

The creature turned and watched the flaming condom fly through the air and land at its feet. When it burst, it set the vodka on fire as it splashed over the beast's feet and legs.

The creature screamed and tried to slap the fire out as Lauren hurled another flaming condom at it, striking the beast's head. That followed with another and another.

The creature jumped to the side and the last one missed its target. The beast yelled furiously as it beat its burning hair with its hands.

Lauren couldn't tell if it was feeling pain or just mad. Less than half of the monster was burning. She didn't know how thick its skin was, or how long it would have to burn before it really hurt it.

Deciding to attack with overwhelming force, she lit the vodka-soaked tampon string and rolled the flashlight/bomb towards the beast. It came to rest just behind its right foot before exploding.

The shock wave knocked the creature on its back. Its arms flailed in the air as if it were being held under water and drowning.

Lauren ran to its side and pulled the trigger on the taser. The nitrogen cartridge propelled the two tiny darts into the less hairy part of the creature's chest. One hundred and fifty thousand volts of electricity flowed from the gun into the beast for thirty full seconds. It was enough of a charge to drop a full size moose. She hoped it was enough for this monster, too.

The creature shook violently, gagging as it choked on its own tongue while howling in pain.

While the beast lay immobile, Lauren took the two cargo straps she'd already connected, and strung it around the creature's neck. After pulling it as tight as she could, she cranked the ratcheting buckle until it dug deep into the skin of its neck.

The beast came to and instinctually grabbed for the strap, accidentally coming in contact with Lauren and knocking her down to the ground.

She sprung up and dived for the taser, pulled the trigger and sent another high voltage shock through the creature. It went limp after the charge sent it into another series of spasms.

She emptied the pepper spray straight into its face, then backed away as the beast struggled to breathe.

As it started to move again, she waited out of reach, and prayed that the taser still had enough charge to take it down when she pulled the trigger.

As the body of the mighty beast shook, it let out a yell that sounded like all the vile inhabitants of Hell had been unleashed at once. The beast's head flopped to the side, eyes sprung open and vacant of life, its tongue hanging down the side of its mouth. Its lips were smeared in frothing spittle.

Lauren waited for what seemed like an eternity for the monster to move, watching for any flinch that might indicate that it was returning to consciousness, ready to pull the trigger again.

The creature remained still. A breeze kicked up and blew the hairs on its face. As she stared, Lauren thought in some ways it resembled more of a human than a beast in its serene state of death.

"Hello? Anyone out there? Hello?" Donna called from within the cave.

Lauren waited for several more minutes before she was convinced that the beast was truly dead. She stood on shaky legs and brushed the dirt off her hands and knees.

As the sun parted from behind a cloud, Lauren felt that a great weight had been lifted off her shoulders. The birds around her began to sing and a pair of butterflies flew around her, enthralled in courtship.

She entered the cave and called out, "Donna?"

"Lauren? We're back here."

Her eyes still needed to adjust to the darkness as she cautiously walked to the back of the cave. "I'm right here. Is everyone okay?"

The light from the mouth of the cave slowly illuminated her three friends. Donna was the only one sitting up. The other two looked asleep, or worse.

"Oh my God, Donna, are they dead?"

Donna made out Lauren's shape silhouetted in the light from the cave mouth, barely able to make out the features on her face. "No, they're still breathing. I don't know how bad they're hurt though. Jenny and Abe tried to put up a fight when that thing went to tie us up. Needless to say, it won."

"Tied you up? You mean that animal out there tied you up with that climbing rope?"

"Yeah. That thing acts as smart as a human sometimes. I don't know what it's capable of."

"It's not capable of anything now." Lauren stooped down and untied Donna's wrists, then her legs. "Help me with the others."

Donna looked up at Lauren, then her eyes went to something over her shoulder…her face became one of terror and she screamed.

Before she could turn around, a massive hairy-clawed hand swept around from behind her, with the force of twenty strong men. Lauren's neck buckled at the impact, to be torn clean off her shoulders.

Donna watched through the veiled light as her beloved friend's head spun in the air, turning flips.

Blood splashed across her face as she watched more blood shoot up like a pulsating water fountain from between Lauren's shoulders. Lauren's body collapsed to the cold cave floor, her limbs spastically twitching.

The beast looked down in disgust at the lithe form of the puny female that had brought it so much pain. The human had fought it with tactics unlearned from the ways of the other creatures of the woods.

She wasn't strong like the mighty buck that attacked with its rock hard antlers, nor the black bear, which Bigfoot respected as a near equal.

But despite the superior tactics of the human, the creature had prevailed using cunning, like other animals of the forest. Such as mimicking the tiny possum and pretending to be dead until the opponent assumed victory.

Bigfoot knew itself only as *Hunter*, and proved today that it was the mightiest creature in the entire forest, superior even to man.

A NEW CALLING

MATT KURTZ

Rocking in the passenger seat, Milt popped open another beer, shoved a stick of beef jerky into his mouth, and cranked up the Metallica tune on the radio. His brother Joe was behind the wheel, driving the pickup through the winding country road.

The two boys were on their way to Joe's cabin for a weekend of work and play. With both brothers recently completing multiple tours of duty overseas, they had put in their eight years of military service and now just wanted to take full advantage of civilian life. First thing on their list was to run off into the woods so they could act like kids again.

It was Milt's first time to see what his big brother had done to the cabin after inheriting the property over a year ago from their Uncle Wendell. Joe had renovated the small, single room cabin by himself but needed help installing the solar panels on the roof since there were no power lines in the isolated region.

The place might not have running water, but it sure as hell was going to have electricity to power a portable A/C window unit. Not having climate control during the Texas summer was plain asinine. Besides, they'd sweated enough overseas and saw no reason to continue doing so once back home, reminding themselves they were now allowed a pampered life as civilians.

Joe suddenly whipped the steering wheel to the right and pulled off the tree-lined road. The pickup began bouncing on the rugged terrain at the same moment Milt took a sip of his beer. The can slipped away from his lips, spilling Budweiser down his chin and across his barrel chest.

"Damn it!" Milt yelled, swinging out and punching his brother's beefy arm.

Joe hooted and immediately swung back, aiming for a shoulder. Milt lurched away, hoping to dodge the blow but wound up slamming his head against the metal frame of the door, then bounced back and met the full force of Joe's punch.

"Damn it!" Milt screamed again, laughing at his stupidity while rubbing his aching head and sore shoulder.

A mile down the winding dirt path, the pickup skidded to a stop, kicking up a cloud of dust. Joe climbed from the vehicle and approached the rusted gate that secured the property. He unlocked the padlock, removed the chain, and…froze.

His head cocked to the side. Swinging around, he drew a .357 revolver from seemingly out of thin air—actually from his rear waistband. He fired twice into the brush, the shots echoing in the distance like rolling thunder.

Picking at a stubborn piece of jerky stuck in his molars, Milt watched from the pickup as his brother grabbed a stick and poked the weeds. The entire business with the gun was second nature because of the feral hogs that roamed around. They were a far cry from the cute little ones in children's movies. They were mean and hungry and capable of an unprovoked attack that could kill a man easily.

Joe lifted the stick and showed off the rattlesnake dangling on the other end with half its head blown off.

Sometimes the gun was needed for lesser threats.

Milt grunted his approval. Although Joe couldn't hear it over the engine, he saw his brother's nod which was good enough. Dropping the dead snake, he returned to the gate and swung it open.

With the wild grass that had grown three feet high scraping the pickup's undercarriage, the vehicle bounced from side to side over the uneven ground as it continued on until finally reaching the cabin.

After unloading the beer and food, they hopped back in the truck so Milt could get a tour of the property. Joe pointed out their uncle's numerous hunting blinds that faced the small pond and various feeder stands. Although neither said it, the thought of hiding in a wooden shack to wait for an unarmed creature to wander close so you could take a shot at it just didn't seem like much of a sport. In fact, it seemed downright boring compared to the action they'd seen while serving.

Moving on, they made their way to check the motion-activated cameras that Joe had strapped to a couple of the trees. They wanted a preview of what possible game lurked on the property at night and in Joe's absence.

Joe pulled the memory card from the unit with his thick, sausage-like fingers and plugged it into his digital camera.

"A week's worth of pics," he said, looking at the counter. "Two hundred and sixteen of 'em. Let's see what critter's set it off." He began to scroll through the photos.

One hundred and ninety-eight of those pictures showed nothing but a tree branch waving in front of the camera, for both day and night. Joe looked up and saw the cursed branch in question and planned on taking care of it when he returned the camera to the tree. The other snapshots were a few nighttime pics of a raccoon at the feeder, a few mangy coyotes crossing the frame, and numerous shots of wild pigs—where every one of them seemed to be runts and not some Hogzilla the two brothers were hoping for. The final picture was a night shot. Just outside the camera's LED flash range was a pair of glowing eyes that stared back from the murky void.

"Huh…" Joe said, offering his brother a look.

Milt squinted, his nose and cheeks, scrunching like a rat. "Coyote?" He pronounced it *kie-yoat*.

"Too high. Its eyes are eight, nine feet off the ground easy."

"Then maybe a 'coon?"

"On steroids maybe."

Milt shook his head. "Could be sitting in a tree."

Both men looked up in the direction the photo was taken. It was a straight stretch of open field.

"So where's the tree?" Joe asked.

Milt shrugged. "Probably an owl swoopin' in."

"Probably." Joe licked the sweat that was already beading on his upper lip. It was only nine in the morning. "C'mon, let's get goin' before it gets too damn hot to do any work."

As the sun set behind the trees, Milt snorted awake from his drunken stupor. Sitting up on the couch, he knocked the dozen beer cans surrounding him to the floor. The commotion woke Joe, who was asleep in the recliner and surrounded by his own dozen cans that completed their recently polished off case. He glanced at the window unit blowing cold air and smiled.

Milt bobbed his head in agreement. The air conditioning sure felt good.

They had spent the first half of the afternoon frying like bacon in a pan while on top of the scalding roof. The heavy and bulky solar panels were a bitch to get up there and Joe almost fell off twice—Milt, once—but their mission was eventually accomplished. After waiting an hour for the sun to charge the portable battery, Joe plugged in the air conditioner and fired it up. They cranked the temperature down, plopped themselves on the couch and recliner, and started drinking heavily to re-hydrate.

"I'm hungry." Milt said.

Joe grunted. He reached over to the floor beside him, grabbed a large box of matches, and tossed them to Milt. "Make a fire." He nodded beyond the front door.

Milt nodded back.

Both men slowly stood, groaning in unison from their already aching muscles. Milt headed outside to start the fire pit in the yard while Joe went to the corner of the cabin used for dining. He dug through a cardboard box sitting on the tiny kitchen table and removed two cans of chili, a large can of Spam, a can opener, and a cast iron skillet. Stooping to the large cooler on the ground beside him, he fished out a six pack of Bud from the icy water then headed outside.

Milt already had the pit lit but his full attention was on the shadowy treeline beside the cabin. He looked as intense as a bird dog pointing out a flock of quail.

"What's up?" Joe asked, stepping beside him.

"I thought I heard somethin'."

"Pig?"

Milt shook his head. "A howl."

"Coyote?"

"None like I've heard."

Joe nudged him. "Your 'roid 'coon?"

Milt shrugged and looked down at the canned goods in his brother's arms. "Forget it, I'm hungry."

Joe nodded. "Good, let's eat."

They both returned to the fire to heat their meal.

The full moon shone down on the brothers as that sat around the pit, finishing their meal by firelight. With their bellies full, they exhaled and licked their lips.

Joe tossed Milt a beer. He caught it one handed and popped it open, not even flinching when it sprayed him with foam. He just sucked up the bubbly that spewed from the top before any more was wasted.

"Tired," Milt said, exhaling.

Joe grunted in agreement.

"Huntin' tomorrow?"

Joe nodded. The work on the cabin had been done. Now there was nothing else to do but hunt.

Milt yawned like an old dog. "I'm beat. Sleep?"

Joe nodded again. "Why not. Gotta get an early start before it gets too hot."

Both stood, groaning from their even sorer muscles. Milt chugged his beer while his brother kicked some dirt over the flames. A crack of a tree branch sounded from the woods, just over their shoulders.

The brothers froze, eyeing one another.

"You packin'?" Milt asked.

"Nope. You?"

"No."

"Shit…" they both whispered in unison. Their guns were inside on the kitchen table. How could they be so stupid as to go outside unarmed? Maybe it was from exhaustion, not to mention all the beer that had them getting careless.

Joe had his back to the treeline while Milt was facing it.

"Anything?" he asked Milt.

Milt's eyes shifted over his brother's shoulder. After scanning the woods for any sign of life, he simply said, "Nope." Then his eyes clicked to the right. "Wait."

A pair of glowing eyes broke the darkness.

"Pig?" Joe asked.

"No."

Joe waited for a further elaboration.

Milt squinted. "'Roid 'coon?"

Joe subtly bent his head to the fire. Milt glanced down at it also.

"Dibs on the pan," Joe said.

Milt was hoping his brother wanted the greasy, cast iron skillet. He had been eyeing the thick stick poking out of the pit that they'd been using to stir the fire. The tip of it was red hot and perfect for searing through flesh with minimal effort.

Milt looked back up at the woods and noticed the eyes were brighter. The eyes are larger. "It's comin'," he said.

"Count of three?" Joe whispered.

Milt nodded. "One."

"Two," Joe said.

"Three!" they yelled together, quickly grabbing the items from the fire. By the time they swung around with weapons raised, nothing was there.

The woods were dark—silent.

The brothers sprung onto the cabin's porch and raced inside. Seconds later, they returned with flashlights and fully armed—Milt with his pump action shotgun, Joe with his Winchester lever-action rifle, and both with pistols shoved in the waistbands as backup. They sprinted to the edge of the woods with Milt taking the lead.

"Here!" Milt called, aiming the flashlight's beam at the ground.

Both studied the tracks in the dirt.

"Thought you said it was an animal," Joe said.

"It was."

"Then you need glasses."

Milt looked back at the tracks and saw the enormous, five-toed, humanlike footprints leading off into the brush. "Well I ain't never seen a man's eyes glow like that."

The brothers stared at each other then cracked smiles. No words were needed to understand that they might be going after a new breed of animal. Something big. Dangerous.

"Ready for a hunt?" Joe asked.

"Hell yeah."

They stepped into the darkness of the treeline. Joe took the lead. About a hundred yards in, the tracks vanished.

Joe shone his light around. "Shit."

"What?"

"No, I mean I can smell shit. You?"

Milt took a couple whiffs and grimaced. The odor seemed to be all around them, permeating the darkness.

Joe looked back at the ground. With the prints ending at the trunk of an oak, it only made sense to look up into the treetops. The flashlight beams only reached so far, unable to penetrate the shadowy abyss above.

A crack of a branch came from somewhere within the canopy of thick treetop foliage. The men whipped their lights in two different directions. A few loose leaves floated down into their beams.

The surrounding crickets suddenly fell silent and the brothers glanced at one another.

"Ambush," Milt said.

Joe grunted. It sure felt like one.

They clicked off their lights and let their eyes adjust to the dark, then slowly backtracked with weapons raised, scanning the surrounding blackness, both around and above. Whatever the animal was, it had enough intelligence to lure them into a trap, and that mad the hunt all the more thrilling.

More leaves fell from above. Scratching and scraping—like claws on wood—sounded overhead. Something was definitely on the move up there, they just couldn't pinpoint it.

Milt and Joe quickened their retreat to get out from underneath the suspicious activity. A deafening roar echoed overhead that chilled their blood. The falling leaves stopped, then a loud thud came from somewhere in the darkness ahead. Whatever it was sounded like it weighed a ton when it hit—or landed on—the forest floor.

"Pickup or cabin?" Milt asked regarding where they should go.

"The cabin," Joe said. "Better shelter till we know what we're dealin' with."

A snarl echoed in the murky woods and the brothers halted with firearms raised.

A loud crack rang out. Joe glanced over his shoulder to see if Milt had fired off a shot. He hadn't. He was too busy gaping into the distance where even louder cracking sounded. Joe spun back around and caught something enormous moving within the shadowy landscape.

A tree was falling. Upon its descent, it swiped and tore off the surrounding branches in its path, causing all the other trees around it to sway. When it landed, it bounced on the ground and vibrated like a fish out of water until finally going still.

"We're dealin' with somethin' big here," Milt whispered.

Another roar came from within the shadows.

"Ornery too," Joe added.

A series of cracks rang out as one tree began to fall, then another. Something very large was approaching. Something with enough strength to push small trees out of its way.

"Move!" Joe yelled. He lay down a few rounds of covering fire into the falling timbers while his brother retreated.

Seconds later, Milt darted out of the woods and into the clearing as the roaring continued, but the gunshots ceased. He swung around, dropped to one knee, and raised his shotgun to cover his brother's withdrawal, hoping he wouldn't have to fire since he'd probably hit Joe with the spray of pellets. A rifle would be much better suited for the job.

In the blink of an eye, something raced out of the black void, startling Milt. He swung the shotgun, leveled its barrel at his brother's chest, then quickly raised it to get Joe out of his sights.

Joe ran to the cabin and leapt onto the porch, immediately swinging around to cover his brother. "Move!" he yelled with his rifle aimed at the woods.

Milt sprung to his feet and ran through the cabin's front door. Following, Joe ducked inside, slamming the door behind him and locking it.

Running to a window that faced the oncoming juggernaut, Joe drew the curtain while Milt killed the lights and covered the front door. The snarls and roars seemed to be growing louder, echoing just outside the cabin.

"Shit almighty…" Joe said, peering between the curtain's seam. "Milt, come over here."

Milt joined his brother and peeked out the window. Wild pigs, deer, coyotes, skunks, raccoons, and other critters scuttled from the treeline, dashed across the cabin's clearing, and disappeared into the dark woods on the other side. They were all fleeing, getting out of the way from the approaching behemoth.

A tree fell into the clearing, landing mere feet from the cabin. Both men knew they would be in deep trouble if any trees in the immediate vicinity were pushed down. If the cabin—their refuge—wasn't demolished, the pickup truck—their only means of a quick escape—would be.

There was another crack of splintering wood just outside the window. Milt glanced out and saw something that resembled a gigantic ape pushing against a tree trunk. Having the height of a basketball player and the width of a linebacker, the beast snarled—revealing razor sharp teeth.

Milt pulled back the curtain and raised his shotgun, shoving its barrel through the glass pane, the shards falling to the floor.

"Hey!" Joe yelled about the breaking of his window. But when he finally caught a glimpse of the beast, he quickly forgave his brother's action. While Milt's intent was to get a kill shot, Joe was more concerned with the tree that was falling away from the creature and toward the cabin. Milt fired a shot, but before he could see if his aim was true, Joe grabbed him and threw him to the ground, landing on top of him.

A deafening crash rattled the cabin. The roof above the low lying bedroom loft collapsed in upon itself, sending a rain of dust and splinters into the air. Luckily, the sturdy ceiling joists prevented the cabin from pancaking in upon itself.

When all had settled, Joe and Milt slowly sat up, looking above.

"Shit," Joe said.

Milt raised his shotgun. "You smell it again?"

"Nah…the cabin, it's ruined."

A snarl came from outside. Crawling across the floor on their bellies, the brothers went to the window, each taking a quick look from opposite sides. They caught a fleeting glimpse of hairy muscular legs loping up the fallen trunk, heading for the roof. It quickly disappeared before they could even raise their weapons.

There was a thud overhead, then the sound of splintering wood. It was clawing its way through the damaged roof, trying to get inside.

Joe pointed upwards then motioned for Milt to stay put. Milt raised his shotgun at the ceiling, waiting for the thing to show itself.

Joe ran outside, leapt off the porch, and dashed across the yard before the thing had a chance to spot him and attack. Once at a safe distance, he spun around and raised his Winchester, aiming it at the roof and closing one eye. Shock was his initial reaction to seeing the cabin with a tree on top of it after he had invested so much blood, sweat, and tears into the place. But that shock was nothing compared to the sight of the huge, eight foot tall, ape monster on top of it, tearing through the roof like a dog digging for a bone in the dirt.

His eyes shifted to the cabin's open door. Through it, he could see his brother crouching, swinging the shotgun's aim back and forth then…BAM! Milt's shotgun exploded, sending down more wood splinters and debris from above.

Back on the roof, the creature lurched out of the hole from the impact of the blast. It rose up, roaring in pain and clutching its chest. Milt always was a good shot.

But Joe was better. He raised his rifle, setting his crosshairs on the beast's throat. Slowly exhaling, a bead of sweat rolled down his brow as he gingerly squeezed the trigger. There was a loud *crack* and the muzzle flash blinded him temporarily. He used that time to chamber another round by throwing the lever on the Winchester. Once his eyes quickly re-adjusted, he saw the creature holding its neck with its taloned hands. It collapsed to its knees, somehow keeping its balance on the lopsided roof.

Joe lowered his aim to the beast's chest, dead center, for the kill shot. A headshot would've been more ideal but he wanted to keep open the possibility of a head and shoulders mount of the creature, and obviously needed to keep the skull intact. How many taxidermists could accurately reconstruct a Sasquatch head when the creatures supposedly didn't exist, and the only pictures that prove *they* might only show them as blurry fur balls?

Since it appeared to be a cross between man and ape, Joe felt pretty confident that its heart would also be located dead center of its chest. He fired another shot.

Bull's-eye. Blood, bone, and fur exploded from the creature's chest. The beast went limp, slumped forward, and rolled off the roof, landing in the brush with a heavy thud.

"Got him!" Joe called out, letting his brother know that the coast was clear.

Milt stepped out onto the porch with shotgun raised. "Is it dead?"

Joe fired another shot into the creature's chest from a distance. It didn't move. "Yeah, should be."

Both men kept their weapons aimed at the beast lying still on the ground. They had enough hunting experience to know that just because it wasn't moving, didn't mean it was dead.

"If it starts twitchin'," Joe said, "I'll handle it." Thinking about that taxidermy mount, he nodded to Milt's shotgun. "Yours will make a mess."

Moving closer for a better look, the stench of the beast became unbearable. It smelled like a rotting skunk caked in feces. They quickly shuffled back to a more tolerable distance.

"Now what?" Milt asked.

"Take a breather. Then we can load it up and leave."

Keeping their eyes glued to the prone beast, they walked to the front of the pickup, climbed onto its bumper, and plopped down on the hood to keep their feet off the ground. The last thing they needed was to get bit by some rattler or gored by a feral pig making a sneak attack.

They sat for a long moment of silence then Milt slid off the hood and began walking to the destroyed cabin.

"Where ya goin'?" Joe asked.

Milt gave him a look as if he was stupid. "Where else? To see if there's some Bud left."

Joe nodded. "Get one for me, too."

Milt nodded and went hunting for some beer.

An hour later, after using a makeshift pulley system to hoist the dead beast into the rear bed of the pickup, they threw a tarp over the hairy corpse and tied it down. They really didn't know if they'd get in trouble for killing something so…rare…but when a wild beast mistakes you for a midnight snack, most people wouldn't object to the 'you or them' rule of thumb.

Anyone doubting the mortal danger they were in just needed to take a look at what remained of Joe's cabin and the woods surrounding it.

Inside the cabin, they gathered up anything of value in case trespassers came across the half-demolished structure with greedy fingers. They piled the items by the front door with the pickup waiting on the stable-side of the cabin.

When it came time to start loading the pickup, Joe dropped his box of pots, pans, and skinning kit on the ground by the rear bumper.

Milt came up behind him with a crate of ammunition. "What's up?" he asked, staring into the bed of the truck. Then he lost his grasp on the crate, letting it drop to the ground.

Both stared into the rear bed like two village idiots. The tarp was shredded and ripped back, the corpse of the beast gone.

"Playing possum?" Milt asked incredulously. There was no way that thing was still alive.

"No," Joe said, scanning the dark treeline. "Its kin took it." He pointed to the numerous large, fresh footprints around the rear of the truck.

"Time to go?" Milt asked.

"Hell yeah," Joe agreed. One had been hard enough to fight, he didn't want to think about a battle with a group.

They quickly loaded up what they could gather using one hand, the other needed to hold their guns. Joe started the engine while Milt held a pistol in each hand—a shotgun being too bulky to swing around inside the cab of the vehicle if another attack were to occur.

"Kinda makes you wonder about the other things out there in the world," Joe said. "Things that most don't believe in but must still be out there, huntin' us."

Milt smirked. "Then maybe we should hunt them back."

Joe cracked a smile, catching a glimmer of excitement that he hadn't felt since becoming a civilian.

As the pickup drove away across the shadowy fields and back to civilization, the darkness of the woods was broken by dozens of glowing eyes of all shapes and colors. Yes, the night held many secrets, and some that just might be discovered in the near future by two good ole' boys from South Texas looking to raise a little hell.

ALGERNON WOOD

NICKOLAS COOK

1888- August 20th

I am traveling by cart to my new home. The unnamed town where the loggers come for supplies is a muddy, stinking haven for the destitute and lost.

A fitting place for me, then, this swampy forest in Northeastern Florida. Father thinks to let me rot here, but I have my own plans.

I have come here to help survey and raze this hidden land in the name of commerce. My employers claim we are the first white men to invade this place. It is here that I hope to start my fortune.

For I cannot hope to receive any help from my father. He has disowned me, thrown me from the house; from his heart. Somehow, he found out about the women, and doesn't understand. The *hideous acts of depravations*, as he terms the experiments, he's thankfully kept secret from my dear mother. His reasons for secrecy…because my 'indiscretions' would dishonor the family name and cause her no end of grief. I think he'd be surprised at what mother could, and, indeed, has endured without his knowledge. After all, she's a woman with needs— physical needs—father has not been able to perform for some time now.

The dear girl has sought comfort in the arms of those that she finds familiar and safe. So they both keep their secrets about me from one another.

I would laugh, if only I did not miss the feel of her next to me during the dark and lonely nights. Here, I have only black nights, far away pinpoint stars, and the stink of men without culture and seemingly no social graces.

When I was forced to leave with no explanation, she was beside herself with confusion and grief. But I couldn't stay there with *that man* one more day. Our hatred is mutual and all encompassing. Besides, my 'dearest' father threatened to call the authorities down upon me. An irony from a man who has done more injustices than could fill the pages of that Holy Bible in which he puts so much faith.

As if I have done anything wrong. I have only done what men have done since God created him. I have explored the unknown. Something my father calls 'evil,' I would argue is only simple experimentation in human desire, a way to test the threshold of pain and pleasure. To know these boundaries of human experience is to see the face of God himself. And I firmly believe that He compels each of us to find our own level of worship, to seek our own understanding of His word.

Father will never understand. The authorities would have me executed but He understands. Or else wouldn't I have been punished for my so-called 'evil indiscretions' by now?

August 21st

Today I met the troop of sixteen men with which I am for some time to share my camp. They are a disgusting lot, every one thoroughly filthy with encrusted dirt, stinking like animals and entirely moronic. The half-grunted conversations I hear remind me more of pigs than men.

Violent men, they are also given to drunken brawling, and seem to feel that a knife is as good as a fist when it comes time to settling even the slightest disagreement. Already there has been one death: a man hit over the head by a blasting powder keg during a fracas. The others stood over his dead body, laughing, and then turned away to continue the card game that had been the cause of the turmoil.

It sickens me, being around such vileness. This is death with no theory. It is cheap and tawdry and it has no purpose, no soul. These children shrouded in the filthy skins of men have no true understanding of the power of death.

My father wished to punish me, wished to send me to Hell, as he said. Well, he has done so. I am lost as to how I will survive giving orders to this heathen troop. They would rather spit tobacco residue than speak.

This morning we must begin construction of a base camp in this vast unknown territory. We will create such from the plentiful materials around us. The pine, the oak, and the cypress shall be our walls and roof, the limbs and leaves our rugs and shade.

August 27th

It has been some days since we completed construction of the camp— as if calling a single communal bunker, and a pen for our mule, Jehovah, a camp.

We're surrounded by giant trees—behemoths of a time out of mind. Or in the eyes of the office I represent, we're surrounded by profit. Each fall of timber means dollars per head. The civilized world beyond will rise from the destruction we leave here in God's backcountry.

This is no place for the weak of nature.

This forest is strange. It somehow seems darker than any I've ever seen. Whether it is the twisted thickness of the pines, the gnarled gargantuan oaks that seem to scrape the sky, the ubiquitous Spanish moss that smothers everything, or only a peculiar aspect to the oppressive air, it is the first thing I noticed upon my arrival in this lost forest of the Florida outback. At night the effect worsens, for it is as if the real world—the world to which I once belonged—disappears. It is a sensation both terrifying and liberating in its own way.

The sweltering days are like cumbersome giants stepping along your tired back as you stoop and grovel through the sticky humidity. The only relief we've had so far has been the two nights of rain. But it stays humid here at all hours, for beyond our primordial forest is the swamp depths. One can smell moisture in the air, if the infrequent stirring breeze is just right. It is a dank stench of still water, rot, decayed life, and boggy death.

I dislike being here. It is sheer mental torture. However, in all fairness to these hardened excuses for men, there are among this example of the lowest order two with which I may share some degree of a kindred soul.

During our few conversations, or when I've been listening in on them through the cracks in the walls, I catch hints that they might understand my penchant for exploration of the darker side of sexual lusts. Although surely they would never be able to convey their feelings thusly, I think that we are, at the root, made of the same stuff. It seems they have concerned themselves at times with the same experimentations I've plied, although obviously their methods are rough and without the purposeful intent as mine own.

The first man, Wilton, is short, standing only five-foot-one in height, but he's wide, built like one bourn of the oxen. One would think that his unnatural brevity of height would make him the target of some of the others' violent inclinations, but he's given a wide berth when he saunters into the room.

I hear the others whisper dire things about his past, stories that almost rival the Seminole tribesmen's tales about this place. In general appearance, he's not much different than many of the other men. His face is perhaps more livid with criss-crossed scars than any of the others; his hands are similarly scarred, portending years of tough manual labor. The scraggly black beard he sports is tangled and dirty; his clothes, rags hanging upon his thick muscled frame. His eyes carry an unspoken message that perhaps keeps the others away as well. They stare from the grimy cave of his face like two bits of eons-dead coal, glittering out at the world in the same emotionless way, whether he's killing a chicken for dinner, or scaling one of the towering giants that hold sway in this arboreal hot-box.

The other man, the only man in camp that Wilton seems to allow near him, is Snyder. Physically he's the exact opposite of Wilton. Tall, lanky, his muscles stand out upon him like twisted cord rope. Despite his thinness, I surmise he's the toughest man in the camp. I've seen him take down men twice his girth, purely because he's willing to go one step further than they to accomplish his goal. His is the ferocity of a jungle cat, the roughness of a bear. He has no qualms about knifing a man to death during even the most innocuous of arguments. The others treat him as if he's possessed in some way. Wilton is the only man in the camp that will work with him, the only one I can be sure that Snyder won't kill while working in the field.

My curiosity grows daily about what has driven these two out into this hellhole. Is it possible they, too, have found themselves unable to live among so-called civilized men because of their predilections for experimenting with the flesh?

Oh, dear mother…how I miss the taste of your skin on my tongue.

September 5th

Something odd has happened this night. I feel the event is important, so much so, that I feel it must be noted before I attempt sleep in this sweating Hell.

As we sat round the campfire outside our communal sleeping quarters, as has become our custom these long lonely weeks, several quiet shapes stole upon us from out of the shadow-strangled forest.

These shadow shapes crouched within the brush and watched us for some time before Norton, who was sitting across from me, suddenly grew very quiet and watchful. He called our attention to the fact of their presence as he leaned forward in the guise of getting more coffee.

The word passed quickly in whispers from one man to the next, until everyone was on the alert. For some time we sat in a nervous expectation of violence, loading and checking weapons on the sly, while trying not to show that we were none the wiser of our silent watchers.

Wilton made it known, by hand and facial signals, that he was all for rushing the shapes and attacking them. Luckily, we were able to talk him out of such a foolhardy maneuver. Instead, we waited for the hunched shapes to come closer.

As the fire died down, I threw on another log. The wood sent bright, dancing embers into the night air. It seemed that the sudden flaring of the log as it caught aflame was too much for our strange visitors and they moved back into the forest beyond, leaving us unmolested.

We were only aware of their departure because they made enough noise so we would know they were leaving, whereas they had made none upon their earlier approach.

Once we were sure of their departure, we doused the fire and retired to the cabin, barring the door behind us.

Now, as I lie in bed, writing by a dying nub of candlelight, the creatures of the forest outside call loudly across the dark expanse of benighted woods. I'm sure I am not the only one this night sleeping with a loaded pistol in hand.

September 6th

It is the morning after our strange encounter with the sneaking shapes and the general consensus is that it was the native savages, commonly known as Seminoles. Perhaps they only wanted to see what these new pale squatters are all about. I hope for their return, so that we may start friendly trading with them.

They have things I require. Things for which my appetite has grown into a state of hunger.

But I will have to be careful. Very careful, indeed.

I understand these savages have their own brand of justice. They might not look kindly upon my predilections for fleshly pleasures.

September 12th

We lost a man today.

Andrew Norton was last seen in the East quadrant this morning, marking trees for cutting, as per his assignment. Sometime after noon, another logger, Markos, half a mile away, heard what he describes as a 'blood curdling' scream emanating from Norton's area of the wood. He raced to Norton's aid only to find no trace of the man. He claims there was nothing left but his tools lying scattered at the base of a giant oak tree. Markos hurried back to camp and told his story, upon which three of us followed him back, armed and cautious. But it was as Markos said. There was not a drop of blood, nor strip of cloth, to indicate what had become of our companion. My suspicion is he was waylaid by a passing bear; perhaps a panther. They are the two most prevalent species of predator in this part of the country. We've seen numerous skeletal remains belonging to both, enough evidence of their presence.

It occurs to me, of course, that Norton's disappearance might be attributed to our visitors from last week, stolen away for some savage purpose of their own. I have heard they have been known to eat the flesh of humans. But why would they attack now, and in broad daylight, when they could have done us all in the other night before we were even aware of their presence?

Of course, there is another theory that might bear some thinking upon.

Perhaps it was one of our own small crew that has killed Norton.

And I grow more certain with every passing hour that he is, indeed, dead. We may find remains at some later date, when the carrion birds begin to circle some distant area, but I'm sure we won't see Norton alive again.

I will keep my eye on Markos. Maybe the two of them quarreled and his story is to cover an act of unplanned violence.

The long hours in this dismal place, with its heat and constant cacophony of screaming birds, does nothing to displace the sense of homesickness that has gathered inside me lately. I miss the streets of Atlanta. I miss especially the opportunities a big city affords me in testing the limits of my strange desires for blood and flesh. Here, there is nothing, unless I can convince the savages to trade for one of their own. Preferably a young girl, for their flesh is sure to be tender. I need something to distract myself from this damnable place.

Dear, sweet mother, do you also dream of our nights together? Am I never to feel your pulsing flesh wrapped around me again?

Damn the man to his own Hell for getting lost.

September 12th—night
The natives returned to watch us again tonight.

I write this entry by the sheltered light of a single dim candle, so as not to disturb the others. They have had an exciting night and need as little disturbance as possible. It was hard enough to keep them from rushing the silent shadows lurking in the bush, especially Wilton. After Norton's disappearance, some of them want an eye for an eye, although, thus far, we have no proof that Norton's disappearance has anything to do with them. Thankfully, some of us—too few of us for my taste—have been able to talk the others out of a foolhardy attack. But I don't know how much longer our talk will keep them if there is another disappearance.

Until just an hour ago, most of the men were still awake, whispering stories back and forth in the semi-darkness. They speak tales of the horrible things the natives do to their captives. Their nervous mutterings played an oddly sinister counterpoint to the forest sounds outside the cabin walls.

Their stories make me anxious.

Some are patently ludicrous, fables of magic and brave warriors, which I find difficult to credit that these degenerate savages possess anything like what I have heard of, such as their great minds and strength.

However, it is the darker tales the men whisper amongst themselves that have me gazing with concern out at the dark rectangle of the window of the cabin. Stories of evil forest spirits which these savages can supposedly call forth.

I don't know if I believe in such demons or not, but I do know I prefer not to decide my beliefs in the dark of this forest. There is a spiritual comfort in blazing city lights and busy streets; they allow men to cast off the fear of the unknown. Here, I am confronted with that fear at every turn, day or night. Must sleep now...

September 13th

I have slept badly, my dreams dark and disturbing.

One dream, in particular, has me quite nervous this morning.

After the others had fallen asleep, and the full moon was slipping from its sharp impalement of silhouetted treetops on the horizon, I dreamed that I awoke to see something lurking at the window. A dark face was pressed against the glass, while two burning red eyes shifted back and forth between the sprawled forms of the sleeping loggers. When its burning eyes found mine, I sensed an evil power emanating from the creature that was not unlike an electric current running through me. The power of this dream demon paralyzed me, so that I couldn't move to warn the others. While I fought against the unnatural paralysis, the nightmare creature gave a final curious snort and then shambled back into the midnight forest.

A horrifying dream.

Most likely brought on by the men's dark tales.

But a dream, only.

Perhaps at best an illusion of moonlight and shadow, which my exhausted mind turned into this demonic presence.

It, of course, couldn't have been real. But there is one remembered detail of this nightmare that still troubles me this morning.

Vividly, I recall the ubiquitous forest sounds had ceased; the world beyond the shadow-filled cabin was quiet as a tomb. I remember only the snoring or dream-filled muttering of the men in their restless sleep.

It does now seem to me an awfully poignant detail for a simple night-mare. My hands tremble as I write this down. I can't deny it is fear which makes them do so, whether real or imagined.

I think I will keep my gun near for a few more days.

September 13th—continued in unknown PM hours
Two more men have disappeared today.

This time there were not even residual screams to lend a clue to the time or cause of their disappearance. At least none of us in the camp heard anything.

However, I can't be sure they met with any sort of violence. It's entirely possible the two left of their own recognizance. There's some speculation among the remainder of us—fourteen now—that the two men may have run off with whatever money they had on their persons.

Although I'm sure it couldn't have been much, if any. And with their monthly pay due to them in less than two weeks, it just doesn't seem logical for them to have left before they had money to spend. Especially if they decided to make their way back to that pitiful excuse of a supply town that lies nearly twenty miles to the east.

Then, of course, there is the question of supplies, for they took nothing with them if indeed they have decided to leave on their own. Wouldn't they have taken some supplies with them other than the shirts on their backs?

I let the others talk, but I don't share my thoughts with anyone but this journal. But I don't think the two have run off to spend some imaginary money. I don't think they ever left this forest.

I believe that they, like Norton before them, have been swallowed up by something out there. I think upon my supposed nightmare again and the fear sits heavy in my gut.

September 14th
No other disappearances. No sightings of the natives. The men are set-tling back down again after a quiet night.

September 18th
This morning several of the men report having heard strange noises in the wee hours of the night. When asked to describe the sounds, they said something large was shambling back and forth outside the bunker walls, rustling along the roughshod wood. Although I heard nothing myself, I made it a point this morning to check the grounds surrounding the cabin for

tracks. I found some odd prints, some animal larger than a man, although the feet look strangely human. Five toes, like men…but enormous in size. I'm not sure what they are. I also found clumps of dirty, sodden, stinking black hair caught in the walls' rough bark. The smell of the hairs remind me of the slaughterhouses on the docks of Chicago. Vile and stomach churning, and at the same time, oddly heady and exciting, something that I can't place right now. Something that reminds me of the backstreets of Atlanta as well, those same alleyways which I plied my experiments.

I'm not sure what to make of the evidence, nor the queer sensation which the oddly human looking prints gave me. I want to believe that the others are only frightened by their belief in the fables of the savages and their forest spirits. But they each have the same story, and these hardened men are nervous as kittens now.

Those foot tracks, the hairs, are proof which is hard to dismiss. I keep trying to convince them it was only a bear. But do I believe my own explanation? However, the most telling sign that something occurred last night is not the fearful men. Indeed, it is our company mule, Jehovah. This morning his fear is plain enough. He shivers and cowers in the back of his small stable, whinnying and braying as if mad with fright.

His behavior bothers me more than the twitching faces of the men, for he has proven himself a solid and faithful beast, thus far, not intimidated by the depth or darkness of the surrounding landscape.

But now he is terrified of something; that is plain.

Tonight, I will post a watch.

September 23rd
Supplies are low. Against my better judgment, I had to send six men this morning to get more. They would not agree to go without at least that many on the travel crew. I have outfitted them with our sole source of transport: the cart, pulled by Jehovah, and guns and plenty of ammunition. They have been warned that if any living thing approaches them, especially the savages—for I am still convinced they play a part in this—that they are to shoot without warning.

September 28th
It has been five days and the wagon has not returned. It should have taken only three days at most to return with the supplies. We have little food and will need to hunt soon for meat, if the wagon doesn't return.

September 29th

There is still no sign of the wagon or the men. The remaining eight of us discussed the possibility that they may have run into problems with the wagon, the mule, or both. A couple of the more stout-hearted individuals of our dwindling company insisted nothing at all has happened to our comrades, that they are off gallivanting in town, with no regard for our urgent need for supplies, nor our fear as to their late return.

But I don't share their optimism.

In my heart of hearts, I fear they, too, have met with some violent end.

But who is to blame?

No one speaks aloud the theory they might have been killed or captured by the savages, but it's on all our minds. The stories of their heathen ceremonies of blood and flesh resound in our collective memory. But dire mumblings of the forest natives as perpetrators don't hold much ballast with me any longer, no matter what stories they repeat over and over again at night, for I sense a darker party to blame.

I don't speak my mind aloud; in fact, I dare not even write down my fears, for they are unreal and insane. I fear to give them voice, even in the deepest parts of my soul. But I still can't seem to shake that dream of the face at the window, those red eyes and the power which they seemed to have over me. Those hideous crimson bright eyes peering in at me.

Will I ever leave this forest alive? Will I ever hold her in my arms again, or feel her passionate breath mixed with mine during our shared lust?

October 2nd

As a group, we have come to terms with the fact that whatever has happened to our six workmates—and the wagon and mule—they won't be coming back. Even the stouthearted individuals I mentioned before now agree it's likely that the six men have met with a bad end. Scalped and eaten by the savages, most likely, is what the others seem to believe.

Work has stopped altogether now. Nothing has been done for several days, for I can't convince any of them to go beyond a few hundred yards from the camp, and most certainly they won't wander outside of shouting distance of the cabin. All the men carry weapons at all times. Guns, axes, knives—we verily bristle like Grecian soldiers of old, ready to kill any shadow that moves in the forest.

What are we to do now? We have very little supplies, even for such as what remains of our party, and I don't think they will last till the end of the week. I have tried to get the men to hunt for meat, but they won't venture far enough into the forest to get more than the occasional errant squirrel or rabbit within range of the camp. Oddly, no larger game seems to inhabit the area. I can find no footprints, no scat, no evidence that larger animals come around at night. The only prints are those strangely human-shaped, but impossibly large, footprints…which cannot be ignored or dismissed by even the most illiterate among us as bear tracks. No bear ever laid a print such as the ones we found all around us upon waking.

And I have to wonder how came the bear and panther remains we have found? How did they come to be in this part of the forest? Something has brought the skeletons to this area, but what?

One of the men put forth the theory that it is one of the savages sneaking around our camp while we sleep. But no one pays his theory much attention, for we have all seen the savages, and know they aren't near large enough to be responsible for these impossibly large prints.

The meat we are able to procure is tough, stringy, and unsatisfying. But at least it is food. In a week, I'm sure even the most-vile squirrel will taste like heaven, when there is nothing else upon which to eat. Water is not yet a problem. With a few days of rain here and there, we've been able to catch enough in the rain barrels to last for some time. But we can't live on water alone.

The men grow more and more apprehensive at the hours which preclude the coming of night. As the sun sets each night, I witness all manner of nervous reactions among the others. The unspoken fears are bringing out the worst in all of us. There have been more frequent and more violent fights for the last few days, Wilton and Snyder originators for the most part. No one has been killed yet, but I suspect the reason for such restraint has nothing to do with Christian morality. I think it's because there are few enough of us as it is. Plain common sense dictates the more of us there are, the easier it will be to protect our dwindling numbers.

I can't say I blame them.

There does seem to be some new foulness to the air, some heavier oppression than the ungodly humidity that speaks of things unseen all around us. Even the forest birds seem to have deserted our immediate area. Silence reigns all round now. As if even the wood fears what watches from within its very shadowed realm.

Now we all hear the odd movements around the cabin at night, heard but never seen. When we go out as a group to investigate, there is nothing to be seen, only those inhuman footprints. It's as if we suffer from some form of mass hysteria.

I think we're all going a little mad.

Terror causes men to react strangely, does it not? What a driving force it can be. I know from my own experiments in those remembered back alleyways, where the glint of moonlight on the silver knife drove each of those frightened women into ecstasies or horror…

By God, I must leave this forest soon.

My own demons must be fed before I go mad!

October 2nd—night

The native savages came once again this evening.

When they made their presence known this time, we sat very still, waiting for their inevitable attack. But there was no such attack. In fact, they approached us with that same purposeful carelessness as before, so that we would know they were upon us. They rustled bushes, muttered among themselves in their heathen language from behind massive tree trunks, and stood tall among the gathering night beyond our meager campfire. Perhaps it is our dwindling numbers which makes them brave enough not to care.

After a few minutes of waiting for them to finally come into the circle of light cast by our fire, Wilton muttered something under his breath and stood. No one tried to talk him out of approaching them this time. But when he moved toward the nearest of their number, the dark-skinned, half-naked savage grunted something to the others, and two dozen more of the natives suddenly stood as one from the darkness.

I must say that my amazement was evident at that moment.

If I had to swear upon the number of Indians 'hiding' in the brush before that moment, I would have said no more than four or five. But it was evident that they had us surrounded from the beginning, but we never knew it.

Half a dozen of the savages moved to stand around Wilton, glaring at the surprised man, silently daring him to step into their midst.

Wilton was no fool. He gave them a watery, near toothless grin and cursed them as he backed away with his hands before him to show he had no weapons. Stoop shouldered and humbled, he returned to his place by the fire with the rest of us.

One of the dark-skinned bastards came forward then. Unlike some of the others, this one was mostly clothed in cured animal hides that hung to his knees. The clothes were stained with dirt and sweat. His face was no different, grimy and shiny. His dark eyes glittered in the light of our fire as if he were a barely covered cauldron waiting to boil over.

I felt as if he wanted to speak to us, but he was evidently wise enough to know it was a waste of time since none of us knew his heathen language and he knew nothing of our civilized English.

When he tossed a pile of white man's clothing into our circle, we all let out a collective gasp of amazement. The shirt and pants were bloody and torn, ripped to bits as if a large beast had been at them. We recognized the rags as having belonged to Fletcher, one of the men who'd been part of the supply run.

Someone muttered that we should attack right then, a notion at which I could barely hold back my derisive laughter. I doubted we had even two dozen shells left between us at the moment and we were completely sur-rounded by at least twenty of their warriors. They could easily have slaugh-tered us like whores at that moment had they wanted to do us harm. We didn't have a chance in hell of making a go of it.

Long-faced Snyder, despite his violent tendencies, knew our chances as well as I, and told whoever had voiced the attack plan to shut up. Wilton agreed and went on giving the savages his sickly, fearful grin, showing his tobacco- stained, rotting teeth.

The stinking, sweaty redskin who'd thrown the bloody clothes in our midst became frustrated with our continued silence and attempted to communicate with us, despite his lack of English. When it was evident from the confusion and shrugs he received at his gibberish, he tried using hand signals and facial gestures. We all sat in confusion still, but through his histrionics I gathered he was trying to tell us to leave the forest. Grunting uselessly, he kept pointing at the woods beyond…or perhaps he was pointing at the night…I'm still unsure which he meant.

Finally, sneering in disgust at us, he gave up and joined his fellow tribesmen in the brush once more, and without even a backward glance at us, they melted soundlessly back into the night. We discussed the event well into the night, but no one had any real solutions that didn't involve getting slaughtered, so we turned in, apprehensive and restless.

So now I lay here in bed, with my gun cocked and ready, feeling the night pressing in upon me, wondering if we will survive another encounter with the savages.

October 3rd

It—whatever IT is—came back last night and this time I know for sure I didn't dream it. The lurking shape, which I have now seen twice, is real enough, and I believe it means to kill us all.

As the night wore on, I and several of the men who couldn't fall asleep, heard something land upon the roof of our cabin. Wide-eyed and frightened, we sat shivering silently, listening to the heavy mass above move along the timbers of the roof. Each thumping step the creature took was heavy enough to shake the cabin. Guns were cocked into readiness. The thing kept moving back and forth and I felt sure that the entire cabin was going to fall in on us at any moment.

I was trembling so badly I could barely hold my pistol in place as I attempted to follow the thing's plodding steps above. I heard someone sobbing and praying and I wanted to shoot the bastard to shut him up. Foolishly, I thought surely if the thing did not hear us, then perhaps it would leave us in peace.

I'm afraid my terror was master of me at that moment. Strangely, I always thought my ability to instill terror in others would make me immune to the sensation of pure terror, the sort of bone deep fear I felt at that moment. It was not.

The roof trembled above us. There came an animalistic snuffling noise, followed by several pig-like grunts, which oddly enough reminded me of the savage's earlier attempt to speak to us.

"It's trying to find a way inside," one of the men whispered in horror, his voice ragged and terror filled.

Wilton replied from across the room: "It's them goddamn injuns tryin' to get in at us."

I knew he was wrong. I knew right away what was on top of our cabin roof. I had seen it in what I convinced myself was only nightmare. It was some black beast seeking entrance. It had been responsible for the disappearances and the deaths of our companions as well.

The moon was a thin, useless sliver in the sky beyond the trees, the darkness complete around our little cabin. Someone struck a match in preparation to lighting a candle. I hissed for him to put it out. Damned fool! For some reason it struck me that the idea of letting that thing know we were awake and aware of its presence made me even more fearful than waiting in the dark.

Above, the movements became more frantic, a scratching at solid pine wood, and that searching snuffling began anew.

With a yelp of furious terror that surprised us all, Wilton leaped from his bunk, waving his pistol madly, and ran to the front door of the cabin. Before anyone could stop him, the fool had thrown open the door and he ran out into the night. We could see his capering form, insubstantial in the dim moonlight. He turned to gape up at the roof, aiming his gun. He yelled some incoherent curse and began firing his pistol, shattering the deep, tense quiet of the night with thunderous explosions; he fired over and over again at something only he could see. The rest of us were still too stunned to move from our bunks.

What he was trying to kill, only he could see, but we all saw what happened next.

A massive black furred hand reached down, snake quick, and snatched Wilton into the air in an irresistible embrace. I saw Wilton's eyes grow round and insane as he stared into the eyes of the unseen thing above. The last image I had of him was his arms and legs kicking and then his torso disappeared past the doorframe. His scream was cut off in mid-agony, as if by some unseen savage axe of fate. Then there was silence again; a terrible nightmare residue of quiet that left us all jarred and shaken.

The terrible silence didn't last for long.

From above we heard the most horrible wet rending sounds, as if something fleshy and still living was being torn apart. Meaningfully sickening thuds followed—pieces of Wilton hitting the timbers above.

One of the men, Hunsucker I discovered later, moaned like some pitiful animal in pain, then jumped to his feet, ran to the open doorway, slammed it closed, and barred it against the nameless horror beyond.

Those sickening, dreadful eating sounds soon ended, and in this new silence, we all gaped in the dimness, waiting for the next horrifying thing to come. But there was nothing else.

I felt trapped in the cabin, not knowing if the monstrosity still crouched above, wondering if it meant to kill us all this night. I could almost sense Wilton's carcass above my head, dripping and lifeless, torn apart like some hapless forest prey. But I couldn't even conscience the notion of leaving the claustrophobic security of the solid wood structure. Not even God himself could have made me take a step into that appalling night.

No one slept for the rest of the night.

We sat like frightened children. Some fool muttered and cried in a corner of the cabin, though I didn't bother to look to see who it was. His wet sobs went on for what seemed like hours. I would have gladly staved in his head had I not been terrified of moving, perhaps drawing the attention of whatever may be still waiting above us.

When morning finally arrived, we were still alive.

It has been unanimously decided the time has come to vacate the camp altogether. The thought of spending even one more night here is too much to contemplate.

Six hours has passed since sunrise and we have collected everything needed for our travel. We will leave behind anything too heavy or too frivolous with which to worry. All the men are anxious and fearful. We watch the trees and shadows with shaking apprehension.

I think I understand now what the savages were trying to tell us.

One last note: Before leaving the cabin this morning, Snyder went to the top of the roof, but found no evidence of Wilton's death. No blood, no torn clothing, just deep scratches along the timbers. His steps ended at the door. It was as if foolish, mad Wilton had never existed.

I write this now, as we hurry along a rough trail through the woods. In places, the trail is barely visible but several of the men are excellent trackers and they have little trouble leading the rest of us along the winding path.

I have not prayed since I was a child. The Great Truth is that all is death and love, and all is meant for fools. I refuse to pray now that I face what may be my last days on this Earth. I am a Machen. I will not bend for some invisible plaything meant for simpering fools who can't deal with that truth.

October 3rd—afternoon
Several hours into our escape, we've found the wagon. It was deserted. No bodies anywhere. The mule is also gone, too. Snyder took two of the men to search the immediate area, but they found only a rusted pistol, the cylinder half-empty.

I ordered the search quickly ended. Night comes all too soon in this arboreal Hell; the canopy cuts out most of the sunlight. Dark will descend in less than eight hours. The further away we are from this cursed forest, the better for us all.

October 3rd—early evening
Disaster has struck our party again! We are slowed to a crawl now that Hooper—that damned fool!—has broken his leg. What will become of us now?

October 3rd—near sunset
Our problem with Hooper and his broken leg was solved rather succinctly and simply by Snyder a few minutes ago. He shot the moaning bastard in the head. The others gave Snyder dire looks, as the body jerked

and quivered, the gunshot still echoing into the long shadowed distance. When the body was still, a couple of the men demanded we give Hooper a Christian burial, but Snyder dared any man to pick up a shovel to do so. He told them he'd put a bullet in the head of the man who didn't pick up his packs and start moving. I stayed silent, but I wanted to yell at those who dissented. They were fools! This was life and death! What good were their primitive rituals of putting a body into the ground now?

We're now on the move again. Hooper's body lies slumped against a pine tree, meat for the predators and scavengers.

As leader of this ragtag band of rough survivors, I expect trouble from the men later. They hate Snyder and Hooper was well-liked. I would not be surprised if one of them tried to kill him for his actions this day.

October 3rd—night

We have several miles left to go before we find civilization again. I'm afraid that this may be the last entry. I can only hope that someone may read my journal and take heed against exploring the dark corners of the world. Perhaps they will raze this place to the ground and put an end to the evil which calls this land home.

Since we stopped for the night, for fear of running headlong into the savages, a deadfall, a swamp—or worse—the thing which lives here, we have gathered stacks and stacks of firewood to ward off the night. Tonight we sit back to back, guns ready, shaking with terror as the darkness closes in on us.

I can only hope…no…perhaps if I were to pray for anything in this life, I would pray that somehow my mother knows my end.

Salva me ex nocte

Let that be my prayer then, and whatever gods hold sway in this damnable place, hear my silent entreaty.

October 4th—early morning

Perhaps my prayer worked. We have survived the night. I'm too frightened and exhausted to record more.

October 4th—afternoon

We've lost another man.

This time it was to a more mundane terror of this swampy forest.

This morning we decided to stay away from the darker parts of the forest, and we deviated from our original wagon trail by a half a mile in an easterly direction. It was there that we found we had to cross a stretch of dank swampland, a scabrous suppuration of pine and cypress giants. They were twisted, tortured skeletal trees, with grasping roots that thrust up from the black still waters. We proceeded into its misty depths with careful apprehension.

Silence reigned as we sloshed through the stinking watery pit of black moss laden waters. As we passed what I took to be a large floating log, the last man in line began to scream and thrash, churning the dank stinking waters into a gray churn mixed with red. The thing which I had taken as a log suddenly came to horrible life and snatched the unfortunate last man to his death beneath the waters. The log had been one of those monsters of the swamplands that the natives called an alligator, enormous reptilian creatures close in nature to the lost reptiles of eons ago.

There was no way to save the man. He was dragged down in a tumult of crimson water and a long wail of agony, until the great reptile's teeth closed horribly together at his midsection, bursting his lungs, stopping his terrible screams. Ragged clothing and parts of him floated in the sudden wash as the great beast sank below the surface once more. We hurried from that place, fearful that the bloody black waters would draw more of the fearsome creatures down on our small, huddled group.

I now find that it was stupid of me to allow one man to carry the entire water supply for our team. Now we have no water left, very little food, and at least ten miles yet to trek through this stinking dismal hell of sweat and fear. Will any prayer save us tonight if we find ourselves still here?

October 4th—evening

We are being watched. The Seminoles have been pantomiming our every move through this godforsaken place, for who knows how long. One of their numbers was so bold a few hours ago to step ahead of us in our rough pathway and motion for us to come near. We were much too exhausted at this point to be afraid of him or his companions—of which I had no doubt there must be many more than we could see—so we staggered to meet the lanky, dark-skinned savage.

When we were closer, he reached up slowly to snatch at a long brown vine hanging from the tree next to him, and using a shining silver knife, he sliced the vine in two and placed the severed and dangling end above his mouth. He looked at us expectantly as he made drinking motions and then he sucked at the vine. With a smile, he pulled the vine from his mouth and we all muttered in astonishment at the water that dribbled heartily from the severance.

We spent the next hour or so grabbing at any vine similar to the one he had shown us, cutting and sucking at them with desperate thirst. The heathen watched us gleefully sucking at the vines for a time and then he silently shambled off into the forest again.

Thank whatever gods live here! We know water exists now!

We may have filled our constant need for water, but it did nothing to solve our escalating food problem.

Night comes quickly in this forest and it was less than two hours before sunset. Soon, we will have to decide whether to make a hurried camp for the night or continue on, heedless of what the darkness may hold.

October 4th—evening-addendum

It has been decided that we should keep going. Snyder insists we continue. He insists out food problem is easily solvable should it come to desperation. The remaining fools most likely believe he refers to hunting for food, living off the land, only I have heard Snyder's whispered conversations with himself. I know what evil meat he has eaten in his past.

I wonder which of us he has chosen to become his next meal.

I don't blame him for keeping his head and knowing that there is only survival to consider and no price too high which one must pay to stay alive. But I will kill him if he comes near me with that evil smile of his. That I swear on the same swamp gods who call this place home.

At his insistence, no one argued. No one wants to think what will happen if we stay still for too long. Of course, I don't dare remind them that the wagon had been moving as well, and it had done nothing to save those men. Still, it's better that they have some hope rather than none at all, I think.

We'll continue our trek despite the fact that we're all near death with exhaustion. We dare not stop, even for rest.

October 5th—dawn

Blessed dawn has come and I'm the only one left alive.

I'm squashed down inside the bole of a gigantic tree, back as far as the tree will allow me to squeeze into its hollowed-out body. Here, in this insect riddled sanctuary, I await death.

The night has brought horror upon horror. If I live to be a hundred—which I highly suspect will not be the case, for I doubt I shall see another sunset—I will never forget the things I saw last night.

It came for us while we were trying to get away from the forest. Its attack happened so quickly that all I heard was a volley of terrified screams all around me, then the two men behind me were suddenly gone.

The thing did not wait long to come for the rest of us.

Snyder had two men beside him. I stood not far from their position, so I can say I finally saw the creature in all its monstrous impossibility as it made a snatch from the shadowed trees above to take Snyder's companions, the men diving out of the way.

I will try to describe it, though much of the details escape me now as I shudder to remember its horrible aspect.

It was like a bear and gorilla all at once, with the face of a man, and the glowing red eyes of a demon. Those crimson eyes glared in hatred at the small flesh things called 'man' which it easily tore apart. Its gaping massive mouth was filled with rows of yellow twisted teeth. Its massive muscled body, covered with course black hair, was power personified. The thing's strength must be great, indeed, for it hurtled men aside as if they were mere grain sacks of flesh and bone.

I saw it wrench away the very flesh of Holister's face in a flash of razor claws.

When it had decimated most of my crew, I witnessed the creature swing down from the trees overhead, its huge legs bulging with muscles. It gave a low hateful growl as it landed next to Snyder. Then, like a lightning strike in the night, his two companions were hoisted bodily into the air. I saw only their legs kicking in terror; their screams were muffled by the creature's twisting, churning body, as it scuttled up into the shadows of the treetops again.

Then it was silent once more, but it was a silence heavy with waiting death. The creature was there, watching us. I could feel its horrible stare on Snyder and myself, the last survivors.

It wasn't until I turned to see Snyder looking not at the trees above where the thing had disappeared, but at me, that I realized my true immediate danger was to come from my companion, rather than from the hands of some ungodly forest monster.

Snyder's face was stretched into a tight mask of insanity, his rotting teeth bared at me like a cornered and desperate dog. His pistol swung towards me. I had no doubt about his sudden gutless plan for survival. He intended to use me as bait!

My own gun, already aimed at him before I knew it, fired without conscious thought, my finger squeezing the trigger in a nervous tic-like motion.

I saw a red blossom appear above his left eye, and I knew he was dead before he hit the ground.

I watched his body for only a second before I dove for cover into the tree bole. It was a short time before the thing came for him. Its great giant hairy hands clutched Snyder's limp form against its black body.

Then it turned for a moment, to gaze at me in my small hiding place. Its red eyes glittered like dying stars. It felt as if we locked eyes for a long time. It didn't seem overly concerned with my presence inside the tree. It shifted its massive body and then the thing was gone, scurrying back up the nearest oak tree, Snyder's limp form held closely to it. Within seconds it was gone.

October 5th—afternoon
I have sat in this tree for hours now. My body is slowly dying from forced starvation and dehydration. Outside my hiding place, many of those hanging vines filled with life-sparing water await me, but I'm afraid to leave for fear the creature is only waiting above for me to come out. I won't be its next victim. I have one bullet left in my otherwise useless pistol. I will use it on myself if it comes for me.

If I am able.

Truth is: I'm very weak, sick from exhaustion, no food, no water. I can barely hold my pen upright. I may be long dead before it comes for me.

What prayers now?

Mother will never know how I died. I will never feel her touch again.

Will I pay for my own supposed crimes against the flesh?

October 5th—evening
How long have I been here? I can't be sure of anything anymore. I mark this entry as the 5th of October, but I have no way of knowing if that is the actual date or not. My waking and sleeping moments have all become like a liquid spill, running together in a mesh of half-seen, half-heard, half-remembered fantasies of escape, fantasies that dissipate when I come to this half-wakeful, miserable state to find I'm still trapped and dying.

Am I even writing now, or am I only dreaming the act? I feel the pen in my hand, but I don't trust my senses anymore.

Perhaps this is all a dream.

I will have to brave the outside soon, even if the creature is waiting for me. I have to try for the vines with water. I dream of great oceans of crisp clear water. I want to drown myself in their depths.

October??—evening

I have been told by the savages that it's been days since I left the safety of my hiding place to try for the water vines, even in my weakened state.

I recall staggering out of the tight hole and then falling a great distance with nothing to catch me for miles around.

The next half-recalled sensation was of being lifted into the air, and wondering why there was no pain if the black beast of the forest had come for me. It seemed as if there should have been some pain. My eyes were gummed shut so that I couldn't open them to see the thing pulling me to my death.

Of that I remember feeling a great thankfulness. I didn't want to know my death.

Then there was darkness again and I was thankful for that as well.

I remember thinking how I had outwitted the beast by dying before it could kill me. Or some such ludicrous thought. I was out of my mind.

Some time later, my eyes opened, and I saw a vast sky, cluttered all around by dark clouds. A storm was coming, but I thought nothing of why I was moving, why I was floating on my back through this cloudy sky. There was no ground, only that gray, godlike canopy ready to receive me, to exonerate me from all my sins, to whisper like my mother about The Great Truth.

It was only after the dark-skinned forest natives gave me water and food, and my body began to heal, that I realized I hadn't been floating at all. The savages had carried me back to their village, which is some distance from the abandoned logging camp.

Now, they are slowly nursing me back to health.

We don't talk much, and use hand signals whenever the need arises to communicate in our limited fashion.

Their village is surprisingly well-ordered, clean, and quiet. They have cut their home from the very heart of the woods and subsist mainly on fruits, vegetables and deer meat that they get from the surrounding land. Their homes, their clothes, their tools are all made of animal hide and bone.

They are friendly enough, but seem to fear me. The elders of the tribe come to visit me from time to time, and gesticulate wildly as they try to tell me something. I can only nod and smile. Eventually they lose their patience and leave me alone again.

They allow me out now and I walk among them, watching their little daily rituals which they must perform to fill their heathen bellies, to make things run smoothly for the tribe.

I say they allow me out, but they don't allow me freedom.

When I limp towards the surrounding woods to see if anything lies beyond their camp, invariable one of their old men hurry to stand before me and they make excited gestures to push me back to the center of the cluttered domiciles. I allow myself to be led back, wondering why they won't let me near the woods.

Not that I want to go out into that bleak depth, mind you.

For that stinking hairy creature is still out there; I can feel it waiting and watching even now. I have no need to test its power again.

The women I see walking throughout the encampment stay well clear of me. A shame, because as my strength grows, so do my secret hungers once more descend upon me, ever demanding, ever growing. It would seem that facing my own death has caused the controlling force within me to break down. Something is happening to me and I don't know how to explain it. My taste for experimentation is a kicking, screaming beast within, seeking release once more.

I must find some way soon to get at one of them.

Preferably one of the little ones, one which won't be able to defend itself.

That way there won't be much of a fight to get her alone, to do what I need to do. I've been sharpening my knife on and off for days, to be ready if the opportunity presents itself.

October?? —morning
It has been several days since my last entry. I wonder if I'm still trapped in the bole of that damned tree, still dying slowly, that my rescue by the savages was only a dream?

I must be mad. There is no other explanation.

It came to me last night and spoke.

But not in words.

The giant, man-like creature showed me through a series of glorious sensations what it could give me if only I would agree to its infernal soul contract, an agreement so hideous that I can't make myself write it in words for this entry. Suffice it to say that this beast requires a servant and it has promised me much to do its bidding. It knows things about me that no living person could ever know. It knows all about my fun with the wayward girls in Atlanta. It knows all about my need to experiment upon the flesh of whores. It knows every cut I ever performed on their writhing, whore-flesh.

This thing is the devil, surely.

And what it promises is the devil's work.

But it is either me or them, an easy enough bargain to make when all is said and done.

October?? —evening

The deed is done. I belong to this creature body and soul now.

I still live.

The savages are all gone.

But I live.

Last night, the thing came for them, took them all.

With the exception of one upon my hungry request—one little girl of about ten years of age was spared.

I was its way and guide. Now it shows me how it is going to give me life; a long and fruitful life. All I need to do is find a wife and get her with child. My fortune will be no problem, so I can buy a wife if need be.

But don't I already know exactly who will bear my first child?

As for my father?

To quote the famous bard, himself, *"Is this a dagger which I see before me, the handle toward my hand?"*

When the child comes along, there is the rest of the contract to be fulfilled. This Black Beast has given me the ritual words and signs which I will need to use for the ceremonies. I write them here, so I shall never forget them. These precious things it tells me must be passed from one male Machen to the next, to forever be remembered, for I have now placed every Machen heir in direct line of the agreement between me and the Black Beast that owns my soul.

There is one final catch to this infernal contract, and it is to be explained only to the surviving male members of the Machen lineage.

The women wouldn't understand the need for such things, and could not, I fear, condone such actions as must be taken to fulfill the contract.

This power is great.

To break the contract means death for another Machen male.

I set forth for the nearest town and then to home, to love, to the glorious future for the Machens and this Black Beast in Algernon Wood.

AREA CODE 51

WILLIAM R. D. WOOD

The smell was the worst part.

It got on your skin and held on for dear life. A disgusting reminder that nature did everything without regard for human standards of hygiene. In fact, if anything, nature abhorred cleanliness altogether.

Garcia sniffed at the air and scowled. The changing room was supposed to be almost as sterile as the examination bay, but if he could smell the beast in *this* room, nothing in the facility was truly sanitary. Why the Americans had chosen to build the facility in Peru, he didn't know, but Garcia was sure they had used state of the art methods back in the mid-twentieth century when they'd constructed the place, intending it to last. But everything breaks down.

With a sigh, he fastened his rubber boots to bright yellow hazmat pants and looked up at the antique monitor hanging from the ceiling. The creature lay unconscious on the modified surgical table in the next room.

Garcia rubbed his right side. Three months and his ribs still ached where he'd been backhanded by the soulless beast.

He and Cordoba had been using a modified patient lift, the kind employed by nursing homes to lift the obscenely obese, to move the creature from the transport pallet to a powered table. The creature's eyes flickered open. Still doped with enough tranquilizers to bring down ten men, the brute had lacked the strength and coordination to pull off an escape, but one haphazard swipe with its massive hand had lifted Garcia from his feet and sent him slamming into the monitoring equipment surrounding the table. Cordoba had been quick, ramming an assault taser into the creature's chest. Two additional shocks later and the men stood side by side over the hairy, apelike mess, Cordoba sporting his killer smile and Garcia four cracked ribs and a torn isolation suit.

"You okay in there, Garcia?" Cordoba asked over the intercom. "You look a little pale."

"I look pale because I haven't seen the *maldito* sun in three months." And the only reason he'd been outside then was the week-long trip to Villa Trompeteros for a local doctor to patch him up and check him for contamination after such close exposure to the creature.

The doctor, under constant instruction from officials in Lima by SAT-phone, had drawn all but a single drop of blood from his body, Garcia was sure. Then the doctor had ushered him into a room on an abandoned ward and locked him in while they awaited test results. The doctor hardly talked to him that week and when he did, it was in broken Quechua. Something about *tunnels* and his own *ácido desoxirribonucleico*. The department really knew how to pick them.

"Fair enough." Cordoba's laughter popped from the overhead speakers. "At least you *have* seen the sun."

"The sun through barred windows is not the sun."

"You're like an old woman, my friend." A series of muffled dial tones came through the speaker as Cordoba established a link to Lima. "Only you could complain about such a quick recovery."

Garcia laughed. The banter did help him relax, somewhat. Despite his lack of comic delivery, he knew Cordoba meant well. Garcia thumped his chest. "It's my superhuman constitution. You should take better care of yourself and you could be as healthy as me."

"And you shouldn't get in the way of an angry imaginary creature just so you can shirk your duties for a week."

"Next time we'll trade."

He and Cordoba had worked together for years. You had to stick together when you were cut off from society so often. You helped one another out, too, whether that meant Garcia buying a bottle of Scotch from a street vendor on their last mission, or Cordoba paying off the doctor so Garcia's new bride could slip into the hospital room for the night.

They'd tracked the creature for months before coming across the beast by chance in a stretch of dense jungle several hours drive from the facility. Unconscious beneath a copse of trees, it appeared to have given up, surrendering to its pursuers or the jungle. The undergrowth shook angrily in places when the two of them had arrived, small scavengers fleeing their prospective meal. Had they been a day later, or perhaps only a few hours, the jungle could have picked the creature's bones clean. For all its lack of cleanliness, nature was efficient.

Garcia eyed the monitor. Creatures in pharmacological comas should not be able to lash out and throw people across the room. And that included curinquean—or *Bigfoot*—as the Americans called them. He rubbed at his side.

"You can't ask for a better twist of fate, eh, Garcia? You'll be out of here in no time."

Garcia nodded, trying and failing to keep the grin from his face. "Si." He could still hear the encrypted warble of his superior's voice in Lima. *Get the job done, Agent Garcia. Get the job done and return to your pretty wife. Retire. Be a papa.*

Now their leaders were the ones shirking the mission. There was still so much to learn yet he and Cordoba had been ordered to destroy the creature and lock down the American research facility.

The beast's sickening musk triggered his gag reflex and he fought the urge to heave. The only thing he liked less than the smell was the fact that the people he worked for kept tabs on his wife; enough that they called her *pretty.*

With a gloved finger, Garcia triggered the airlock open and stepped inside. Huge air handlers hummed to life somewhere on the surface, causing his ears to pop. Filtered air rushed into the room, stirring the stench free in copious amounts. Garcia hurriedly pulled the transparent hood over his head to keep out as much of the odor as possible. With a firm swipe of his hand, he sealed himself in.

"You ready to get this done?" Cordoba's ghostly image looked down from the observation bay, the plate glass acting as much like a mirror as a window from Garcia's standpoint.

Even though Garcia had initiated the airlock cycle, Cordoba had to complete the sequence from the observation room. "Yeah, open it up."

Another protocol designed to ensure objectivity and safety should things go *other than ideal.*

Clanks reverberated through the floor and the door slid up, eliciting images of a guillotine blade being raised by a rusty hand crank. He rubbed the heavy plastic visor just below chin level, holding his breath as the inner door disappeared into the frame.

The room was large, done up in smooth stainless steel, glass, and white ceramics. Equipment lined the walls, some pieces modern, most not. Articulated arms hung from the ceiling, holding lighting fixtures, monitors, and scanning equipment. When they'd arrived, the plan had been to install one of the experimental Rembrandt surgical robots but that had been defunded in the same breath as the project termination, he was sure.

He sighed. *Así es la vida.*

The curinquean, though unconscious, panted like a dog. Clumps of matted fur, the color of wet straw and interspersed with dirty white, covered the creature's scrawny body except for the palms, soles, and face. Garcia had to remind himself their captive was two and a half meters tall, and even though it appeared disproportionately gaunt, its forearm was still as big around as a bodybuilder's thigh. Heavy brows and sunken eye sockets dominated the wrinkled face below an expansive forehead extending to mid-crown. From the sides of the mouth, stringy tufts of fur hung like a Fu Manchu mustache. Garcia couldn't help but think of the wizened masters from the kung fu movies he watched as a child. The pointed upper lip dropped into a cleft in the lower, as if God hadn't quite made up His mind between lips and beak.

This specimen was old. The timing of their capture could not have been better. Months ago he'd felt pangs of guilt at pursuing the tired old beast, but the blow he'd received at the creature's hand was a game changer. He just wanted to get home in one piece. Now, he'd be glad to see its mangy chest heave a final breath.

A rattle like shaking chains startled Garcia. Heart racing, he barely heard Cordoba laughing at him from the speakers in his headset. "He is restless today."

Sweat beading on his brow despite the suit's cooling fans, Garcia checked the suit's seal indicator. Still green. "Back on the horse now, as the Americans say."

Cordoba's chuckle was strained, half drowned by the flurry of taps from a keyboard. "He can't hurt an *hombre* as tough as you, my friend. Not a second time."

"*It* is not even a *he*." As near as they could tell, anyway. There were other anatomical indicators, but the lack of clear genitalia made it easy for Garcia to see the curinquean as genderless.

One of the creature's legs flexed, the clink of metal straps against the stainless tabletop louder than before. Garcia watched the creature's eyes darting beneath leathery lids, like wild animals trapped at the bottom of adjacent pits.

"Maybe it knows this is the last dream it will ever have."

"*Tal vez,*" Cordoba said. The typing stopped abruptly, followed by the sound of chair rollers. "We've received no emails. No phone calls. No stays of execution."

Garcia nodded. He made his way across the operating theater, skirting the edge of the table. The wire mesh restraints pulled taut with each breath, tufts of fur working their way through the metal strands.

Despite his dislike for the creature, Garcia didn't understand the order from Lima. In their morning conference call, he'd asked why they should euthanize the creature just because of political tension between governments. Didn't the Americans finance this facility for just this sort of operation? Why should their own politicians get upset because their financiers wanted to send in a few scientists?

This is above your pay grade, Agent, had been the answer.

After relaying their final findings on the creature, the voice on the other end had lowered to a whisper and offered one last comment. The Americans were not coming to study the creature. They were coming to take it.

Garcia shook his head. There was no understanding the machinations of governments or the politicians who claimed to control them.

Time to finish the job.

Below the observation window, recessed into the metal wall, were a half-dozen glass drawers, each etched with a single word to describe their contents in the often vague vernacular the Americans relished. Garcia made his way to the center one, giving a nod to Cordoba in the window.

The other man released the drawer marked **PHARMA**. The drawer slid open, tiny fluorescents along the left and right side illuminating the contents. Two racks of pressurized vials sat side by side, their caps color-coded. A printed list on a clipboard in the middle detailed their contents. Resting on the clipboard were several syringes sealed in plastic and a box of Triad alcohol prep pads. The rack on the left was full. Except for four vials, their stoppers bright red, the rack on the right was empty.

A grunt came from behind and he spun in time to see the creature's body stir like a wave of fur. Arms and legs tugged weakly against their restraints and the overhead lights glinted from its bald pate as its head moved in tiny jerks.

"He's still unconscious," Cordoba's voice wavered.

Tearing open a syringe, Garcia slid a red vial from its cradle and pushed it into the base. The tube seated with an audible hiss.

A louder hiss came from the direction of the creature, followed by a bellow that shook the vials in their racks. Garcia's pulse pounded in his ears and he could taste the salt on his lips. A few meters away, the beast twisted on the table, neck craning, back arched.

The muscles in Garcia's shoulders bunched, the hairs on the back of his neck standing on end. He inspected the needle with shaking hands and glanced at Cordoba. The other man was speaking into the observation room's SATphone. "Hey, *cabron*. I've got a situation in here."

Cordoba glanced at him, then the curinquean. His eyes widened, reacting to something Garcia couldn't hear. Without a word or gesture of acknowledgement, the other man turned away, phone clutched to his ear with both hands.

The creature wailed. Garcia felt the noise in his chest, his aching ribs throbbing at the same frequency, his heart rattling around in his chest.

We will settle this in a minute, Garcia thought, scowling at Cordoba's back. He gritted his teeth, fear mixing with anger. First the curinquean, then the asshole of a partner.

He moved to the creature's side and flipped the safety cap from the needle. Pinpoints of electric gold glinted from behind the milky cataracts obscuring the creature's eyes. Its lips pulled back in a snarl, cracked yellow fangs exposed, the point of its upper lip quivering.

"You and me both," Garcia spat. He took an alcohol pad from the table's edge then let it drop to the floor, realizing the absurdity of prepping the injection site.

Garcia aimed the needle at the shaved portion of the creature's neck they'd used a hundred times. Its head whipped at him, fangs snapping together, connecting across the needle, almost snatching the syringe from Garcia's gloved fingers.

The creature's face twisted amid sudden violent coughs, sending spittle spraying around the room. A glob of mucous struck Garcia's face plate, separating as it oozed down the transparent plastic. Cherry red liquid ran ahead of the stringy yellow saliva. The toxin from the syringe had partially discharged into its mouth.

The needle was bent and broken halfway but there was no reason to get a new one. Body convulsing, muscles bulging, the creature howled.

Veins stood out on its scabby arm like tree roots. He'd just…

The strap holding the left arm wrenched free with the sound of tearing metal. The back of the clawed hand struck him in the chest and he was airborne, tumbling over a wheeled supply table and into a bank of flat screen monitors. Sparks flew amidst the shattering of glass and the clang of crashing metal.

Blackness crowded the edges of his vision but Garcia shook his head sharply, using the splitting pain behind his eyes to fight away the darkness. "Cordoba," he gasped, unable to breathe deeply enough to scream.

Metal screeched and he forced himself to focus. The creature, squatting atop the table, heaved at the strap still holding its left ankle. Even in a crouch, its head reached the lowest of the booms mounted to the ceiling. A shred of metal from the table struck the cabinet door above Garcia's head as the last strap came free. Garcia's arms went reflexively over his head as large pieces of glass rained down.

The creature roared, spittle flying from the hook of its lip as it swept its gaze side to side, head tilting back and forth. It couldn't see. Garcia nodded. The cataracts had grown far worse since they had brought it in. Possibly in response to their drugs, possibly nature at work. One more thing they'd never know.

"Garcia," Cordoba said. His voice was quiet, calm. "There's a problem."

Garcia inhaled sharply to laugh and immediately regretted it, wincing in pain.

Another roar reverberated in the room and Garcia launched himself clear as the curinquean pulled a boom from its mount in a shower of sparks, and sent it hurtling in his general direction. The improvised missile wouldn't have hit him but that was no consolation. The room was large but the threat of the creature, feeble or not, was far larger.

Garcia slid along the arc of the wall toward the airlock door on the far side of the room, hoping his movements were subtle enough that the creature couldn't track him. Blinking hard, the beast looked in his direction. It took several deep breaths, brow ridges furrowing even deeper. Dropping to the floor, still in a crouch, it let out a series of barking noises, warnings maybe. Or trying to flush him into movement.

Not today, pendejo, he thought.

He'd get out the door, seal the abomination in the room and gas the place the way they should have when the word came down. The room would be unusable, the way many of the other facility spaces were, but that was a small price to pay.

The creature went silent, head leaning to one side. For a moment, Garcia was certain its near-blind eyes bore right into him. With several sideways gorilla-like hops, the creature took up a position directly in front of the airlock. The only way in or out. Gnarled hands traced along the razor-thin seal of the door, coming to rest on the keypad jutting from the frame. With a flick of its wrist, the panel was torn from the wall.

Is it reading my mind?

Damage to the circuitry locked it down hard. Now he was trapped in the room with the creature until Cordoba could manually operate the door.

"I need your help," Garcia whispered into his headset mic.

"Protocol…"

"Protocol be *damned*," Garcia snapped. The creature's gaze swept across him like an icy wind. He lowered his voice until barely audible. "I'm going to make a run for the drawers. Get ready."

"I don't think…"

Garcia scrabbled to his feet, taking several steps before gaining traction in the awkward suit. Glancing back, he dove to the floor as another boom whizzed over his head. One articulated joint snatched at the back of his suit, flinging him hard to the floor, as the boom crashed into the observation glass.

New pains erupting from every corner of his body, Garcia pushed against the floor, rolling until the airlock came into view. The curinquean remained crouched there, an ever vigilant guard.

"It can't see me—not exactly," Garcia murmured. "Turn off the lights."

"I need to tell you…"

"Turn *off* the lights."

The brilliant glare of the overhead fixtures disappeared, replaced with a shadowless orange.

"Turn off all the lights."

"I did," Cordoba said. "That's what I'm trying to tell you."

He'd just never seen the room with the lights fully off before. They'd kept the overheads on over the beast twenty-four hours a day. Still, the ambient light seemed way too bright. He looked around. Where the hell was it coming from?

"What are you talking about?"

A few meters away he saw the drawers. The **PHARMA** drawer was still open, but he'd never get close enough to the creature to use those again. He wanted the drawer next to it. The one marked **MEASURES**. The lights in the supply drawers were off just like the overheads, but he could still make out the black grip of the Colt M2021 beside a taser and assorted blades. He moved.

A blur caught his eye. In an instant, the creature, bathed in orange light, was on him, pinning him to the floor. The weight of the world pushed on his chest. Its horrible face pressed against the outside of the visor, hot breath steaming the plastic. Claws like daggers raked across him and he screamed, his voice a roar in his ears. Gagging at the hellish odor flooding his nostrils, digging into his lungs, Garcia felt iron hands clamp around his ribcage, lifting him. The hood peeled away from his head as he slid along the smooth surface of the observation window.

Dangling in the beast's crushing grip, Garcia's hands grasped wildly at his sides. The cold glass seeped in through rips in his suit and he could hear Cordoba's voice as distant cracks of static from the headset now hanging inside his suit.

The curinquean roared, mucous and blood splattering across Garcia's face. He screamed back at the beast, his anger swelling inside him like a tidal wave. A huge hand clamped across his skull, covering his eyes, and his neck began to twist.

Then the pressure eased, stopped, and the floor came up beneath his feet. Vision clearing, he gasped, taking in gulps of air, oxygen flooding into his lungs.

The creature knelt before him, eyes level with his as Garcia stood unsteadily before it. Cocking a massive head to one side, the point of its lip bobbing, the creature chirped. A noise one might use to calm a baby.

What the hell?

Senses continuing to clear, Garcia now felt the weight of the gun in his hand. His frantic flailing moments before had connected with his goal and he had grabbed the weapon on instinct alone. In one fluid movement, he placed the barrel between the two clouded eyes and pulled the trigger. Thunder rang in his ears as chunks of brain and bone peppered the room behind the massive head.

The curinquean remained motionless for endless seconds, a small hole splitting the continuity of its brow. With a floor shaking thump, it fell.

The muscles in his shoulders relaxed and Garcia slowly turned to look up at the observation window. The gun shook in his hand and he fought the urge to raise the weapon a second time. The glass was more than just bulletproof though.

"You have no idea how…angry I am," Garcia said. His throat hurt and his words sounded like a growl. He could sense Cordoba's fear. He seemed like a small animal on the far side of the glass, about to bolt.

"I really must talk to you, Garcia, my friend."

"Friend?" Garcia barked a laugh. "Open the door."

"I can't."

Garcia's jaw tightened, the taste of blood in his mouth and the stench of the fallen creature in his nose. He could *taste* the smell. "Oh, I think you can.

The Americans will get their prize and I'll go home to my wife, to my family. First you and I need to have a little chat."

"They will have their prize, yes." Cordoba held up the SATphone. "New orders from Lima. The Americans will have a living prize."

"What?"

"The tests, my friend. Lima has figured out how this creature reproduces. The doctor in Villa Trompeteros, he saw the activity under his electroscope. Dispatching him will be my next assignment."

"I…don't understand."

"The creature's cells are rich in a new form of volatile genetics. They are calling it *tunneling DNA*."

Garcia stalked to the window, lips pulled back in a snarl. He raised the gun, catching a glint from its polished metal surface at the same instant he caught his reflection in the glass. The golden shine of his eyes.

The weapon clattered onto the floor.

"But…"

Cordoba nodded. "Every bodily fluid, my friend. Even the odor itself."

No.

Yet, what was a smell except airborne particles of a substance?

Tears welled in his eyes.

Cordoba shook his head slowly then flinched, startled by a buzzer from a nearby panel. "The Americans are here."

"Wh-what will they do with me?"

Cordoba shrugged. "Before I let them in, I think you should know…"

Garcia looked up at the window where his friend held a laptop, the screen swiveled to face him. On the screen a small animal like a monkey or a bear cub squirmed in a glass bassinet—the kind hospitals used for new-borns.

Golden eyes blinked up into the light. "The Americans will have you, my friend. And we…we will have your son."

Garcia was only vaguely aware that the roars of rage filling the air around him were his own.

ABERRANT

PATRICK FLANAGAN

Number 48930 tried to scream, thrashing its head back and forth as much as the restraints would allow, but no sound came from its mouth. They gathered around it, two standing on either side of the examination slab, the rest adjusting their personal gravities so as to hover overhead.

One of the standing ones gestured its slender fingers, remotely manipulating the prosthetic tendril as it methodically flayed 48930's pectoralis major and minor muscles from its clavicle. The specimen writhed in agony on the slab, again trying to howl in pain, again failing. A spherical suspensor field bobbed just over its left shoulder, containing the creature's tongue, mandible, maxilla, and twenty-seven extracted teeth, floating in a gelatinous soup of protein-based analyzers. Another sphere contained the specimen's legs, severed from the kneecaps down; a third, its penis and testes.

Small black eyes peered at the specimen from all directions. Minor gestures summoned more implements of dissection from out of the walls and ceiling; the telescoping tendrils encircled the slab, their tips sprouting razor-sharp scalpels, acid injection systems and whirring drills. The specimen's eyes bulged in horror, a reaction which the project observer diligently noted in his report. The tendrils descended, waiting for the command to proceed with Radical Visceral Analysis.

All eyes turned to the Project Leader. Here, thirteen hundred light-years from home, his word was stronger than law; he was the living embodiment of Science Itself, and he was obeyed instantly and without question, hesitation, or remorse.

They waited.

The tendrils hung motionlessly. The specimen made a valiant final effort to free itself, hurling itself up from the slab and actually managing to rise nearly a foot before its gravity doubled, pulling it backwards painfully. After a single wrenching, silent sob, it lay there, exhausted, resigned to what was coming.

Finally, the Project Leader narrowed its eyes, and the thought came: *Proceed.*

The tendrils stabbed downward. Radical Visceral Analysis had begun. The Grays leaned forward intently, their minds synched to each tendril and absorbed the data they obtained in real-time; they felt the tearing of each muscle, the splintering of each bone, and the splattering of bile, marrow, and blood. It took nearly ten minutes for the specimen to be completely analyzed. When it was over, nearly twenty spheres had materialized, bearing off limbs, organs, bones and blood for storage in the specimen archives. Each piece would be tagged with the specimen's DNA sequence, the local geographical coordinates where it had been obtained, date of obtaining, and level of resistance to being obtained.

The ship's archives existed in a pocket of subspace. Forty-eight thousand specimens obtained only took up a fraction of the storage space available.

The Project would continue until the Grays obtained Comprehensive Understanding of this world's dominant species. The Project Leader was determined to see to that. Science Itself demanded it.

48930 was the last fresh specimen onboard, one of the blood-spattered surgeons thought to the others. *Should we descend and acquire more, or process the latest data more fully?*

A heated discussion—by Gray standards—ensued. The surgeons argued for more specimens; the researchers wished to contemplate and sift through the results of this recent batch of eviscerations. There were security concerns and fuel concerns to take into account, as well. For four Earth days, they floated silently in the surgery chamber, their minds intertwined in debate.

The Project Leader blinked twice. The other Grays, mildly shocked at such an outburst, stilled their thoughts and disentangled their minds. The Leader cocked his head to one side, then the other, weighing the consequences of either course of action.

Two more days passed. Then the Project Leader sent a thought to the ship's pilot, loud enough for the entire assembly to hear.

We shall retrieve one final set of specimens, he proclaimed. *Then we shall depart Sol for the outpost in Proxima Centauri.*

The pilot tapped his fingertips together, to acknowledge compliance. *Leader, where shall we descend? Moscow? Beijing? Mexico City?*

We should find a highly diverse cross-section of human genotypes within their largest megalopoli, the sociologist replied.

The Project Leader tilted his head in disagreement. *We do not wish to provoke a panicked reaction from their laughably crude aerospace defense networks,* he thought, *or inspire more puerile works of filmed entertainment. We will return to the rural areas of the landmass we last visited. Accounts from witnesses in these locals are dismissed as the result of mental conditions incurred by generations of incest, or hallucinations resulting from the abuse of psychostimulants.* The corners of his mouth twitched slightly at his own uproarious joke.

Pilot, prepare for descent, the Leader ordered.

The pilot nodded. One by one, the Grays drifted off to their respective stations aboard the ship. By now, they'd been immersed within their work on the Project for so long that they no longer felt a need to cleanse themselves of the arterial spray from the specimens they studied. Deep down, in the private corridors of their minds which they kept walled off from the casual examination of the others, some of them derived a sense of satisfaction from the feel of blood on their skin. It gave them a pleasing sense of…accomplishment. Yes, accomplishment. At all of the progress they were making on the Project, of course.

Of course.

The ship dipped and sluiced down from its perch in the lower exosphere. The Project Leader narrowed his eyes in contemplation. Proxima Centauri was a long ways off. There would be many weeks without any examinations to conduct. His crew might grow restless with the lack of intellectual inactivity. Perhaps they would find something unique on this descent, to keep their minds fully engaged.

Louie Denton's lungs were on fire. He was twenty pounds overweight, a bad ankle, and a pack-a-day smoking habit, not to mention the claw marks bloodily gouged across his back, and yet he'd been running at a breakneck pace for nearly a mile without stopping. If he stopped, he would collapse. If he stopped, he would double over in pain, vomiting until the acrid taste of puke and bile filled his throat and nostrils. If he stopped, he would lie where he fell for a week.

If he stopped, the bear…

It's not a bear. Don't kid yourself, Denton. You know what you saw, he thought.

The bear would get him.

Tree branches whipped across his face as he ran headlong through the darkness. His eyeballs were scratched red from pine needles. His will began to flag, and the seductive thought of slowing down crept back into his mind. Then he remembered what had happened to Mike, remembered the look on his friend's face when the…the…*bear*…had knocked him flat on his stomach, and with one crunching step had broken Mike's back; his feet rose and fell, rose and fell, faster than before. Chris had gotten a shot off, though.

Louie had clearly heard it echo behind him after he'd started running, but he hadn't dared to turn and look.

I should, though, I'm a coward.

He was so tired, so thirsty. His throat was bone dry. Surely he'd out-run…IT, by now. Surely it was safe. And it was probably too busy…

Eating my friends. Don't hide from it. It's tearing Mike and Chris limb from limb right now.

To busy to have chased him all this way. It couldn't have.

I left them to die.

Maybe…maybe it was safe…if he could just be sure…

Louie slowed a bit just to crane his neck and look behind him. Nothing was coming.

He turned back in time for the pine tree directly in his path to break his nose, crack one of his teeth, and knock him out cold. He spun around and sprawled forward, landing on his left shoulder with enough force to dislocate it, and lay still. Blood trickled from his nose down over his lips and chin.

The forest was deathly still for a time.

If Louie had been conscious, he would have eventually heard leaves and twigs crackle underfoot, tree branches snap and splinter, and a low rumbling moan that sounded nothing like a bear…or a man. He might have smelled its pungent musk as it approached. If he'd been awake, his eyes would have bulged wider than Mike's had, just at the sight of it.

The creature looked down on Louie's prone body. It flared its cavernous nostrils and snorted the man's stink in a deep inhale. It detected sweat and blood, and beneath that, the scent of flesh that had drawn it to their campfire in the first place. The beast's hunger had overcome its fear for a few moments, and then rage and pain at the stinging bullet wound to its arm had done the rest.

It bent over Louie, close enough that fat droplets of Chris' and Mike's blood fell from its muzzle onto Louie's cheek. Louie began to stir.

The creature wasn't hungry, but perhaps it should crush this man and drag him off for later.

Then the light was everywhere, blinding the beast, searing its eyes, and the large creature crashed backwards onto the forest floor.

Out of the blinding whiteout, two spheroid suspensor fields popped into being like soap bubbles, expanding to ensconce the two limp bodies. One of them took twice as long to coat its target, the hairy specimen twice as large as the other body. The fields rose up, carrying their charges through the tree cover, up over the forest, into the swirling iris in the underbelly of the ship. The iris closed and sealed over behind them. The ship rose up without a sound into the North Carolina sky. Peace returned to the forest.

The 'taxonomer' looked down at the two specimens in confused delight. 48931 was a standard adult male, possessing the color pattern and infirmities common to this particular habitat—the standard self-induced damage from a poor diet and abuse of stimulants and depressants, nothing new there. But 48932…

48932 was something different altogether.

A new species, he mused, carelessly forgetting to shield his speculation from the minds of the others. *Not human at all.*

The taxonomer ignored the mocking doubts from the others. *DNA confirms my observations,* he insisted, pointing to the holo of the specimen's genome that filled the examination chamber. *There, there, and there. Major differences from all previously gathered specimens.*

Merely an aberration, insisted the others. *A mutant. Look at its brain. This biosphere has been thoroughly studied, there are no other sapient hominids remaining. This must be a human.*

Perhaps a relict population hidden in the remote wilderness, the taxonomer suggested. This is an important find. *This is not a human. It must be preserved whole for observation.*

Angry thoughts from all directions—most notably the surgeons, the taxonomer noted.

We must operate. We must cut. Radical Visceral Analysis, he stated.

The taxonomer tried to dissuade them, but his mind was drowned out by the overwhelming chorus. The Project had decided. 48932—or 48932A, rather, A for Aberrant—would be sent to the examination slab, and whatever secrets it possessed would be extracted by scalpel and laser.

The taxonomer tried to appeal to the better judgment of the Project Leader, floating high overhead, but his thoughts went unanswered. Reluctantly, he yielded to the consensus. *I would like some time to finish my own examination,* he stated. *Examine 48931 first.* He hoped his demand was not taken by the Project Leader as a challenge to his authority.

It was not.

Examination of specimen 48931 is hereby authorized, the Leader replied. The surgeons waited anxiously.

And 48932A? the chief surgeon asked.

You have your directive, chief surgeon, the Leader added.

The taxonomer privately cheered. He descended through the floor, drifting down the decks towards the storage archives. He had to make the most of what time he had with the new species. Perhaps he would find something that would persuade his colleagues from following the course they invariably pursued.

Louie blinked. Bright. So damn bright. He squinted, trying to filter out some of the blinding light so he could see where he was, without much luck.

His nose hurt.

Hell, his whole body hurt.

He was lying strapped to a plastic table in a large, oval chamber, maybe twenty feet across and forty to fifty feet high. The walls, the tables and sloping panels protruding from the walls at various heights—everything was phosphorescent white.

It took a few minutes for his eyes to adjust, to discern the subtle differences in brightness each object emanated, so it wasn't all just a blinding field of white. Small details began to creep out to him: what looked like veins embedded within the walls and ceiling, pumping a gold-white fluid at timed intervals; gleaming metal circles set into the walls, at roughly the same height as the table to which he was strapped; far up, almost at the ceiling, a platform with a handrail, sprouting from the wall. No, actually…

He squinted, trying to see further details of the distant object. It was crazy, but it looked like the platform wasn't attached to anything. It was just hanging there. Maybe it was attached to the ceiling by a pole he couldn't see. It's not like it could just *hover* there.

He tried to move a bit beneath his straps, but they must have been too tight. He swiveled his gaze forward to look down at his body, which made his broken nose throb with agony.

He was naked. He seemed to have been scrubbed clean. Something was odd, but he couldn't place it at first…then it hit him—harder than he'd hit that tree. No straps. He was just lying there, yet he couldn't move. Something was pulling him back flat against the table.

Louie mustered as much strength as he could and threw his right arm forward. It rose about three inches off the table, then slapped back down flat, hard. "Ouch," he whined. *I'm not gonna do that again*, he thought.

He heard a hiss, like a door sliding on a metal track. He struggled to crane his neck to either side, trying to see where the door was. It was useless. He looked back up.

Five people were jumping down off the platform. He thrashed against whatever force was pinning him down, trying to move so they wouldn't land on his abdomen and burst his stomach open. He calmed down when he noticed that they seemed to be falling…very slowly. No, they weren't falling, they were drifting…and they weren't people.

They were naked, with gray skin, huge black eyeballs, and bulbous, bald heads.

Aliens, of course. He absorbed the notion far more calmly than he'd thought himself capable of doing. Little green men. Sorry. Gray. Had to be. He was going insane. That was it. The certainty of it had a calming effect on him. Either he was out cold, lying in the woods with a lump on his forehead—and possibly a bear gnawing on his intestines—or he was hallucinating to an extent that fantasy and reality were totally indistinguishable from one another, and there was nothing he could do about any of it.

He should just relax and wait for Chris or Mike to come along and shake him awake. Then they'd have a laugh about the whole thing, head back to the campfire, drink the rest of the Miller Lites in Chris' Igloo, and laugh and laugh.

Not Mike, though. Mike's spine had been crushed by the *bear*, hadn't it. And Chris was probably…

And when he got back home, he'd tell Stacey about it, breaking the Guys' Code and sharing what they'd done on the trip, and she'd laugh, too! Louie forced himself to smile as two of the aliens drifted down over him. They'd laugh and laugh and laugh.

Mike's dead.

Louie admitted it was true to the voice of reason in his mind, that quiet voice that wouldn't shut up.

Chris is probably gone, too. And it wasn't a bear that got him.

He knew this was true.

And this is serious.

Yeah, I know.

I'm not leaving this room alive!

Louie's eyes brimmed with tears.

"No," he whispered. "I won't, I won't." *I won't believe that*, was what he was trying to say. But he couldn't force the words out.

There was a shockingly loud metallic *click*. From either side of the chamber, two telescoping arms emerged from beneath the disks on the walls. Their tips were studded with needles, curling blades, and drill bits.

Louie began to laugh, a mirthless sound of someone trying to brace themselves against an imminent beating. Stupid Internet stories about cattle mutilations in Nowhere, Arkansas floated up to the surface of his mind. He'd rolled his eyes at that kind of nonsense. Stupid meth-smoking rednecks, Louie Denton had said. Those words came back to him as the drills began to whir and whine. Stupid hicks.

"Moo," he said, and this time the laughter and tears were genuine, and he couldn't stop.

One of the aliens nodded and the arms descended towards him, to begin their work. After a few minutes, he realized that the screaming he heard—dimly, through a haze of pain that slapped him hard and receded and slapped him again like a tide—was coming from his own throat.

He watched the arms slice into the meat of his thighs, cutting down to the bone. The blood spurted at each incision, but didn't keep gushing; he didn't succumb to unconsciousness, he didn't slip into numbing shock, he didn't die, he just lay there and watched as the rapidly darting arms sliced down his legs, then shouted in agony as their ice-cold digits sunk into the incisions and jerked downward, shucking the flesh from his legs as if they were cornhusks.

"*Oh God! Aaahh! Oh God, please stop! Please stop!*" One of the aliens, drifting a few inches off the floor, leaned over Louie, peering at him with its eight-ball eyes. The right side of the alien's face was drenched in blood—Louie's blood. The being didn't seem to notice. Or maybe it didn't mind. It waved an arm down towards Louie's chest, and a screaming lightning bolt of agony seared Louie's skin and drove into his chest. They were cutting into his ribs now. The pain was so intense, so exquisite, he couldn't speak, couldn't plead with them to stop, couldn't even think the words in his mind, all he could do was open his mouth and scream and scream again.

Steel fingers dug greedily into his chest cavity, looking for buried treasure. He couldn't bear to look. He was going to die, and all he wanted was one last Miller Lite around the fire with his friends.

And he *hated* Miller Lite.

The cutting continued. The pain continued.

Unable to think of any other course of action, Louie screamed some more.

The taxonomer ignored the screams echoing throughout the ship. The examination chamber was soundproof, of course, but the Project Leader had decided that those members of the crew unable to witness each examination owing to duties elsewhere should be able to watch and listen to it wherever they were. In case they had any observations or conclusions to contribute, of course. That was the only reason.

He peered down through the suspensor field at 48932A. It was rare for consensus to evade Project teams for extended periods of time. Gray culture was devoted to Science Itself, to logic and reason, and when a minority opinion on a matter emerged, the Project members devoted themselves to straightening out those who disagreed, stamping out any threats to intellectual harmony before proceeding onto the next task. In fact, this Project assumed that consensus on 48932A *had* been achieved.

That conclusion had been reached because the taxonomer had deliberately shielded his thoughts of doubt from his fellows.

As the Project had ground on, cycle after cycle, the taxonomer had begun to suspect that perhaps, just perhaps, the Project had become contaminated. His fellows had performed thousands of examinations of specimens gathered from every landmass on the planet, both genders, all age groups, all ethnic clusters. At first the specimens were mind-wiped and returned to their natural habitats. Then the surgeons began to argue for Radical Visceral Analysis—not here and there, but in every case. The taxonomer was a scientist; he understood that some animals needed to be regrettably sacrificed in the quest for knowledge.

This was something different.

The taxonomer suspected that it was not knowledge that the rest of the Grays sought.

There were no words in the Gray language to describe what it was they sought. And now that they'd finally found something unique, a second sapient species, the…he struggled vainly, but there were no insults in the Gray language…the *curiously mistaken fellow scientists* were insisting that 48932A was just a big human! An impossible mistake. The genetic template was there! It was indisputable!

Yet they were all in agreement. All of them.

The taxonomer had picked up a stray thought from one of them, while he'd struggled to convince them. One of the lesser surgeons had sent a flickering image of 48932A being flayed and dismembered, a dozen remote tentacles messily butchering the specimen as it wailed.

The image was drenched in a sensation not unlike…hunger.

Something had gone very wrong with the Project, the taxonomer realized, and there was no one with whom he could share his thoughts on this. Not even the esteemed Project Leader.

The taxonomer beheld his discovery. The creature had been heavily sedated and lay slumped across the floor, its chest rising and falling heavily, its huge hands and feet stretched wide. The Gray adjusted his molecular structure and phased through the field, solidifying to touch down on the floor. Something was stirring within him as he watched this poor, primitive brute sleep.

This was something unique. Not just another human, but something decidedly rare. Perhaps even the last of its kind.

It would be…*criminal*, he tried to think; *immoral,* but again his language failed him, those words having passed out of common usage millennia before his birth. It would be *scientifically unsound* to subject 48932A to the tender mercies of the surgeons.

Yes. He would do something. He would go against the group in order to spare this animal's life.

A profound and dizzying sense of compassion and altruism filled the taxonomer's mind. He was unused to these feelings and struggled to process them. He just knew that he liked feeling this way. It was good, to do the…the *right* thing.

It was at that moment that a particularly loud scream echoed from far off. 48932A's eyes snapped open.

The taxonomer didn't have time to compose a rational coherent thought. If he did, he might have withdrawn behind the containment field. Or changed his molecular structure to attain intangibility. But he remained where he was, the better to observe the specimen's reactions. Or he trusted his instincts and reached his mind out, seeking to communicate.

But there was no time for any of that.

The room went dark as the specimen wrapped a large hand around the taxonomer's face. Callused fingertips pressed against the sides of his head like steel dowels. Inky clouds of pain squirted out from his nerve endings, blinding his brain in a murk of confusion.

Most Grays went their entire lives never feeling a single sensation of pain. The taxonomer had no idea how to react. His spindly arms and legs flailed and kicked as the specimen easily lifted him from the floor and slammed the back of his skull against the containment field. Then more blinding pain.

Friend, he managed to think forcefully, projecting it outward in all directions. The specimen didn't understand, or chose not to. The second battering against the containment field tore his flesh, and his mind cried out as the silvery blood began to flow freely from the torn flesh of his scalp. The pain was going to overwhelm him, soon. As the hairy beast swung its massive arm to bash him into the field again, the taxonomer willed the field to discorporate. It shimmered and vanished.

The specimen was startled and thrown off-balance, and loosened its grip on the taxonomer. The alien did his best to wriggle free. He tried to shift his molecular structure and sink through the floor, but the pain was too great to concentrate, and before he could pry the creature's fingers loose from his skull, the beast had grabbed his left foot with his other hand.

48932A sniffed the Gray up and down.

The taxonomer, still ensconced within the darkness of the enormous shaggy hand, heard the specimen growl.

Then there was a sudden wrenching sensation, and his left leg went taut and was torn from its socket in an instant. Slimy silvery-black blood splashed everywhere, drenching the creature's densely matted brown and black pelt, the floor, and the taxonomer's own face. The pain was too intense, too soon, and it overloaded his mind, as he felt himself slipping into unconsciousness. He was dimly aware that the animal had torn his left arm off as well, and was now pulverizing his body with its fists.

It didn't matter anymore.

His role in the Project had concluded, just when it was finally getting interesting.

48932A gnawed on the Gray's thigh muscles for a few minutes, not exactly enjoying its meal but too hungry to stop. It tore open the corpse's burst abdomen, looking for intestines to chew, but the alien didn't seem to have any. To the creature, the taxonomer was the strangest man 48932A had ever seen. No hair anywhere it noticed, and barely even a stink at all. The notion of a man, or any animal at all, with no odor to it was somewhat frightening to the creature.

The small gray man stared up lifelessly with huge black eyes.

It made 48932A uncomfortable. The beast raised its palm and smashed it down hard, the blow cracking the man's bulbous head open. More blood-that-wasn't-blood. More meat that had no smell, and probably no taste made the creature wince.

Its stomach was rumbling.

Wait…there. 48932A flared its nostrils and sniffed the air. There was a real man nearby…the man he'd been chasing, back in the forest. Fat and greasy, the scent of sweat and real blood.

The beast drooled.

A few uncertain steps convinced the creature that the flat, white rock that spread out over the floor and rose high into tunnels was safe enough upon which to trod. The beast loped down the corridor, following the scent of blood. Not too far. Not too far at all.

Louie looked down at his body. He had no choice, his eyelids had been peeled back and stuck in place with a gummy blue gel. He hung by his head in a suspensor field, staring down at his hollowed-out husk of a torso which lay on a table.

Half of his spine and various internal organs dangled from the stump of his neck, hanging like damp laundry; his lungs shriveled and billowed rapidly as he struggled to process each nightmarish new development.

It was impossible that he was still alive, and yet here he remained, still conscious, still alert. How could he exist without a body, merely a head and hanging organs? By now he'd wrestled the pain somewhat into submission; it was still there, but he'd been able to mentally stuff most of it into a box and not deal with it. He was grateful to still feel anything at this point. Pain at least meant he was still alive.

The remotely operated tentacles had plugged various clear plastic tubes into his wrists and what meat remained on his legs, and a thicker one into the gaping hole in his torso, where his heart lay beating. The aliens peered down at the operation. One of them, floating up beside Louie's head, reached out and turned his head from side to side, like a slave trader examining the merchandise.

Louie's eyes bulged as the tubes began to pump a fluorescent purple fluid into his former body, making the arms and legs twitch and flop around. The alien standing beside his body produced a slender silver rod and waved it over the body. Clumsily, the headless body sat up, swung its flayed legs around, and took a wobbly step away from the table.

Louie felt something like embarrassment on behalf of his poor body. This was humiliating. He tried to shout at them to stop, but his voice was only a raspy whisper. They made the headless body walk around the room, waving its arms up and down. It picked up a gleaming scalpel from a nearby table, turned, and marched haltingly back towards Louie's dangling head.

The field holding him in the air began to settle and sink down, so that he was within reach of his formerly loyal body

Oh, God…oh, God…

They were going to make him dissect himself! Cut open his own brain. It was insane. This can't be happening. *This can't be happening, please, someone needs to wake me up! Wake me out of this. It's not real, this isn't real, this isn't real…*

His body stopped walking. Louie looked down at his hand—his former hand—holding the scalpel just inches away from his face. The hand was frozen in place. The aliens looked distracted by something. Then some of them fell to the floor. Behind him, he heard the hiss of a door sliding open.

*W*ait, the Project Leader broadcast. *Something unscheduled is occurring.*

The others reached out and felt it. Distorted thoughts were bouncing around the ship. What was worse, three of their number were silent, and remained so even in the face of direct abashment by the Leader to respond.

I have one of them, the psionicist said. *The taxonomer. His thoughts…aaah!*

The Gray stumbled and fell back against the wall. Concern vibrated across the room.

The Project Leader locked eyes with the psionicist. *Share,* he ordered, and the psionicist distastefully complied. The final thoughts he peeled from the taxonomer's dead brain flickered through the minds of everyone present.

Violence. Wanton violence. The panic and terror of their fellow Gray, the brutal rage of his murderer, scarred their placid, pristine minds like splashes of acid. Their thoughts swirled together. *Murder/No, not murder—animals do not murder/Humans are different, humans can think, we all know that/We don't know that, if humans can think then what does that make us, what does that make this Project/Coming for all us, we need…*

Silence! The Project Leader landed on his feet in the center of the chamber. The others bowed their heads, embarrassed at his directness. We need information, the Project Leader stated. *All personnel are ordered to remain at their stations and seal their chambers, and scan at maximum range. Overexert yourselves if possible. Any alien thought-patterns or instincts detected are to be reported at once to both myself and the Project psionicist…*

Four, the psionicist interrupted. *Four minds are now missing.* He shuddered again, his body convulsing as he tried to wretch. *Awful…please, do not make me…*

Keep scanning, the Leader ordered. He stood calmly as the others strained their minds, searching…searching. He felt their fear and understood it, but did not share it. The Project Leader feared nothing and no one, especially not some unintelligent beast looking for a meal. Something in the room brushed against his mind, an irritant; he looked over at the disembodied head of 48931 and felt thoughts of terror, pain, and rage.

The Leader came as close as a Gray could to smiling.

The other Grays in the room flinched, and he reached out and yoked their perceptions to his own. And he opened his eyes and…

His stomach gave way as a hairy fist smashed into him again, his vertebrae cracked, the breath was squeezed from his body as the beast hoisted him overhead, and he looked down into those savage, mindless, brutal eyes, to see cunning and cleverness staring back. Then he felt himself being torn…in…half!

He staggered back, himself again, and all around him his fellows had toppled to the floor, some from a great height, and he felt fear.

Fear, in fiery script seared across the flesh of his brain. It was coming. The blood of their fellows dripped from its paws.

It was coming. Their flesh and their brains filled its stomach.

It was just outside the chamber. A peculiar urge came over the Project Leader and once he'd thought it, he couldn't dispel it. He ordered the chamber's door to open.

48932A roared and charged in…

Louie wanted to cheer. The 'bear'—whatever it was that had stumbled across their campfire, broken Mike's spine and probably killed Chris, too— had appeared out of nowhere, picked up one of the aliens, and had bitten its head off at the neck, throwing the body aside like a ragdoll.

Yes! he mouthed silently. Another alien went flying against the wall, its hairless skull cracking open loudly as it struck. Its blood was like quicksilver. The monster's huge foot rose and slammed forward into the chest of a third one, knocking it flat on its back. Its tiny arms and legs wiggled like eels as the beast leaned forward and stomped down. The alien's body burst open, its insides ground into silvery paste.

Kill 'em! Louie screamed in his mind. One of the aliens had the presence of mind to look at him, and Louie threw it right back at him. *Yeah, you heard me, didn't you, you little gray bastard? Go get 'em, big guy! KILL 'EM ALL!*

The beast was on a tear now. Silver blood drenched its pelt up and down its arms and striping its belly and chest. Three of the aliens surrounded the creature and extended their tiny hands forward, causing the beast to slow for a moment.

Some kind of mind control thing, Louie realized.

The creature slowed and seemed uncertain for a moment. Was it afraid? In pain? *Don't let 'em box you in, buddy*, Louie thought. *Fight. Fight back!*

The creature took a hesitant step backwards...

Then charged forward, grabbing two of the aliens by the neck and jerking them off the floor. Its roar echoed across the room as it *squeezed*...and squeezed...and squeezed... One of the aliens' heads burst and tore free from its neck. The creature angrily smashed the headless one against the floor and seized the other with both hands. The alien's spindly legs cracked like dry twigs. One of its black eyes popped out of its socket. The creature sank its teeth into the alien's side, tearing off a huge bloody haunch with a wet snap. It hurled its meal by the ankles and the body flew end over end, knocking two others down.

Now the aliens' leader waved his hand. From the sides of the room, four robotic tentacles emerged. One of them lashed forward and wrapped around the creature's left arm as another sank into the back of its neck. It howled as smoke began to curl up from the drill, blood spurting and running down its back. It reached back with its free hand and wrenched the tentacle from its housing.

The aliens tried to press their advantage now. A brave one stepped forward, hand extended, trying to push the creature's mind as its fellows had done earlier; a third tentacle shot forward and tried to pierce the beast's heart.

It caught the tentacle even as it flinched and almost fell over backwards, and again tore it free from its socket. It whipped the tentacle across the room; the alien attacking its mind fell back as its face and jaw were torn from its skull.

By now the creature seemed immune to the aliens' mind-tricks. It tore through three more beings that attempted to rein it in, smashing heads and crushing bodies as the rest fell back.

Louie could sense their panic now. They looked at one another, and then...

He thought he'd seen everything, but the aliens began to float right through the walls, like ghosts. Hell, maybe they were ghosts. It wasn't as if anything about this day was sane anyway. UFOs, something that had to be a Bigfoot, why not ghosts, too? He almost wanted to laugh. What was going to be next?

The whipping tentacle flashed towards him, catching on one of his exposed vertebrae and pulling the rest of what remained of him free of the suspensor field. He was flying, flying through the air, and everything was spinning, and then the entire universe slammed into the right side of his face. His skull gave way, and everything went still. What was left of Louie Denton dribbled out of his fractured skull onto the cold white floor.

The Project Leader looked at the creature.

The rest of his fellows were slaughtered, or had fled. He felt their minds even now, consumed in terror as they dove through the decks. If they weren't careful, they'd fly right through the hull into the hard vacuum of space.

It had taken nearly fifty thousand specimens before the Leader had found that for which he'd come to Earth.

The world of the Grays had been at peace for a hundred thousand years. No Gray wanted for anything. All material and intellectual needs were met. It was a life of plenty and tranquility, all in the service of Science Itself. Of understanding reality.

It was a Hell.

This was *reality*. Fear. Uncertainty. Blood. Risking your life and triumphing over something that wanted to rip you into pieces and feast on your carcass. All else paled into insignificance compared to this. He thought he'd inured his fellows to violence with the thousands of specimens they'd examined, but that had been controlled, carefully measured, sterile, unsavory violence.

Some of the surgeons had started to come around to the Leader's sensibilities, but they hadn't been willing to go further, they'd still deluded themselves into thinking they were cutting and dissecting to find answers. *They* had been the ones upon whom *he* had been operating; his orders were meant to change them, open their brains up, show them just how stultifying and meaningless Gray life was. Radical Therapeutic Psychosurgery, just without the laser and the blade.

The Project Leader had been too timid, he realized now. He should have shared his…his *aberrant* thoughts with the others, to make them ready. This specimen, this brutal beast—this was the *universe*. This was *reality,* bearing down on the Grays with bloodied fists, and there was no cowering before it.

The Leader lashed out his powerful mind, pressing the animal back a few steps, and summoned two more surgical tentacles—the last remaining, he noted—out from their wall housings. He also directed a thought-wave at 48931's headless, flayed body, which had stood forgotten during the beast's rampage. The body turned unsteadily towards the beast now, raising the scalpel still in its hands. The Leader prodded it to step forward, and again.

The Project Leader looked into 48932A's eyes.

Their minds touched.

The drills and flexing scalpels of the operating tentacles stirred to life. Behind the beast, the headless corpse of Louie Denton lurched awkwardly into battle.

The Leader's mind was clear. He was ready to face the *fear*, and either conquer it or be destroyed.

Proceed, the Leader commanded.

The beast roared and charged him.

The battle had begun.

UPRISING AT RED HAWK RESERVATION

SEAN GRAHAM

Duncan Gerard believed in Manifest Destiny, the ideal of romantic nationalism, American Exceptionalism. You couldn't leave the Academy otherwise; it was pressure cooked into your subconscious. And Duncan had welcomed it, gone through the motions, played the game, but it was all unnecessary; as a fourth-generation officer in the Union Army it was all he'd ever known.

The dirigible drifted slowly towards the ground, hauled downward by thick hawser lines and steam winches. From his vantage point, he could see the vastness of Red Hawk Reservation sprawling to the west as far as the eye could see. To the south sat the squalor of Fort Ticonderoga, its hovels and leaning pine walls representing the greatness of civilization. Disgraceful.

Government propaganda painted an entirely different picture of the frontier efforts. Posters and signs showed shining images of steel walls and shimmering glass homes, children playing and on and on. If the people saw the reality, there would be riots in the streets of D.C., Philadelphia and New York.

Lies from the first word to the last, all lies. But they were his lies, too, weren't they? Lies he had taken an oath to uphold.

Maybe, possibly, Duncan was the man to change all that, bring honor to the west. *Expand the frontier, Lieutenant, by any and all means.*

He intended to do just that.

"Moored!" cried the boatswain, and the crew exploded into a flurry of action tying this, securing that, and making a grand show of it all as only the Navy could. Duncan's boots were the first to hit the gangway. He was greeted by a fellow lieutenant nearly a mirror image of himself in stature and presentation, a testament to the Army.

The officer extended a crisp salute. "Lieutenant Gerard, I presume."

Duncan snapped to, heels popping, and responded with a crisp salute to make any Academy instructor proud. "At your service, sir."

"Come with me, Lieutenant. Your bags will be waiting for you at your quarters."

The pair walked along the clapboard pathway from the landing pads into the fort proper, a shantytown of ramshackle structures pieced together from scrap and debris.

"The USS *Ulysses* made several unsuccessful attempts to raise you on the Low Frequency."

"Ah yes, the LF is in need of repair, sir. Many things at Ticon are in need of repair."

"I trust your travels were uneventful," the lieutenant said, shifting the conversation and making small talk as they followed the walkway between two buildings to the intersection of a main avenue of sorts; a dirt road, reeking of sewage and muddy from God knew what, flanked by buildings of all purposes—administrative, supply, infirmary.

"Fine…it was…" but Duncan couldn't finish. Ahead of him, a two-wheeled cart was being pulled across the road by massive figures— two red-furred Sasquatch. He stopped cold. "What's the meaning of this?" he almost shouted. "Why, those heathens should be behind walls!"

His chaperone had stopped with him, but now continued on, leaving Duncan gawking in the mud. "Ah yes, you should find plenty to write home about," he said over his shoulder.

Duncan quickstepped and caught up with his guide as the two beasts and their burden disappeared behind a building sporting the signage 'Quartermaster.' The road turned and they followed it past the reservation gateway and its sentries, then to the post command office. The gate and razor-wire crackled with direct current. Steam generators chugged at regular intervals along the fence line, maintaining a steady amperage in the line, packing enough lethality to drop an elephant. Beneath that the subtle grunts and throaty clicks of the ape-men residents drifted over the wall.

In the early years, the Union's position on the Sasquatch was summed up in Sherman's immortal words *pacification through force*. But the application of force proved to be a Sasquatch's strong suit, and before long the program turned to pacification through cajoling and subterfuge. Unable to either subdue the beasts in outright combat or accept the realization that the greatest fighting force on the continent could not defeat ape-men, the Union adopted a combination of tactics. In the end it was alcohol, shiny trinkets and the threat of disease that managed to coerce the giants onto reservations, and the continued flow of these items kept them there; liquor, belt buckles and tasty fruit-flavored placebos that prevented all manner of illness.

"No time for dilly-dallying. The major would like to see you immediately."

"This is all highly irregular," Duncan pressed. He had seen two more Sasquatch digging irrigation paths between buildings.

"Indeed, sir," the lieutenant said without missing a step.

They left the reservation gate behind and stood at a gravel path that split into a Y, one way led to the command office, the other to a building labeled 'Harvester Corp Indigenous Relations and Development Department.' Outside, a woman in a broom skirt and white blouse sat with a Sasquatch twice the size of the largest man Duncan had ever seen. Despite the animal's size and the tailored suit it wore, Duncan found it hard to take his eyes off the woman.

"Highly irregular," he said again, but the bluster had left him, brushed away by a certain broom skirt.

"Indeed," the lieutenant smirked.

They stepped through the command office door and both men snapped to attention. Sitting behind a massive desk covered in papers and refuse was a slovenly excuse for a military man. Hair disheveled, stained undershirt exposed beneath an unbuttoned tunic, the man spun in his swivel chair, completely unperturbed by the presence of others.

"Sir, Lieutenant Gerard to see you, sir." The escorting officer saluted.

The man brought his chair to rest with a socked foot pressed against the desk edge. The sock had been white at one point, but was now a charcoal black and apparently served as storage for random lint and animal hair. Bleary eyes looked both men up and down and he saluted limply. "Yes, yes, Lieutenant Gerard…so good to see you. I trust you have become fast friends with the good Lieutenant Scotts." He resumed his spinning.

Both men paused. Duncan was completely unsure of how to respond to the oddity before him.

Scotts stepped in. "Yes, of course, sir."

Still spinning. "And you have briefed him on his first mission?"

"Not just yet, sir."

"Well, what are you waiting for?"

Scotts cleared his throat. "Yes, sir." He turned to Duncan with no more expression than a stone. "It seems a…supply party…has gone missing."

"Yes, yes, a…supply party," chimed the major. "Medication for the sick."

"Your *second* act of duty as Fort Ticonderoga's executive officer is to retrieve the goods…the uh, medication…and the party if possible," Scotts continued.

"I see," Duncan said. "All very good, but what might my first act be?"

Scotts handed Duncan a set of papers. "To sign the release orders of the exiting XO."

"And who might that be?"

Scotts snapped a salute. "Lieutenant Roger Scotts, executive officer, Fort Ticonderoga." The major began humming and conducting an invisible orchestra with a pair of wagging index fingers. Scotts leaned in to Duncan and whispered, "Good luck."

Under much protest from Duncan, Scotts left that very night on the same airship Duncan had arrived on. His bags had been loaded before the two of them reached the command office. Duncan guessed Scotts was somewhere over the Arkansas Territory now, and there was no small part of him that wished he was along for the ride. Major Hamlin, the commanding officer of both the fort and the reservation—and the tip of the Union spear on the new frontier, for God's sake—was a blithering idiot and half out of his mind. In the days since his arrival, Duncan could hardly steal five minutes of the man's time, and within those small windows his commanding officer hardly had a minute of coherent thought.

True to form, Duncan was making his own way despite his failed superior's leadership and things were already on the mend. Under his guidance, several buildings had been repaired and the sewage line rerouted. Now he saddled his horse in preparation for the search party that was days overdue. "Find my bloody medication, Lieutenant!" the major bellowed in one of his rare moments of clarity.

But there was one thing that needed addressing before his departure. Duncan stuffed the area maps into a saddlebag and made for the Indigenous Relations building. Using his most authoritative strike, he knocked on the door. Even the executive officer was expected to employ manners, and besides, the facility was civilian run and the lines of authority were gray at best. Harvester and other corporations funded much of the Union's press into the frontier, and one couldn't bite the hand that fed them. Not very hard at any rate.

Broom Skirt opened the door.

Duncan cleared his throat awkwardly. She was striking. "Good evening, madam. My name is…"

"You're the new XO, Lieutenant…Gerard, is it?"

He bowed slightly. "At your service."

"I was wondering how long it would be. I'm Amelia. I'm sure you're quite eager to see what we're up to here. Positively bursting." She opened the door and motioned for him to enter. "I mean, our treatment of the indigenous population has been less than…regular, shall we say. *Most irregular,* your predecessor was fond of saying."

"A fine choice of words," he said and stepped into the room, which resembled a cross between a laboratory and a day care center. Cages occupied by small primates lined one wall while larger, heavier cages, empty cages, lined the opposite. Most of the room was reserved for activity, however, and not storage. Large blocks of all colors lay in piles, flash cards of basic shapes, colors and objects leaned on easels: a red apple, a yellow canary, a square, a circle.

Several Sasquatch of varying size, age and color milled about the room. Two younger specimens the size of adult human males sat at a chalkboard. A young woman used a pointer to indicate which words on the board she was speaking as she spoke them: "I-would-like-to-use-the-loo."

At the far end of the long room more Sasquatch worked on simple clockwork machinery using basic hand tools. Others sawed and planed wood into awkward-looking furniture.

He motioned to the chalkboard "You can't be serious, madam. Teaching these beasts to speak? I would lock you up, but I'm not sure whether prison or a sanitarium is the better fit. I needn't remind you of the Union's official stance on the Sasquatch dilemma."

"Dilemma? Since when do we refer to a people as a dilemma?" Amelia snapped, placing her hands on her perfectly proportioned hips.

Duncan was puzzled. There was a time and a place for the opposite sex, but that time and place was always *displaced* by duty. He quoted federal regulations from memory. "It is the policy of the government of the United States of America that all indigenous people to the North American continent are to be reserved to approved geographic locales or put to the sword." He took a breath. "These…indigenous peoples are neither detained nor dead, madam."

"You are quite observant. But you can save your nationalist rhetoric for someone who cares."

Duncan had stopped listening. A stuttering, slow speech had cut the room like water running through a creek. He watched, jaw agape, as the young Sasquatch, the larger of the two students, struggled with the words on the chalkboard.

"U-u-se…da…da…loo." The words were nearly unintelligible, but there was no denying that the thing had made a credible attempt at the English language.

"Amazing, isn't it?" Amelia asked.

He turned and realized that he'd actually taken several steps towards the student animals. "They can speak." It was half question and half statement.

"Well…somewhat. The Sasquatch people are astonishing mimics. It's instinctual to them—the chirping of birds, a babbling brook, a deer mewing. Given time, they can re-create any sound found in nature. It's a form of communication as much as it is a survival tool for them, a way of blending with nature, with their surroundings. Something best translated as *oneness*."

"Oneness. And they told you this, I suppose? Very rich."

She ignored him. "As for Bear Paw here, he's young. We're fairly certain he doesn't understand the words, but give him a few more days and he'll be able to recite Shakespeare as well as you or I."

Duncan was dumbfounded not only by what he'd seen, but by the audacious treason that was taking place right under his very nose. She pressed on.

"Come with me." She led him out the back door through a courtyard and to the door of a house styled like a quaint cottage but much, much larger. Amelia knocked on the door and a pleasant female voice told them to enter.

They did and Duncan instinctively reached for his pistol. Standing at an open window in an arrangement of giant-sized furniture complete with stove, bed, table and assorted other fillers, was the large Sasquatch he'd seen the day of his arrival.

It still wore a suit, but retained the traditional native-Sasquatch feathers and beads in his thick, tangled mane of auburn hair. Rough scar tissue protruded through its matted facial hair and one of his lower tusks had been broken off near the lip line. Duncan guessed the creature's age at over one hundred years old, judging by the remaining tusk, which was yellowed and ringed. A sparrow, infinitesimal in comparison to the red giant, perched on its cuff. It chirped and sputtered, and a second later, the beast returned the identical sound to the exact twitter.

It turned to greet Duncan and Amelia and in Amelia's perfect voice, without a hint of accent or throaty pitch, it said, "Welcome. I'm so glad you could pop in."

Duncan watched the creature's thick, crevassed lips and extended maw move and work like the sack of a cephalopod shifting and undulating to force out the unnatural sounds. The scene instantly destroyed his paradigm of reality, of what was and what should be. Before him stood a two-ton ape man wearing a custom-tailored suit and speaking in a voice so feminine, so gentle and so utterly alien to its physique that it made Duncan's head hurt.

"Does it understand the words? Can it comprehend?" Duncan gasped, clutching the handle of his still-holstered Colt.

"*Its* name is Red Hawk. He's a chieftain, a general if you will. Three thousand of his tribesmen live on the other side of that wall of yours. To answer your question—we're not sure, to be honest. Most often what they repeat is inappropriate for the moment, such as greeting a stranger with a request to use the loo, but as you've just heard, sometimes not. Sometimes it's dead on, indicating some level of comprehension or social awareness."

Red Hawk's eyes were a bright green and on the surface congenial, matching the voice it had perpetrated precisely, but underneath Duncan saw something more. From those eyes set deep in the tough folds of dark skin emanated a raw hatred every bit as instinctual as any mimicking. It glanced at Duncan's hand, his weapon, and a palpable tension filled the room.

"This is…blasphemous," he managed. "And illegal," he added after a moment. "I'll have this, this *house of treason* closed before sunset. Pack your bags, madam—you're going home and these things are going back to the reservation. You can put lipstick on a pig, my dear lady, but a pig it remains."

Amelia smiled the smile of a woman who knows something a man does not. "Blasphemous? Oh come now. That's rather dramatic." But Duncan had turned his back and left the cottage, making straight for the front door of the facility when she stopped him midway through the Sasquatch training center.

"Lieutenant Gerard, I have something you should see." She stepped over to a small desk and gently pulled a document from a drawer. "I admit I may have taken advantage of Major Hamlin's, uhm, impaired faculties, but one must do what one must." She handed Duncan the paper. As he read the document his cheeks grew flush, and his neck reddened with his rising blood pressure.

Signed with Hamlin's name and a series of Xs and Os were standing orders allowing one Mrs. Amelia Jennings of Harvester Corp, Indigenous Relations Division, and her people to handle operations with the indigenous peoples of the frontier as they saw fit, including but not limited to the rescindment of the Sasquatch Appropriations Act of 1851.

Duncan shoved the orders back at her. "This is not over, madam."

She winked at him.

Fire had consumed the cabin and most of the crop fields. Embers still struggled for life in the deep crevasses of the thicker logs. What was left of the bodies was unrecognizable as human remains, but no one disputed it. Duncan and his men followed a river of massive footprints to the northern edge of a clearing, where they found the severed heads of eight people: a white man, woman and two children and four more males. Corporate employees by the look of it. Duncan found fragments of Harvester gray riding coats amidst the blood and gore.

But why were they here, this far from the protected lines?

Painted on a tree in blood was a simple hieroglyph drawing of a large bird: Red Hawk tribe.

"Bury the remains. We leave as soon as the stores are loaded," Duncan said.

"That would put us in the open after dark, sir." This time it was his senior enlisted man, Sergeant Mallory. He had honest fear in his eyes despite years of combat service.

"Concerns, Sergeant?"

Mallory shifted nervously, his eyes darting from the mounted heads to the depths of the forest. "Well, sir, the frontier is quite untamed."

"It wouldn't be a frontier otherwise, Sergeant."

"Uh, yes, sir, but we should lay over here in the protection of the cabin. Anything is better than nothing. The Sasquatch…they…"

"Are animals and nothing more. And that cabin is of no use to anyone. Are we the Union Army, Sergeant? Are we soldiers? Are we men?"

Mallory nodded.

"And are we the greatest military power on this continent?"

Nods from the sergeant and the surrounding men.

"Very well then. We travel as we see fit. *We* dictate the time and place of our actions, not some overgrown chimpanzee in a suit." Duncan turned and walked back to the cabin, leaving the men to tidy up. In less than a week, his entire perception of the world had been shaken to its foundation. The Union's might was a mere shadow of the image portrayed back east, its leaders half daft, its soldiers left shaking in their boots at the thought of spending the night in the field. Absurd! And to top it all off, civilians were stuffing monkeys into suits and teaching them to talk!

She's a good-looking civilian though, isn't she? he thought. *But just as loony as Hamlin, by God.*

Yes, there would be a reckoning soon. Tonight, perhaps, in the wild where steel would meet tusk for the thousandth time over, but certainly upon his return to Fort Ticonderoga. There was a new sheriff in town and he was no halfwit. Lt. Duncan Gerard would make his mark on the frontier and Ms. Jennings and her ape-loving indigenous relations would bear the full brunt of his coming. The government policy was clear and purposeful. Just ask these dead pioneers, these children or their parents or the countless others before them who had lost their lives in the colonizing of this land, whether government policy is just or fair, whether the Sasquatch should be reserved or be put to the sword wholly and in total.

An hour later they were ready for the return trip. Six soldiers; four on horseback and two manning the wagon full of Major Hamlin's precious medication. Several satchels were found unmolested; bricks wrapped in butcher's paper.

Sunset was three hours off. Duncan watched the bright orb for a moment, wondering what fate would bring them. A bird of prey screeched, the shrill cry piercing the moment. He dropped his gaze to the treeline and thought he saw a figure standing just beyond the first trees where the canopy clipped the sunlight.

The cry came again and Duncan remembered the mimicry of Red Hawk and the fumbling children at the chalkboard. He searched the sky, the treetops, but spotted no bird of prey, no birds of any kind for that matter. The cry sounded again and now the figure, the shadow among shadows, was gone…if it had been there at all.

Not looking back at his men, he gave the order to move out. He was afraid to look back, look into their eyes, not because of the fear he might see in them, but because of the fear they might see in his.

They left the marauded cabin, each man feeling eyes on him, deep-set eyes protected from the branches and foliage by thick rolls of black skin. Tree trunks became massive legs covered in matted fur. Branches became beefy arms that could squeeze the life from a man, and hands that could crush skulls like overripe melons. One jittery soldier actually discharged his weapon into the woods and was threatened with court martial if he couldn't control himself. The unseen hawk cried once more, as if taunting them.

The sun sat above the mountain ridge, a thin crescent of light and life. The soldiers made camp, ate a pitiful meal of hardtack and coffee, set their sentry and tried to sleep. But sleep was difficult with one eye open.

Duncan lay on his bedroll, awake. Outside, the fire cast jerking shadows across the dingy canvas of his field tent. They hadn't seen a single verifiable sign of danger, yet the entire squad, including Duncan, was on edge. He had no doubt they were being followed, stalked, but would it materialize into action? Academy lectures told of Sasquatch followings that lasted for days, weeks even, culminating in nothing more than a vanishing of the animals, a simple ceasing of the act.

But tonight felt different. It felt…*imminent.*

"Sleep easy, Lt. Gerald," Amelia's voice said, and a single hulking shadow consumed his tent. He drew his revolver from his holster and fired three rounds through the canvas, but the shadow was gone.

Gunfire erupted and Duncan scrambled from the tent, expecting to see all manner of battlefield carnage. But there was nothing, no enemy. His men were circled on the wagon, firing blindly into the night. Terror filled their eyes.

"Cease fire! Cease fire!" Duncan yelled, but he had to physically tear the rifle from a private's hands before the command was heeded. "Conserve ammunition. Fire only on confirmed targets!"

Burning wood in the campfire popped and the squad let loose a volley of lead.

"Damn it, stop shooting!" Duncan screamed.

The fire cast light in a twenty foot circle. Beyond was utter blackness. Trees and rocks were only darker patches against the larger darkness. Outside the reaches of the light might as well have been beyond the edge of the Earth.

Shifting of darkness. Black moving against black.

Duncan pointed. "Fire, there!"

More movement to the left and he shouted again. Grunting, excited whooping came to him.

"Reload!" he commanded. The movement in the darkness increased and before they were ready for the next volley, he could hardly discern the darker patches from the lighter black shadows. All was ink black and swimming.

"It was a mistake to bring him here. He's not the pliable, young Academy graduate corporate thought he would be," came a voice from the darkness. It tickled Duncan's memory, but the owner of the voice couldn't be placed.

"Perhaps, but time will tell. He may be more pliable than we think. Most men are." That was Amelia's voice, and within that context Duncan identified the first voice as the assistant teacher at the chalkboard—*use-the-loo*.

Giggling, girlish laughter came from somewhere in the night.

The darkness crept closer and Duncan picked up a burning log from the fire and flung it into the night. As it flew, the log torch threw a spinning wedge of light across the field, a small, weak flame, but more than enough to see by.

Like the spinning blades of an airship's propeller, it revealed dozens of Sasquatch in brief slices of light. Eyes, a field of glowing eyes like dandelions filled the night. Hulking masses of fur-covered muscle clinching and flexing in tense anger. The nearest of the beasts, a large bull, raised his arms and roared into the night and beat his chest in a display of raw, animalistic rage.

Then the flame went out.

"Fire!" Duncan yelled, but the command was unnecessary. The frightened soldiers unloaded their weapons as fast as they could, but it was clear the effort was futile.

The last thing Duncan saw was the onrush of giant ape-men, their canines bared, dripping with saliva, bullets peppering their tough hides like spit balls.

The herd smashed into the weak phalanx of Union troops. Mallory's head was torn from his body. The sergeant was battered, pulverized by flailing fists as the Sasquatch pounced up and down, beating the man like a drum. Then all was black.

Duncan woke to find the wagon destroyed and its contents strewn about the field. Most of the men, his men, were pulpy piles of flesh and bone.

The few that weren't crushed to sludge, including himself, had been propped up against what was left of the wagon's shell.

The words *I-would-like-to-use-the-loo* were written in blood on a board placed in front of them. Other boards had been written on as well.

Thank you.

So pleased to meet you.

Cup of tea?

What weather we are having.

Isn't it atrocious?

The horses had been set free or been eaten by the Sasquatch; either way, he was on foot. It took him two days to walk back to Fort Ticonderoga carrying what goods he could. He'd dug through the remains of the major's supplies and oh yes, there would be a reckoning. To say that something was wrong at Fort Ticonderoga was the understatement of a lifetime. The voices he'd heard, Amelia's and her aide's, meant that certain Sasquatch were leaving the reservation.

But how?

Hundreds of miles of electrically charged wall kept them in, kept them reserved. But more than the renegade Sasquatch, it was the words themselves that troubled Duncan. Harvester was up to something.

Bleeding from a gash on his head, dizzy with a concussion, he stumbled through the main gate, brushing off soldiers' attempts to help him.

"You and…you, come with me. The rest of you to the Harvester building. Arrest everyone you see," he commanded.

"If they resist, sir?" a man asked, knowing the reputation of Ms. Jennings.

Duncan walked off with the two men he'd pointed out, two of the bigger men in the Ticonderoga contingent. "Shoot them."

Minutes later, he shouldered through the door of the post commander's office to find Hamlin asleep at his desk. Duncan placed a booted foot on the edge and pushed the desk over onto the major. Hamlin hit the floor and woke with a start. After fumbling for a moment he blustered, "What is the meaning of this, Lieutenant?"

The two soldiers with Duncan were stunned, but didn't intervene on their commanding officer's behalf. This was long overdue.

Duncan reached in the satchel he'd carried from the massacre and pulled out a book-sized package wrapped in brown butcher's paper. He tossed it among the trash that had flown from Hamlin's desk. It burst open, covering the major in fine white powder.

"Do you realize what you've done? What your negligence has wrought?" Duncan circled the toppled desk. He grabbed Hamlin by his soiled tunic collar with one hand and a handful of the powdered opium with the other. "Ticonderoga is lost. The frontier is lost." He smashed the powder hard into Hamlin's face.

Hamlin hardly noticed the blow. He began laughing and madly licking at the white dust covering his face. "Silly boy. Silly, silly boy. The frontier was never found." He descended into uncontrolled laughter.

Duncan released him. "Take him to the stockade," he said to the two enlisted men, who smiled and saluted.

Hamlin was a disgrace. He was a simpleton, a mere puppet to be manipulated, his… *impaired faculties* to be preyed upon by womanly wiles backed by corporate dollars. Now it was time to deal with the puppet master, or madam as it were.

Duncan left the command office and cut across the grounds towards the Harvester facility. He could hear the shouting already punctuated with random gunfire.

Two soldiers were dragging the young assistant from the building. A second woman, unknown to him, was already in custody and shackled.

Inside, the smaller primates screeched and bounced violently in their cages. Their panic echoed through the fort. A single Sasquatch stood in the yard, batting at soldiers who prodded and jabbed at it with their bayonets. Blood trickled from cuts and bullet holes. This was the animal Amelia was teaching carpentry to. There was no sign of Amelia, however, or Red Hawk.

"Sergeant, bring your men and come with me," Duncan ordered, maneuvering past the Sasquatch standoff and entering the development center. The large cages were empty as expected and the room was a shambles. Duncan led the squad through the back, and without missing a step, kicked in the door to Red Hawk's new home.

Inside he found Amelia lying on the floor, her legs sprawled out at angles impossible to the human anatomy. Blood ran from a cut over her eye. The room was a shambles. Red Hawk's ridiculously huge bed lay on its side against the wall. Where it would normally be was a giant hole in the floor. Duncan walked past Amelia without a word and peered into the hole. It went straight down ten feet before disappearing into darkness to the west and the reservation.

He shook his head, turned, and took in Amelia's damaged state. "Looks like school is out."

Amelia glared at him. The hint of a Southern belle he'd seen earlier in the week was gone, washed away by bitter pain and apparent failure.

"You knew he's been leaving then, I suppose, Red Hawk and others?" He leaned against Red Hawk's giant chair. He looked like a toddler using his father's chair to manage his first steps.

She nodded, her face contorting in a grimace of pain. "I suspected something when the attacks began picking up."

Waving his hands at the Sasquatch-sized room he asked, "Why? Why did you do nothing? Why all of…this? Men died." He motioned for the troops to collect her.

"Money. Why else?" she said bitterly. She yelped like a kicked dog, then growled through clinched teeth against the pain as the men tried to lift her. "Harvester stood to make millions on their labor. It was my job to prepare the pilot specimens."

"Slaves you mean," Duncan said, more to himself than to Amelia.

"We prefer the term *high-margin labor force*," she smirked. "Think of the possibilities—laborers, pack animals, soldiers…no more men dying on the battlefield, not Union men anyway. As a nationalist I'd think you'd approve."

"Oh, I'm a patriot, and the *nation* I fight for would never stand for this. Turning monsters into men is not the kind of ungodliness the Union would stand for either."

The soldiers had her on a makeshift stretcher; her legs, unusable, had to be lifted individually. "Wake up, Lt. Gerard," she said. "The Union you believe in doesn't exist. It's a shambles, imploding from the top down. And the nation—ha!—the nation wants only to stick its head in the sand and keep its coffers filled. How do you think we were able to operate? Are we that sneaky, that covert? Sasquatch walk Ticon streets in broad daylight!"

"It was Hamlin's incompetence, of course. He was completely unfit for duty."

She laughed out loud. "Incompetence is putting it mildly. The man is a ten year major, for crying out loud. Hamlin was the obvious choice."

"Choice?" Duncan followed them out. More gunfire sounded from out front, a roar, screams, then silence.

"He was a plant. A plant, Gerard. Money paved the road all the way to the highest office. An idiot like Hamlin kept both sides happy. The Union had their scapegoat and Harvester had its research facility far away from the prying eyes of civilization."

The pieces were coming together. "Scotts. He would never…he was a dedicated officer, a…"

"A pain in the ass. Started writing letters, no doubt. Luckily they never made it to anyone significant," he said.

"But he's home now. The jig is up. Union cavalry is no doubt en route."

Amelia shook her head. "Lt. Gerard, please. That airship was never going to make it back. No way in hell. They'd never allow it. There are headlines proclaiming Indian marauders or some such nonsense on the newsstands as we speak, mark my words. There'll be headlines for us too, Gerard, don't think there won't be.

"I hardly think so. I'm taking you and Hamlin in myself. We leave in the morning. I'm not one to be swept under the carpet, like some troublesome schoolgirl to be shipped off."

Outside, the carpenter Sasquatch was lying face up in the gravel, riddled with uncountable bullet holes. Two soldiers lay dead at his side, one with his smashed head still gripped tightly in the beast's steel grip.

"Ha! We're not leaving tomorrow. We're not leaving ever!' she yelled. "It's over. The student has become the teacher, Gerard. We've been had by primates, played. This entire exercise has been a university for them…for years!"

Just then the constant hum of the electrical detention lines fell silent, the generators sputtering and stopping. All eyes turned to the reservation gate. Primitive horns sounded. Loud, droning, the sound reverberated in the ear, shaking a person's skull.

Amelia laughed. "It's over, Gerard."

The ground began to shake.

"Earthquake?" one of the stretcher bearers asked the man across from him.

"That's no earthquake, men," Duncan said. They all stared at the wall a moment longer, then at each other. "Run!" Duncan yelled. "To the armory!"

And they did. And in that moment any inkling of chivalry died at Fort Ticonderoga. The soldiers dropped Amelia's stretcher and the men holding the teaching aides bolted. The reservation gate hissed as steam power was released, then the gate began to open even as Sasquatch poured over the wall. The bulls first, massive and powerful, tusks bared and worst of all filled with hate over years of humiliation, abuse and genocide. But they were a warrior society, make no mistake, and behind the bulls followed the cows in waves and any pups old enough to walk behind them.

They've taken the engines down, Duncan thought. *Bloody Harvester training. Three thousand Sasquatch on the loose!*

They washed over the Harvester Corp staff like a tsunami of fur and muscle, not stopping to kill, allowing their ample feet to do the work. Amelia caught Little Bear Paw's eyes in the sea of Sasquatch. After years of working with the creature, developing it, teaching it the ways of civilized society, she saw no familiarity in those eyes, no recognition, no mercy. His giant, thick calloused foot blotted out the sun before it pressed her skull flat into the dirt.

Many of the soldiers were caught from behind and torn limb from limb; legs plucked out of their sockets like the wings of flies, their screams of agony washed away by the bestial howls of joy and frenzied anger.

Duncan and a small group of survivors averted the main flow of Sasquatch and made it to the armory. They barricaded the doors and windows and began emptying the weapons lockers—nothing but small arms.

"Where are the real guns? A cannon, anything but this. This is a fort, is it not?" Duncan said, loading a carbine rifle, one he knew from the attack in the wild would do him no good.

"Oh, we got guns, sir," a young soldier said, the armory clerk. He rolled out a pair of canvas-covered wheeled carts with the help of his mate. He yanked the tarp off, revealing a multi-barreled, trailer-mounted weapon. "This here is the Gatling 500, sir. Twenty rounds a second in the right hands."

"Well, I hope you've got the right hands, Corporal. We're going to need every round and every second we can muster," Duncan said. "Position one at the southern bay door and one at the main door and don't stop firing until either the bullets run out or the ape men do."

They took up positions and waited, knowing it would not be long, that their time was short. This was no great final stand of good versus evil, of right against wrong where right prevailed simply because that was the way things should be.

This was war, lopsided and imperfect, and they were all going to die here in this shabby warehouse on the frontier.

What would come of this? Duncan wondered. *How far would it go?*

Man had mastered his environment through intellect, logic and science. He was no match for even the smallest Sasquatch physically, and now thanks to corporate and government corruption, the scales had been tipped in the wrong direction, brought nearer to an unfathomable balance.

Of course, it would be generations before the Sasquatch could truly wield this new knowledge, but what then, and would man last long enough for it to matter? Elk Horn, Iron Mountain, the other reservations…would they follow suit? Union records held the reserved Sasquatch population at over fifty thousand. Would the uprising at Red Hawk Reservation go down in the history books as the start of the world's next great war?

The howling grew louder, the horns blew on, the ground trembled. The bay door burst in first and the young corporal kept true to his word, sending hundreds of rounds into the horde of Sasquatch.

The large caliber rounds ripped the beasts apart, but numbers prevailed and the herd descended on the boy and the gun crew.

Duncan gasped in shock, not at the horrendous way the boy's spine was ripped from his back, but at the Sasquatch behind him spinning the Gatling 500 around on its axle. It fumbled with the loading slide for a second and squeezed the dual triggers.

The rounds tore through several of its comrades before the Sasquatch was able to train the weapon on the other Gatling gun station and rip it to shreds.

When the ammunition ran out and the barrels free-spun, dry clicking, the beast pushed it over, beat on it with heavy fists and rejoined the melee.

The building seemed to evaporate as the huge monsters stormed through the very walls.

The ceiling had begun to come down around Duncan as he fired his revolver feverishly for all the good it was doing.

Two bulls bounded over the destroyed Gatling gun and charged him. From somewhere in the chaos he heard his own voice say, *Does it understand its words? Does it comprehend?*

UNCLE JOE

ANTHONY GIANGREGORIO

The Fourth of July party was in full swing in Topsfield, Mass, in the yard of one Mary Simon. She held the party every year, figuring it was one of the few times her and her friends could get together. With people always so busy, it was rare for everyone to set aside some time to get together, but at least one time a year (excluding Christmas) they did just that.

Mary's husband Dave was on the grill, flipping hamburgers too early as usual. They broke up and left bits of themselves on the grill bars, the scorch marks barely visible. He was one of those cooks that couldn't leave the food alone, but had to roll the hotdogs, flick the sausages and of course, flip the hamburgers five times before even one side was cooked.

A few feet from the grill were three coolers filed with ice, each one holding something for the appropriate audience. The first carried beer and wine coolers, the second soda and ice tea, and a few lemonades if you wanted to dig around a little. The third held bottled water, for those too finicky to drink from the tap.

The party had been going on for hours, everyone eating and having a wonderful time. There had to be over fifty people easy, all laughing and catching up.

A dozen children ran about, playing ping pong on the set-up table or basketball near the end of the driveway. It was a warm day but not so warm it was uncomfortable in the shade, though most of the older men with balding pates would have been better off if they'd stayed out of the sun altogether.

Some of the guests had brought friends of their own so everyone didn't know each face they saw, but that was okay. It was a party, a time to meet new people, to eat, drink and be happy.

While everyone was going about the serious business of having fun, a tall figure hovered near the edge of the yard. See, Mary's yard was in the middle of the forest, with only a few other homes surrounding her.

In times past, she'd seen deer and rabbits, owls and raccoons and one time could have sworn she'd seen a bear. But Dave had told her she was mistaken, for bears didn't live in this part of the state. Overdevelopment had chased them away to easier hunting grounds.

On the edge of the treeline, the tall figure went from tree to tree, slowly making his way closer to the party. On closer inspection, the figure was clothed in an odd assortment of attire.

The shirt he wore had a Red Sox logo on the front, but the arms and shoulders barely fit, the girth of the figure too wide. The figure wore a pair of pajama pants with small trains on them, too baggy even for his ample frame. No shoes were on the large hairy feet and a Yankees baseball cap and dark sunglasses rounded out the attire.

When the figure was right at the edge of the yard, he stood tall and strode out of the woods and into the party as if he belonged there. No one noticed him, all having fun, and from a quick glance, he was just another guest, albeit taller and with more hair than the rest.

The figure towered over the tallest person by almost a foot so he hunched over so as not to call attention to himself.

The figure went to the buffet table where Dave had just put out the plate of cooked meat. As stated before, the burgers were overcooked, because after playing with them continuously, Dave then left them on the grill for too long.

It wasn't his fault really; he had gotten into a conversation about the new Hybrid cars and became distracted. The hotdogs were charred on the edges but that was all right—some people liked them that way.

The figure picked up a paper plate and began heaping meat onto it, taking more than half of what was on the serving tray. Next came the macaroni salad, fruit salad and finally, hamburger and hotdog rolls—a bag of each. He even went to the cooler with the beers and grabbed two.

He was a Coors man by what he grabbed, totally ignoring the Budweisers and Coronas. Then, going over to the side and a little away from the main group of partiers, he sat down in a wooden chair—which groaned, and if it could have talked would have begged for mercy—and began to eat.

Dave's brother-in-law Bob was making his rounds and he finally came upon the eating, hairy figure.

"Hey there, I'm Bob. I haven't seen you around here before," he said as he looked down at the Yankees cap, the figure hunched over, his face hidden. Bob could see a thin beard and a thick mustache covering almost the entire face by his quick glance.

He wasn't a big sports fan so to him the cap and Red Sox shirt was just fine, though he knew many of his friends who would have exploded at the sacrilege. Then recognition came to him. He knew Dave's uncle liked to wear his hair long and was such a hairy bastard that he looked more like a bear than a human being. He said, "Wait. You're Joe, aren't you? You're Dave's uncle? I remember you now. Wow, I haven't seen you in what, three years?"

The figure didn't reply, but continued eating in silence, enjoying the hamburgers, not at all unhappy with Dave's cooking. He was a sloppy eater, bits of meat and crumbs from the bread rolls falling onto his lap.

Bob sat down next to the figure and pointed to a woman across the yard. She had bright red hair, a frumpy looking blouse on, and her makeup was simply garish. "See that woman over there?" Bob asked. "That's my wife of over thirty-five years. Man, I tell ya, I could use a change of pace; know what I mean, pal?"

The figure simply grunted.

"She's always nagging me and complaining, as if she's so much better. I swear, one day I'm gonna simply run off with another woman." Then he regretted what he'd said and he glanced at the eating figure. "Nah, I'm not gonna do that, sorry for even sayin' it. I'm just blowin' off some steam." He patted Uncle Joe on the shoulder, a little surprised when he felt the taut muscles rippling beneath the shirt. "Thanks for letting me vent, Joe, I appreciate it." He leaned a little closer. "I hope we can keep this conversation between us."

The figure merely grunted again, but whether it was because of the food or what Bob had said was unknown. Either way, Bob took it as a sign that his secret was safe. He stood up and began to walk away. "I want another beer." He was soon lost in the crowd of revelers.

The figure didn't look up as Bob left. He'd just finished devouring everything on his plate and was still hungry. Then he looked at the paper plate covered in juices and ate that, too. He'd already finished one of his beers off and he popped the second one, guzzling it down in one quick breath, after which he let out a loud burp that had a few guests chuckling at the sight of the hairy man with the beer making a scene.

When he was finished, he stood up, wiped his mouth with the back of his hand, turned, and loped off into the forest, his arms swaying back and forth by his sides.

Bob returned from getting a beer and looked for Uncle Joe, wanting to talk a little more. After all, if Joe was willing to listen, he had a lot more stuff he'd love to get off his chest.

But Uncle Joe was nowhere to be seen, the figure having disappeared from whence it came.

Dave walked up to Bob and patted him on the shoulder to get his attention. "Hey. Bob, what's up? You look like you lost someone."

"Well, yeah, I kind of did. I was talking with your Uncle Joe but he seems to have disappeared."

"My Uncle Joe? Here? That's impossible. He died two years ago," Dave said, wondering if Bob was drunk.

Bob's face went blank and he shook his head. "But if that wasn't your uncle, then who was I talking to?"

Dave shrugged. "Who knows? We get party crashers all the time around here. Campers hear the party and come in from the woods, then they leave after they've gotten fed and drank all my beer. Sometimes I kick them out, other times I let them stay. Hell, one time a guy had a guitar with him. He entertained us for a free meal."

Bob nodded slowly, understanding. "Oh, okay, that makes sense. I guess it must have been one of them. He was a nice guy though. Not much of a talker but a great listener."

"Sure, that must have been who it was, one of them freeloaders coming by for some free food," Dave said. He was going to say more but Mary called out to him.

She wanted him to put on more burgers and hotdogs. It seemed they had gone through much more than usual for this time of day, the data taken from past parties how she gauged how much was gone. Dave patted Bob on the arm and walked away, leaving Bob alone.

Bob's forehead creased in thought as he sipped his beer, gazing off into the forest. "Huh, campers, that must have been it. Still, that guy sure was hairy for a camper. And he needed a shave real bad."

THE JOKE'S ON HIM

SCOTT SHOYER

His head was throbbing as he woke up. As his mind swam to consciousness he began to remember. He faintly remembered playing some kind of joke and then remembered the blow to his head. After that, nothing. The blood from his head wound caked his eyelids together, making it impossible to open his eyes. He then felt a gentle to and fro motion and realized he was hanging upside down.

What the hell happened? he asked himself as he tried to focus his thoughts on how he ended up in this place, but it was no good. His mind was swimming in a thick fog.

Suddenly, a surge of adrenaline jolted him like an electrical shock as he felt he was in danger.

He squeezed his eyes tighter together to try and remember but only felt consciousness leaving him like the disappearing waves on a beach. Slipping back into a dreamless sleep, his mind still tried to remember.

1

"Come on, dickhead!" Jerry yelled as he threw his backpack and sleeping bag into the back of the truck. "I don't wanna burn anymore daylight waiting around for your lazy ass."

Robby walked out of the house yawning, giving Jerry the middle finger. "A man needs his beauty sleep, asshole." Chris and Bob walked around Robby, carrying the packed-up tent and cooler full of beer and hotdogs.

"If that's the case," Chris said as he walked past Robby, "then you better stay in bed for a month or two."

"Fuck you, too," Robby said, smiling. Robby grabbed his oversized pack and put it next to the other equipment in the back of the truck. He lit a cigarette and leaned next to the front tire, watching the others gather up the remaining supplies.

It was July 4th weekend and the gang had decided to have a *guys' weekend*. No girlfriends, no bullshit, and no cell phones. Getting Bob to agree to leave his cell phone behind was no easy feat. His job required him being tethered to that damn phone, and the guys told him that if he took it with him, it would be no different than being at work. Now it was just a solid three day weekend of male bonding, reliving the good old days, and making new memories.

Jerry and Robby had known each other since the fifth grade and instantly bonded, while also getting into a lot of trouble together. Harmless, boys-will-be-boys trouble, but enough to give their parents huge headaches. They met Chris and Bob in college, and after their first night playing pool, drinking too much, and hitting on girls, the four were inseparable. Now in their late twenties, they would get together every other weekend to hang out; mostly with their girlfriend's around. But this weekend they made a pact: Just the boys.

Looking over at Robby smoking, Jerry yelled, "Hey, Robby, do ya think you could give us a hand here?"

"I don't want to interfere!" Robby called back with a grin on his face. "Besides, you all look like you're having fun." He snubbed the cigarette out on the bottom of his hiking boot and joined the others.

2

Living in Southern New Jersey didn't have too many advantages but at least they were only two hours from the Pine Barrens. Being largely undeveloped with many areas not even being mapped out yet, the Pine Barrens had always been the guys' preferred camping refuge. They would go to the same spot every time they went camping. It was deep enough in the Barrens to have some privacy, but not too deep or remote where they would be in danger of getting lost.

"One of these times," Chris said as he opened a beer, "we're gonna have a guys weekend in Atlantic City. This camping thing is getting old."

"Yeah good luck with that, Chris," Jerry fired back. "You try convincing Amanda to let me go to A.C. with you knuckle heads. Hell, try convincing any of our girlfriends!" Keeping his eye on the road, Jerry opened another beer. "The girls think camping will keep us out of any real trouble, so I'm good with that."

As Jerry lowered the bottle of beer from his mouth, a deer dashed out in front of the pickup. He swerved hard to the left to avoid the animal.

"Holy shit, Jerry!" Bob yelled. "What the fuck are you doing?"

"Didn't you see that?" Jerry screamed back. Bob just stared at him in the rearview mirror. "Well then, I guess it's a good thing I'm driving, douche bag."

"Maybe it was the Jersey Devil," Chris said as he looked over at Robby. Everyone in the truck started laughing.

"Ha ha ha," Robby said sarcastically. *Here we go again,* he thought as he rolled his eyes. "Can't you guys just drop it? It happened over a year ago."

Robby sat back in his seat and thought about what had happened last year. He'd always had an interest in alternative history, conspiracy theories, and unexplained phenomena. The guys knew this and really rode his ass about it. Last year he was on a huge Jersey Devil kick and was reading all about the mysterious beast and all the encounters people had had with it over the decades.

Then on last year's camping trip, Bob and Jerry rigged a plastic Halloween Jersey Devil doll to swoop out of the trees and 'attack' Robby. While Chris kept Robby occupied, the others rigged up the doll and when Robby was getting ready to go to bed, the Jersey Devil jumped down at him from the trees. He was taking a leak at the time and was so scared that he pissed all over his legs while screaming 'like a bitch,' according to Jerry.

Everyone had a huge laugh at his expense. As his urine was drying on his legs, Robby made the promise that he was going to get them back. He decided to wait and let them think he'd forgotten about it and then he would strike.

"Oh yeah, guys," Robby said, forcing a laugh, "that was pretty hilarious." But Robby just smiled to himself, knowing that by this time tomorrow night, he would have had his revenge. What the guys didn't know was that in one of his bags, Robby had packed the most realistic Bigfoot costume he could find. It was expensive, but he reasoned that you couldn't put a price on sweet revenge.

His plan came together while reading an obscure book about the Jersey Devil titled, *Jersey Devil Sightings in the Early 1900's.* One person's account of a sighting really stuck with him. A young couple who lived near the edge of the Pine Barrens reported seeing a 'gigantic, hairy creature eating a deer' in their backyard. The author of the book took the story to be just another Jersey Devil sighting, but to Robby that was a bona fide Bigfoot sighting. And why the hell not? There had been tons of Bigfoot sightings in the Pine Barrens over the past decades. Maybe not so much in New Jersey, but the Barrens stretch from New Jersey to Maine and from the Midwest to Canada. The damn thing could travel to Jersey, right?

And besides, he knew Jerry, Chris, and Bob wouldn't know the difference.

Robby just sat back, opened another beer and let the guys rip on him and have a laugh at his expense. He knew that revenge would soon be at hand.

3

That night after unloading the equipment and setting up the tents, the guys made a camp fire and cracked open the hotdogs and more beer. They were all having a great time reliving some of the crazier times they'd had in college.

"And who could ever forget that beast Robby banged sophomore year?" Bob said laughing. "What was she, Robby, three hundred, four hundred pounds?"

"Oh come on, she was only like one-eighty to two hundred pounds max," Robby said defensively.

"Yeah," Jerry said back, "but she was only four feet tall!" The guys erupted into laughter. Even Robby spit some beer out at that one.

Laughing, Robby fired back, "You guys are such assholes," and flicked his cigarette into the campfire. "I gotta take a piss."

As he was walking off into the woods, he heard Bob call out, "Be careful, Robby, I hear the Jersey Devil is out and about tonight looking for some love." Robby gave them the middle finger over his shoulder as he walked deeper into the woods.

Robby had already taken the smaller bag holding the Bigfoot costume out of his backpack and set it up about thirty feet away from the campsite.

He grinned as he walked towards it.

4

The guys continued drinking and telling stories around the fire. "Let's lay off Robby," Jerry said after taking another bite from his hotdog. "God knows we've all had our own Porky Pigs over the years. Besides, he's probably still humiliated from pissing all over himself last year."

Bob couldn't help laughing and choked on his beer. "Sorry, sorry, but that was fucking hysterical, ya gotta admit."

"Well no shit, Bob, of course it was hysterical," Jerry stated. "I just think we need to lay off him. I think it's pretty cool that he never tried to get us back." Then looking at Chris and Bob, he said, "Because you both damn well know that if he wanted to get us back he would make pissing his pants look like nothing!"

Bob and Chris agreed, knowing that Robby was the creative, artsy one of the group, and if he ever put his mind to getting them all back, he would scare the crap out of them and make them all shit their pants, just to one-up them.

"I'll apologize when he gets back," Bob said somberly.

"Hey, while you're at it," Jerry said, "why don't you change your tampon! I didn't say we should be pussies, just that we should lay off of him a little."

"It's a shame, Jerry," Bob said as he stood up. "Usually guys with no personality or looks have a great sense of humor. You don't have either." Not looking back, he walked off into the woods to urinate, smiling when he heard Chris laughing.

5

Bob walked thirty feet away from the campsite. He was stumbling back and forth as the beer attacked his senses. Being careful not to trip over any tree roots or get smacked by any branches, he didn't hear the raspy breathing not far behind him.

A branch snapped, making him bolt upright and he turned around, trying to see the source of the noise. "Very funny, guys," he slurred. "Are we seriously gonna try to play the same trick twice? Real original."

He started walking again and had the odd feeling that someone was masking his footsteps. He would stop walking and the other footsteps would stop as well. He stood still for two minutes and didn't hear anything. "You're a little paranoid there Bobby-boy," he said to himself. "Good thing we're not gettin' high tonight." He began walking towards an overgrown tree in front of him. "This looks as good a spot as any," he said as he looked around. Unzipping his pants, he adjusted himself and started peeing.

Closing his eyes and leaning backwards, he tilted his head back to stretch out his shoulders and neck so that he was now looking straight up if he opened his eyes.

Feeling a warm breeze on his face, he opened his eyes and tried to focus on what he was seeing. Two fluorescent-yellow, blood shot eyes stared back down at him. Whatever the thing was standing behind him was tall. Bob stopped his flow of urine but still held his equipment as the beast lowered its face towards his.

He was frozen in fear as the creature slowly raised its tree trunk-sized arms over its head. Before Bob could stand upright, the creature brought its arms crashing down towards his chest.

It felt like a freight train had slammed into his body and he felt his sternum snap like a dry twig while his body folded backwards. His spine snapped from the force of the blow as the back of his head met the heels of his boots. His crushed body remained upright for a second and then fell over.

6

Robby was feeling good, real good. He had the right level of alcohol in his system, he was out on a male bonding weekend with 'the boys,' and he just looked at his Bigfoot costume again and thought it looked even more realistic in the dark than it did in the store.

I'm gonna scare the shit out of them, Robby thought, laughing to himself as he walked back towards the campfire.

"Jeez, dude," Chris said as Robby approached. "What took you so long?"

"I had to take a crap," Robby said, lying. "Besides, Chris, I didn't know I was being timed."

Chris tried to think of something clever to say but the alcohol was dulling his mind.

"Talk about being timed, where the hell is Bob?" Jerry asked.

"How long ago did he leave to take a piss?" Robby asked.

"About five minutes after you left," Jerry answered. "We thought you guys were having a secret rendevous in the woods." Jerry tried to keep a straight face.

"If I was gay, dude," Robby said confidently, "I could do way better than Bob. But seriously, has he been gone long?"

"He's probably just taking one of his patented 'Bob Dumps,' " Chris chimed in. "And if he is then we may not see him till morning."

Jerry thought about that but was skeptical. "No, guys, even for a patented 'Bob Dump' he's been gone too long."

"Well, I'm gettin' tired," Chris said as he yawned. "If we're gonna go look for him, let's go. If not then I'm hittin' the sack."

Before Jerry could say anything, Robby cut him off. "I'll go out and see what he's doing. He probably smuggled his cell phone up his ass and is checking his emails."

Chris and Jerry shook their heads in agreement and were mumbling about Bob as Robby walked back into the pitch black woods away from the camp.

This is perfect, Robby thought. *Bob is probably walking back to the camp right now. I'll get the costume on and scare the shit out of all of them.* He was grinning from ear to ear. *When they see my costume they won't know whether to shit or go blind!*

7

After the beast carried off Bob's shattered body, it feasted on the flesh of its kill. It loved the thigh meat but always ended up eating everything but the bones. The creature had lived for a very long time and knew it could be a while before it ate again.

Wiping a chunk of flesh from the fur around its mouth, it heard more voices and heavy footsteps. Twigs snapped and tree branches jostled. It sounded as though the footsteps were coming towards him.

The beast froze.

It was amazing how a creature nine feet tall, weighing almost five hundred pounds of pure muscle, could suddenly become 'invisible.' But camoflauge and becoming invisible in plain sight is what had kept the creature alive for so many decades.

Whatever was walking close by smelled like smoke. The beast saw something willowing out from the human's hand as it walked by. It *was* smoke. The creature remained perfectly still for a few more minutes, just to make sure the human wasn't coming back.

It then heard two more voices from the opposite direction from the first human. The other voices were laughing.

The natural hunter knew that finding the human with the smoking hand would be easy. All it had to do was sniff the human out. It decided to forget about him for now and go check out the other voices.

8

Robby lit up another cigarette as he walked back to the spot where he'd hid the Bigfoot costume. *I really need to quit*, he thought. *These things are gonna kill me.*

He found the overgrown tree hiding his costume. He put out his cigarette and started to take his shoes off.

"This is gonna be great," he said, getting giddy at the thought of scaring Jerry, Bob, and Chris.

9

The beast quietly approached the campfire and saw the owners of the voices that had drawn him in. It stood perfectly still as it watched and learned the human's behavior. The creature had survived for many decades on its own, after its companion was killed. It thought about that day and felt sadness for its companion. They were together for a very long time until a chance encounter had ended her life.

Luckily it was able to get his mate's body and run off before the killer had a chance to find them. After many decades of being mateless, the creature knew it had to find one soon. It didn't understand why or how, but it knew that it was hardwired to do two things: eat and mate. Not being able to mate had made it more aggressive as each year passed. But it knows it would one day find a mate. There were many of its kind all over the world and it would eventually find more like it.

For now it knew he must stand perfectly still, be patient and observe.

The beast's stomach rumbled in excitement, knowing it wasn't going to be hungry for the next week.

10

Jerry and Chris built a brick wall around the fire. Now they could let the fire burn all night and not have to worry about starting a forest fire. They were talking about what kind of players the Philadelphia Flyers needed to add to their roster to have a winning season next year when Jerry suddenly bolted upright.

"What's wrong?" Chris asked.

"I'm not sure," Jerry said, not taking his eyes off the surrounding woods. "I thought I heard something."

"You probably did, douche bag. Bob and Robby are out there playing grab-ass or something. Remember?" Chris said.

"Yeah," Jerry agreed hesitantly. "I guess you're right."

"You *guess* I'm right?" Chris shot back at him. "Who the hell would it be if not them?"

Shaking his head to try and clear it, Jerry looked at Chris. "Yeah I'm sure it's one of those idiots." He turned around to look back into the woods. "It just sounded bigger than either of those fools."

When Jerry turned around to look at Chris, he was gone. "Chris!" he shouted. "Chris. I don't think this is very funny. Lemme guess; you're all gonna come running from the woods to try and scare the shit out of me. It's not gonna work," he said as his voice faded on the last word.

Looking at where Chris had been last, Jerry could see something shimmering in the light cast by the fire. He walked closer to the spot. It looked like some kind of liquid. *Those guys get so friggin' clumsy after a few beers,* he thought. When he kneeled down to check it out closer, he realized it was thicker and darker than beer. He thought it kind of looked like blood.

Just as he reached out to touch the puddle, he caught a very slight motion not five feet away from him. As his eyes started adjusting to being away from the fire, he realized what he was staring at. Two very large and hairy feet. His eyes began to travel up from those feet as he began to understand that whatever was standing in front of him was over eight feet tall. Tall and hairy, kind of like...

But he never got a chance to finish the thought. As his eyes gazed up to the creature's face, the beast raised a manhole cover-sized hand and swiped at him. The force of the blow and sharpness of its claws opened Jerry's stomach. Intestines spooled out of the deep wound as Jerry gasped in shock, watching his insides tumble out. A coldness gripped his entire body as he watched the creature bring back its hand and swipe at his head.

He never felt the blow.

11

Robby was laughing inside the Bigfoot mask. He couldn't help himself. This wasn't some lame Chewbacca-looking Bigfoot costume. This thing had realistic-looking claws on the hands, real looking hair, and even came with some heels he could wear to make himself taller.

After putting in the yellow contact lenses, he was ready to go scare the shit out of his buddies. *If they thought that crappy Jersey Devil gag was classic, he thought, then wait till they see this. The Jersey Devil can suck it.*

He walked back to the camp, being sure to make a lot of stomping noises. He crushed twigs under his Bigfoot shoes and violently shook branches.

He saw they'd already built the brick wall around the fire, but he couldn't locate any of them. He looked over at the tents and didn't see any flashlights on.

"Where the hell are they?" he said.

12

The beast had dragged Jerry's corpse away from the campsite and now only chewed on a few feet of bloody intestines.

The beast knew it didn't have time to savor the kill because the one with the smoking hand would be coming back soon.

Throwing the lifeless body over its massive shoulder, the creature heard a loud racket not too far away.

It sounded like something stomping in the woods. Twigs were breaking and branches were rustling.

The creature quietly and cautiously walked towards the racket.

It peered through the trees to see the source of the noise over by the tents. Its eyes lit up in happiness when it realized it had found one of its own.

13

Robby was getting angry. Where the hell had Jerry, Chris, and Bob gone? It's not like they went down to the corner store to get some more beer.

Wanting to keep the element of surprise in order to scare them, he started walking back towards the woods, away from the tents.

Turning his head back to look at the tents one more time, his body slammed into what felt like a rock wall. Expecting to see a tree right in front of him, he lost all his senses when he looked up into the eyes of a monster. The thing had the mangled corpse of Jerry over one shoulder and the faceless body of Chris on the other.

It stood there looking down at him; almost as if it were smiling.

Robby turned to run but the creature reached out and held his arm. He tried to scream but could only get out a hoarse-sounding croak.

The beast looked confused. It reasoned that it had met up with a female based on her puny size. But why, it wondered, was it trying to run away from him?

Robby purposely avoided looking in the beast's eyes. If he looked in its eyes then all this would be real. But it couldn't be real. It's too ironic and horrific to be real.

I'm standing in a Bigfoot costume while a real Bigfoot is holding my arm, he thought.

Growing more frustrated that his new-found mate was trying to run away, the creature hit her on the head just hard enough to knock her out. He then readjusted the two dead bodies on his right shoulder and carried his new mate on his left side.

14

Hanging upside down, Robby now remembered everything leading up to this moment. He used his fingers to pry open his eyes from the dried blood and saw he was in a cave with a tiny fire in the corner. Underneath him was the mangled bodies of Jerry and Chris, and next to the fire were the remains of what he guessed were Bob.

Struggling to get his feet free, he didn't notice the creature entering the cave from behind him. He again saw what looked to be almost a smile on the creature's face.

Oh my God, Robby thought. *This thing thinks I'm like it. This fucking costume...he thinks I'm a Bigfoot!*

The creature effortlessly lifted and stood him upright. It was petting his head in a friendly gesture.

Oh no, Robby thought as he began to panic. *It's not petting me...it's caressing me!*

Looking down at the creature's groin, Robby could see its huge, hairy beast-cock becoming hard. Its member had to be fourteen inches long and as wide as a full roll of paper towels.

The monster grabbed him by the shoulders and threw him over a bunch of large rocks.

Robby started laughing maniacally as he wondered whether it was going to be worse before or after the monster found out he wasn't a Bigfoot.

But after feeling the monster pressing against his backside, he had a feeling that he wasn't going to make it that far.

ABOUT THE WRITERS

Nickolas Cook lives in the beautiful Southwestern desert with his wife and three pugs. He is an editor in chief of The Black Glove Magazine (http://the-black-glove.blogspot.com/), a free monthly blog magazine devoted to horror culture and entertainment. He is a well-respected horror critic and reviewer, with hundreds of articles in print. He is also the author of a few dozen published short stories and three novels, THE BLACK BEAST OF ALGERNON WOOD (Dailey Swan Press), BALEFUL EYE (Stonegarden.net Publishing) and ALICE IN ZOMBIELAND (Coscom Entertainment) and a forthcoming novel from Dailey Swan, PAINT IT BLACK. He also has a new short story collection from Damnation Books, 'ROUND MIDNIGHT AND OTHER TALES OF LOST SOULS.

To contact the author email Nickolasecook@aol.com or stop by his official website: The Horror Jazz and Blues Revue: http://thehorrorjazzandbluesrevue.blogspot.com/

Patrick Flanagan is believed to be currently be working on his next work of mayhem and horror in an undisclosed location somewhere along the Eastern Seaboard. Authorities believe he is also one of the perpetrators behind ALIEN ABERRATIONS, DARKER THAN NOIR (both from Grand Mal Press), IT CAME FROM HER PURSE (from Sam's Dot Publishing), and ATTACK OF THE 50 FT. BOOK (from Library of Fantasy). Junior G-Men are advised to purchase these works at once, so as to better familiarize themselves with this dastardly fiend.

Anthony Giangregorio is the author of 36 novels, almost all of them about zombies, and has edited over 25 anthologies.

His work has appeared in Dead Science by Coscomentertainment, Dead Worlds: Undead Stories Volumes 1-7, and Wolves of War by Library of the Living Dead Press. He also has stories in End of Days: An Apocalyptic Anthology Vol. 1-5, the Book of the Dead series Vol. 1-6 by LDP, Zombie Zoology by Severed Press, two anthologies with Pill Hill Press and Metahumans vs. zombies by Coscomentertainment.

He is also the creator of the popular action/zombie series titled Deadwater and his action/ horror novel Dead Rage is being optioned for a movie. Check out his website at www.undeadpress.com.

Sean Graham lives in central Oklahoma with his beautiful wife Tammy. They share their home with a couple of short-haired felines and a pair of three-legged dogs. His short fiction can be found in various anthologies and e-zines.

Check out his blog at seanegraham.blogspot.com.

Dane T. Hatchell lives in Baton Rouge, LA. He has stories appearing in over fifteen different anthologies from Living Dead Press.

You can contact him at Enadious@gmail.com.

Matt Kurtz: Originally a part-time independent filmmaker and screenwriter, decided to narrow his creative energy to focus more on short stories and future novels. He writes twisted tales for fun when not working at a small advertising company somewhere within the big state of Texas.

Adam P. Lewis is an author within the horror genre. He has written numerous short stories, essays, and reviews published by Wicked East Press, Pill Hill Press, Living Dead Press, Static Movement, Dark Quest Books, and Ambrotos Press. Follow him at http://www.facebook.com/adamlewis518.

Patrick MacAdoo is an author of supernatural thrillers. He currently lives in Portland, Oregon. His influences include Stephen King, Elmore Leonard, Shakespeare, Plato, and David Milch. He is currently seeking a publisher for his novel, "Big Box Byzantine." You can find Patrick on Facebook and email him at aspergo321@aol.com

Dustin Reade loves Bigfoot. He lives in Port Angeles, where Bigfoot walks.

Suzanne Robb's debut novel Z-Boat will be released by Twisted Library Press, under their Lbrary of the Living Dead Imprint. Her stories are in current and upcoming anthologies with Coscom Entertainment, Pill Hill Press, Wicked East Press, Rymfire eBooks, Library of the Living Dead, Library of Fantasy, Norgus Press, May December Publications, Living Dead Press, Panic Press, Hidden Thoughts Press, and Static Movement. In her free time she reads, watches movies, plays with her dog, and enjoys chocolate and Legos.

Scott Shoyer is a long time horror fan ever since seeing The Last House on the Left and Cannibal Ferox at the tender age of nine.

Today he runs the popular website http://www.anythinghorror.com and has short stories published in various horror anthologies and is editing his first zombie novel for publication. He lives in Austin, TX and can be contacted at the following address: anythinghorrorscott@gmail.com

Rebecca Snow lives in Virginia with her husband and a small herd of inherited cats for inspiration. Her fiction can be found in various anthologies from Books of the Dead Press, May December Publications, Library of the Living Dead, Static Press, and Pill Hill Press. She has a Bigfoot lure in the backyard and plans to teach him how to do yard work and brush cats. You can find her on Facebook (look for the bloody hand print) and Twitter @cemeteryflower and at cemeteryflower.blog.com

Alan Spencer is a horror author from Kansas City. His novels include "The Body Cartel," "Ashes in Her Eyes," "Inside the Perimeter: Scavengers of the Dead," and "Zombies and Power Tools"—The last two published by Living Dead Press. Keep an eye out for his forthcoming book "Cider Mill Vampires." Seek him on Facebook or e-mail him at: alanspencer26@hotmail.com

J. D. Stanton's work has appeared in Mount Zion Speculative Fiction Review, The Indianapolis Star, Compuserve Magazine, MIND, Static Movement, Theatre of Decay, Yellow Mama, and other print and on-line magazines. His photographic art has been used as covers and internal illustrations for Not One of Us, Black Petals, Twisted Dreams Magazine, RAZAR I and II, True Police, Literally, and the anthologies Of Shadow and Substance, Requiem for the Damned, Studies in Scarlet, and House of Horrors' recent Tales of a Woman Scorned, among others. He was a field investigator for APRO, the Aerial Phenomenon Research Organization and maintains a blog on all things Fortean and synchronistic at http://johndstanton.blogspot.com/

He explores graveyards, abandoned and haunted sites with his wife Flo for inspiration. They live next door to a house haunted by the spirits of a murder-suicide that happened as they slept just a few yards away. Find out more about him at www.3amblue.com.

William R.D. Wood lives in Virginia's beautiful Shenandoah Valley in an old farmhouse turned backwards to the road. He was born in South Carolina, grew up in the US Navy, and has spent a fair amount of his life fixing things. His love of science fiction and horror routinely leads him to destroy the world, whether by alien artifact, zombie apocalypse or teddy bear. If you're looking for stories about gleaming utopias, you'll probably want to look elsewhere. Check him out at http://writebrane.blogspot.com/

CLAN OF THE BIGFOOT

ANTHONY GIANGREGORIO

BOOK OF CANNIBALS **2**: THE HUNGER
Edited by Rebecca Besser

Forbidden meat, but the sweetest when you take a bite...

Dark desires remain hidden deep in the human consciousness, waiting to be set free. Why not let them?

What recipe would you use to cook your neighbor? What cut of your girlfriend would you try first? Would a human steak be more tender on the grill than any you've tried before?

No matter how you boil it, roast it, or grill it, human meat is what we're serving up. Cannibalism at its best and worst are contained within this book.

Will you be able to stomach the contents as the innocent are served up for your dining pleasure? Or will you cringe with disgust at the wicked and twisted creations the sadistic chefs and butchers are making for your palate?

Next time you sit down for a meal at your neighbor's house, or are enjoying a cookout at your friend's, will you look at your plate and wonder...is it human?

MONSTER PARTY
Edited by Anthony Giangregorio

Zombies, vampires, werewolves and ghosts are just a few of the monsters in this anthology.

But this isn't any anthology, you see, this is a party.

Or to be more to the point…a *Monster Party*.

Ever wonder what would happen if a werewolf and a zombie squared off? Or perhaps a vampire and a Frankenstein monster? Or better yet, how about a world where every conceivable monster is real and humans are their prey?

If those burning questions have been driving you mad, then look no further than this book.

So go on over to the buffet table, grab yourself a plate (the shrimp looks good) and get yourself a drink, and enjoy the fun ride that is the *Monster Party*.

THE WAR AGAINST THEM: A ZOMBIE NOVEL
by Jose Alfredo Vazquez

Mankind wasn't prepared for the onslaught.

An ancient organism is reanimating the dead bodies of its victims, creating worldwide chaos and panic as the disease spreads to every corner of the globe. As governments struggle to contain the disease, courageous individuals across the planet learn what it truly means to make choices as they struggle to survive.

Geopolitics meet technology in a race to save mankind from the worst threat it has ever faced. Doctors, military and soldiers from all walks of life battle to find a cure. For the dead walk, and if not stopped, they will wipe out all life on Earth. Humanity is fighting a war they cannot win, for who can overcome Death itself? Man versus the walking dead with the winner ruling the planet. Welcome to *The War Against Them*.

ETERNAL NIGHT: A VAMPIRE ANTHOLOGY
Edited by Anthony Giangregorio

Blood, fangs, darkness and terror...these are the calling cards of the vampire mythos.

Inside this tome are stories that embrace vampire history but seek to introduce a new literary spin on this longstanding fictional monster. Follow a dark journey through cigarette-smoking creatures hunted by rogue angels, vampires that feed off of thoughts instead of blood, immortals presenting the fantastic in a local rock band, to a legendary monster on the far reaches of town.

Forget what you know about vampires; this anthology will destroy historical mythos and embrace incredible new twists on this celebrated, fictional character.

Welcome to a world of the undead, welcome to the world of *Eternal Night*.

DEAD HISTORY 2
A Zombie Anthology
Edited by Anthony Giangregorio

From the dawn of mankind, the walking dead have been with us.

The greatest moments in history are not what they appear.

Through the ages, the undead have been there, only the proof has been erased, documents destroyed, and witnesses silenced.

The living dead is man's greatest secret.

In this tome, are a few of the stories of what really happened all those years ago. History isn't alive, it's dead!

INSIDE THE PERIMETER: SCAVENGERS OF THE DEAD
by Alan Spencer

In the middle of nowhere, the vestiges of an abandoned town are surrounded by inescapably high concrete barriers, permitting no trespass or escape. The town is dormant of human life, but rampant with the living dead, who choose not to eat flesh, but to instead continue their survival by cruder means.

Boyd Broman, a detective arrested and falsely imprisoned, has been transferred into the secret town. He is given an ultimatum: recapture Hayden Grubaugh, the cannibal serial killer, who has been banished to the town, in exchange for his freedom.

During Boyd's search, he discovers why the psychotic cannibal must really be captured and the sinister secrets the dead town holds.

With no chance of escape, Broman finds himself trapped among the ravenous, violent dead. With the cannibal feeding on the animated cadavers and the undead searching for Boyd, he must fulfill his end of the deal before the rotting corpses turn him into an unwilling organ donor.

But Boyd wasn't told that no one gets out alive, that the town is a death sentence. For there is no escape from *Inside the Perimeter*.

KINGDOM OF THE DEAD
by Anthony Giangregorio
THE DEAD HAVE RISEN!

In the dead city of Pittsburgh, two small enclaves struggle to survive, eking out an existence of hand to mouth.

But instead of working together, both groups battle for the last remaining fuel and supplies of a city filled with the living dead.

Six months after the initial outbreak, a lone helicopter arrives bearing two more survivors and a newborn baby. One enclave welcomes them, while the other schemes to steal their helicopter and escape the decaying city.

With no police, fire, or social services existing, the two will battle for dominance in the steel city of the walking dead. But when the dust settles, the question is: will the remaining humans be the winners, or the losers?

When the dead walk, the line between Heaven and Hell is so twisted and bent there is no line at all.

RISE OF THE DEAD
by Anthony Giangregorio
DEATH IS ONLY THE BEGINNING!

In less than forty-eight hours, more than half the globe was infected.

In another forty-eight, the rest would be enveloped.

The reason?

A science experiment gone horribly wrong which enabled the dead to walk, their flesh rotting on their bones even as they seek human prey.

Jeremy was an ordinary nineteen year old slacker. He partied too much and had done poorly in high school. After a night of drinking and drugs, he awoke to find the world a very different place from the one he'd left the night before.

The dead were walking and feeding on the living, and as Jeremy stepped out into a world gone mad, the dead spotting him alone and unarmed in the middle of the street, he had to wonder if he would live long enough to see his twentieth birthday.

THE CHRONICLES OF JACK PRIMUS
BOOK ONE
by Michael D. Griffiths

Beneath the world of normalcy we all live in lies another world, one where supernatural beings exist. These creatures of the night hunt us; want to feed on our very souls, though only a few know of their existence.

One such man is Jack Primus, who accidentally pierces the veil between this world and the next. With no other choice if he wants to live, he finds himself on the run, hunted by beings called the Xemmoni, an ancient race that sees humans as nothing but cattle. They want his soul, to feed on his very essence, and they will kill all who stand in their way. But if they thought Jack would just lie down and accept his fate, they were sorely mistaken.   He didn't ask for this battle, but he knew he would fight them with everything at his disposal, for to lose is a fate worse than death.

He would win this war, and he would take down anyone who got in his way.

ZOMBIES, MONSTERS, CREATURES OF THE NIGHT
OPEN CASKET PRESS
OPEN CASKET PRESS.COM
THE NEW NAME IN HORROR